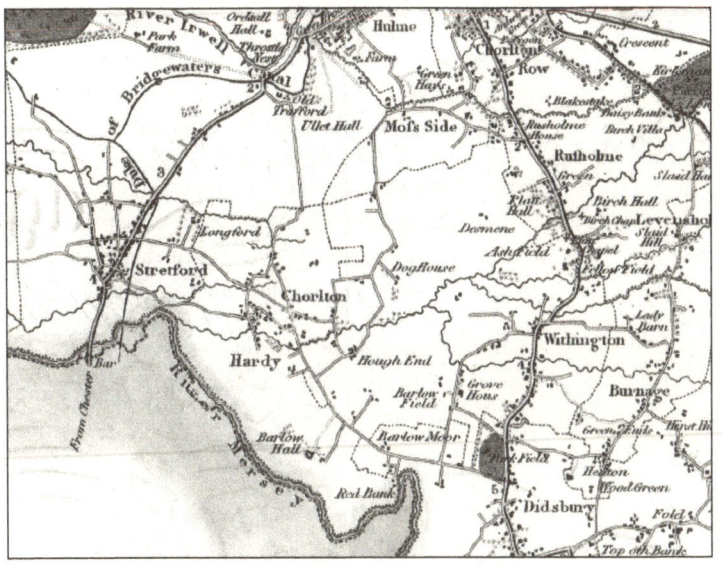

Detail from Greenwood's 1818 map showing
Longford in the Manchester hinterland

First Published 2024
Copyright © Juliette Tomlinson 2024

Published by The Squeeze Press,
an imprint of Wooden Books Ltd,
Red Brick Building, Glastonbury, Somerset.

A CIP catalogue record for this book
is available from the British Library
ISBN13: 978–1–906069–30–8

Typeset by Wooden Books Ltd
Glastonbury, Somerset.

Printed and bound in the UK
by Clays Ltd, Elcograf S.p.A.

www.woodenbooks.com

the
SQUEEZE
PRESS

Longford

a Manchester love story

Juliette Tomlinson

Lyon, 1867

ENRIQUETA SAW THE BOY FIRST.

Before she saw the hard grey wall and before she saw La Castilla. She saw him waiting, chucking his heels against the black dust. The silt puffed into the air, mustard yellow in the moonlight.

The horses trampled to a stop. The driver shouted an apology, his voice brutal in the empty night. Enriqueta's clothes stuck to her, the journey's grime a film on her skin. The carriage smelled stale and her head was sore, her breath sour. Beneath the chat and introductions between the boy and her driver she pushed away the sense of oddness. An apartness that was cleaving; reason and misgiving tumbling over each other in a circus.

The driver and the carriage rattled away, leaving just Enriqueta and the boy – gentle and pale – who belonged to the place. Through the gates of La Castilla, the driveway sloped upwards, tunnelled and black with thick trees. Branches moved in the wind, nearly noiselessly under the moon. A grey building that she had seen on her approach was huge, ugly, and sat outside the walls of La Castilla. It made Enriqueta think of a prison: something municipal and threatening. It could be full of mad men, their rage suppressed by drugs and binds, dumbed and unaware of her arrival.

The driveway suddenly turned, to set La Castilla in view, a row of lights flanking the path. Enriqueta supposed the boy had lit them sometime before, and she was thankful for him again. Though they had said little apart from his quiet pleasantries, he was reassuring company. He told her his name was Jules. Bravery, she found from somewhere, but the turn of her stomach and the spider stretch of apprehension pulled at her every step. Betraying her.

La Castilla was solid and unyielding in the darkness. The windows were blind and unlit. It was a heavy building, a typical Lyonnaise country mansion. Unadorned and sturdily handsome, painted in a buff cream so old that it failed to glow in the lamp and the moonlight. All the lustre from the finish had gone long ago. The roof – even, solid and balanced – was much like every other in the locality. Possibly bigger, and definitely blacker in the subdued night.

Enriqueta was sensitive to beauty and order, noticing untidy gardens, cast in shadows by the shabby bushes and the stones of the driveway, not neat at their verges, but spilling over onto the untended grass. A pond somewhere close by emitted a fetid scent. Mosquitoes gathered, juddering beneath the peeling lamps, whose wet, dangerous bases crawled with earwigs humped one on top of the other.

Jules went before her, pushing open the front door. Like the house, it was vast and outsized. Coarsely carved into the wood, the deep whorls in the surface were lumps beneath her fingers, and Enriqueta swallowed her disappointment. Tannin and something else laced the air in the porch and into the hallway. It was a bitter scent, wintry and male, like myrrh. The odour settled on her heavily and Enriqueta was weary again, standing still as fatigue and unease swaddled her close. La Castilla was rigid and stifling, and her hopes of a contented and radiant new life were fast diminishing.

Jules lit a few of the lamps here and there. As he moved around her he instructed, and listed, while Enriqueta stood motionless, stone like the floor.

'Madame Bardin is not at La Castilla until Friday. She sends her regards and apologies. I'll be here to help you with everything until she returns. Not now, of course, it's too late and you must be tired. And my sister Madeleine will be around tomorrow too.'

His glances were shadowed by the lick and flicker of the candle lamps. Guiding them into the pantry, his hand only touched her back lightly. While Jules didn't look at her much as he spoke, his purposeful movements were soothing.

'When it's light, I can show you around properly. Our home is nearby but we often stay to help guests. Maddy will help with your unpacking, showing you where things are.'

The brown and grey pantry was cramped, with a sink and cold shelves, an ice box and a doll-sized table, four chairs crammed around it. A large, cold glass of wine was set down in front of her and as she took it, she watched him prepare her some bread, butter and ham. There was also cake, grapes and cheese, which he plated for her so simply and with such kindness that a great sadness chimed in her like a bell. When Jules slipped out with her luggage to arrange her room, the food stuck in her throat. In the small space, the same dark fragrance clung to everything. Something like sandalwood, or wax. Enriqueta felt wretched, lost in the foreignness of an unknown place. The bell that had been rung could not be un-rung. She longed with a sickness to be back in Paris.

La Castilla, 1867

OPTIMISM ARRIVED with the forgiving morning light. Madeleine's knock to wake her was as soft as magic, loosening the ties of Enriqueta's dismay. Really, the siblings were only children—Enriqueta guessed ten and maybe seven years younger than her twenty-four. Conducting themselves with calm and measure, they seemed like slight adults, wise beyond their years. Sweet, humble self-possession—what she wished for one day in her own children. Would she ever be the mother, the wife that she saw so clearly, knitting and stirring, stroking and bathing, sighing with wonder into faces like theirs.

They were surprisingly delicate for country people, their narrow figures a contradiction to the bulk of the house. With their mistress Madame Bardin still away from La Castilla, Jules and Maddy presided over it with ease and without interruption. They worked busily and faultlessly, anticipating what the other would do next.

The full gleam of mid-morning sunlight polished the remarkable light fitting that went from the bottom to the very top of the house: a rod of iron decorated with lamps and curls of jade forest leaves held parrots, enamelled in red and green in groups, clinging to the fixture. Their eyes were preternaturally white and knowing, beaded with a black marble centre which appeared to swivel at her as she turned on the banister. Up and up through three floors it went, and a set of see-no-evil, hear-no-evil brass monkeys sat at the base, each covered in gold and wearing sparkling patchwork trousers over their muscled haunches. Their hands, carved in polished wood, closed off their senses. Maybe they were the source of the bitter scent that saturated every surface.

Enriqueta dared to call out.

'Hello! Hello! Jules? Where are you, Madeleine?'

Pleated pistachio silk covered the walls, faded and spotted in a rust that may have been blood, or the careless flicker of an empty soup bowl rushed down the stairs in the dark. The pearl of it was remarkable, making a Greek theatre of the morning, and at last Enriqueta saw the peculiar beauty in La Castilla's eccentricities. A portrait of Madame Bardin, powerful in her absence, was pinned like a curse to the fabric.

How had she not seen the huge, decorated structure that shot through its core when she arrived? The perfumes of the previous night had dissipated. The windows were open and a fresh, wet, grassy smell came through. Enriqueta heard the gardeners, men chuckling and snipping. Their low hum was light and normality, real and reassuring. Imagination and nighttime, such mischievous bedfellows, had been chased away by the benign order of the new day.

'Is anyone here? Jules?'

The doors to each room through the hall – three each side of the large, square space – were mirrored from top to bottom. Where there could be glass, or panels, or patterned wood, were mirrors. The house bounced off itself from every corner as the Verdigris metal gate, layered against the door, shut with a clang that hailed vastness behind it. The beauty of Lyon. The city was some miles away but clear, the domes and spires, and rows of roofs etched in watercolour against the mist. It was astounding, like a painting, and on the air she could smell the divine scent of milk and people.

Madeleine emerged from the shadows of a thick vine, china cups paper white in her hands, her apron the colour of blood that had been bleached again and again.

'What a trip we could have, Madeleine!'

'We rarely get to town Mademoiselle Tennant.'

Madeleine pulled out a chair and Enriqueta sat, obedient in the moss green damp of the garden.

'Call me Enri. Like my friends did, and might I call you Maddy as your brother does?'

Again, the invasive pull of homesickness. The garden, slippery with moisture, hummed with creatures. A slug, with its fat frilled rim of orange, hung from the beak of the bird on the bush. Enriqueta's mind shot to the white, clean, straight lines of the capital. Lyon blurred in the distance, grey and dank as a monstrous cloud, snuffing out the sun. Enriqueta recalled a brighter sky, a better sun; an orb skidding on the polished lanes of Paris. City of light.

The breakfast was a country meal and nothing that she was used to. Sweet, curded cheese of Lyon, with black jam and dark, dense bread. There was a short glass of syrupy local apple juice and – a small mercy – a pot of pressed coffee. She could drink that, and she did so quickly, thirsting for more straight away. Madeleine leant over her, mixing hot chocolate, but she whipped the cream too thickly and it fell badly into the bowl, a sliding lump. She rushed away, apology blooming red on her face. The unborn mother in Enri rose with ferocity, and she fought her away, resisting the urge to race after Madeleine, past the mirrors, the dumb monkeys, the billowing green walls and the endless iron pole. Wasps settled on the smears of breakfast, and Enriqueta trudged to the insufficient safety of her shut door at the very top of the house. There was still another day until Madame Bardin returned, and after being awake for only two, lonely hours, Enriqueta Tennant, far from love and far from home, fell asleep until dusk.

MANCHESTER, 1864

'YOU ARE ALL JOHN to me, whatever you call yourself.' Caroline Castiglioni's voice was muffled at his neck as she stroked his bare stomach. Laughing, he pulled her to him as if to trap her and the moment in time, a stamp and a lock on their love. There was nothing else to do; she said it to make fun of him, but he wanted so keenly to please her. Yet, undeniably, he felt a searing jealousy. The thought of her with other men filled him with a rank sickness.

John's arm was under her head, his free hand lifting her dark hair over and over and letting it drop through his fingers.

'When can I see you again, Caroline?'

This was the third time he had been with her like this. As he watched his own hand picking and dropping her hair, he wondered when he had begun to feel so strongly for her. Stroking her face, his finger shook as it moved. He tried to steady it, meek as a child. Was this love? If so, it was at the worst time with the wrong woman. But God help him, as John looked at Caroline, with her beautiful skin and her silken voice, he was sure that this was as close to love as he had been since Dinah, his first wife. Grasping her warm, full body he didn't think at all about moving onto her again. The eiderdown slithered to the floor, covering their discarded clothes like a magician's trick.

'When?' he asked again.

Making her weak with bliss as she clasped him was easy for

John. Smiling a long smile, she tried to push him away – she was sore, he was sore – but each time there was a selfish and battering heat that started again in them both.

'Everyday, John,' she said, moving his weight off her and feeling him stick against her thighs. 'Come and find me every day.'

His heart hurt and the pointlessness of making plans— the blank page that fluttered—unwritten with any sort of future between them, made him ache. It was chapters of pain, that they kept trying to make good. Secrecy and danger ill-afforded a haven for true love. And he knew that she knew that 'everyday' was impossible for him. The grave mistake of a marriage to Martha, fixed by the conventions of a societally good match, had trapped both him and his second wife by a bond of misery. Both of them still tethered to the memories of their first spouses, made even more wonderful in their deaths. Their commonalities were grim; babies dying before they could walk, parents who pressed them up the aisle together, hoping a union, convenient to both the Rylands and Carden family, would mend past sadnesses.

John never forgot how Martha left their bed, weeks into the marriage. The kiss at the alter was their last. Martha wrapped her shawl around her like a shroud and took the candle from the bedside table. In the gloom, she made the small chamber two doors down the hall her own, and never returned to the marital bedroom. John made daily efforts, thinking he could salvage something with trips and affection, but the closer he came to her, the further away she turned, flinching at his touch, and paling with irritation at everything he said. Charity work took the place of a marriage in action, and she found her leisure and pleasure in the leaves of the begonias she bred and spliced relentlessly. She stood before the grave of her first husband, Richard, and pushed primroses into the plots of her babies, while John took a coach into town and watched out for someone else to love.

If he mentioned a word as huge as love, Caroline would laugh him out of the door and onto the road like the last two times.

'It is you that isn't free, John. I'm here whenever you want. I'm here all the time. You know that.'

Caroline lived in a small cottage just behind the main road that ran through Ancoats, to the north of the city of Manchester, before the thoroughfare panned out like a star towards the outlying villages of Gorton, Droylsden, Longsight, Crumpsall. The cottage had only two rooms; John and Caroline lay in the crooked little bed at the back, lit by the street lamp. It sputtered and hissed, singing to the hushing cotton shift of the bedsheets. He loved the smell of this room, partly her and partly the drifting scent of the city. Bodies and bread, the yeast of the breweries and the tang of the muddied hooves from a hundred passing horses. There was a dichotomous mix of her carbolic cleanliness and the scent of warmed skin, a fragrance owned by her alone. Above all was the pure delight of association. Excitement jumped through him when her fragrance hit him, an exquisite shiver that ruled him absolutely. Increasingly, she was a queen over him; he, a serf, weakened and dominated by her beauty.

They had met some months ago, in a room he had forgotten even existed, in one of his charities, Wood Street Mission. John had rented the vast cellars of 2 St Peter's Square. The location was central, with plenty of bays for traffic, and the space was dry enough to store all the belongings that were donated to the cause. He had chosen the place as it rang loud with a veracity so stark, he felt it in his heart. The sabre wounds of Peterloo still ran deep, the political earthquake that saw hundreds of working men and women slain at the bloodied hands of the yeomanry in St Peter's Field. John loved his city, and he was its son. *Concilio Et Labore.*

Newly recruited, Caroline Castiglioni had stopped selling her body for gin and foraging buns out of bins. This had been all the life she had known since the age of seven, when her father had pinched out the light in her room, climbed into her bed and snuffed out her childhood for good.

She had begun as a fervent volunteer, directing all her anger into sorting the bags of clothes into packs to send out to the needy. The needy in Manchester were copious, and the range of packages they put together reflected the desperate sectors of the burgeoning city. There were bundles for newborn babies and fallen mothers, containing cloths, blankets, knitted boots and hats and underwear. There were boxes for the elderly, with shawls and blouses, woollen socks and bedding. For working men, suits were roughly compiled. Things may not have matched, but everything was mended, clean, pressed and tied up as decently as was possible. Caroline put a penny in each pocket of each parcel, and any moment that she craved the burn of gin in her throat, she imagined the joy of the cool coin in a poor palm.

Caroline was a natural leader, and it was not long before she was granted a small but fair salary to direct all the practical, day-to-day duties of sorting and allocating the goods that were donated. She had a rare gift for management: the ability to shine even the dullest stone of a person. Responsibility given out generously and packaged with praise produced remarkable results, as she encouraged others with brightness and humour while steering altercations away from disaster with a firm touch. Caroline operated with love and consistency, free from the dismal shackles of the relentless work of sex for money. She had locked danger and fear in the box that contained her childhood and its china doll, her placid face smashed by the fist of a stepfather.

John had complete trust in the directors of Wood Street, but it was always his way and his want to keep a close hand on everything. In this spirit, he visited the charity every week, an aspect of his duties that was usually tedious to him. Until the day he saw her, and the world turned.

Caroline had caught his heart with her first glance – as brief as a breath – before she turned back to the bulging sacks on the bench before her.

John forced himself to concentrate on the drone of the Buildings Manager, who plodded alongside him explaining every last detail, every little benefit or each small improvement that had been made since his previous visit. John nodded, pained to take his glance from her glorious form that had not once – not once – turned again to him. He was utterly unused to invisibility, and he strained again to catch her voice as the manager led him to the next room. Endless rooms.

The tour ended with a final agonising hour in the manager's office. A full potted history of the site, his (admirable) enthusiasm at being able to, in his own small way, help to support *such an estimable charity, Sir*'. Peter was, as ever, polite and patient but John was absurdly distracted, all the time thinking that if he didn't leave this meeting soon, she would be gone. She would disappear, swallowed by the crowds and the hot smog of the city while it clenched itself for revolution. He checked his watch. Past five o'clock.

Where this fire for a stranger had come from was a mystery. But John's heart was beginning to thud with an agonising mixture of irritation, consternation, and lust. Finally, the chairs were scraped back and Peter and John returned down to the cellars to collect the week's paperwork.

John's blood quickened with his pace as they went through the tangle of rooms and doors and infuriating corridors to the sorting hall. He didn't register a word of Peter's steady conversation behind the stifling pounding of his heart. And then finally he was there. And she was there. Kneeling in the middle of the piles of clothes. In her grey everyday dress and her dusty apron. Her cheeks were dark with effort against her smooth face and her incredible hair was dropping out of the topknot on her crown. She was breathing as hard as he was, and this singular unified rhythm ran from one to the other across the emptied room. Everyone – everything else gone – even the colour from the walls. She pulled her head up to meet his stare. 'John Rylands. I have been waiting to meet you properly.'

That perfect moment was just three short, sweet months ago. He knew he had to get out of her bed, get dressed and return to his normal life. His wife, his magnificent home, his work. His reputation as a good man, a Godly man, a charitable man, a fine employer, and a masterful businessman. Her last kiss, pulling her to him was wasted. His practical mind reigned over the torment of his body. With one squeeze of her hand, his passion for Caroline was suspended. Until the next time, he would try to dampen fierce sentiment. Love, whatever it was, had to be shut firm behind the closed door of his own, secret, self.

In this way John grew his empire with a rigour and a zeal that expelled itself from the amulet of grief that he carried with him. His dead children – and it appeared there was no longer any chance of more to come – sat daily in his thoughts. Being with Caroline reminded him of them all. He saw them in their tiny boxes, still and waxen, and he grimaced, pulling on his boots.

Paris to Lyon, 1867

ENRIQUETA CRUSHED THE LITTLE gilded pot of cacao powder beneath her heel, relishing the crack of the glass and the puff of chocolate across the floor, spoiling the white tiles. She didn't care. At the same time pain rippled through her abdomen, the dragging discomfort of womanhood; punishment for all. It didn't matter anymore; Monsieur Lejeune, the owner of the commercial library in Paris where she worked, had modern ambitions. He planned to convert the ambling rooms into a splendid coffee house with painted windows and the very latest in hot chocolates and scalloped sandwiches. Insufferably unfeeling, he strutted through his property, having rarely been seen in it before, while his red waistcoat strained as he boasted of his expensive, radical, coffee machine. She swept up the mess as her womb griped against her, and she thought of children and blood, and the blitheness of men. The voice of Padre Esteban, an elderly Spanish priest she had become particularly fond of, rang out, calling to her to stamp his almanac for the last time.

Her final week of work dwindled amongst the boxes and the smoke from the flames in the yard, stoked with the bibliographies she had spent so many hours compiling. Enriqueta poked the fire with a broken umbrella. Words curled up into the blank Paris sky, brittle on the breeze.

The month that followed was listless; hours wasted in the apartment waiting for Marianne and Jeanne to return from their days at work. With clement weather, Enriqueta wandered the streets, which were changing their shape by the week. Haussman had begun his work on modern order, bringing formation to the city. Construction of the Palais Garnier was underway, an opulence commanded by Napoleon. Circling the Boulevard des Capucines, men would sometimes dart towards her, and she knew they enjoyed her fear. So much of her was disappearing, with her meagre savings vanishing almost to nothing.

Soon she was down to free apples from her friendly grocer, and shoes that were looking worn. She had pennies left; Jeanne and Marianne paid for the Friday treat of the harshest, cheapest cherry brandy. She drank it while she wrote letters, licking the glass clean. Young, healthy, educated, unmarried and personable, Enriqueta soon received a reply to one of her many applications. A Madame Bardin of Lyon, who needed someone to help her with her charitable work. The babbling, excitable letter insisted that she must begin the job as soon as possible. The role involved cataloguing her book collections; a fortuitous, timely situation that even Enri, in all her caution and reservation, could not afford to deny.

'You must go! Lyon is a wonderful city. We will write, we can visit you. Be brave!' Jeanne and Marianne shut her suitcase for her, closing up her life in Paris.

Two weeks later, Enriqueta was in the Blue Room at La Castilla, some three hundred miles away from the Parisian fireside she loved so dearly. The azure crystal lights in the ceiling and the pale Lyonnaise sky at the window cast a watery shimmer over the space. Motes of stale dust settled on the trestle tables and teetering piles of books.

The morning bought the muffled boom of action from inside and outside. Different horses, foreign men then the new bark of the mistress of the house.

Madame Bardin was short and squat, with a wide waist and small bust, hard and shelved in her bodice. Her frock was a rich red and her shawl was emerald, with lace birds sewn into it, like the ones that crawled up the iron lamp. In late middle age, she was a plain woman made startling by her eccentric dress.

'I am a woman of means, and my purpose is charity. I spend much of my time travelling to meet with people who, so generously, want to gift to me all or part of their libraries and collections. For example, when you arrived, my dear, I was a week in Rouen. An acquaintance of mine was dying and had no heir, but he passed peacefully knowing his books would go to me.'

Enriqueta recoiled as discreetly as she could. Madame Bardin was too close to her.

'When I am here at La Castilla, my time is occupied with relentless correspondence, which I do from my office across this hall. I also host functions – lunches and soirees – for people of means and of charitable minds.'

The position notice had said little more than that the post would be of an administrative and clerical nature, with a modest salary and board included. The skills required were a fine eye for detail and a sound literary knowledge. The rest – trustworthy, reliable, hardworking – were standard elements for every position for a single woman.

Madame Bardin busied herself with propriety over the tea that Jules had brought them. She fussed over the sugar cubes, grumbling that the set was not the one she usually favoured, and that Jules should know by now. Enriqueta smarted at the small, inconsequential criticism of him.

Madame Bardin's civet odour mingled with the cloying scent of the sugared lemon slices in the saucer. In Paris, they had fresh bright lemons for their tea tied in sheer white muslin. Here, the fruits were dark and syrupy, kept in jars and coated with a brittle granular sugar. Madame growled and grizzled over the pots, dumping a thick slice of the fruit in the cup. Enriqueta winced as she sipped it, the greasy lemon bobbing at her mouth, the tea—so foreign and sour—leaving oil and grit on her lips.

MANCHESTER, 1825

DINAH RABY JUST WANTED to be grabbed and kissed. She was a back room seamstress, pulsing with desire and intent, much like the twenty other young women who tapped and sewed and needled the working hours away. One of many whose wet eyes gazed at John Rylands. Though he wasn't tall, he seemed to fill the draper's shop. When Dinah pictured her body pressed to his, her breasts stung and she could almost feel the tweed on his shoulders beneath her palms.

Unlike most of the men she knew, who blustered around their way through the world pronouncing orders, finishing the food meant for tomorrow, belching beer as if it were an opinion, John had never appeared hurried or undignified, angry or impatient. His shirts – daisy white – were always pressed, his shoes conker bright and his collars straight and stiff. Dinah breathed him in, a delicious blend of soft laundered lavender and hard amber. On warmer days, he shed his jacket and rolled his sleeves up, leaving Dinah so flustered she could hardly thread her needles properly.

She scowled, pushing her foot to her machine. Twenty-four this year. Something, anything, had to happen. She would make it happen. She was sick of wanting, and waiting, bleeding and turning over and over at night. Her body longed to be filled up, and she dreamed of long conversations with him in the sunshine of Turn Moss, before his hands delved into her skirts.

She burned at the thought, and the dacca skidded from under her needle.

She refused to countenance the alternative: maids, thinking they would be fair forever, fell for a man and played the waiting game, letting other, less impressive suitors pass them by. Thirty years old came on the turn of a penny, their choices narrowed to widowers and the sad, motherless children that hid behind their coattails, smelling of dust and streaked with tears. While many men circled Dinah's orbit, none had John's blue eyes, his exquisite manners or his deep, melodic voice. Tommy McGuire from school had made his intentions clear, doggedly pushing Valentine's cards under the Raby front door for a decade now. Sam Kenyon, at four years old, had kicked hard balls at Dinah in the schoolyard. At twenty-four, he cast wary, yearning glances at her over church pews. A local businessman, Joseph Holt, had pursued her so frequently of late she had begun to fear his tread on her way home from work. Handsome, dark, sanguine and insistent, Holt was wealthy. Full of the swagger born of money and looks, his family was in calico block printing and property, and he had made it clear that he wanted Dinah as a part of his empire.

In the rattle and the shafts of light in the shop, in the grime of her nails and the desperate smoothing of her hair, she wondered if John Rylands would ever notice her. Dinah pressed her hands over her apron, gripping her hips. She simmered with envy as girls fluttered around him, pestering him with pointless questions and mindless gabble, confident in their brassy yellow ribbons, pretty as parakeets. Where did they find their nerve? She wondered whether such conviction was handed to them alongside their beauty, dropped into their bassinets as a blessing from some indulgent angel. Her mother always said she should put herself forward more. Mrs Raby told Dinah that it was more cheek and spirit that she needed, not a larger bust or longer hair.

Where her figure was full and healthy, she thought that she

was dumpy and inelegant. When it occurred to her that she should stop eating, she meant it only as a short-lived rule. Maybe a few days without lunches and sweets would gift her with finer skin or a neater waist. Her heart lurched as she watched John respond to yet another request, always so kind and chivalrous. She was anguished by the mere suggestion that he might have any sort of feeling for anyone. Mrs Raby had begun to worry about her, as Dinah returned home from work each day more and more wretched.

'Lovesick,' concluded her mother to Dinah's father, putting another batch of cakes in the oven, hoping in vain and exasperation that she could tempt her girl to eat something. Dinah went straight to bed, leaving her mother to get fat on the tray of wasted buns in front of the fire.

Her days of fasting grouped into weeks, and after another hot, sleepless night she had left the house without breakfast. The walk to the drapers was long and shadeless, and at only seven o'clock in the morning, the sun scorched her miserable little face. She sank, tormented, onto her workbench. Dinah's head began to spin and as she rose to reach for her cloth, the room tilted wildly and she collapsed to the ground. When she opened her eyes, Dinah found she was in John's arms. He was kneeling by her, cradling her as tenderly as he might a broken bird, stroking her brow. His face was startlingly close.

'Dinah, are you awake?'

She hardly dared to move, sure she was dreaming. Could she really be in the strong embrace of the man she had loved so much, for so long? Behind her, she heard the fuss of the other women shaped in whispers and giggles, and the clang of the church bell ringing for a rushed Friday wedding. She began to shake, the tension of fruitless desire released all at once. John held her closer, and Dinah began to cry, tears of the deepest, truest, most overwhelming happiness that she had ever felt.

MANCHESTER, 1865

Longford Hall was a bold purchase, plucked from the Walker family for a fantastical price. They were a riotous lot who had stomped through properties in the area with exclamation and political noise. Something in John admired Thomas Walker's braggadocio and feckless, righteous courage, but Walker's vigorous hubris juddered to a halt in front of a gang armed with pistols over in Didsbury. His son Charles Walker paled at the responsibility of the Longford Estate and John – ever tenacious – grasped a fortunate moment to relieve him of his burden for just short of nine thousand pounds. He had long since paid off the mortgage and at the same time set a dividend aside for new building on the land.

Even after eight years of living here, John thrilled at the sight of it, pale and solid in the gloom of the late night. The hall had an almost paternalistic hold over him; they shared a deep and restless energy and the union between home and master was indefatigable, John taking from it a vitality that fuelled so much of his action and purpose.

The decade had been busy, profitable and precise. He was exactly where he should be, his reach stretching across all he believed in and desired. He was a Fellow of the Society of Arts, a leader of the Manchester Chamber of Commerce, a church builder and patron, and the owner of mills dotted all over the district: Gorton, Medlock, Water Street,Gidlow. He owned streets of houses – buying them like sweets – and industrial chunks of Manchester.

Forty-three acres, bordering Hedge Lane in Stretford, made up the estate, the patch on the world he had increasingly made his own. The Union Church – Rylands. The Congregational Chapel – Rylands. The public library, the coffee house, the swimming pool – Rylands, the Cotton King. Planning and imagining, projects overlapped projects, gains targeted and won. There was no why or when, or solution to the end point of his relentless doing. It wasn't tethered to financial forces, though money pleased him. He met with his accountants twice weekly, once in his office at the hall and once in his chambers at the Portico. Meticulous and involved, he made every fiscal decision; from the purchase of the seeds for the greenhouses, to the donations for aged gentlewomen, to the deeds of the Cheapside warehouses in London. His wise and judicious reach touched all he owned.

He smiled at the annotations in his diary. Peter O'Hara's loyalty and fine brain had ricocheted him from his footman to director of many of the businesses. John shared himself with Peter as though he was turning out his pockets to him. Only Caroline was hidden away, like a peg doll he could curve his fingers over in as she lay hidden in the dark of his palm.

Peter O'Hara and his family saw the best in John, and their unerring good faith buoyed and comforted him. He was, he really believed, a mostly good man. He tried so hard to be. Peter's wife Leone inhabited the kitchens of Longford, cinnamon in the air and flour on her apron. She was as constant as the magnolias in April. She shared Peter's loyalty. But there was the day she had seen John with Caroline. Chance and errors, falling on people as unexpected as the hailstones of spring.

The rain came so hard, that it had seemed that the alley near

St Mary's Mulberry Street would collapse in on them. John had Caroline's wrists in his hands and her lips just a stain away from his. Brackish water from the pipes slipped onto them and down their necks in thick droplets. Their embrace pressed hot breath out of them in wet clouds.

'Thank God, thank God, I have missed you so very much my love!'

John had to let her go – both of them knew that it was ferociously dangerous for them to hold each other, so openly, in the eyes of the city centre. John, maybe moved by guilt, looked up. Where the alley narrowed, it led to King Street, whose expensive light framed Leone like a portrait. She glowed; she was a good woman. Away from Longford, her pastries and her aprons, she was on a rare errand away from Stretford, or her village of Chorlton-cum-Hardy. When John's eyes collided with hers, her shape flitted away like a bat, too fast for him to trace her expression or the colour on her face. Seeing his demeanour fall so suddenly, Caroline froze. John's palms prickled as he sprang back from her. He stared into the gap onto King Street where Leone – dear, constant, busy Leone – had been imprinted just seconds before.

Leone never mentioned it to John; no moment of shame or abnormality ever slipped between them. For some weeks, he checked her expression, searched for meanings in her words that were never there. The whole taut and sorry scene finally drifted away, leaving nothing but the grip of vigilance on him.

The O'Hara's deserved more than the two dusty dark end rooms of the Longford west garret. Tynan, at fourteen, was beckoning at manhood. Bridget and Michael, at nine and eleven, were shedding their childish years. Worse off were the wider staff; the gardeners, the maids and the hands, the porters and the groomsmen, all still housed in the older wooden structures on the estate, ghosts of the house John had pulled down. Wind whistled through the cramped rooms, dampening the children's bunks and the straw beds for the horsemen, who cursed and turned in their sleep, scratching the fleas as they suckled on their waists. Billy McNamara, one of the senior grooms, had died in his paltry bed last Easter; the straw smelled sweet; rotting from the warmth of a ruddy Lenten. Billy's dog had pushed open the door, barking into china-blue skies and scaring the doves on the cote. It was undignified, and an affront to John.

Peter, Leone, their families and every single person tied by life and wage to John's home would one day be properly housed, he promised himself, to die in beds of white cotton, their deaths housed in brick walls and under tiled roofs. A bright bank of land lay to the west of the hall, situated perfectly to catch the very best of the seasons and the always dewy dawns of the park. Warm and sheltered, John had already named it Sunnyside.

Days that were littered with appointments ended late, and John's parlour in the evenings was a cradle to his sighs, witness to his hands passing over his face, sometimes in despair. Midsummer kept the fire low but his supper warm. Leone had made two warm sausage rolls and chopped apple and salad cream, with a flask of stout nearby. Discreetly, John watered it with neat whisky.

In his days he kept occupied, and thoughts of Caroline could be suppressed. But as soon as he sat in the parlour, the whisky set his misery alight and the heat in him rose. He longed for her so morosely that pain pulled across his chest. A red flag of terror flapped, signifying the uncontrollable panic that said *maybe tomorrow will be the start of the end.*

Obsession was an ugly companion. A whisper of a moment – taking her boots off and feeling the supple leather on her ankle bone, the recollection of releasing her from her dress – would intrude as he stacked the papers of a contract, making him want to run to her immediately. Her voice, her opinion, her body. All her mannerisms had caught hold of him so fast. He had always wanted someone like her – pretty, maddeningly pretty – bold, and clever.

Just as Dinah had been.

'Get it done, John. That's right.'

He could still hear her, and feel the weight of her breasts in his hands.

'Go on, John. They could be back, go on.'

What a habit it had been, frantically on each other in locked cupboards and under trees, rich with abandon in the weeks before marriage. The joy it gave him to see Dinah buck against him, her skirts rucked on her back, her moans huffing over the daisies. He remembered roaring into the sky, scattering the crows.

Denial was a useful master, distracting him while his buildings were burning and his accountants were mithering and his wife, Martha, was withering. Love exhausted him, and while Caroline was only three miles from Longford, John felt wretchedly far from her.

LYON, 1868

IRRITABLE AND DUSTY, and pulling an unfair weight, the horses were slow up the drive to La Castilla. At least it was his sister, Madeleine, and not the Madame who came out to greet Jules. He winced, his back aching from miles of terrible track. Madeleine had the wisdom to stay quiet until her brother's temper subsided.

'It's a bloody farce. Eighty miles off the main roads to pick up a ton of rubbish. I'm a wreck – the horses are spent. Look at the state of their shoes.'

'Well don't leave the beasts to me, Jules. Mighty, angry things – look at them flaring their nostrils! I'll help you get them to bed.'

The animals whinnied in gratitude at the pleasing stable scents of motes and sweat. There was a pot of potatoes and onions how he liked it. Parsley in the middle layer and beef fat underneath. Butter on the top.

The pokey range had warmed the parlour and the wine.

'You've not missed much.' Madeleine said. 'I feel sorry for Miss Enri, Jules. Don't you? I don't think she really knew what things were like here.'

Jules sighed and took a long draught of the Cotes.

'Yes, well, I don't know what to say. Who could prepare themselves for La Castilla, with all its ghosts, its hall of mirrors, its witch-in-residence!'

Riding over rubble, and hunching through gales, tipping his glass to his mouth, had all served to make Jules gently drunk. With Madame Bardin out of their way, there was even a chance of a quieter day tomorrow. Feeling a warm boost of contentment, he poured his sister a glass and raised himself, gingerly, to serve them both their supper.

It was an odd bewitchment; a force in the walls that had wiped out, in time, all of Enriqueta's expectations that she had held with such fierce, false clarity in her mind's eye. The ideas and pictures that she had let her mind shape, that rattled with the carriage on the way from Paris to Lyon had fled as immediately as her hand had touched the great door arriving, Jules knightly and quiet before her.

Each morning was the same. The slippers on the mat by her bed, causing her heart to swing back to Paris. A Christmas gift from Jeanne, monogrammed satin, the slippers were impractical, raspberry pink with gold thread. Her breath was mist. The morning sun was weak, yet to blush into warmth.

'Braziers are lit, miss. Blankets if you want. Bread? And try this jam. Look at these big turquoise eggs; the old lady pecked at me when I took them. Maddy could fry you one – with morels? Blood sausage?'

Jules treated her like a child in many ways. Feeding her, questioning her sleep and her spirits with the application of a father. Enriqueta's own childhood had been a twisted cord of neglect and loneliness, formed by an absence of compassion. Despite her early years being abundant with the riches of babyhood: the dolls, the nannies, the long exhausting days out in the parks of Havana, and the private beaches, she was an isolated being from infancy. The challenges of each day in the Blue Room did not overwhelm her, but she feared that she had found herself in a new wilderness of solitude, without any means to escape.

Books, and more books, arrived every few days. She divided

them into three very basic categories. 'Gentry' included pieces in perfect condition, antiquated, first editions, unusual items, rarified titles. Their beauty and intrigue distracted her until the end of the day, when she allowed herself to indulge in their magnificence.

'Library' took the more ordinary books, the popular plays and stories that were produced in quantity, that appeared again and again.

'Ha'penny trash!' bellowed Madame Bardin, scorn creasing her greasy brow.

'La Tempête dans le Coeur again! I spent time with this one before she passed away; she didn't seem as stupid as all that. Tiresome woman. Very thin.'

Madame snorted with derision and tossed the book towards Enriqueta, knocking one of her towers askew. It was right to Enriqueta that there were different types of writing and different desires in readers, just as there were different types of cake, children, curtains, dogs and clouds in the sky. Madame's narrow perception of what was fashionable, worthy, and acceptable infuriated Enriqueta; snobbery and ignorance displayed with practiced pride.

Something quiet came to Enriqueta as she watched Jules work beside her. He was so like her twin. The thread of sibling ties fluttered across seascapes, and she could hardly recall her brother's voice. The thought of a baby in her arms, a Jules or a Jose, was air in the suffocation of the house.

Madame Bardin was a woman without family, and she was at least a decade past any hope of a child. With no elderly charges, friendly local cousins or even sociable neighbours, La Castilla had no story to tell. She crafted a soul for the place by filling it with people as insubstantial as herself. While she was ruthless in the way she repelled intimacy, her parties were a playground for deviance, people unified by her and their aberrancies. The guests arrived, warm palmed and eyes blank; beads of sweat under heavy makeup. The men were largely atrocious, well behaved in their usual daytime positions, but at La Castilla at night, a mask of debauchery descended, and red faced and rheumy eyed, they grasped at the maids and pawed at Jules. Both men and women put their hands on him, trying to lure him into a corner, chemical breath in his face, and fingers grazing his crotch and backside. They arrived at the house pale and perfumed but before long, their painted faces smudged as they swayed and tumbled in the spare rooms, stockings sagging around their ankles. Jules had seen so many men of high society thrusting drunkenly into someone else's wife, her eyes swivelling in her head as it bobbed like a puppet.

Jules first witnessed rape when he was twelve years old. He heard a steady mewing from the coach house when he was taking out the bottles. He thought it was the cat again, pushing out another wet litter. Words of pity for the animal levitated through his mind.

Poor girl, that bad tom should leave you be. It never stops for you. Pain and babies.

There were no kittens in the coach house. There was a man, with huge haunches and a broad, white behind, hunched over Stephanie. She was only seven years old, and Jules wondered if she was dead before he realised the noise was coming from her. She seemed to squeak in rhythm to the assault. The man's fingers were ploughing her mouth, red with the blood from her nose.

'You can have a go next if you want son. Wake up, dolly!'

The man slapped Stephanie hard across her face, which was ivory with agony.

'Suit yourself. Tell le Cure I have started her off for him, lad.'

Stephanie died a few weeks later. Madame Bardin was furious when the tree that she buried her under failed to produce any quinces. She blamed Stephanie, saying that the girl had poisoned the soil.

The parties swelled with danger, and Jules and Maddy always left by midnight, closing the door to the music and raised voices, the glittering jewellery and the burning eyes. They were always instructed to sleep at their family home on the night of the parties, and to return late the next day to clear up the mess. Their unwashed aprons were sticky with splashes of liquor, and their ears still rang with the dead, droning bawl of Lyonnaise high society. Shattered glass crunched beneath their feet and Maddy sighed, wondering how she would remove the hard sheet of candle wax which spread across the blue velvet of the curtains.

Invitations to the parties landed in expensive hallways, and Maddy was tethered to Madame, planning the menus and writing complicated notes for the caterers. The gatherings were not large by local standards – sixty or seventy people, but this was too much for Maddy's scullery. Caterers arrived at La Castilla the day before, sweeping through to the larger, below-stairs kitchen to begin their preparations.

'Am I keeping you up, Madeleine?'. They had been at the office table for two hours, but Maddy knew never to expect thanks or praise from Madame Bardin. Jules and Maddy were parts of La Castilla as much as the monkey at the bottom of the stairs, but despite the siblings working for her since they were just small children, Madame didn't know when their birthdays were, or what their father was called, or how they took their tea. Showing them no sentiment, she was baffled and irritated by any rare day of sickness or fatigue in them.

'Sorry, Madame.'

The more Madame drank, the closer she sidled across the seat towards Madeleine, her breath laced with stale meat and wine. Leaning forward unsteadily, Madame Bardin spoke into her ear so closely that Maddy could hear the click of spittle and teeth and tongue, moving thickly together.

'Look here, Mademoiselle Madeleine, I need everything to be perfect for this one. For the future of the charity. And for you! What would you do without me to line the pockets of you and your idle family!'

She bashed the table with the heel of her wrist. The flowers in the vase dropped some of their petals.

'And now with all your ridiculous huffing and puffing I don't know where we are up to. Where are we up to?'

Madeleine saw the drinker's tremor in her powdered jowls. The smell of Madame Bardin's unwashed skin leaked through her satin frock and the strength of her perfume. Madeleine was close enough to her to see the smudge of breakfast butter on her front, and the angry red ridge at her neck, where her ill-fitting wig was rubbing her.

'Cheese, Madame. We were listing the cheese you might want to order. But also then, we went back to fruit, to go with the cheese.'

'Yes! Last month when I had the pleasure of that dinner in Beziers, I saw a fabulous new way with fruit. Cook had it piled up into the shape of a sphinx, with ice along the bottom. The whole beast was lacquered with gold paint. I don't know how they did it but I need to get one. Jules will have to go into Lyon. I have a name!'

The thing sounded horrible. Even at her tender age, Madeleine had experience enough of Madame's penchant for tasteless, fashionable arrangements with food to know the fate of the fruit sphinx. Guests would 'Ah' their wonder for a while and then forget about it as they sluiced more wine down their gullets. The gilded ice would melt as the evening wore on and the grape eyes and banana legs would begin to sag off the rods that held the gruesome piece in place. Jules and Maddy would next see it again at midday on their arrival back at La Castilla, as the last guests slunk off, avoiding their eyes, and notice the fat flies that had begun to buzz round the flesh. The air would be waxy with the smouldering smell of the last, dangerous, candles.

'Yes, Madame. I can make sure Jules gets along to them for a price. And he needs to take the order to the vintner.'

La Castilla didn't have much of a cellar. What languished there were items from old Madame didn't favour, so each new party bought a new order, every drink drained in greed, leaving nothing to store. Sticky bottles were passed under the morning sun as the parties waned, their last inches swallowed as the pétanque balls skittered off the terrain, clicking the cochonnet into the bushes. Even the vintner's boy, well used to copious drinking, raised an eyebrow as he clattered away the next day with the empties. One of their elderly cartmen had taken an early retirement after a collection at La Castilla. He refused to speak of it, but the other lads still whispered about a horrible scene involving a dog, two of the local aldermen and a young woman, who might have been tied to the buttress of the barn.

Madeleine tapped her foot, and the end tip of her pencil on the paper. Errors – incorrect orders, late deliveries – they always happened, but they were never her fault. Regardless, she was quietly masterful at solving problems long before the Madame discovered them. A young person in a world without power of her own, she wore her wit and her burgeoning wisdom as a cloak. She dared to lean back in the chair, hoping to move the meeting to a close, just as Madame yawned.

'That will be all for now, Madeleine.'

Madame Bardin tottered, ungainly inebriation forcing her forward. She leaned too closely to Maddy and she swayed, blocking out the light and filling the air with a dark, insectish musk. Maddy was as still as a doll. Madame Bardin placed a crooked finger beneath her chin. It wasn't the first time, and it wouldn't be the last.

'Get everything right, Maddy dearest, and we will all be fine.'

Maddy shut her eyes tight and gripped the arms of the chair. The fabric was slippery under her palms, and like a door closing hard, she felt Madame's dry mouth on her lips.

LONGFORD, 1868

IT WAS TOO DARK FOR THE ROBIN to be awake, but the families of the estate were stirring. John could call on them at five o'clock in the morning if he wished, and the stove would be hissing, while children bawled and bayed or dozed after feeding. But he had no wish to hover at dark dawn doors and intrude; far better to come by in the cool rays of morning when the men were gone, and the women had tea in their hands. October, in all its ripe fecundity, invigorated John. Autumn in south Manchester is a golden time. Something in the earth throws up just the right species and the surrounding scents can make a small, inauspicious piece of the world quite beautiful.

The estate was busy by eight. His men had long been at work and their children were up and in their boots. The littler ones bustled about, swamped by their rose and amber hand-me-downs. The bigger children, sturdy in britches and skirts, formed a line to walk into the village to school. It was part of the contract, and where on occasion John had found a child assisting a father in the sheds or a mother with the laundry, they were immediately dispatched back to school. Every child born on the Longford estate could read and write by seven years old.

The early sun's rays shot across the green land, bleaching it fawn; John's boots were mirrored with cold dew. It was an uncommonly easy day, no trips to town or further. No finance meetings. No property committees. No contracts to read and reread and sign.

John had built Longford Hall in an Italianate style, and over these past few years had begun to build up the gardens, allotment, and leisure areas under the same premise of beauty in order. The combination of his own ambition and Peter's voracious appetite for perfection was a powerful one. Now they had more gardeners in employment, though not enough. While his dream of the Sunnyside Villas was not yet nascent, John had been quick to start and build some of these men and their families a row of neat, modern cottages to the back of the hall.

Gerard Tolan had been a disgruntled and underpaid labourer on a dairy farm in Cheshire. Over a few ales at the Frozen Mop in Mobberley, Peter convinced him that he was the man that John needed; a rust-headed Cork-born fellow who was an instinctive horticulturist and a learned groundsman.

Seed catalogues landed in John's mail at an alarming pace and the paperwork written against the newly laid out gardens and arable patches was mounting up vigorously. Ged was sharp and keen and unfettered in his criticism (sometimes, scorn) of the work that had been done before his arrival. The irrigation systems were unworkable, the glasshouses were cheap, the 'no-dig' methods weren't making the best of the soil, the crops were all in the wrong places, facing the wrong way.

Ged paused and glanced at Peter, running a finger round the top of his trousers, and jigging his knee. John nodded and waited.

'The irrigation system is not fit. It's shot. It's…' Ged looked around the room for a word to replace the livelier language that came most naturally to him.

'Poor, Ged?'

'Yes, sir, as Peter says, it's "poor".' Ged smirked and shifted again, resuming the riddling of his belt. Silence, but for the ticking of the grandfather clock and the clink of the spoon in John's tea glass.

'The water is gathering on the roof. That will – would – be a complete disaster for the house. I've been up to look and it's beginning to sag the top gables. And I can use that water. I can drain that off and bring it right down to where I want it. I could pipe all that water into the glass houses.'

John winced. There were 'I's and 'me's coming too quickly and easily.

'We could put the pipes down and sink them low enough to get water into the front meadows. We've followed Chatsworth in the plans as you've favoured and it works here too – it's the same sort of ground, same sort of land.'

The Chatsworth estate in Derbyshire was John's model for Longford. It's pretty, hardworking span created a garden that was leisurely and light of touch, yet yielded crops that Leone would use in the kitchen. The people of the estate could share it too; any child could pod a pea.

John's tea was tepid, but Gerard's voice was warm with zeal. He flipped another page, pulled on his breeches, propping his well-padded backside on the walnut of John's desk.

'So, I think – I know – I need, that is you need, upwards of twenty men on this land. It will cost of course, as they would need to be housed.'

Gerard put his hand up in a dramatic defence to an objection that didn't come.

'I have seen it before, sir. Big houses like these, just this size – new gardens and no plans. Lord of the land makes the shortcuts. Ten, fifteen on the ground and most of them living out. Never works. Mark me, sir, it never works. The savings you make, you lose again just trying to keep up with who is coming and going.'

John had long ago made his mind up that he would pay for twenty men with families, and house them generously. He could afford it. He would enjoy it. Though this decision had been made, John was interested in hearing Ged's reasoning behind it. Maybe even letting this foreigner adopt part of his dream.

'We could double the glass houses – and I have the right contacts to make this work for the right price. I can call in more favours, sir, than you have them fancy tea jars.'

Ged laughed, and Peter frowned, made nervous by the new confidence and growing colour in Ged's face, wondering if there was more than coffee in the man's flask. He was relieved to see him roll his papers up.

'Think about what you want, Mr Rylands. From this place. From me. I know I am the right man for the job. I've done this before, and I've done it well and I'm not a lazy sod who will just do all that again like a copy. I see why you feel for this place. There's something in it. It's special but I could make it perfect for you. I can do your lawns, I can do your courts, I can do your glass. Do you want vines, or peaches? Anything. By God, I can even bring pineapples to Stretford, if that's what you want, Mr Rylands.'

MANCHESTER, 1870

UNFORTUNATELY FOR MARTHA, when they married, love
didn't much live in John. It was as though he had forgotten
how to feel it at all. Dinah's death had defeated him. Her grave
was full, cold home to her and five of their children.

Martha Carden was a widow, also navigating grief and a
mistrust of the shallow promises of life when she was pushed
towards John by her bullish father, who was tired of her taking
up his space by the fire, weeping for Richard. They married in
1848 at St. Peter's Church, Newton le Willows. Martha was of
the Greenough Brewers family; a fine stock, but not without
the similar rifts and scandals that had riddled John's own
Pilkington line.

On paper, the match was feasible, even admirable. The
Cardens and the Rylands were known to each other, and they
moved in similar circles. The north-west was always a close
community. John had liked her enough at the start, and he went
into the marriage with hope at his heels and a wish for more
children. The autumn that framed their courtship had been
spectacular, a series of warm days and of amicable moments
that together, imitated the beginnings of love.

John had missed the small things of marriage; conversation
in the dark, choosing flowers together for a party, mild disagree-
ment over a headline, or the final pages of a novel. His bed was
vast without Dinah. At only forty-seven years old, the thought

of not having a woman with him again to share his home and his embraces made him wretched. Martha Carden had a dry wit, and a reputation as a good hostess. The autumn romance illuminated them both well; he, eager to map her into a future made with babies and anniversaries. Martha, thinking of the fear of empty years ahead, her beauty diminishing and her position in the world fading in vibrancy as it inevitably would; as the young widow shrinks to the lonely spinster, voiceless in a corner. She would have only her father for company, and the invitations to wider society would stop, before long. With this at hand, she filled their October and November together with her sunniest smiles, her roundest knowledge and best-chosen gifts of books and trees to plant in the spring at Longford. They were married by January.

Martha was conveniently childless, and John soon found out why. He tried to please her in bed, though it was more of an effort for him than he would have wanted. John's body and his thoughts turning to it whenever there was a lull in business. He was not a predatory man. Not the type to leer at women or show any outward signs of lust; he kept all his thudding desires hidden within him.

Their incompatibility between them was severe, and kept John melded to Dinah's memory. This huge and dangerous fact started to rupture them from the beginning. A seam that began as a small tear, grew and grew, creating the yawning rent that Caroline would reach in to.

Martha only allowed him on top of her; she would not let him attempt to please her, in any way. He had tried to talk to her in the dark of their bedroom, persuading her and assuring her. Caroline, at once his saviour and his downfall.

'We could have children, Martha? Is that not want you want?'

She pulled the bed covers around her.

'I hate it. All the fuss and effort. It makes me ill. Richard never bothered me like this.'

John looked at her.

'What? Never, Martha?'

Her lips were a tight line.

'Never. He was a gentleman. He never asked any of this of me. Not once.'

He made sure it was over as quickly as he could. To get it done with for himself as well as for her. On his elbows in the black of their room, his head ached, the vestiges of attraction he had for her dissolving. An admirable match meant nothing to him without any sort of love. Martha was dry and closed, a board beneath him.

He wanted her to be willing, to reach out for him as Dinah had. In the first years of their marriage, he kept trying to seduce her. He arranged for flowers, wine, evenings in town. Martha laughed with the waiters with ease, yet when he asked her about her day she yawned, looking past him. Over tablecloths and by ponds, at theatre bars and on walks through Valentine's orchard, he asked her how he could please her. Martha shrugged and visited Richard's grave with bouquets. As months passed, John's passion dwindled, and he found he didn't even want her anymore at all.

It was no surprise to either of them when John's ministrations began to falter. The pitiful coupling had finally limped to a complete stop some years ago, and the last time was memorable. After another costly evening, where the wine was plentiful but the conversation arid, John reached over to caress her hand. He hoped she might at least allow him to hold her. At that moment, the moon cast aside a cloud and John saw Martha's face. Grimacing, her teeth bared and her eyes screwed shut, she looked a portrait of repulsion. He moved his hand from hers, and never tried to touch her again.

Intimacy was shed like a cusk. The poison of distaste which began as her waning interest in him, rapidly turned into patent hatred. Martha – as his second wife – became obsessed by his first. Benign curiosity curdled in her then grew, assuming a spiteful energy which feasted on Dinah's memory, eroding the little goodwill that was left between them. John found her staring at Dinah's portrait in the library – taken off the walls, leaving the greasy ghostly outlines on the paper where the picture should have been – instead propped on Martha's neat, angry lap.

For a short while, John had endeavoured to manage her jealousies, thinking that by entertaining them he could exorcise them.

'Was she as dark as a gypsy, John – did she sound as coarse as she looked? Did she sit on you the way you wanted me to? Was she heavy, John? Her picture looks like she had a taste for cake and wine.'

She insisted on a ghoulish tour of all the residences that he had shared with Dinah, starting with Cheetham Hill, Hilton Street and finally the grand mansion house, Gorton Villas. Dinah was dead by the time John moved there, but Martha's appetite for his past was voracious. Yet she had no interest in his living sons, and even less so in Dinah and John's lost, unbaptised infants.

It had been a grim late November day when John, exhausted by yet another evening of Martha's questioning, had risen very early and asked Peter to pack the coach. In the freezing black of the morning, Martha was subdued and silent, her fire from the night subsided.

'Get in. I am sick of your questions. Get in and we'll go to Gorton and by God, that will be the end of it.'

As the horses tramped through silent streets, Martha began to interrogate him all over again. The flask of coffee juddered in her grasp as she spat out her anger, ranging over his past. Dinah, his sons, his dead babies, his business, his properties; she cast them all in a terrible light so unrecognisable to him it caused a spear of pain in his chest. He leaned his weary head against the carriage seat and stared out into the distance, seeking the comfort of the dawn.

The groomsman dropped them in the gloom outside of Grove Villas. Taking the keys from his pocket he gripped Martha's arm hard, nearly dragging her up the path to the door. John started as he saw that there was a low candlelight coming from two of the bottom rooms.

'Be quiet! Be quiet for pity's sake! Anyone could be in there, Martha. I haven't checked the villa for weeks and I have had no man to come down here since summer. Stay back here.'

Mercifully, for once she obeyed him. The heat from the interior hit John. His tread was cautious, Martha silent behind him, as they heard a noise from the front living room. John pushed her back firmly with one hand and pushed open the door with the other.

John Garthwaite, his eldest son, was supine on the beautiful rug that his mother Dinah had chosen for Hilton Street. John had forgotten how rich the colours were and for a speck of a moment he loved her fiercely again for everything, and her perfect good taste in this rug that his son was sprawled naked upon. There was a man above him, bouncing on his white torso, long fingers crawling in and out of his hair. Time stood still for a pin and then all things changed forever.

Martha's screech pierced the silence, then tapered away into panting, and whimpering. She clutched at herself, convulsing. John Garthwaite's face bore no shame, only disgust.

'Oh, look who we have. Visitors. Do shut up, Martha.'

John Garthwaite didn't move to cover his lean white body, marbled in peach and grey from the licks of the open fire.

His companion whipped his clothes from the floor, grasping a blanket to his modesty. His eyes darted with alarm and his mouth hung open in shock.

John Garthwaite stood, his body beautiful and frightening in front of his father and his father's wife.

'Father, just go and take your stupid, whining, insane bride with you.'

John saw his son, in a way he never thought possible. Naked, John Garthwaite was a stunning specimen, Vitruvian and astounding. His arms were solid, and his stomach and loins were taut. His father could hardly bear to look at him.

'John, I'm sorry. I didn't know you would be here.'

'Clearly not, Father. This is Isaac. It looks like he is going now anyway. Are you, my love?'

Isaac dressed. It was a harsh pantomime, and John felt the oddest sense of disappointment in his son's choice of lover. Isaac – if that was his real name – was a weak-looking individual. John knew well enough the look of drug-addicted prostitutes. While they were never to his taste, he was familiar with their hungry ways and desperation from his work at Wood Street. He saw in Isaac what he had seen time and time before – the pallid gleam of an opiate sweat, the rickety arch of prematurely aged shoulders, and a paranoid twitch in the eyes.

An idea scattered back through his mind that he should have given his sons some form of guidance, some idea of how to conduct this sort of thing. John Garthwaite had plainly inherited the curse of his own powerful drives. Should he have sat him down, at the start of his youth, and imparted the limits he adhered to himself? It would never have been possible – if he had offered such advice, it would have been the most unbearably open admission of his hidden truths, something he could never divulge. It would have been like publishing the book of himself, an author of secrets and shame. And where the message of the tale might have served them all for the better, it could have never happened.

Martha leaned against the wall, rubbing her hands over her face and sobbing. John Garthwaite found his robe and once he had dispatched his boy, came back into the room with force, the door bouncing off the wall.

'I think this show is over, Father. Martha? Kindly stop snivelling your mucus over my family property and get back to your ill-begotten marital pile in Stretford. You have his wealth, yet you make him miserable. You escaped your moronic father, yet you bring nothing. I know what love is, and my mother loved him. You don't. You never did'.

Strands of her hair stuck around Martha's face, which was swollen with anger.

'You disgusting, filthy, Godless pig. You sicken me. This house belongs to your father and to me and you dare to use it this way!'

Dinah's rug blushed gold in the different light of the pink sun, and the shadows of the weakening fire.

John Garthwaite's laugh was hollow as he turned to his father.

'I feel for you, Father, saddled to that witch. You are a fool, and you are as unhappy as I am. But at least I have not tied myself to any person for good. Doubtless she has her hand in our pot, but not in your bed, I think. This is an end for us, Father.'

There was too much truth in the room for John to endure. He had a fierce urge to return to Longford and lock Gorse Hill down forever. He could barely countenance anything further than the next few moments, quitting here and dragging Martha with him. Then everything happened at once. John Garthwaite had turned to stoke his fire, and John, too late, saw Martha reach for a heavy vase. Her aim at John Garthwaite's head was lucky and it hit. He swayed and gripped his forehead, snarling in pain and fury.

'Take your demented wife away from me, Father. And take my name off anything to do with either of you.'

'Son, don't say that! Wait. We can meet, you and me and Peter. None of this matters. None of it!'

Hot tears fell from his eyes, and he reached for his child, not seeing him now, but feeling him, remembering and knowing him as his beautiful, perfect, warm little boy. He had held him in his arms. Taught him to read. Kissed him with such love every single night. Wrapped his tender knees when they were scuffed, sat with him when swaddled in his cot, stroking his velvet skin as Dinah put her baby to her breast. He loved him still, just the same.

'What has happened tonight matters nothing to me. You are my boy, John! You are my boy! Please, take my keys. Have the house, John. It's yours. Don't say anything else, please!'

Martha launched into John, pulling the keys from him and running out into the orange of the dawn. John took a last look at his son. His precious baby whom he had once cradled, kissed so often, so preciously. His lovely, exquisite, little boy. He looked long enough to see John Garthwaite turn from him in rage and disgust. The slam of the door was final and short in the air. John had no choice but to leave and to follow Martha, leaving his son in the destruction of a house in pieces, glass on its floors, and a fire dying in its grate.

John left early the next day, his shock and pain driving him away from Martha and the trials of Gorton Villas. Martha's nightclothes stuck to her and she could smell herself; unwashed, fetid, a sweet musk turned to a bilious bloom. She heard Leone in the room – when had she arrived? How long had she been here, moving so silently as she lay stinking and exposed in her pathetic bed.

Leone felt the arduous weight of pity. Martha's bedroom, once so neat and fragrant, was dank and horribly untidy. Discarded clothes lay in rumpled mounds, and her bedside cabinet was stacked with soiled cups and tissues. The curtains were drawn and the room was airless, locking the stale odour in and onto everything.

'Mrs Rylands? Shall I help you up?'

Martha turned in her bed, keeping the eiderdown clamped to herself.

'John is out again, I suppose.'

Less of a question, more an admission of bitter defeat.

'He is. He went with Peter on business'.

Martha spat out a hard, mirthless laugh.

'The great John Rylands and his great, great business. What today, Leone? Buying up more blocks of London? Laying the first brick of another mill? Spending his millions on yet more tiresome books for his bottomless library? Or is it the charity? Oh yes, I can picture it now. Our dear John Rylands, spilling his hospitable kindnesses into the lap of some deserving whore.'

Leone swooped to gather up some of the clothes strewn around the place. Leone had once felt something akin to love for Martha. Well, if not love, a kind of loyal, womanly affection. She had been a pretty bride with a strong mind and had briefly brought a sort of optimism to Longford.

Martha had at first taken an interest in the estate and in John's business. Leone was no expert on much at all, but she believed that in those early days Martha was behaving just as she should and as was expected. She was not the first Rylands wife and knew she was not the most loved either, but she fitted the role and made herself as likeable as she needed to be.

Leone had been in service all her life and was under no illusion as to the nature of her relationship with Mrs Rylands. They were never going to be dear friends. It happened, of course.

Leone knew of some girls who were the absolute confidantes of their employers. In her previous house, she had even known of a maid who slept with her mistress. She herself had heard how very close they were night after night; a querulous, triumphant wail came through the walls. But the amicable, mutual, cheerful alliance between her and Mrs Rylands had started to dissolve some time ago and would never return.

'Shall I help you to your bath?'

'I'm not a cripple, Leone. He may wish me dead, but I'm a long way from that yet. I'm staying alive and in this woeful marriage just to spite him.'

Venom was etched in the lines of her scowl.

'Dearest Dinah was adored by him, was she not? Blasted, saintly, Dinah. Mother to the heirs. Littering the graveyards with her dead progeny. My chances were taken from me by Longford and him – an endless memorial to her.'

Martha didn't shock her anymore. Much as she smarted at how viciously they were expressed, Leone recognised that much of what Martha felt was perfectly true, and her mind seemed to be fracturing. John and Dinah had been fiercely in love. Sex and births and deaths kept them close and made them closer and John's determination to please her never wavered. He impregnated Dinah over and over again, and the terrible demise of each blue, sacred and loved baby set him back to the task with a furious, dark, energetic passion.

But all that was past. While Leone had not been witness to his first marriage, she knew enough to suppose that after Dinah's death, any further happiness for John was going to be hard built on his misery. And what for her own life, thought Leone, as she left Martha heaving herself from the bed. There was a new school opening down the road in the village of Chorlton-cum-Hardy, funded, in part, by Rylands money. They would need teachers and that felt like more of a future for her than this. Her mind's eye took her to a bright, white classroom, peopled with little faces upturned in an eagerness to learn. She imagined it so vividly she could almost reach the scent of fresh, new wood and the powder of the chalk. There were curtains in green lawn and spicy aniseed balls in her apron. It swam to her head and for a moment of hope she could nearly forget the dolour and anger that was beginning to seep and grow in her beloved hall. Her will had grown short and she was finding Martha, in her illness and her anger, almost impossible to like. Something in Longford had to change.

La Castilla, 1870

THE LETTER CAME FROM NANTES. Madame Bardin had been clearing the home of another dead, generous aristocrat. Books and maps and musical scores and an array of orphaned, high-value items magically appeared in La Castilla following these trips. A costly glass vase, diamond brooches and valuable paintings would suddenly become part of the fabric of the house, and nothing was ever said or explained. Enriqueta doubted that any of the innumerable objets d'art housed at La Castilla, apart from the actual fixtures, were the original family possessions that Madame Bardin so readily boasted of.

'Ah, the scene of old Lyon in oils. Great Uncle Cesaire was so terribly fond of it.'

'My dear little St Louis decanter? My darling Grandmother Elodie had such a very, very refined eye for fine glassware."

'Girandole is my chosen style for earrings and the grey pearls do suit my complexion, you are quite right. They are just like the ones favoured by the Empress Eugenie.'

Madame Bardin had a sound knowledge of period and style, so each of her finds blended well with the others, and it never took long for a new piece to become entirely absorbed into the sham family history.

The rain soaked Jules as he unloaded the cart, and together with the courier, who swore in fury at the puddles on the drive, they bought in stack after stack, until Enri's long table was filled and she had no idea where to start. With every surface covered, even cataloguing them would be hardly possible.

All would eventually be placed or repurposed. The truly valuable ones could be sent to auction, or sold to museums, galleries, and private collections. The academic tracts and maps often found their way to colleges, universities, or specialist teachers.

Madame Bardin had many contacts and she black-booked all their fancies and peccadillos. There were ladies who always wanted bird books, or collections of fashion drawings. Gentleman who wanted engineering books or particular histories. She kept the little pocketbook, the leather bald with use, under her pillow or tucked in her skirt. The information it contained about the great and the good of France was incendiary, detailing a significant handful of men who paid a high price for erotica, of all classifications. These books arrived at La Castilla already wrapped in brown paper. At first, it had been a mystery to Enriqueta, and she had carefully peeled the corner of the paper away, thinking that it was the correct thing to do. Sketches of pudenda, thick with hair and plunged with devilish items, children tied and gripped by demons. Lately, even sheaves of photographs, ghostly images of naked girls, their eyes lowered in shame, captured by the rare few that were rich and depraved enough to own a Phoebus camera.

She never mentioned them, placing them in a designated box, which was soon full to the top. The box got emptied overnight when Madame Bardin was in residence, presumably to be shipped in secret to varying addresses, and whichever hot, wealthy hands were waiting for them.

The general process of redistribution could be prepared for: Enriqueta and Jules knew how to divide the spoils and box them accordingly. But the final decisions always had to wait for Madame's return, when she would stalk her way through each of the piles, approving them or otherwise. On the odd occasion, she would quickly retrieve one, putting it slyly aside for herself or someone else. Mostly though, through sheer hard work and their dogged, tedious learning, Enriqueta and Jules knew instinctively where each item should go.

Enriqueta had come to love Madeleine and Jules dearly, and it wasn't just because she was stranded without anyone else to care for. They were wonderful company and the three were bonded by the bizarre and irregular life of La Castilla. Jules, for all his staid and ordered manner, would, on their luckier days, suggest an evening trip to Lyon.

'She's gone – for at least a week. I know it for a fact. If we get all our business in order and call in a few favours here and there, we can take one of the traps into town for a night. A whole, proper, night. No one will know.'

There were plenty of favours Jules exploit. He was always willing to take in and bed down a horse for a tired rider, quick to take the boucherie pots back on his way into town. Maddy was wise too: making almond cakes and iced biscuits as gifts for the maids or gardeners' wives, wrapped up in ribbon and so delicious that people asked for her secret recipe.

Between them, they had enough goodwill to cover excuses, absences, lock stables and light or snuff out the relevant lights. The sleight of hand wasn't absolutely necessary, as Madame Bardin was often so far away, but it added to the thrill of escaping the confines of La Castilla. In the last few months, they had got away with evenings to see the Saltimbanques, the last of the Goguettes, the touring Saxophonists and even the Ba-ta-clan.

On those occasions they rushed through their duties so that by five o'clock they could start to get ready. Maddy ran Enri a deep bath and threw in walnut oil and a drop of the rose scent that Madame insisted they kept in the store cupboard for polishing the wood.

When Maddy pressed powder onto her cheeks, Enriqueta felt as close to happiness as she ever could in the peculiar, stifling walls of La Castilla. The nights away from La Castilla were rare, but for the three of them, they were enough to make all the trying times bearable.

Madeleine bought in tea, lemonade and biscuits for them and once these were finished, Enri rose to start again. Weary and bored, she nodded at Jules to rise himself too. But she wondered how long she could stay. The work neither challenged her nor held her interest. It was an isolated, tedious situation, and the days were insufferably long and without any sort of variety.

Her learning, at first on such a steep trajectory, had rapidly flattened and become stale. Not yet completely lonely, but certainly stuck. Not exactly afraid, but disturbed and unsettled by Madame Bardin.

The house itself had daunted her from the beginning. She was not foolish enough to believe in ghosts, yet La Castilla, she was sure, was enthralled to a negative force. A dark spirit, a malevolent presence. She increasingly fretted about what would—and could— be the next part of her life. Enriqueta had not had the benefit of any governing wisdom in her life for a very long time. Her father had died some years ago. A remarkable railway accident in England quashed him, and her mother had always been too busy for her multiple offspring. Her stepfather, the great composer Julian Fontana was as weak and selfish as he was talented. When her mother Juana died, he packed her children onto a ship, bound for England where they were sent to live with their Tennant relatives, in houses where they were foreign, burdensome and silent.

In one of those rare, mind-reading moments, Jules stayed seated and looked sidelong at her, saying, 'You never talk about your family, Enri. Do you miss them... want to visit them? He stopped, his shyness taking over. 'I could take you. Madame must allow you some time to go and see them. If it is what you want.'

He saw her redden and take a breath as she sat back down again.

'Look, I'm sorry. That was a stupid thing to say. And none of my business.'

'No, Jules. We are friends.'

Looking at his thin, sensitive face, furrowed with anxiety, she felt a rush of affection for him.

'I don't miss my family at all. My mother and father were much too busy for me when I was little. They had their hobbies and their parties and their sugar. They seemed constantly surprised to see me if I emerged from the nursery, or when I came home from school. As though they had quite forgotten they had children at all. Maybe they loved each other too much to think of us.'

Enri's smile was wan.

'I miss my sister Leocadia. I miss my brother, Jose. I miss friends. Jeanne, and my cousin Marianne. My time in Paris. It was a gilded period of my life, too good to last forever. Of course. They were happy days. But I knew things would have to change for all of us eventually. Being twenty-one lasts for months, not years. Weeks, really, a lot of weeks. Marianne is married now, and has her son, Arthur. She lives in England, in a seaside town called Truro. Jeanne is still in Paris, though recently I have heard that she is also to be married.'

Jules wanted to ask – what about you, Enriqueta? When will your tall husband and fat babies come? There were no secret, magical corners in La Castilla for a suitor to appear from. Their covert trips to Lyon were not long enough to strike up the beginnings of a passion with anyone. And Madame's parties, though full of men, were the type rightly avoided by Enriqueta. There were no cracks or small spaces for romance to seep into her life. And even if opportunity were to present itself, thought Jules, would Enriqueta respond?

He saw she was small and guarded; the natural cast of her glance was downward, making her appear more reserved than she truly was. Her smiles were warm and genuine, but rare. She never rushed at anything or anywhere, and her conversation was spare – measured and thoughtful. Despite her sober qualities, just beneath her careful surface was a witty sense of energetic fun and a constant good humour. Compared to the swinging, volatile, often unpleasant nature of Madame, Enri was all the best of calm, warmth and kindness to Jules and his sister.

But where she could conceal her nature, she could not shade her beauty. Even Jules, in the fig green of his youth, saw that she was a pearl. There was not a dim side to her. Her cheeks were pink, her eyes a piercing ebony and her face arresting. She had a holy face, smooth and even, her features delicate. Moreover, she had not the first notion of how untouchably beautiful she really was. Jules wondered whether it would be long before the dark reach of a lover would invade the prison walls of La Castilla and snatch her up.

The names of her friends in Paris were now familiar to him, and because of her vivid and fond descriptions of her apartment there, he felt he had walked through every room. She occasionally referred to her birth country but when Jules sought out Cuba on the globe, and traced its mountains on the maps, it still meant little to him without the detail she so readily supplied about Paris.

Indeed, there was much more to know about Enriqueta Augusta Tennant. Born in 1843, in a white hillside mansion built on her mother's sugar money, above the heat and the hustle of

Havana, Enriqueta had an upbringing more unusual and exotic that anyone could ever imagine. There were hints to her French heritage in her dark hair and her soft ecru complexion, but even then, her father's Yorkshire bloodline balanced and diluted her looks, lending her some firmly Anglo characteristics. Her nose was small and narrow, but her lips were full.

Her father, Stephen Cattley Tennant, was a restless and talented man, who represented his employers, a Liverpool mercantile firm, robustly and judiciously in all his dealings. He would have continued multiplying his moderate but solid wealth around the world at a leisurely pace had he not met the remarkably beautiful Juana Camila Dalcour, a day before he was to leave Cuba to begin the long and broken journey back home to England.

Stephen had spent a stifling two weeks prowling a tobacco farm with its owner, Señor Puerto, recording every detail of costs, labour, production and supply chain. The aim was to secure enough information to take back to the board, so that they could consider a distant investment in the place. The days were long, and Stephen had fallen into bed each night exhausted, swiping away the flies who were already fat on his thin English blood.

The last day of business came, and they were no closer to any sort of deal or plan. Though he was replete with information, Stephen was uncharacteristically far from procuring a conclusive, profitable package to take back to the board. Frustrated and tired, he was thankful to shake Puerto's hand for the last time. Puerto gripped it, chugging his arm nearly out of the socket, kissing Stephen roughly on each cheek. Although there had been no real business at all done between them, Stephen had grown to like the affable, wily man. For the duration of his stay, his bone-deep fatigue – and the unrelenting heat – had afforded him a decent reason to excuse himself from the Senor's tireless offers of hospitality. But this was his last night and Puerto pulled Stephen to him, grasping him against his bearish chest.

'No more no Señor Tennant!' He growled, battering Stephen's narrow English back with his massive fist. 'Come with me tonight and we can drink together. No refusal! It's our last night together, my friend.'

For once in his life, Stephen didn't agonise or rationalise or think much of the decision. He allowed himself to be led by Señor Puerto to his favoured bodega at the end of the Calle Obispo, just inside the Havana city walls. Stephen had passed by La Pina de Plata several times while in Havana – its distinctive pink walls housing all that was beautiful about the city – the people, the uplifting sound of Changui, the Son Montumo, the games of Monte played at nearly every table. All of it drenched with the sweet, intoxicating scent of rum and lime, sultry bodies and satin fragrances. Everyone was welcome and a part of La Pina: man, woman, soldier, prostitute, artist, banker, farmer.

Puerto swung open the door and Stephen was assailed by the warm blast of laughter and the rhythm of the Guajeo. The long central bar was full of people waving notes for their drinks, and the waiters, dressed in their famous red jackets, served up rum cocktails with dizzying speed. Couples and groups of women danced the salsa in the space in front of the band, their exquisite bodies syncopated, so close to Stephen he could detect their mix of perfumes; mariposa, vetiver, tobacco and rose. Their shapes glowed under the golden sheen of the star shaped lamps that hung from the teal ceiling. Stephen's spirits lifted as the rum hit his empty stomach, and he no longer cared that he would be returning to his seniors, stiff and cold and bristling under moustaches and the weight of finance, and the chill Yorkshire wind, with little to show for his trip.

He was knocked out of his trance by Puerto's hard nudge.

His mouth was close to Stephen's ear, so that he could hear his urgent whisper below the thump of the music.

'There she is, Juana la Cubana. The Sugar Queen.'

Stephen turned to see the most splendid woman he had ever set eyes on. It was the biggest shift in his life, set to alter all. Juana Camila Dalcour was tall and radiant in a deep pink gown, finished with white frills. Stark around her wrists and her neck, the snowy lace lit her skin and pooled in the reflected light of her eyes.

'Something else, right?' Puerto chuckled. 'Not just beautiful, Señor Tennant. She is rich, rich, rich!'

Stephen watched her move through the room, and he felt a certainty and a confidence that came to him suddenly and with an outrageous ferocity.

'Introduce me, Señor Puerto.'

Sometimes, just sometimes, thought Stephen, you get lucky. He crushed the diffident timidity which usually thrived in him until he heard an inner voice instructing him which was born just at that moment, and for just one purpose.

Stephen Cattley Tennant did not return to England until many, many years later, and when he did so, he returned with Juana as his wife. Against some considerable odds, Juana fell deeply, quickly and equally in love with the pale, handsome, earnest Yorkshireman. While their backgrounds were staggeringly different, they had much in common. They admired each other's robust intellect and wit. She was a born businesswoman, and it did not take her long to discern in him a kindred mind. Unified by marriage only weeks after they met, he also joined her in her family plantation business 'Le Reunion Deseada'. He brought to it his considerable skills and he felt at long last fulfilled and utterly content. They were a passionate couple, and swiftly, the marriage began to yield very beautiful, healthy progeny, including a perfect pair of twins, Jose Esteban and Enriqueta

Augusta Tennant. The ancient Dalcour motto, displayed with pride above the doors of 'Le Reunion Deseada' was lived in him. 'Le Bon Temps Reviendra'. Let the Good Times Roll.

The conversation between Enriqueta and Jules, the most intimate they had ever had, was cut abruptly short as they heard the dreadful stomp of Madame in the hallway. She was back again, which meant their peace and small freedoms were over for a while. The doors slammed shut behind her, adding chips upon chips to the delicate paintwork.

'My dears, you are such quiet little mice, I didn't know if you were here or not! Good Lord, we are rather overwhelmed.'

Madame Bardin at least had enough grace to grimace at the sheer number of books in the room. There were tottering piles on every surface and stacked all over the floor. On her travels, it was easy for Madame to get carried away, and to keep sending cart loads back to La Castilla. It was fuelled by greed, at heart. A collector, she was good at taking, less at giving. The only time she ever displayed anything near to generosity was when she hosted one of her parties. Even those were more an opportunity for her to seek favour with those she considered useful.

Her time at chateaus and spas and holiday homes around the country were spent deep in drink and conversation, and she frequently woke, clothed and still inebriated, quite forgetting what cartload of books she had sent off the day before. Thus, she kept adding more to the booty, just for good measure, and was – without fail – baffled by the pile of goods that filled La Castilla to bursting when she returned.

'We need to move some of this on. I need the room back by next weekend! I am hosting a marvellous event for some very important people, and I will need your help. Both of you. And Madeleine. Where is she? Go and fetch her. I need her to do me a list for the catering. Oh, and Enriqueta. I forgot. A box just arrived for you.'

Madame turned to look slyly at her. Enriqueta felt a futile rage begin to simmer in the pit of her stomach.

'It had been damaged. I tried to patch it up for you, but I couldn't help but notice what was in it. A most beautiful gown.'

Since her cousin Marianne had given birth to Arthur, she had taken to sending her older, before-baby dresses to Enri. Marianne insisted that she could never regain her old shape, her ribs forever expanded by the callous burden of pregnancy. Enriqueta felt sickly despondent at the thought of Madame's crimson fingernails raking through the pretty frocks, sent to her with a pure love and intercepted by Madame's covetous gaze.

'Oh, and a letter. Here you are. Quite the popular one, aren't you?'.

The writing and the mark were Leocadia's, her sister, writing from London. Shutting her bedroom door, Enri delved into her apron, joyful to see four fat pages of her sister's comforting script. Pinned to it was a cutting.

Englishwoman's Domestic Magazine
Wanted: A respectable, genteel, steady young woman as a useful companion to a lady. She should be educated and willing to travel abroad. She must have twelve months' character from her last situation. Apply for name and address at the office of this paper.

Enriqueta's thoughts were quite blank; there was scant detail in the notice, but such was her unhappiness at La Castilla, she felt a small flame of hope.

Enri, the house may be in London! It most probably is – I can't think there can be many places of grandeur outside of the capital. It could even be somewhere near me in Kensington! Think of that – we could meet on your days off. We could explore the city together, the shops and the galleries. You must apply, Enri – write to the paper quickly. You are so very educated and so very well-travelled, you shouldn't be trapped like you are in that terrible French place. Please, please, please at least write to them. This is the right thing to do.

Enri smiled with joy; a sensation so foreign that it felt forgotten. She heard her buoyant little sister's voice jump with certainty from the page. Despite being younger, Leocadia had always been more sure, more vocal and far bolder than Enri ever could be. Leocadia's pert confidence and wild enthusiasms felt like home to Enriqueta. It imbued in her a revived sense of purpose. Leocadia's urging words were an abutment to her nerves. Enriqueta craved the foundation of her sister's surety, and just as soon as she had put the letter back in its envelope and hidden it away, Enriqueta knew exactly what she should do.

MANCHESTER, 1870

IT WAS AN UNPROMISING START to the day's business for John
and Peter. Thunderous clouds obscured the morning, and
only minutes into their journey to Manchester, rain began to
thrum onto the roof of the coach, the driver pulling the horse
against the sleet. The weather was too noisy for any sort of their
usual, companionable conversation. Besides which, Peter knew
that his master was in no mood, of late, for talk of *any* kind.

Weeks had rolled by untethered by the routine they thrived
on. They had always worked together with equilibrium. Yet this
all depended on John. And now, it appeared, the centre was
not holding, and misery danced like the devil in the place of
harmony. Peter saw that John was bending, thinner than he was
just a week ago. Lines were sketched across his clear forehead
and anguish drew his peaceful mouth into a line. Peter spoke in
a whisper against the rattle of the rain, knowing John, with his
head turned from him, would not hear his words.

'*You have secrets, John, holding you in this sad, sad place. I
wish I could lift them from you.*'

Peter sometimes worked late at Longford, finishing clerical
tasks in the office. Stiff with hours of work, he would rise to
hear the scuffle of John taking a horse out under the pull of the
moon. Other nights, Peter heard the dismount on the drive from
a public cab, long after Peter himself had returned to the hall in
the house carriage. The receipts from trips to Wood Street, back

and forth, stacked up on Peter's ledger spike and if the strength of John's torment had not silenced Peter they may as well have been scrawled *Caroline! Caroline! Caroline!*

'I can't do this for much longer, Peter. Look at the bruises on my arms, the scratches. Martha is strong; she tears her sheets and flies at me. I could cry thinking of the days ahead. The years. Once she was just unhappy with me—which was bad enough. Now she is ill, also. What a mistake we made. I am at fault. I thought I was above greed, but I wanted love and children at her cost. Oh, if only I could undo it all! There would have at least been freedom in solitude, for us both.'

Martha's illness had come in quickening increments. There was no up and down to Martha anymore, as there once was, but instead an exponential slide down into matters so inward and so dark that there was no retrieving her.

Leone had said to John that there was nothing to be done about Martha now. When her black moods and strange obsessions had first started to appear, John had not ignored it. Quick to act and logical as ever, he sent for his doctor, and consulted the wide range of medical books in his library. There were few subjects that didn't interest John, and rather than disregard his wife's dangerous gloom, he spent hours studying the condition, trying to understand what was driving her moods, and fuelling her discordant sorrows. He knew he was much to blame, but the things she had once loved – the garden, her work, and reading for hours – had drifted from her reach. Beach's Family Physician painted exactly Martha's mood: 'A low kind of delirium', often without real occasion or reason. Her gloom; taciturn and sometimes violent, did not appear to be caused by the Beach's list of suggested causal circumstances: 'A sedentary life, and solitude, acute fears and other diseases.'

John scoured the tracts of Blandford, Yeoman, Flint.

According to Beach, Martha's mania and delusions could be the fault of a hereditary disposition, a poor diet, lack of activity and too much time spent indoors. Her fears, suspicions and angered outbursts could equally be the expression of a 'neuropathic affection', or a diseased mind.

Though all the learned men had varying opinions on the contributory factors behind melancholia (not least that it was most virulent in the female sex), they were united on many of their solutions. Fresh air, activity and a regimen of rest.

John had all the tools to hand: money, people, his own sharp mind and rich experience. His business had survived multiple mill fires. When he needed machinery, he built it; his factories in Gidlow and Gorton loud with the grinding of burning metal. The Rylands business was thriving under the family motto, 'Not the Last', and as well as the mills he owned prosperous farms at Skelmersdale and Heapy. His commercial tenet was ravishingly simple—he did not enter any market or trade in which he could not excel in price or in quality. He had never passed a year without profit and his interests were global, with offices and outposts proudly scattered in Lyon, Cannes, Paris, La Spezia, Trastevere, San Remo, Genoa, Florence and Germany. He prayed, looking to God to hold him in the energies of his work, and lift him onto the paths he knew to be right.

Not slothful in business, fervent in spirit, serving the Lord.

But solving Martha was to be one the most uncommon challenges of his life. The truth was that although John had the money and the means to alleviate her sufferings and anger, he lacked one thing most vital to her recovery, because he no longer loved her. He knew this most definitely, and so did she. The most expensive physicians and the most radical treatments were feeble without the supporting power of tender, true, enduring love. Their union was irreparably damaged, and it was made worse by Martha's dark infatuation with Dinah. The legacy of devotion that had existed between Dinah and John was tacked to his present marriage like yellowing lace.

Was John to blame for her deep, savage misery and the loathsome cycle that trapped them and bound them? Their compass swung fruitlessly, Martha at the north – cold – and John at the south, burning and melting as he grew more obsessed with Caroline. His visits to her were frequent, and he could only find happiness when he had her in his arms. In his mind, he put her in bed with him at Longford. In his head, she strolled down the great staircase, she poured him wine by the fire, she sat with Leone, talking. If he concentrated hard enough, he could hear her laughter in his library, clear as a bell. Her image was so strongly imprinted in his eyes, he could often turn to see her disappear around a door, hear the whisper of her dress, and scent her, as if someone had crushed a meadow of spring roses across every floor in Longford. His was a vision pure enough to partially smother the noise that came from Martha's room every night.

Caroline knew of his wealth and his situation, and they talked often of his business plans. The trough between their fortunes was lit by the tiny candles of ordinary things. His gold watch gleamed next to her thin copper bangle on the bedside table, his wallet thick with folds of cash, fat next to her meagre little purse, sagging and empty but for coins. Her velvet boots had seen four women before her, while his shoes shone like the globe, made from a last with his name on it.

'You are the most patient, beautiful woman in the world. All my tedious talk of plans and work. And yet, you never ask me for anything, Caroline. Never.'

John had no right to caress her with one hand, hiding the rest of his existence in the palm of his other, crushing it dead. He knew that it was likely that, one day, her patience would expire. She could end it all and be free of him and the agony of their fruitless affair, and the thought of it made his heart bound with despair.

The city loomed ahead, and the clouds loosened to let the sun create playing-card rainbows in the wet air.

'Read this, will you, Peter? And post it for me when you are next at the office.'

Wanted: A respectful, genteel, steady young woman…

John struck his fist against the carriage.

'I can't keep vainly hoping things will improve, Peter! Both you and Leone have seen how Martha is, and the situation – if that's what I can call it – can only get worse. I have spoken to all the medics in the region and beyond and their only resolution for her at this point is the asylum.'

He shook Peter's hand from his shoulder, pressing the tears in his eyes with the same fists that could hurt and harm, but never would. Though his body raged, and his words cursed his fate and that of his wife, his spirit could still hear his God somewhere, and the voice was willing him to find strength to reach peace.

'I can't send her there, Peter. It's no place to die. I know there is no marriage left in us if there ever was one at all. She feels nothing but fury and disappointment towards me and for that I do not blame her. I know that I've failed her in many ways, and I keep failing her. But there is duty. I do not want to abandon her.'

Wisdom shut Peter's words tight within him. Often life doesn't allow for choice. Duty, at least, can be managed.

'She doesn't want my company, Peter. My presence agitates her. Riles her. Leone has such patience with her, but she can't continue to shoulder the burden alone. I will find Martha a companion. I must.'

The actual moment that he had decided to end everything with Caroline was shrouded in a grey, impenetrable mist. It was coloured as steel as the skies of the day. He could never clearly recall the exact reason or moment that pushed him into the most painful decision of his life. It might have been the persistent rain, Manchester damp around him, the madness of the mud and the bluster of the darkening city. It was Peter next to him, and Leone, in their example of a good marriage. It was Dinah, in the arms of his memory, shaking her head and holding their babies, offering up their small forms, limp like quiet prayer. It was Caroline, the woman he loved, but must leave, so certainly. She deserved all the riches that an honest love could yield, and selfishly, he was her gatekeeper, disallowing her the chance to find it. Or it was his God, and Martha, imploring him to turn from his base greed and be the decent man he ought to be.

The Lord stood with me and strengthened me.

Somewhere around that time, he had found himself at her familiar doorstep, knocking softly on her pale door, his heels on her two shallow steps. The agony in his heart was acute, and he was sickened with the hard task of taking the hammer down on both of their hearts. He heard someone shout his name from a passing carriage, and shame hid him under his hat, and twisted the certainty of his decision tight like a steel screw.

Caroline wrapped her arms around him, violets and the sweet promise of her wet breath at his neck. The noise of the world was muffled, leaving only them; so familiar and precious and he could feel her fingers shuddering. She was wearing a peony-blue scarf, as though she was on her way to a fair.

'Caroline. I don't think you will ever, ever know what this is for me. How difficult it will be for me not to see you. Not to hold you. I must walk away from this'.

The tears spotted the scarf dark.

'I always knew this day would come. John, I can't see how

we will live without each other. Oh! I feel like I am dying. I think I will die without you. Can't we just carry it on? I know how it is with Martha, but aren't we willing to keep each other? Be happy, like this, as we are?'

A milk cart rumbled behind them, passing the window, and mocking the scene with its terrible, normal noise. She raised herself on her toes, pulling John as close as she could.

'I love you, John. Know that I will always love you'.

John bent his head.

'I love you. I have the same agony. I am so very sorry. I am ashamed; I don't deserve your love and loyalty and I am tormented. This choice I make – believe me, I do it because I can't live with what I have become. A man governed by selfish motives. If I saw it in another, I would think badly of them, yet I continue, and I must stop. I can't pray to God and look to Him for approbation when I am living in the shadows of sin. Not you, Caroline! You are not a sin to me; it is how I have slipped so far from grace, and I need to resolve it. Absolve it'.

'Then go, John. Go and be a better man. Tend to your wife. Build your empire. Sow your seeds where you should. There is nothing more to be said'.

John knew that in the weeks to come he would yearn for her with an intensity so fierce, he would be sorely, desperately tempted to run to her again.

'But we can never see each other again, John, and I will make sure of that. You don't have to worry that I will appear, or that we will pass. And life will continue, the sun will rise, and the spring will come but we can't see those things together again. I will think of you, as I always think of you, and wonder, in agony, of where you are. What you do. But there shall be no maze to find me in, and no corners of the city that will spring me like a surprise upon you.'

John did not recognise himself anymore. Listless, he was

beginning to lose a hold over so much that he held dear. There could never be a complete life with Caroline, and as long as Martha still lived and breathed, he had to be the person he claimed to be and honour their marriage. He had to prove to himself and those around him that he was the good man he purported to be, and the selfish happiness he dreamed he could seek with Caroline could never be a reality. Such happiness would be impossible.

Kept by the power of God through faith unto salvation.

'No messages, John, or changes of heart. Don't do that to me. To us. Go. Don't turn round.'

For the last time in his life, John held Caroline's face up to his. He kissed her, tears falling from his eyes; shut tightly against the pain of the final embrace.

LA CASTILLA, 1870

MADELEINE MIXED A THIRD GIN and French, though it was not yet midday. Madame Bardin was very particular, insisting on the best Lillet Blanc vermouth and imported Gordon's. If only the generosity she bestowed on herself was extended to her staff; Madeleine hadn't had a new frock in months, yet here she was again helping Madame plan for another extravagant gathering. Her wrists shot too far from sleeves that were frayed with wear.

Delusions of a grandeur that were far above her had orchestrated Madame Bardin's life from the moment she had inherited La Castilla by chance from a very distant uncle, when there was no one left in a long line of single-child families. The family tree was so sick it should have been felled years ago; sparsely leafed with misers and thieves, the branches falling foul of great influenzas and airborne poxes. The feeble bloodline trickled to an unseemly end, terminating with the birth of Manette Bardin. As soon as she was old enough to interpret the value of class and breeding, she reinvented herself, smoothing over her tenuous bourgeois upbringing, perennially vague regarding her lack of schooling. Over the years she had modified and elevated her accent, imitating the languorous speech patterns of those she aspired to emulate. When she left the stone home cottage for La Castilla, she lost nothing; bracing herself to crawl up the rotten vine of greed, plucking at the fruits of lust, pride and envy on her way.

Manette Bardin was darkly preoccupied with societal rank; and it was with considerable strain that she maintained the illusion of status, developing a particularly horrible snobbishness which she employed to bolster her defences. Mean and spiteful, she took enormous pleasure in scorning those that she believed to be beneath her. All too often Madeleine had seen Madame Bardin's lips curl in derision at the clothes or the accent of those who served La Castilla. The delivery boys, the washerwomen, the gardeners. She showed them no kindness or grace, but sneered at their broken teeth, shabby clogs and Lyonnaise diction. Madeleine had witnessed the evidence of her cruelty over the years. The mark of the witch all over the house; in the pitiful bag of blind puppies, heavy with death in a bucket of water. The little candle girl, shut in a cupboard for hours because she asked for some bread. The burns on the hands of the deaf and mute gardening boy, who had doubtless dared to sit in the sun for a minute.

The Castilla parties were a playground for the covetous, predatory and aggressive; those that possessed the worst kind of unfounded infallibility. Stories about the parties circled the district, below the stairs of every big house, whispered from maid to maid, butler to groomsman. A game of cards at dawn on a Saturday had passed a row of worker's cottages from one fat pink hand to the next, resulting in the eviction of four families by midday on Monday. A young butler had been found tied and dead in a field, and once enough of the Gentry had claimed loudly that it was a prank that had gone awry, he was forgotten about in the main, though his poor mother cried over his blank grave until her heart stopped with grief. It was said that the occult played games master after midnight, rugs hastily covering pentagrams before the dowager duchesses visited for tea days later, the mustiness of the incense beaten from the drapes and the stains scrubbed from the floors.

Madame Bardin's glass was empty again. Madeleine added Gordons and Lillet to the long list of items she needed to order. She sighed, careful to turn her face from Madame and her demands. Grand gestures – improvident, capricious whims – such was Madame's burning ambition to impress her society. Peacock feathers, twisted to make wreaths. Quail eggs, blown and painted gold then hung from the ceiling on invisible twine, bobbing like celestial jewels. This time, she had requested yards and yards of fake vines, specifying that they must be a very precise shade of forest green, and made of a sheened damask only available at Maison Combier, the finest fabric atelier in Lyon. The list grew, with Meillard Richardier and Debard roses in pink and white from the prestigious Aux Fleurs du Sud on Place Bellecour. Hundreds of them.

Madame slurred.

'Party favours! Back in fashion. For the ladies, we will have Venetian Lanterns made of gilded gauze and real blossoms. For the gentlemen, Jules must go down to Ludovic Marque at Ferronnerie Verrière. He does a marvellous miniature thermometer! Shaped as hunting trophies, no less. On to the menus, Madeleine. Our theme this time is "Ambition and Indulgence". Ha! We could write that on all the invitations. In your lovely handwriting.'

Madeleine thought of the thin daube she ladled into her ancient grandfather's bowl each evening. She concentrated on the scratch of her pen on the notebook as her stomach tightened. Vol-au-vents filled with stewed eels cooked with nutmeg, anchovy paste and port wine. Croquettes of field fares, with white pepper in hard egg and lard pastry. Saddle of mutton glazed with redcurrants. Capon stuffed with lean veal and truffles. Turbot Au bleu. Matchstick potatoes stuck in Camembert, a souffle of sugared spinach.

Madame Bardin favoured the service á la Russe, with a screened table behind which Madeleine, Jules and the auxiliary staff would stash the mounds of plates and dishes. And once the party was over, leaving just the shadows of grease in the linen, there were the endless days of clearing and cleaning. Madeleine was still finding grimy glasses behind the curtains of unused bedrooms after the last gathering six months previously. To his disgust, Jules had once unearthed a pair of lady's undergarments from behind the largest magnolia tree. They looked as if they had been there for years. Stray stockings, garters and socks were frequent finds under beds and cushions. Madeleine stuffed them together and took them to the kittens at the farm to play with. It pleased her to see the tiny animals tear the expensive silks apart.

The following weeks were spent in preparation for the party, while Enriqueta was stuck in the tiring monotony of the Blue Room cataloguing the mountain of books and ensuring that they were all allotted a destination and packaged accordingly. Madame Bardin thundered in and out, sounding pointless, unhelpful direction. Every few days, the cart men would return to pick up another load, packing their vehicles and standing for a few minutes in the sun, drinking idly from their flasks, the afternoon rum escaping into the breeze. Enriqueta watched them from the window with envy, wishing she could jump into a cab and canter away, far from here, never to return. She had done as Leocadia had implored her to and had responded to the advertised position. Enriqueta was waiting, counting the days that passed. With each sunrise and sunset, each cart loaded and each rum flask drained, she felt her hopes of ever escaping La Castilla wither away.

MANCHESTER, 1870

SOTIRIOS HAZZOPULO pulled John into his arms, then Peter next.

'Welcome, Gentleman! John, Peter!'

Sotirios embraced his friends in turn, sheathing them in his familiar scent of cedar and bergamot. The ebullience of his smile and his imposing Ottoman dress was known throughout Manchester and beyond. Children sketched pictures of him, sticking pigeon feathers on to make his hats. Men envied him and his capacity to combine potent masculine allure and exquisite finery. The women of Salford lost their senses at the sight of his well-oiled, startlingly smooth beard, and would always find a chore to do at the steps when they heard the tinkling of his bell-laden horses turn onto their corner.

There were tales of his majestic and unflagging skills, and that his black military headpiece was never off centre, even in the most active of circumstances. Sotirios shunned the conservative shirt and tie, favouring a dark military cape and the thickly embroidered, golden breastplate of his family crest. While he was unstintingly proud of his roots, he had also integrated into his adopted county. He was a frequent winner of the annual Kersal Moor races, and the locals gathered to stare at his outfits and gasp at his prowess as one of the very best of the Lancashire Archers. His accent had become layered with Salfordian vowels, and the result was so ravishing, no one minded that his animated speeches as Conservative councillor and Greek consul lasted far longer than they should have done.

Sotirios Hazzopulo had much in common with John, not least their extensive business concerns. Born in Constantinople, Hazzopulo had arrived in Manchester with his brother, bringing with them a broad and profitable branch of the family yarn and textiles firm. Though his influence had begun in a small way – pulsing through the compact but serious group of Ottoman merchants who lived by him – it was significant enough that Sotirios could now claim John Rylands as one of his most close confidants.

Some years previously, John had watched the beautiful Greek Orthodox Church of the Annunciation rise with grandeur on Bury New Road. He admired every elegant detail – the basilica, the pilasters, the intricate modillion cornice – and set out to seek the beautiful brain that had imagined it. When he found Sotirios, he found a friend.

Their shared fascination for architecture had taken them from men who spoke business in town to friends that shared wine at home. Sotirios had grand offices in the same building as Rylands & Sons. His home, Bella Vista, nestled in the heart of the elegant sweep of The Cliff, in Broughton. The gates were ornate, curlicues of wrought iron flanked by two great sandy pillars. Yet they were nothing compared to the mansion they protected. An enormous villa, erected with pride and great expense, it was built in a Mediterranean style that was so loved by the wealthy Greek inhabitants of Upper Broughton.

A huge hallway ran through to the back of the house, where gardens stretched downwards, a sizable half acre of The Cliff as Sotirios's lawn. The sun made warm milk of the sky, steaming away the rain of the morning. The pelt of the lawn was glassy, with not a bent blade or a thug of a daisy throughout it. He had a man employed for the grass alone, and the summer previously

The Manchester Courier and Lancashire General Advertiser ran a long and detailed piece about the gardener's methods, and how he achieved such perfection with the peal-handled tools that Sotirios imported for him from Corfu. A portrait of Sotirios flanked the article, and the outcome was astounding. Over weeks, the hallway thudded with the sounds of packs of letters, so many that the postman abandoned pushing them through one by one. Instead, he sat on the wall in the sun each morning, binding them up in bundles and tying them with string then dumping the lot in the porch. Countless women, and a considerable number of men, wrote to him passionately and extensively about how they longed to see his beautiful lawn, to stand with him on it, to lie with him on it. Offers of service came without conditions. Many pleaded for the chance to trim his lawn for him, by moonlight or in the rain, wearing boots and tassles in the snow. One claimed she would give anything-just to see Sotirios himself snip at a fresh sod with the enamelled scissors. Alec, his devoted manservant, was used to a few ardent letters here and there about his master, but after the deluge that followed the newspaper coverage, he implored Sotirios to avoid his picture being so widely published again. The strain on his administration time had been ungovernable.

The famous lawn was well used: for cricket, croquet, and to host the finest seasonal garden parties in the Borough of Salford. Summer air simmered with the salty fug of thyme-roasted suckling pigs, turned on fires that put a silver sheen of ash on the cherry blossoms that circled the lawns. A Greek band played on a circular stage, which was automated to turn slowly, filling the Salford skies with the sliding notes of the bouzouki, the lyra, mandolin and psaltery. The colder months were no barrier to his inexhaustible sociability. Alec, resplendent in white cotton bloomers and a tapestry jacket, led a crew of sturdy Cypriots, erecting great buff-coloured circus tents which could be seen for miles, pale and incongruous on the vast suburban garden. The tents were also used furtively after dark, when Salford lasses would swoon in the arms of strong, dark men.

Glossy laurel trees, their bushes hollowed and clipped in places, sheltered the whitest marble nymphs. Granite water fountains shimmered and sputtered rhythmically in the shadows. Alec strode ahead, his white clothes drawing a family of red admirals to hop and flicker in the air around him. A mandarin-orange parasol bloomed open as Alec clipped it into place, shielding the table and chairs. Alec seated Peter first, flapping a napkin into the air like a magician's dove.

Peter had been born and raised in Chorlton-cum-Hardy, to a loving but very ordinary farming family. His childhood had never seen any sort of wealth, and all they had was made, grown, borrowed, or given. The first time he had used real money to buy proper sweets—rather than stealing spoons of sugar from the larder—it was a mystical moment, and he could still sense the weight of the coins in his hands, the sour blood smell that they left in his palm. The rough touch of barley sugar at the tender pink roof of his mouth.

While the O'Hara's had always had just enough, his life and work alongside John had lifted the veil of scarcity to reveal the other side, which housed luxury, elegance, transactions. Even the idea of education as ongoing and pleasurable, far from the pain of sums whipped into the child at a desk. Bella Vista was all of this, and Peter smiled contentedly as the tea – the Tsai Tou Vounou – was poured. He had first tried it some years ago, when the mountain leaves had tasted bitter and difficult for his resolutely English stomach. Peter soon learned that the generous spoonful of honey and splash of dark brandy that Sotirios added transformed the drink from indigestible to delicious. After three or four cups, he certainly felt in extraordinarily fine fettle.

A plate of Koulourakia – a twisted vanilla and anise biscuit – was set down along with the tea and as Alec disappeared, John leaned toward Sotirios.

'Thank you for again having us here, Soti. I need your ear for a few things. But, first, how is business for you?'

Shedding his black cloak, which must have been stifling in the warmth of the midday sun, Sotirios flexed his arms, muscled and toned as a warrior under his whites. His eyes sparkled, his smile widening. There was little he enjoyed more than discussing the strength of his own trade.

'It's good. Business is all good, John. You know, this bad economy, the strikes at the mills. These aren't my big problems.'

He laughed and stood, stretching – pointing a finger at John. From the cote, a couple of doves gurgled and shrugged their wings, as if imitating him.

'Even my competition is fair and agreeable! No, this challenge of mine is transport.'

John and Peter exchanged glances, nodding at him to continue.

'The trains. Bah! I could run with my fabrics on my back faster than they move. The dock charges for our goods are madness. None of this works for me – and you! Am I right, John? Peter?'

John traced the rim of the china cup, his fingertips tingling. The measures in their drinks were growing generous, more honey and brandy than tsai. Sotirios spoke with great arcs of his arms, releasing clouds of bergamot.

'We need to plan, John. Together. A canal connecting us all the way to the Irish Sea. Something big enough to give ocean ships direct access to the heart of Salford, on to Manchester, passing all our mills and factories. We can join everything – Liverpool, the docks, maybe the railways. All inland. It will be a monster, though, John. Miles. Possibly more than thirty, closer to forty, I believe.'

John could listen to his ambitious, voluble friend all day. Though competitors in commerce, they were the greatest allies in aspiration and enterprise. Soti was generous in everything he did and touched, and John appreciated that he saw him and Peter as equals, men he could share his dreams with. From a pocket in his waistcoat, Sotirios plucked out some fat raisins, and the family of doves waddled and hovered to tap around his feet.

'It is, without doubt, our biggest problem,' said John. 'And while I agree with you, it seems impossibly difficult. The expense. The number of navvies, engineers – the amount of time we would need. How would we even begin to get assent? The scheme would be a vicious battle to win, if ever won at all.'

The three friends were silent for a moment, weighed by the enormous prospect.

'It would take decades. At phenomenal cost.'

Peter's even voice was gentle above the tinkling of the waterfalls and the soft cooing of the doves, parchment puppets bobbing around their feet.

'But we are amid a depression that will get worse before it gets better, especially for us in the north and the regions. Think of the jobs that would come from this! As it is, John, we are having to bring the ships in to Hull for us to make margins affordable now, and we are siphoning work off to the south which should sit here, right on our doorstep, in the pockets of our people. Our powerhouse is here. So much good could come from this.'

John's heart swung again to his beautiful, tender-hearted Caroline. There she was, so distinct and lovely in his mind, working tirelessly in her blue dresses, to help exactly those impoverished people that Peter was talking of. Peter, whose valuable business sense was always tempered by a dependable, equable notion of compassion. The love John had for

Caroline and for Peter and his family, and for Soti, and for Dinah and all his perfect, still babies, pounded in his heart with a sickening force.

The mother dove nuzzled at the soft neck of her baby, and her black eyes shut with such distinct contentment that a surge of deep loneliness fell over John like a door shutting hard, quietening all light, all joy, all life. He hoped that comfort would come, some grace from God to assure him that his decision to leave her was right and honorable. Martha's life was diminishing, and he was determined to show her loyalty in the time that was left. In salvaging his marriage, he might save himself from hell ahead, while having to survive the abject punishment of life without Caroline as hell on earth.

'You are quite correct, Peter,' Soti said. 'It will take years to complete. We must think about how we begin. There is a man I know – Adamson. I think you know of him, too, John. John? He has the Newton Moor Spinning Company in Hyde. We have his support, and I am certain we will gather more like him.'

The doves, full of fruit, hopped away, and John saw clarity in their purity – if he was going to be in solitude and despair forever, then he would pour all he had left into this monumental thing. The Ship Canal.

The afternoon stretched over the lawn. The discussions ranged freely, such was the trust and balance that thrived between the men. Sotirios provided the expanse and excitability, his ideas and ambitions bouncing from his fingers and words with verve and boundless energy. Peter, always so measured and sure, tempered his wild proposals with facts, figures and the reminder that at the heart of it all were real people, real places and real money.

John said less than both men but listened intently.

His philosophy was far ahead of its time, led by the notion that the middle way was mostly always the best way. He made calculations and took risks; decisions so quickly that even before the meeting was over, John had already mentally mapped out The Manchester Ship Canal. Yet there was nothing on his face that would have revealed the mechanical, fastidious workings of his mind. A stranger looking on would hear the loud, lively animations of Sotirios. They would see the clasped hands and cocked head of Peter as he interjected. But they could not begin to imagine the deep, quiet, constant genius of John Rylands, who sat with them in near silence.

Peter helped Alec clear the table, the parasol unclipped and turning burned umber in the setting sun. A chill drifted across the lawn, the first touch of frosts sewn in by the breeze. Alone in the grand hallway of Bella Vista, Sotirios held John to his hard, perfumed chest.

'Always a delight to be with you, John. Though I can see you have much on your mind, my friend.'

After years of combative business meetings and deep amity, it was difficult to disguise his feelings under the searing glare of Sotirios's affection. Soti kissed his forehead, palming John's head in his hand.

'John, you know you can come to the house anytime you need to. In fact, from next Thursday, I am away for weeks. Bella Vista would be quite empty, and you would be my guest. And, if you wanted to invite anyone here to be with you, you would be very welcome.'

John shook his head.

'You are kind, Soti. And God knows there is a huge part of me that would like nothing more than to be here. I need to be at Longford. Its Martha. Her health, it is getting worse.'

'Then at least you must both come to see me again when I return in a few weeks. We can talk of the canal again and make our plans.'

John glanced at the sweeping staircase behind Sotirios, envisioning pulling Caroline by the hand, tumbling into one of the deep red bedrooms. For a lucid instant, he saw them on the terrace, laughing and uninterrupted. Feeding her and bathing her, hours in their hands and her body in the darkness of any of these rooms. He caught the scent of her – violets, and the toasted sugar of her tiny scullery.

'Are you ready to go, sir?' Peter shrugged on his cape, and as Alec handed John his coat, a square of peacock blue fabric floated to the floor. John caught it, like a child grasping a feather. In his hands, John saw the faint check of the scarf, imprinted on the high-day and holiday colour. As his fingers brushed it, violets and sugar and meadows, her kisses and the chime of her voice swept over him, gifting the fresh and particular agony of shock.

'Why, she must have left it, Alec! Last week when she came for the bedding. She must have left it in the cloakroom.'

'She, Soti? She? Who? I don't understand.'

'Ah, John!' Soti chuckled. 'Not any amour of mine – though she is a spectacular woman. No, she is our wonderful Caroline. You must know her, surely. She collects for one of your places.'

John thought his heart was going to twist out from his body. His voice was leaving him to make way for tears. The cloth of her scarf grew warm in his hand.

'Yes, yes of course. I know her. Does she visit often?'

Hope sprang in him, an arch of gold, and possibilities spun from his mind in moulten threads, seeing ways and ways of reversing his terrible decision. He had promised he would not seek her out again, and she had sworn that he would never find her. But if they came across each other here, in all innocence, in all purity. At least he could be near her again. Hope and its gold pooled in him, and he breathed again, as he hadn't since he had left her behind her door.

'Yes, every two weeks or so. Alec can always find her things for the needy. And if not, we always give her a contribution. We always insist she stops to sit in the garden for tea, of course. We love hearing of all she does, and the progress she was making with Wood Street, and all her other places.'

Oh, his queen. To listen to her spoken about with such love filled him with a mad sort of joyful rage. Of course, she was loved everywhere, by everyone, and what torture it was that she had stepped where he stepped now. But what a beautiful turn – to think that in weeks she could walk through the door. He would make sure he was there, in the garden, with the doves and the nymphs and the placid afternoon sun, and all would be well. They could abide by their foolish rules but-yes- he would live just to see her again.

Sotirios sighed as he helped John with his coat.

'We were sad, weren't we, Alec, when she said that her visit would be the last.'

John stood; his arms half thrust into his coat. The front door before his eyes was huge, locked with a great key and swagged with brass chain.

'She was vague about where she was going, and I didn't see it was fit to press her. She has left Manchester for certain though. We will miss her.'

John stared at the door, black now in the sinking dusk of the evening. Peter slid the chain and it dropped with a great swing, heavy against the wood. Brushing the scarf to his eyes, he palmed it into his pocket. It was all he had of her. Fate had turned and spun in a moment, and it was as if it possessed a fist, mighty and cruel; a fist so full of vengeance and spite it had floored John with its terrible conclusion. Somehow, he found a voice that came from outside the dread and sorrow of his heart.

'I will see you soon, dear Soti. I have things I must attend to at Longford. I have a duty.'

As the carriage wheeled away from Bella Vista, John clenched his hands hard to his breast, trying to summon a bravery and fortitude that seemed impossible. He turned from Peter, shaking his head at his offer of brandy. His chest ached, and his heart felt hollow. A fight in him had gone on for so long and the only salve to his bruising had been her. And now she had gone. Not only from his arms, from their bed, from all their conversation and their gazing at each other, but gone, most totally, from his city. From Manchester, and from any, last chance of him catching sight of her. His throat was sore with the strain of trying to find an optimism he could no longer conjure. A strength that had left him when he had left Caroline.

La Castilla, 1870

'For pity's sake, Jacques, move yourself. If you could lift tables as well as you can lift your fork to your greedy mouth we would have been out of here hours ago. No wonder your missus is slim, you must squash it all out of her, the poor mare!'

'Funny, because your wife wasn't complaining about me when I was all over her last night!'

The men tramped in with the extra tables and chairs which were stored in the outhouses, parrying insults back and forth. The halls of La Castilla smelled of sawdust and stale sweat, tobacco and horse manure, which stuck like glue as it dried. From the back of the queue, the head groundsman snapped, his patience boiling over.

'Give it a rest, boys! Foul-mouthed time wasters, the lot of you. Get a move on! Sooner we are done, sooner we can get to the bar. Jacques, move it!'

With a day remaining before the party, and staff were stuffed into the narrow hallways like ants in the arteries of a nest. The caterers carted sides of meat into the kitchen, burgundy and black with age and old blood, swinging them onto the chef's blocks, where cleavers were ready to come down hard through flesh and bone. Sacks of potatoes, heavier than children, were heaved and shoved under benches, next to baskets of broccoli and green beans. A sous chef kicked the basket near him and turned to the man next to him.

'Ugh, mine are gone. They stink like pond weed. Yours?'

'Slimy. I dig up fresher stuff when I work the graveyards.'

They sniggered.

'It is the same every time at this place. She is as tight as she is ugly. But once we boil it all up and add enough salt, the drunks won't even notice.'

Florists, musicians, ironmongers, haberdashers came in a relentless procession. None of them escaped the ineffectual wrath of Madame Bardin. Puce in the face, she barked at one then the other, depending on which way she was facing.

'No! Do not put that there! Jules! Jules! How many times must I ask you to organise these people. Where is the piano tuner? He should be here by now. Blind idiot has probably fallen down a ditch.'

The tuner coughed politely behind her, which she ignored.

'The flowers! The flowers! Not there! Not there! By God, you stupid fool! Into the cold room!'

Enriqueta stood sentry at the back door, checking off each delivery on Madeleine's exacting, exhaustive list. Thanking each person, she guided them into the house, surveying the goods, storing all the receipts. Fresh grime was walked into the floors as quickly as she could sweep them, and the mirrored doors of the hallway were smeared with the clumsy handprints of strangers. Taps were left turned on, paintwork scuffed, and the lavatories were a disgrace, some of the men spoiling them out of spite, such was the dislike they had for Madame Bardin. The traders trudged out from the Blue Room, universally grumbling, and disgruntled at how the Madame had spoken to them.

'Treated like dirt!' said the florist to Enriqueta, shifting her bust, swelling a puff of pollen into the air. 'It's not like she even pays well, your Madame. Always sniffing for some cheap deal. I'm not doing this again. No wonder Lavarenne

Fleurs passed it on. I knew she was bad, but not this bad!'

'I'm sorry.' Enriqueta's voice was a whisper in the clamour of doors and people.

The pervasiveness of unease and displacement struck again as she wondered at all the hows and whys of her being where she was. How had she arrived at this point, saying sorry to strangers on behalf of a woman she neither knew at all, nor liked one bit?

But the florist was already gone, climbing into a cab back to Lyon with stiff words and a bat of her hand. The vintner behind her caught the end of the conversation. Florists and vintners judge character well, and they were both pleased to being leaving La Castilla for the sanity of the city.

'It's not your fault, cheri.' He patted her arm, sucking on his pipe. The cedar scent went over the odour of the hot lard of the kitchen, and the steaming piles of manure from the back yard. 'You are doing your best. Everyone knows she is a monstrous pain in the arse.'

A cool, wet wind blew, and Enriqueta leaned on the damp of the porch wall. The sky, darkening with the threat of a storm, rumbling over the hills. It was an unholy, unnatural alliance she found herself in. Enriqueta was unafraid of hard work; she had no ideals or pretensions to superiority over any living soul. She had been raised on cleaning the pigs out in the heat of Havana as much as she had been trained in the classics surrounded by the cool marble of the Lisbon University. And yet again, her heart demanded of her: what now, Enriqueta, what now?

Madeleine tugged at her sleeve.

'Shut the door, Enri. Come back in. Most of them have gone now and we need your help. All the stuff is here. It's on the floor in piles and Madame is useless. Can you come, please, Enri?'

Enriqueta turned to her – little Maddy with a core of copper, her body a sapling whip, always churning with the next job.

She never stopped, running on empty fuel, her pale brown eyes always looking to her and to Jules for approbation. Madeleine was shivering with fatigue, half in and half out of the house. Enri wrapped her in her arms, wanting so much to warm her, to assure her that her life wouldn't always be this way. Yet she wasn't convinced of the truth of that for herself anymore, never mind Jules and Maddy, who were far more entrenched in La Castilla than she was.

'Go to bed, Madeleine. We will get on with it. Don't worry.'

There was so much to do, in so very few hours. There were boxes and boxes of decorations: ornate filigree fans in silver lace, fabric butterflies meant for the gardens, lanterns and candles, all mixed up. Hide and seek favours irritatingly wedged tight in cartons and baskets, piled high in the hallway.

The vines had been dumped carelessly by the offended ateliers. It took Enriqueta and Jules an hour to unravel them and another two hours to get up the ladders, suspend them and place them. Enriqueta pulled at the taut bits of her dress, where it pinched her at her waist and her arms.

'I can't do this with all my stuff on, Jules. Do you mind? It is so hot in here; everything is dragging at me.'

The moon was high in the sky over Lyon, sending clear pearl light into the room. Jules cast off his shirt and his trousers, and even before he turned back, he heard the rustle and thud of her dress falling to the floor.

They worked in the sweet, cool freedom of their under-clothes. Climbing ladders, flinging the ropes to each other, fastening the strands of diamanté and the heavy glass bunches of grapes, their fingers ached with twisting. Their backs strained at the weight of the task as they tried to reach each other across the great, idiotic bows they had made.

The dawn broke to rouse Lyon in the distance, and the elegant early arms of the sun crept towards them. Madeleine found Enri and Jules slumped and pale, rolling broken grape globes like marbles across the floor. She bought them coffee, stiff with milk and brandy. They opened the big back doors and dangled their legs over the patio ridge, the crumbs of their milk rolls dropping onto their dusty knees. Jules laughed as Enriqueta threw the broken glass grapes high in the sky across the garden, and they spun like planets, the black arches of the dawn city birds rising in silent crowds behind them.

LONGFORD, 1870

MARTHA TRAILED THE HALLWAYS of Longford at night, banging on John's locked door. Silence came for a time, and then the murmurs began, whispers and the hissing of years of disappointments expelled through his keyhole. When she tired of her miserable game, he heard her shuffling away down the corridor, the bleak drag of her stick mercifully waning.

He stared into each cruel dawn parched and exhausted, but horribly alive with a desire for another life that he could not quell. He willed his sick mind and his healthy body to stop, for once, and give him some reprieve from his own desperation. John reached across his great, empty bed and pressed hard into nothing. Everything ached in him for Caroline and just as he thought-just as he imagined her hard kiss on his waiting mouth-there was a knock at the door.

'Mail, John. Breakfast.'

John wrapped his dressing gown round him.

'What is it?' John took the coffee from Leone's tray.

'It's Peter, sir, making me laugh. He's seen the writing on all these scores of replies and already decided on the one you will like best.'

She laid out the applications one by one in front of John. As was the fashion, each had sealed her letter with her own stamp. He opened the one with the butterfly and read it. He opened the one with the bluebird, then the dove, then the oak leaf, then he finally settled on the bee. The bee was dear to his heart, like it was to all Mancunians.

It was only in very recent years that this town, formerly merely a Wapentake of the Salford One Hundred, had been granted city status. John had been an active part of the board who designed the heraldic coat of arms, which proudly incorporated the three ribbons, representing the rivers Irwell, Medlock and the Irk. A ship in full sail, marking Manchester's proud trade with the rest of the world. But at the shield's centre was the worker bee, a potent emblem of the hive of activity that was Manchester. A city built on the confidence and determined labour of its people. The motto born by the shield was one John lived by himself: Concilio Et Labore—Wisdom and Work.

John, as a man of nature as well as industry, loved the bee not only as a metaphorical token, but also as a part of the organic world he fostered around him. He had been the driving force behind a huge community of beekeepers in the region, with his hives flourishing in Heaton Park, Marple, Broughton, Kersal and even on top of the city's cathedral. Indeed, even the honey they had enjoyed with Sotirios had come from Alec's thriving, buzzing hives, gifted to him by John.

Peter and Leone stared at him expectantly as he opened the bee letter and began to read it. Surely this had to be the one. The coincidence was too great, the sign was so clear.

'Well, Peter, you are correct. As ever. Please respond to this one. Invite her for an interview.'

'Of course. I will get it out to the post today.'

Leone stepped forward. 'And may we ask her name, John?'

John passed back the letter, the tidy little waxen bee glinting in the morning light.

'You may. The lady is a Miss Tennant. Miss Enriqueta Augusta Tennant.'

LA CASTILLA, 1870

THE BATHROOM WAS WARM with the scented steam that rose from the tub, and Enriqueta wallowed in the peace of a few moments alone, always grateful that her quarters were right at the top of the house. Madame Bardin rarely climbed the stairs to seek her out.

The front of her hair was tied with papers, the heat setting it into coils with the weak sugar syrup Maddy had combed through it. The party was fast approaching and within a few short hours La Castilla would be teeming with guests.

She soaped herself with her sponge, her legs thinner and less defined than they had been in Paris. She didn't walk here as she had there. She remembered with a sorrowful tug in her heart the long, carefree rambles through the steep windmilled hills of Montmartre. Arm in arm, the girls would window-shop their Sundays away, stopping for a carafe of wine here and there, pushing hard against each Monday with their comforting chatter. Her world here was so much smaller, her journeys no longer consisting of miles of city strolls, but merely trips up and down the endless stairs.

Enriqueta started suddenly; sure that she could hear a shuffling outside the bathroom door. A guttural cough.

'Ah, Enriqueta my dear. Can you hear me? Are you beautifying yourself in there?'

A lascivious laugh.

'I've a favour to ask of you, dearest. A revered guest attending my soiree this evening is a certain Monsieur Foncé. A wonderful man. Wealthy, learned. Good-looking, to boot.'

What now? thought Enriqueta, wearily. What is she asking of me now? What sort of situation is she scheming?

'He is always so supportive of my ventures, and I thought that I might introduce you to him. I think you would get on famously. You are such a clever girl. Would you be nice to him, for me?'

Of course, Madame knew she was naked in the water, as she wheedled about men and introductions. Enriqueta wanted to disappear, to float away and diminish into something no-one could touch.

'Yes, Madame. I'm sure I will enjoy speaking to all your guests, including Monsieur Foncé.'

There was a small, definite pause. Enriqueta sensed the irritation emanating from Madame Bardin through the shut door.

'Ah yes, dearest. But of course, I meant the gentleman Foncé in particular. I would be so grateful.'

Madame Bardin hacked again, and Enriqueta was relieved to hear the heavy turn of her heel and the cumbersome tread of her feet begin to pace back down the stairs.

'Oh, and be sure to wear that spectacular gown that was delivered to you lately. I know that you will be the belle of my ball, dear.'

Enriqueta uncurled each ringlet with a slow sort of dread. She thought of her mother Juana, who thrilled at the challenge of a handsome man. Juana, who worshipped at the altar of her own beauty, who courted admiration with a singular determination that left no room for her children. She heard her mother call to her from underneath the passion fruit vines, her voice far away but low with admonishment. Enriqueta's head pulsed, and she pressed it against the wet wall.

The door cracked open.

'Oh, my word, miss. Oh, Enriqueta!'

'What, Maddy? You are making me nervous! Do I look ridiculous?'

'Oh no, you look divine. I can't tell you, Enri! You look like a painting.'

The gown shimmered in the low light, nacreous, the palest empyrean blue nainsook. The jupon was made of fine gossamer, skimming her form, the fabric pulled firm into cascades at the back, the tampico gathered in ruffles. The bodice was tight, her waist clasped by a single sweep of thick velvet, dove-grey ribbon caught at her hip with a sparkling diamanté buckle. The cap sleeves of filmy ivory lace fluttered at her shoulders. Her skin glowed against the pearl of the fabric.

In the quiet of the room, Madeleine wiped rosewater over her brow and cheeks, and patted lemon-scented cream across her face. Taking a brush, she swept powder then carmine onto Enri's cheeks. She darkened her brows and stroked her eyelids with castor oil.

'Nearly finished.'

Madeleine pressed pink onto her lips and then she stepped back, looking over Enriqueta and into her reflection in the mirror.

'Enri, you look perfect. Come now, we must go down.'

They descended the long stairs carefully, Maddy leading Enri, bound by her narrow skirts and the twist of the iron descent, every step bringing the music of the quartet closer and closer. Enri's head felt heavy with her hair piled so high, and so stuffed with the jewelled ivory combs and coloured feathers. Maddy was light and agile in her maid's pinny and plain dress – her own hair just pulled into a neat bun. Jules looked small and far away at the bottom next to the see-no-evil monkeys.

His mouth was round, and Enriqueta, shedding her nerves

at the sound of the music, laughed.

'Not you too, Jules. Was I so plain before tonight?'

He bent to kiss her hand

'I have never seen you so lovely, Enri.'

The double doors of the Blue Room sprang open, and Madame Bardin bustled towards them.

'Perfect, Enriqueta! Foncé is a lucky man indeed. How it pleases me when my plans come together.'

LONGFORD, 1870

'Help me with Mrs Rylands, love. Your dad is in town.'

Tynan groaned, heaving his long legs out of bed, reaching for the mug of tea that Leone held out for him.

'She can still walk, Mother. I know she can – I heard Mr Rylands saying about all the noise she makes at night at the hall. If she can stroll up and down in the dark, why does she need all this fuss? It's a Sunday, too.'

'For one, sonny-jim, you shouldn't be using your jug ears to listen to a grown-up conversation. Secondly, she may be capable of walking, but her night haunts are not the same as proper fresh air and sunlight. We need to take her out in her chair for a short time, and I can't do it on my own. Come on, shift yourself, lad.'

The back west patio did not hold the best view of Longford, but the ground was tiled and smooth and the gardeners stored many of their nursery plants here. Plants that were too delicate for the cold of the front but didn't have enough tropical merit to take up a costly residence in the glasshouses. It was a fragrant, sheltered space, edged with pots of tender herbs – mint and marjoram, dill, and tarragon. Sapling baby apple trees, spindly experiments of foreign seeds pressed in pots, pips sunk into paper cups of compost. It was green and clement, a trap for the sun even at its winter weakest.

When it was truly cold, they took Martha to the glass houses.

The first was packed with hyacinths and freesias, scented so heavily that the cloying fragrance overwhelmed that corner of the grounds. The next was devoted to begonias, a collection so huge and diverse that its only rival in the whole of Europe was the Glasgow Botanical Gardens. Horticulturists from miles around – even abroad – would write long, effusive letters to John, pleading that they might visit the Begonia House. Such was the steady stream of earnest pilgrims, Martha relented some years ago and decided to declare an official, annual Longford Begonia Day, opening the gardens to the public.

Martha had adored the Begonia House from the moment she had set foot in it as a bride, fresh and eager as the young buds. She could be found in the stiflingly warm space, greenly lit and quiet. Working under the tutelage of the gardeners, she spent long mornings and afternoons snipping and singing to the plants, and moisture settled on her lips and under her arms. More than once, in the first years of their marriage, John had found her in the rows, mesmerized, moss in her nails and her eyes glassy with pleasure. Shutting the doors, he would pull her to him, flicking away the bee that buzzed at her ear, trapped in the heat. He would kiss her, knowing where his men were, hoping to harness some of the passion she found in her plants, but she never responded. Those days were gone, but the vestiges of affection for the rooms still lay in Martha somewhere, buried deep in her, beneath the bitterness and defeat.

It was a cool day; Tynan slowly pushed Martha along the narrow paths of the glasshouses, Leone behind them. Martha's fingers, once so nimble and dextrous, now trailed feebly over the asymmetric leaves.

'Dioica, Boisaina, Olivacea, Lutea... Acutifolia.' With a remembered fondness, her voice strolled over each one, as if she was naming lost children. Tropical and subtropical species, far from their homes.

Without fight or rage, Martha appeared even older still. The fury she had directed towards John, to Dinah, to his past, present and to her situation had – in its own way – kept her youthful. She had been upright and strong when she threw pots around her room. Her voice had a vicious clarity when she had raved and screamed at him. Her hands and arms were once muscled and strengthened by the force of her disappointment. But envy, in its sickness, had made a feather-light husk of her. She was bent in her chair, her voice whispering and tremulous. The fingers that stroked the maroon and pink spotted leaves were uncertain and bent.

While Leone did not miss the terror and upset of her mistress's tempers, she was saddened by this new version of her that had come so quickly upon them. Martha's life had seemed to gallop, with the period of happiness – childhood and youth, her first marriage to Richard Carden – lived all too quickly. Leone pitied her, that the largest part of her life seemed to be spent in so much fury. And now, even that energy had gone too. There was nothing much left of her lady but this: a depressed figure, afforded a sort of meagre respite by the quiet and familiar glasshouses.

Even in the oppressive and airless heat of the place, Martha was bundled in layers of fine woollen blankets and a bonnet and scarf. Tynan tugged at his collar, sweat beginning to dampen the roots of his curly blond hair, his face flushing pink.

'I'm off outside, Mother. I'm sweating cobs in here. Come and get me in a bit.'

Leone nodded, but moments later Tynan was walking back towards her, through the narrow walkways, irritably batting away the greenery that lolled at his waist.

'Mr Rylands, Mam. He's outside – asked us to leave him with Mrs Rylands. You can come, now.'

Leone hadn't expected Peter and John back from town until

dinnertime, and even less expected John to be waiting outside the greenhouses. He rarely came here these last months. Not like he used to, when he would spend hours with Ged, stalking the plantings and planning his expansive, exotic schemes.

Years before, when things at the hall were happier, John and Martha had hosted bright summer parties for the staff and local people. They were enormously happy occasions with entertainment and games for the children. The glasshouses would be open for people to wander in and out, to gaze at the exotic ferns and fruits. The odd specimen got taken by a few of the light-fingered residents of the locality, but John never minded much. While jellies glinted and wobbled under the sun, and the thud of the skipping rope hit the lawn, a handful of missing guavas were a small sacrifice to pay.

And when was the last time John had been alone with Martha? The deterioration of the union had been incremental but was now surely beyond any hope of repair. Leone had been witness to all Martha and John had suffered. At the peak of their troubles, the mere sight of John had driven Martha into such an uncontrollable rage, they had all gradually agreed that her care was best left in Leone's hands. Although she was certainly unpleasant to Leone, and an arduous charge to have, she was at least never violent. She still had a respect for her that she had long since shed for John.

'What, son? What do you mean?'

Martha dozed, quiet snores coming from below her head, bent down to her chest.

Tynan shrugged, shucking his head towards the door.

'I don't know, Mam. Didn't ask. He just said we could come out now. So come on. And I'm hungry, n'all.'

He tugged at her hand. This lucky turn of events meant he could slip down to the Bowling Green for a pint. He patted his pockets for coins. Maybe a pie, too. 'Come on!'

Leone saw that Martha was still asleep, satisfied that she looked comfortable enough. John was at the entrance and moved to let them pass.

'Sir?'

John took her hand and squeezed it in his.

'Dear Leone, don't look so worried. You go back to the house and Tynan – this is for you.'

Pressing a shilling note into Tynan's hand, John walked with purpose into the dark green depths of the greenhouse, the begonias bending as he passed.

La Castilla, 1870

THE LAUGHTER OF LYON'S most powerful men boomed above the chattering crowds in the Blue Room. Shrieks from the women, prodding each other in recognition, embracing each other while plotting whose husband they would sleep with next. The air was scented with mingled perfumes and the unmistakable odour of liquor, burned vanilla candles and the garlic and lemon of simmering food in the basement kitchens.

Enriqueta had last seen the room hours ago, when they had left a space in front of the huge windows which looked out on to Lyon. There was now a smart string quartet, their bows gliding, and their heads cocked to their music, their moustaches so sculpted that they looked like painted dolls, tipping this way and that under the strings of a puppet master.

In the sway of the candlelight, the perfectly artificial became eerily organic, fluttering in the breeze from back door. The sunset moved over Lyon and toward La Castilla, animating the leaves in shadow against silver and blue walls. The roses, peaches and cream, that had sat tied and rigid in the cold room spilled over copper bowls and glass vases.

'We made a magnificent hell indeed, Enri.'

The champagne Jules gave her touched her veins. Maddy's tray of hors d'oeuvres emptied swiftly, and she circled back to the staff table, hidden from view behind a curtain. Behind it, the hired staff were bustling, Jules directing them all in and out, ensuring their trays were refilled. It was a neat operation. The most senior waiters and waitresses were pleased to be under the Jules's charge. The few times that Madame Bardin had interfered in this aspect of the proceedings, a handful of the staff had walked out halfway through the evening, not before bagging up a couple of bottles of port in lieu of payment and as recompense for her bullish behaviour.

Even if Jules and Maddy had needed her, Madame had made it clear that Enriqueta was not to align herself with the staff but be present as a guest. Gazes were upon her; every which way she glanced in the room, she was met by appraising eyes. Madame Bardin pushed through the crowd, navigating the bodies like a broad ship in battle. She was ghoulishly alight with excitement, her eyes glinting and her teeth bared in exhilaration. She shouted over the noise.

'Dearest – you are bewitching. There is no other in the room – in the whole of Lyon! None as fetching as you, dear.'

Enriqueta flinched as Madame Bardin reached out to paw her arm and the sash at her waist. To those that have suffered it before, there is nothing so familiar than the disgust of unwelcome touch.

'I just knew that this gown would be perfect for this evening. Are you having a lovely time? I must start introducing you. Some very notable acquaintances of mine have arrived.'

Enriqueta was pulled through the throng; a damp hand gripping her glove at the elbow. Madame Bardin found a corner, and the stale tang of her breath gusted over the soot of a clutch of dying candles.

'By God, Enriqueta, make a bloody effort. All I do for you, and I ask so little in return. Smile! Little wonder you will never get a man. I am giving you the only chance you will ever get.'

The candles hissed to an end, releasing their last dark swirl.

'Have I got you so wrong? Are the menfolk not your cup

of tea? I could put you to work with some fine ladies too, Enriqueta. That could help me as much as anything.'

Madame Bardin's finger down her neck, hooking the satin at her breast, felt like the point of a knife. Unclean. A knife that had been used to chop things up and pick things out.

'To the garden, Enri. Let's see what I have for you there.'

The garden was magically reworked, the wet pungency gone. A thick hessian stifled the grass, making a soft imitation layer, warm underfoot. Every bead of rain had evaporated in the heat coming off the domed braziers. Light came from the lamps dotted about the trees and bushes, the oils emanating warm jasmine in whispers. Lyon glittered in the night, an oil painting of shadows and dots.

A crowd at the bottom of the iron stairs glanced at Enriqueta. A girl with black hair, sheened as a crow, tittered, and made a face to the woman beside her. They touched arms and hands lightly and frequently, checking and reminding each other that they were of one kind. Peels of brittle laughter jetted into the sky from straight jaws, drawn back; indicating to all that they bore hallmarks of the wealthy, privileged and confident.

The man that broke the circle was drawn with the fine lines of good breeding; even his white shirt spoke of a tailor far from Lyon. He bent, clasping Madame Bardin, leaning low to her ear. He used the methods of an expert, linking his eyes with Enriqueta's, his voice a secret, his frame displayed in the arc of a man with command over the air around him. He furrowed his thick fair hair with long fingers, and Madame Bardin simpered. The owls of women blinked meanly at Enriqueta from behind the armour of their evening fans.

'Come, dearest, meet these friends of mine.'

Enriqueta moved into the glow of the lamp, its angle putting the circle into shadow. She could see no face apart from his, above the light. The rarity of a handsome man couldn't be ignored, and Enriqueta knew immediately, as sure of as the stars above Lyon, that here was a person with diamonds at his fingertips, all people at his bidding, any table he desired at the turn of a golden cheekbone. Tailors wanted his numbers, children wanted his knee, musicians wanted to please him, and the seasons waited for him to notice them change first.

'Monsieur Foncé, please let me introduce Mademoiselle Tennant.'

Through the satin of her glove, it felt like his lips were opening over her palm. A word, or a noise, came from the woman behind him, dressed in dragon green. It sounded like a curse.

'I'm enchanted to meet you, Mademoiselle.'

The swoop of a cheer from the house marked the band moving to on to a popular song, and a cymbal crashed. The circle rearranged themselves, turning away and floating off like phantoms and Enriqueta heard the burn of scorn in their laughter. They swung into the shadows of the trees, their colours young, like a box of paints: carmine red, green, cerulean blue. Enriqueta ran her hand across her grey sash.

'I will get drinks for you both.'

A taut seam ran through Enriqueta when Madame Bardin turned with the glasses, leaving her alone with Foncé. The garden had emptied, the lure of the tune and the slam of the feet on the dance floor irresistible.

Enriqueta was all too aware of herself, when alone. She had furrowed memories of her childhood bed, when she should have been safe and wrapped in her tangle of sheets and the bumps of her dollies, while her parents were out at a dance.

That her sweet, young aunt had played with her all evening, tossing dice and spinning wheels. Feeding her dinner and little chocolates before bed. Her aunt held her close and painted pictures of butterflies who could sing, and promised her that if she wished hard enough, she could fly.

Her mother forgot her birthdays in a flurry of apologies. Her aunt baked cakes with Enriqueta, allowing her to sprinkle them with boundless brown sugar. Her hand brushed her hair and threaded pink shells through it while Juana Camilla slept behind a locked door. Her aunt sung the old songs to her, songs of sea and harvests, letting her be the one to sleep last when the little ones were patting their lips together, deep in slumber. Bad – that a mysterious uncle, a stranger to her, came in after the lights were dimmed and ran his hands under the cover and over her body in the darkness.

A cruel, silent man who knew there was no danger she would utter a word, so rigid with shock and fear and obedience was she. He chuckled as he fluttered his fingers over her sparrow chest, and she shut her eyes tighter and tighter until her head ached with the wishing he would disappear. His fingers pinched her small body with spite, searching her out under the blankets like a game, as she lay in abject misery, his brutal palm rubbing on her and making her cry quietly. She wanted to save her aunt, and the children she would have, and tell her that her husband was a wicked man. At breakfast, little Enriqueta meddled her spoon in her custard sadly, and the man grasped her aunt in the kitchen, his palms gripping her skirt, bunched in his great, mad hands. Her aunt laughed and squirmed, and as he darted his tongue at her, he swivelled his eyes to Enriqueta, grinning through his lust. The custard grew cold, a hard skin yellowing on top. In the night, somewhere from downstairs her aunt called him, her voice like the butterflies who could sing, and he cursed, throwing Enriqueta down like a doll. And she breathed again.

The next time was the following spring, a bomb in the buds and the blooms. Enriqueta, five years old, had been sent out into the cane sheds. Her mother, though feckless, wasn't stupid and she knew to keep her girl-children close. But she made them all work in small ways, near enough to the house, and pretty little Enri was no different. In her heavy boots, calico smock and leather cap she was sent out with her older siblings and cousins to the nearby fields and to stock the sheds. Her mother – busy and blithe – had told them over and over to always stay together, as though repeating the mantra would serve as a talisman against all evil. Mostly, they did, but that day Enriqueta had wandered off alone, following a kingfisher as it swooped orange and blue towards the big pond.

Pablo D'Iablo hit Enriqueta hard – a single blow to the back of the head that would never leave a mark, but rendered her nearly, but not quite, unconscious. He had been watching her for months. Or was it years? He couldn't remember. He slept near the donkeys each night, while his mother and idle father languished in the comfort of their bed. As he listened to the mules shudder and snore, he lay awake, eyes stark and his body hard at the thought of taking Enriqueta, who day by day walked by him, her dark hair glinting and her small body just yards from his touch. He loved her leather cap, and he giggled at the thought of it rubbed against his own skin. Once he had it, he planned to keep it forever, like a scalp.

Pablo had chosen that day with care. Good Friday; when the adults would be occupied with preparing for the big weekend. He watched Enriqueta like a wolf as she drank her green tea through her silver straw, shivering with lust beneath the window. Her mother threw the children out after breakfast to their chores, literally sweeping them away with her porch brush. To Pablo's joy, Enriqueta did what he prayed she would. His dainty prey split from the others and rather than heading toward the cane shed, idled off towards the pond.

'Naughty, lazy, Enriqueta'

He stroked himself through the crotch of his trousers, sweat beginning to pop on his brow.

Enriqueta had no thought that day of any danger. The vague warnings about bad men and wild animals floated over the children like mysteries. She was tired, bored of the same days and with Easter on the way, decided to take some small childish liberties.

The smell of the pond reached her before she saw it. It was two turns of the path away and the water birds chirruped amiably to each other through the reeds. The muddy green scent mushroomed, as two electric-blue flies dodged passed her. Pablo watched Enri as she batted away the pond flies, and he grew harder looking at the wobble of her plump golden arms and hearing her free, light laugh on the air.

Sweat dripped from Pablo D'Iablo's face as he tried to push into her. Ages had passed and he was soft, trying to shove his slug of a penis between her legs. Enri had given up crying, her face in the suffocating dust, her pelvis and hips bruised and battered by his weight and the relentless rape. He stank, like a realm of hell. In fury, he pulled her hair, yanking her poor head up so brutally that she thought he would snap it off, like the ball of an over-wintered clothes peg. Her mouth was caked in dust and she looked across the pond, where her huge kingfisher had landed heavily on a palm. The branch bent and curved up again, nodding in the wake of the bird as it launched into the sky in a magnificent arc.

Enriqueta buckled her back and kicked. It didn't stop Pablo, but it was enough to enrage him and he brought an elbow down on her hard. His father had taught him well. As Enri watched the kingfisher disappear over the trees, she dropped to the floor again.

'Tennant is an English name, is it not?'

Enriqueta hadn't been asked about her name in a long time. She had even forgotten how foreign it sounded to most people.

'Your people must be from Yorkshire?'

'Yes. No one ever notices my name.'

She remembered that there had been no one, for so long, to notice anything about her at all. A flicker of pleasure crossed Monsieur Foncé's smooth face. His eyes were curiously dark for such a fair man. Her aunty had a box of marbles, and they had all been the usual colours, green and grey, with flashes of blue and orange. She was allowed to take them into the dust of the front path to play. But among the clatter of the ordinary ones, there had been two special marbles that her aunt never lent to the other children, that glowed like fire in licks of dark tawny brown. Her aunt told her they were made of precious Tiger's Eyes, and they were mystical to Enriqueta, orbs of magic.

'I'm surprised. Surely you are always noticed, Mademoiselle Tennant?'

His charm was polished and administered with such ease, like popping ripe fruit from a skin. She had been seated beside him at the dinner table; a king, stately and tall, wither as his silent pawn, clasping her glass, robed in her nunnery grey.

Jules circled the tables, pouring wine. One of Lyon's most senior judges lumbered past him, knocking the bottle, staining a shock of plum across the whites of both their shirts. Enriqueta watched the judge's mouth twist with fury, as he poked Jules hard in the chest. Where she usually harboured a painful desire for her life in Paris, she now felt a sharp longing for just a normal day at La Castilla, the Blue Room dull and full with books, not groaning with swags and flickering with the malevolent glow of countless candles and peopled with strangers bent on gluttony. A small army of maids and butlers leaked through the door, carrying huge platters of food. The claws of great orange lobsters hung from the plates, the shine gone from their eyes, and their flesh emitting the round, sour scent of deterioration.

'Please excuse me, Monsieur Foncé.'

In the hallway, the clamour of the Blue Room was muffled by the great mirrored doors. Jules appeared from the pantry, blue shadows beneath his eyes.

'Are you alright?' they both said at once.

'I'm fine, Enri. Tired. These parties go on and on and they are all drunk already.'

He brushed crumbs from his apron, not meeting her eyes. A maid ran past them, wiping tears from her cheeks. Her hair was wet, as though liquid had been flung over her.

'Bastards,' he muttered. 'I need to go after her.'

He reached for her hand.

'She was wrong to put you with him like this, Enri. I've seen how the grand Monsieur Foncé works before now and I don't like it one little bit. He's no gentleman. Be careful.'

She wondered at this dear boy – younger than herself and far less experienced – so earnestly warning her against danger. She put her arms around him.

'I'm not a girl, Jules. You don't need to worry about me.'

There was no time for this, and Jules packed up his pain and put it away again, shutting a door to it.

'I know what you are saying – I do. You are a true friend and ally to me in this madhouse.'

They sprung apart at Madame's bark.

'There you are! Come now! Monsieur Foncé will think you have run away from him!'

Emboldened by the kindness from Jules, Enriqueta dared to defend herself.

'Madame, I am surely not indebted to the good monsieur already? Am I not just another guest, as he is?'

Madame's face darkened with a lethal combination of displeasure and contempt.

'As well you know, my dear, Monsieur Foncé is a very particular friend of mine. Such a generous benefactor to so many of my worthy causes. All I ask of you, is that you show him how charming you can be. Not difficult, Enriqueta.'

Madame Bardin's bulbous eyes skimmed over her, wet with disdain.

'What stops you, Mademoiselle Tennant? What keeps you so uncommonly cool and distant? So irritatingly closed? One would think you had something to hide.'

Tugging her dress to straighten it, Enriqueta replied, 'I shall return to the dining room immediately.'

'Marvellous, my dear. The band is playing again soon. I would hate for you to miss any opportunities.'

The band had been joined by more players, swelling their numbers with a piano, cornet and violoncello. They opened with a lively polka. Couples swarmed towards the music, the women, coloured beetles in the arms of the men, black and twitching in their suits.

'Well, Mademoiselle Tennant, shall we dance?'

The music leapt around Armand and Enriqueta, as Madame Bardin's withering words dissipated into the perfumed air. Enriqueta's nerves evaporated too, and she was cross with herself for her brittle confidence. There had been no moment in her childhood for anyone else's swing in disposition apart from that of her mother. Children born of selfish parents learn quickly to dispel the worth of their own instincts, like water through hot sand.

Monsieur Foncé held Enriqueta expertly, the weight of his hand at her waist as light as the notes of the violins. As they moved around the room together, he didn't bother her with whispers in her ear, or catch her skirts in his feet. The music changed to the Mazurka and he glanced at her, silently seeking her permission that they stay. She laughed and nodded, exhilarated by the music, thinking that this was the first time in a long time she had found pleasure in new company.

When they walked out together once more into the garden, the strewn jewels of Lyon sparkled brighter than they ever had. Her feet were hot with dancing. Foncé held glasses of champagne, and a tiny plate with glazed chestnuts, wafers and bonbons. The sugar on them snowed them to the plate, like the paper mâché and varnished toy shop sets she had played with in Havana.

'Thank you, monsieur.'

Their knees were an angel's breath away.

'Please, call me Armand.'

The fingers of mourning that she knew would touch her tomorrow were beginning to meet the honey of the champagne in her blood. She wanted to stay in this moment forever, banishing books, routine and the chorus of women who bounced on their toes in their finery behind her.

'Tell me more about your work here. So different from your life in Paris, I imagine?'

The shadow cleaved his face in two. She was alight; he must know more about her than she imagined. From Madame Bardin, she was sure. An army of unease and alarm readied their pistols; what fantastical portrait had been sketched, then laced with some scandal and intrigue that had never existed? Madame Bardin embellished everything.

Enriqueta had long been witness to Madame's soup of untruths. One Sunday, over tisane and almonds, she had blithely announced to the Lady Mayor that she had found Jules and Maddy orphaned in a fox lair, gambolling naked with the cubs, before she so heroically rescued them. Another time, Madame had told a supper guest at great length that her dear departed family were exiled Prussian royalty, who had been viciously tracked to Lyon and slain in the grounds of La Castilla. She gestured to a large, rust coloured smudge under one of the iron railings that fastened against the side porch.

'The blood of my grandfather,' she had whispered, wiping her dry, pink eyes.

Once, Enriqueta had stopped to pass by the door of the drawing room and had heard Madame Bardin sobbing, describing to the owner of the most popular ice cream parlour in town that her husband, a military man, had been captured and killed by pirates on the Aegean Seas. None of this – not the wolves, the blood, the husband, the pirates – had even the slightest speck of truth in it.

'Just stop, Henri. Enough!'

The woman's voice was shrill. It came with a scuffling sound from behind the bushes, but Armand's gaze stayed on her. To her fingers, the stuff on her face was grease and heat. Her past was not as thrilling as she remembered it. The glamour of her memories leached out as the days in Paris reduced in her mind to cramped, irritating, cashless and pointless days. She felt her heart tumble – she had been a woman for years already, childhood so long ago, and nothing to show for any of it. She felt dull under Armand's shine.

'Mademoiselle Tennant? Are you well? I'm so sorry – asking questions of you. The last thing I want is to distress you.'

Her heart raced as his thumb stroked her wrist. She imagined he saw her blue veins jumping.

'I know nothing about you, but I would dearly love to.'

The bushes broke, and the couple tumbled through the leaves, Henri picking the woman up as she pivoted to the ground. He swung uselessly to save her, but she fell like a stone, her teeth clattering against the primrose shapes of the iron stairs. A howl of agony just as the band picked up again.

'I am sorry, I have to go and take the next dance. Duty calls, but I won't be long. Will you wait for me out here? Are you warm enough? We can talk when I return.'

Armand bounded back up the stairs into the house, stepping

over the woman. A maid bent, patting at the blood on her jaws. One of the district judges lifted her at her armpits. He shouted for help, shoving Enriqueta to one side.

'We need to move her. She's gone. Useless. Can't take a drink. Shift yourself, darling.'

The voices from the Blue Room had taken on a new magnitude, above the vigorous melody, as the guests grew more bloated with wine and thick spirits. The woman on the stairs, her mouth ruddied with blood, was lifted away, and the maid took a foaming brush to the steps, swiftly pushing the stain into the black of the soil. Enriqueta had begun to recognise the endless guests and the various agency maids over the months, none of whom knew how to treat her. She did not fit neatly enough into the social hierarchy that they lived by. Neither staff nor peer, their dealings with her were at best clumsy, and at worst unkind.

Yet Foncé appeared unaffected by the normal social constraints. Her temples began to throb as a lady, towering in red velvet, swept passed her, scenting the air with brutal perfume. The pain in her brow reminded her of her mother, who had scolded her so often for thinking deeply about every matter.

'Lighten yourself Enri! So tiresomely serious. You are pretty when you don't scowl.' The peal of her mother's laughter, gilded by buttered rum and the powders she sniffed from the silver pipe against her knuckle. Twelve years old was a disastrous age to wake to find a mother gone. Although Juana had been a disinterested parent, her death seemed like another punishment, a strike of shock that hit her while she was still mourning the father she worshipped. The news of Stephen's death, so bizarre and brutal, was delivered to her when she had limped back to La Reunion Deseada, the stench of Pablo all over her. Her mother was pale on the veranda, and drunk.

Your father has been killed. By a train. In England.

Five year old Enriqueta pushed her skirts between her legs, hoping the blood would not show through and she thought her poor heart would stutter to a stop. The wonder that God could hate her so very much, to make things happen to her that were more dreadful than anything she could have conjured. A Holy Day, too, which should have been full of light and fruit. Until that day, horror and death, monsters and fear occupied the safety and brevity of her storybooks, where they could be shut and placed back on her shelves. And like a story, her mother's death had been finally bookended by the suicide of her stepfather, Julain Fontana. It had happened just as she left Paris for Lyon, but she cared so little, Enriqueta left the announcement on her desk, next to her empty ink bottle, where Jeanne found it, days after she had gone to La Castilla.

The stairs back up into the house were wet with lemon and turpentine, all blood and people gone. Enriqueta heard, above her own better sense, the echoes of her mother's bold voice, urging her on to seek Foncé out.

Pushing through the throng, her skirts twisted in the heat, as though she was walking through a swathe of wet fabric, and at every movement she caught the incantation of a lustful greeting.

The sound of 'mademoiselle' hissed in her ear, as she squeezed against hard crotches, hands swiftly ungloved to slyly pinch her body in the weft of the crowd. The thick fingers of old men dove in between her legs, taking the chance to stroke her as she passed. Enriqueta searched the room for him, her heart pounding.

Armand Foncé was in a corner, bent in discussion with a glamorous woman, someone Enriqueta had seen before. A confidante of Madame Bardin, a stalwart of the parties and a frequent visitor to La Castilla. Madame Faucher would sit for hours with Madame in the drawing room, toying with pots of tea, which became cool as they reached for the best brandy. They kept the door shut, allowing Madame Bardin to harvest her tales of scandal, and snippets of gossip to use as trade, and to subvert connections to her advantage.

Adelaide Faucher had long been a fixture of Lyonnaise high society, and her succession of three, wealthy, deceased husbands meant she had found herself in a position of considerable affluence, through astoundingly little effort. She had born one of them a daughter, who had grown into a beautiful young woman, as haughty and advantaged as her mother. Madame Faucher's business interests were strewn here and there, small but solid investments that yielded her an enviable, reliable income that sat untouched, floating like curd on top of the cream of her inherited fortunes.

As Madame Faucher had no call to work for her fortunes, nor the need to manage them- her accountants were paid to do that- she had an abundance of time and money on her hands. Her existence was crafted by her wealth: her food, furniture, clothes, carpets, jewellery, shoes were all the costliest money could buy. Her maids were thought to be the luckiest in Lyon, and whenever there was a position at the house, there were girls lined all the way down the road in the hope of securing a job. Because as soon as Madame Faucher bored of something, she tossed it into the maid's cupboard under the stairs. The Faucher staff stood out in the marketplace in their velvet boots while others wore clogs to town.

Where Madame Bardin looked unkempt, despite her fine clothes, Madame Faucher was a picture of elegance. Slight and willowy, her figure was kept small by a regime of tea, brandy and very little food. Dr Palomer, the most expensive medic in Lyon, attended her weekly, prescribing her a range of pills and potions that kept her birdlike. Once, after returning from a trip to Switzerland, he had convinced her to install a steam room at the house, where she languished daily, hoping to sweat away any threat of weight or age.

Madame Faucher was celebrated and courted in all the refined fashion houses of the city, where she had regular appointments with the designers, perusing the collections well ahead of each season, so that she could be assured of complete exclusivity over any gown or hat she loved. She paid her favourite shoe-smiths a retainer, so that she didn't have to endure the indignity of visiting the shops. Each had her foot expertly modelled into a last, and a range of brand-new boots, shoes and slippers were delivered each month to her door in silver boxes, tied up with paper flowers. Those she liked, she kept. Those she despised were slung into the maid's cupboard, not once touching her feet, so childish and pink, and the objects of the district judge's wildest fantasies. On his rare days off, Judge Alarie whiled away his afternoons with her toes in his mouth and his trousers at his knees, and Adelaide Faucher had trays of sapphire and ruby rings to show for it.

While she was famed for her preposterous extravagance, she was also hailed for her great, enduring beauty. She was unusually fair for a woman of the region, her hair a mass of flaxen curls. Her skin was a shade of alabaster, and her exquisite face could have been painted by a Dutch Master. Society women mused and speculated on her true age, sipping their Gamay with resentment. With a grown-up daughter and three marriages behind her, she was certainly no longer a maiden. And yet, the way she looked, moved, and spoke was so incredibly youthful, it baffled them all. The men didn't care for her numbers, content to bask in the gleam of her company, listening to the cleverly personalised praise, strewn over them like spring flowers. They enjoyed it immensely when she leaned in close to impart one of her very secret bits of information. Madame Faucher was a skilled socialite and made whoever she was talking to think themselves the most important person in the world, and the only one at that moment that was held close.

Madeleine arrived at Enri's side like a soft ghost; her voice urgent as the cymbals clashed with triumph around them.

'If you want to slip off to bed, Enri, I can bring something up to you. Just go. Nothing good here happens after midnight.'

The see-no-evil monkeys at the bottom of the stairs eyed her grey dress mockingly, when Enriqueta felt the magic of a touch at her shoulder. Foncé was smiling down at her, just as he had in the short moments of the garden.

'Mademoiselle Tennant, can I speak with you before I go? It is getting late, and the company is becoming a little wild for me.'

In the reception room, the lights were low and there were couples occupying the love seats, deep in hushed conversations, punctuated by giggles and the rustle of skirts, away from the muffled jump of the music.

'I wanted to talk to you about a project. I am sure I can be frank with you. I am asking for the honour of your help and assistance. Your expertise, if you will, and your time.'

Enriqueta flattened the napkin she was twisting hard in her palm across her lap.

'Madame Bardin speaks so highly of you, Mademoiselle Tennant. Your complete command over all the books that come to her. You would be the very best person to aid me in the programme. One of my many charitable interests is the plight of the poor, orphaned children of Lyon. I own properties on Rue Sainte Catherine; I walked past the orphanage building next to my offices for years without even realising that there were upwards of a hundred children behind the doors.'

His face was like sheened milk in the candlelight. The beauty of his hands made her shudder, and she wondered when his birthday was, and what his parents looked like. She imagined what he did all day in that office of his, perched up high over the Rue Sainte Catherine, making money to buy bread and cakes and paper for the little orphans next door.

'I became a patron two years ago. Shortly after, some criminal men managed to infiltrate the place. The swines stole some of the children away, forcing them to work as agricultural slaves in what was essentially a prison at Ille du Levant, near Toulon. Even very little children – five, six years of age – were spirited off, to share cells with delinquents and mad men and to work hard labour in dire conditions. No surprise: they've never been seen again. Even when we reported them missing, the authorities were uninterested. In fact, they seem resigned and even relieved that their numbers in state care were fewer.'

'This was one terrible thing, but there are many more. Things that are enough to make you weep. I set about organising a kind of committee of benefactors that could use their influence, their skills, and of course their wealth to try and alleviate some of the suffering of these poor little souls. Many of them are present this evening, thanks to the generosity and tenacity of your Madame.'

Before she could stop herself, Enriqueta said.

'Like Madame Faucher?'

She crunched her toes in her shoes, trying to pain herself to divert the blood from flushing her cheeks, and waving the red flag of jealousy in front of him. He brushed his fingertips over the back of her clasped hands, so briefly she wondered if she had imagined it. Books and stories flooded into her-tales of thwarted lovers and romance-and Shakespeare's Juliet, and her mother, standing together in gowns and beauty gazed at her, wanting her and willing her to be the most perfect version of herself.

'Yes, clever mademoiselle. How observant of you. Madame

Faucher has joined the committee very recently. She was at first somewhat reluctant, and it has taken me some time to convince her how much we would value her contribution.'

'To convince her? Surely it is a worthy cause.'

She pulled at the napkin, folding it in squares. Henri, from the garden, was pulling up a different woman from the chair next to him, fondling her out of the door as she swayed against him.

'For a long time, Madame Faucher insisted that she was not a suitable benefactor of this particular, distressing cause. Historically she has aligned herself with more...shall I say... cerebral, delicate foundations. The ballet, The Guilds, The arts.'

Irritation prickled under Enriqueta's skin. The orphans – dirty, disabled, unlovable – were not an attractive enough proposition for Madame Faucher. How poorly a sick infant compares to a lithe Russian émigré in snow-white satin.

'But enough of others. I want to talk to you about how we may work together. That is, if you agree', he added.

The room had emptied; people left to find more wine and, by the sound of the footsteps on the stairs, the privacy of dark and distant bedrooms.

'We have many ideas about how we can improve the lives of Lyon's orphans. I wish that the children are provided with at least a basic education. There is some thought that a child has a better chance of improvement if he can read.'

Enri plucked away the wafer of shame; that she would only be ever thought of as a woman of books, rather than a woman of beauty.

'I intend to recruit some teachers. They need to not be trained to a particular academic standard. In fact, it is more important that they can care for children with good hearts and a degree of patience. Encourage them towards reading rather than take a harshly didactic approach, for it will be a very slow process.'

'As well as the teachers, we need some books. And this is where Madame Bardin, and you, mademoiselle, fit into the scheme. Manette said, generously, that the foundation may have any of the children's books you have at La Castilla, and any that she comes across from now. Of course, these books will need to be sorted by way of subject and age, and she has recommended that you are the very best person to help with this. Of course, I would not expect you to undertake this task all by yourself. I would be delighted to work with you here at La Castilla to take some of the burden. Unfortunately, I am no reader. Books are not really a habit for me.'

Thoughts dashed into her mind, crowded, battling with each other for space. Enriqueta did not know which to alight on first, all the time also desperately trying to keep a hold of her expression, lest her features and her face gave away the joy that had begun to swirl within her.

When she had first arrived at La Castilla, she had harboured a hope that the position might improve with time. It never did, instead becoming harder and more stultifying week by week. Worse, it had been clear to Enriqueta from the outset that Madame Bardin was a duplicitous, ignoble character. She recalled ruefully the fantasy she had crafted before the reality of La Castilla and Madame Bardin were presented in all their reality. Now distant, a concocted vision of a warm and welcoming home, presided over by a gentle, interesting lady of intellect and vast wisdom. A kindly person she could learn from and talk with. *How quickly our invented pictures drift from us in the face of the cold truth*. The scenes she had envisaged in that long coach ride to Lyon, the dreams, and fantasies, now long gone.

She had posted the reply to the position in England, which must have arrived by now. As each day passed, her hopes of a response faded. There would be hundreds of others eager to take up that chance, likely better qualified than she. Doubtless they would be younger, more local, more skilled, and more than enough to make her chances slight. England was deep in depression and few of the grand houses were taking any people at all.

Stirring within all these muddled notions was a tiny voice that reminded her she was a bored, lonely woman who could not deny that the thought of working closely with Armand Foncé was one of the most attractive propositions that had been put before her for a very long time. His fingers were hope on the ivory of her glove.

'There is no need to reply to me now, Mademoiselle Tennant. I can see that you have lots of thoughts in that clever, complicated head of yours.'

He read her so easily, flipping her thoughts before her eyes like a coin. Like the pages of a novel, rippling in all their might under a swift thumb.

'I want you to think it over, and I have made that very clear to Madame Bardin. I have insisted that you must be completely content with the arrangement.'

He stood to smooth the invisible creases from his suit. A dart of disappointment pricked her and the booming bell of silence rang between them.

'I will call on you next week, Mademoiselle Tennant.'

Henri tottered into the doorway, a different woman, as drunk as the last, tight against his groin. When she swayed and banged her head hard against the metal of the staircase, Enriqueta knew there was nothing she could do to save her, and she stole herself away to bed.

LONGFORD, 1870

'MARTHA, I NEED TO TALK TO YOU.'
The steady shred of the water sprinklers, the buzz of insects and murmurs from Martha as she continued to sleep thrummed in the warmth of the greenhouse. John wondered what dreams were walking through her mind. Were they like his- did she walk through streets with Richard as he did with his Dinah, hands melded and voices so pleased with each other that they lapped and met. Bending before her on his haunches, he gently shook Martha awake.

She examined him in confusion, her face as pale and parched as a sea-worn shell. Martha was not yet sixty years old, but frailty had taken hold of her and shaken all the softness out of her. On the mellow April morning of their wedding day, she had been regal. Her strong face was even and calm as she stood waiting for him at the aisle, the spring sun streaming through the church windows, illuminating her in a pool of gold. She wore her gown like a medieval saint – plain and faint.

A sharp stab of regret and guilt pierced him as he looked at Martha. He would deal with his own shameful shortcomings in time. He would find a way to repent, and he prayed that it was not too late to atone for his base, selfish activities.

She was as changed as he was, both man and wife tumbling through the ruckus and fissures that all marriages present. From the placid widow she had been when they had met, then to the furious, jealous, lonely woman of her middle years, to most recently this version. A sad, silent, wretched creature, prematurely aged and exhausted of all joy. The woollen wraps and shawls were mounds on her.

John had been through this conversation so many times in the recesses of his conscious and subconscious, yet on facing her, his words failed him, his rehearsals insubstantial and lacking.

Her eyes-milky and wan-focused on his and she attempted to sit upright in her chair. Cradling her body in his palms, she felt as light as eggshell; and it repulsed him. John forced himself to grasp her properly. For years, the only woman he had been intimate with was Caroline, and touching his wife again was terrible. He caught a stale scent as he shifted her, lavender cologne and the vegetal, sour smell of unwashed skin. He knew how hard Leone battled to insist on her bathing and wearing freshly laundered clothes. Day after day, night after night, Leone fought a tiresome war with Martha, and John knew that Leone, as steely and devoted as she was, would soon lose her will, just as he had so long ago.

'There, Martha. You are sitting well and straight. To hear me better, I hope.'

Martha's face was darkly alert, set with a grim determination as she stared at her husband. Even in her muted state, Martha had enough fire left in her embers to put him ill at ease. He knew that a wrong word from him would serve as oxygen to her flames. He picked through his sentence.

'I thought you might like to know about a plan I have for you. For us.'

She met him with the same white stare, unwavering and powerful. No flicker from her wet mouth, but for the constant tremble of her lower lip. A long wasp settled onto Martha's lap, and her finger pressed it silently to death into her blanket.

Starkly intimate thoughts of Caroline came to John, and he tried to steer himself from them; Caroline under covers with him, on top of him. His hands were running along the soft plane of her back, his lips fluttering over her thighs. She was kneeling before him, looking up at him as he pulled her hair together, watching her dark locks drop again from his fingers.

The sprinklers stopped, and but for the small, fuzzy sound of the flies, the greenhouse was silent and expectant, as if every single quiet plant, and every piece of Longford was waiting and listening for John to begin.

'I want us to take a trip abroad. It has been so long since we have been anywhere. You can choose where we go, Martha. Anywhere you like.'

Martha snarled her words out in a low growl. Hers was a rough voice, unaccustomed to being used.

'Business or pleasure, John?'

Her teeth were bruised with grey.

'A holiday for us. But yes – if there is a chance, I would like to visit the offices on the continent.'

He watched her carefully, his answer hanging between them. The moments ticked and she moved her mouth, as if forming words and ideas like a child learning to speak.

'Menil-Hermei.'

The insect she had crushed waved its sting feebly, and she killed it again.

'Good. As you wish. France.'

In his relief, John had nearly forgotten.

'Martha, there is one other thing.'

A wet cough rattled out of her chest, and she pressed a handkerchief to her mouth.

'Leone can't come with us. I need her at the house; the children and Peter can't spare her for so many weeks. We will need someone to accompany us, so I have advertised for a companion for you. I will find a suitable woman to make sure that everything goes to plan.'

He didn't need to tell her that he had replied to Miss Tennant already. He gripped himself in expectation for a torrent, but Martha only smirked at him, her eyes flinted. She reached under the folds of her knitted shawl and felt for the letter that Peter had left in the pile of post for Tynan to take. She crushed it, feeling it crumple reassuringly in her weak fist.

'Doubtless you will, John. Doubtless you will.'

La Castilla, 1870

'WELL, HELLO, MY DEAREST. Where has dull, shy Mademoiselle Tennant gone, and who is the charming, cunning creature that has taken her place!'

Enriqueta turned away, pretending to busy herself with ancient maps of southeast Asia.

'Come now, don't be so coy. You set your heart on him and your courage has paid dividends!'

'Set my heart on whom, Madame? I don't know what you mean, I'm sure.'

Madame Bardin moved towards her, a hunter stalking succulent prey. Madame flapped a letter in the air, fanning the pulse of excitement that had not left Enriqueta for a moment since the party.

'This came just now. From dear Monsieur Foncé. Addressed to you but I'm sure you don't mind that I opened it. He is my friend, after all.'

Enriqueta excavated patience from deep within her.

'And what does the letter say, Madame?'

Madame Bardin pressed against her, grasping at her waist, waving the letter at her face. She made a noise like a grumbling purr and giggled like a child. Enriqueta winced when Madame pinched her arm with force.

'Your Amand is coming to visit you tomorrow! Now promise me you will do the right thing. You will help him with our worthy project, won't you. I'm depending on you, dearest!'

Enriqueta prayed that Madame would not notice anything in her expression, willing her to go away so she could be alone with her letter, happy without her tainting it all. She shuffled the maps in her hands, concentrating hard on the main river systems on the papers: Irrawaddy, Salween, Chao Praya, Mekong.

'I would be happy to assist Monsieur Foncé with his work for the orphans, Madame. Of course.'

'That pleases me, dear. Though don't forget it is I who created this plan in the first place. Foncé is such a good, precious friend, but let it not be lost on us that these orphans are benefitting from my charity.'

Enriqueta bent over her maps, wondering what she would wear. And how she had found herself, so long used to the lonely spaces of La Castilla, so suddenly occupied by one, very particular man.

She hardly slept that night. Enriqueta abandoned any hope of rest by dawn, the tug of worry waking her early. The vinegar of Jules's words would not evaporate, even in the new light of the day.

She stepped down the long staircase, the metal vines twisting down elaborately to the see-no-evil hear-no-evil monkeys. The marble under her feet was cold, until the warmth of the pantry as she rounded the last curve of the stairs, feeling the familiar heat of Jules's early morning fire, that he stoked from embers to flame as each moon made way for the sun.

'I heard about the letter, Enri. So, he is coming today.'

'I believe so.'

Jules sighed, long and low, pouring the coffee. He speared his bread and turned it in front of the fire.

The coffee pot sputtered, and Jules pushed the first of the toast across to Enriqueta.

'There is new honey for you there. You should take some

for your bread. Farmer Luc swears it cures every ailment. Influenza, whooping cough. Broken hearts.'

The scent of all the flowers it was born from sprung from the honey between them. Jules huffed, irritated by the drips of the coffee pot on his table. He dragged a cloth, his thighs filling his thin trousers, which fell short of his ankles. The muscles in his back were defined through his shirt, and his face had changed. No longer sleek and angelic, his jaw was lower, his handsome nose longer and more generous. He wasn't her little Jules anymore and Enriqueta's eyes fill with tears. She longed for her brother, and for a mother that should have loved her more finely.

Her face crumpled, and she pushed her plate away. Jules caught Enriqueta up in his arms, crushing her to chest. He kissed her head and muttered into her hair.

'I'm sorry. I'm sorry.'

The tears that shimmered inside her burst forth all at once, so thankful that it appeared he still loved her.

'It's not my place to instruct you on who and who not you can be friendly with, Enri. I should never have said a word.'

'Jules, I don't know what I would have done here if I hadn't had you and Maddy. It has broken my heart these last few days, thinking you were cross with me. It felt like I had lost you. Maybe Maddy too.'

Jules held her shoulders.

'I could never, ever be angry with you. It's not that at all. The only person I am angry with is that witch, Bardin. She has put you where she wants you. I can't help it- she cannot be trusted, and as for Armand Foncé…'

Jules sawed at the bread again, and finally the sun was creeping in its familiar arc. One of the cats jumped up to the table in the hope of affection.

'I've said enough. You know what she is like, I realise that.

But at least Maddy and I have family around. I mean, there is only so far she can use her cunning and greed to mess us around. We are siblings. You are alone.' The cat jumped to Enriqueta and padded her lap. Her belly swung with the weight of a clutch of kittens. 'Please, be careful. We love you, Enriqueta. They could mistreat you so, so easily. You might not even notice it happening at all.'

The doorbell clanged, and a cockerel's call cracked out from across the yard. From the parlour, they heard laughter echo against the glittering mirrors of the hallway, Foncé's deep baritone against Madame's obsequious chuckle. There was conversation, though Enriqueta could not distinguish what they were saying. Heat flushed into her cheeks, and she regretted her plain, navy day dress.

Armand Foncé was taller than Enriqueta had remembered. He was magnificent and his looks stunned her. The memories of being in his arms felt impossible, as if they belonged to someone else.

'Mademoiselle Tennant. I was just thanking Madame Bardin for the wonderful party the other evening. It really was an unforgettable occasion.'

'The pleasure was all of ours, dear Foncé,' gushed Madame Bardin. 'Maddy is always so late with the tea things. Hopeless.'

She rustled away, shutting the door firmly behind her, the catch clicking in promise.

'Monsieur Foncé, do sit down.'

'We agreed you would call me Armand.'

The cat twisted at her feet and Enriqueta thought that she had never been so happy to see someone. To see him again, in the smallness of the kitchen, with Luc's honey and the empty pot of coffee, items so usual, in the frame of someone so astounding.

'Have you had time to consider the idea? It's all I have been thinking of.'

The exhilaration of flattery rushed through her.

'I have, Armand. Yes, I would be very pleased to help you.'

A huge smile broke over his face and he took her hands in his.

'This is the most wonderful, wonderful news. Thank you sincerely, Mademoiselle Tennant. As I said, I don't know anything about books at all. I was looking at the lovely trees on the way here today and I realised I don't know much about nature either. Strange, isn't it? The things that entice us, and the things that don't.'

The cat turned, arching her back. She ran to a shrew and slammed her paw down, her unborn kittens tumbling over each other in the safety of her fur.

Tea was served, and they spent the next two hours in discussion. He explained his vision for the orphanage. The committee he had formed consisted of many of the great and the good of the city of Lyon. There were doctors and lawyers, businesspeople and landowners. A few of them, like Madame Faucher, were unskilled, but monstrously wealthy.

After the scandal of the missing children of Île du Levant, the spotlight had landed on the orphanage, and the local inspectors decided that a blind eye had been turned long enough. They raided the building unannounced, horrified by what they encountered. The children were starving, their bodies jumping with fleas. Maggots crawled in and out of sores on their knees and elbows, which had been caused by the physical work they were constantly forced to do. Beaten so frequently, the children were covered in suppurating, fiery wounds.

The institution was overcrowded and unsanitary, and children died daily from the typhus they caught from the rats that scattered down every wall, and from the tuberculosis that spread through the air, from cough to bloodied cough. As fast as the children died, more were dumped at the door. Frequently, these poor souls had living parents who abandoned them, unable to care for relentlessly expanding families. Many of the poorest women of the city expelled their infants from their wombs in alleys and outhouses, and after burning through the cord with a candle end, left them still blue and greasy in rags on the steps of Sainte Catherine.

Often as soon as the children were able to walk, packs of them ran away from the orphanage, the older ones pulling the little ones with them. A grim and freezing life on the streets was preferable to the myriad dangers that lurked behind the locked oak of the Sainte Catherine orphanage. Homeless and alone, the street children were prey to the criminals who would use and abuse them with abandon.

As the inspectors went from room to room, new evils lay behind each door. They found a row of iron beds with putrid mattresses. There was a little girl tied like a star to each, the ropes on their wrists so deep into the lesions they had caused, the inspectors could not free them at first, the threads of the binds matted and joined to the open welts on their skin.

They found one room that at first seemed empty but for boxes. In the boxes, they made the gruesome discovery of many little bodies, swaddled tightly in oily lengths of flour sacking. The newborns had been mummified alive, many of their faces set in their last, anguished cries. They were covered in coal dust and ash.

People were arrested and jailed, though it was soon very clear that many of the perpetrators themselves were a pitiful, damaged lot. Some were older children, driven mad and cruel by years of unrelenting, institutionalised abuse. Some were men, frequent visitors to the orphanage for many years, who used it as their own, inexhaustible brothel, with no one to stop them mounting, mauling, and sacrificing any child they chose.

The orphanage had unashamedly supplied the children and had even hired out the healthier ones to be taken away for days by a cabal of monsters and perverts. The inspectors listened to the children's stories for hours, painstakingly writing out each terrible tale. There were memories of being chivvied into fine carriages late at night. Blindfolded, they were taken up into the hills, the children sensing the cart resisting against the steep narrow tracks and feeling a change from the warm city air to the sharp damp of the countryside on their silent skin. Arriving at the grand houses, they spent days and nights enduring endless assaults and torture for the entertainment of the braying men and women who loomed over them, laughing at their agonies. They spoke of rituals and stones, blood and chanting, endless attacks and the final whimperings of sisters and small companions in corridors painted in ruby and gold and symbols laid out on floors. And when many of these children inevitably died at their hands, these dreadful, heartless demons were handed yet more. Those who lived to impart their experiences to the inspector's records often vomited while recalling them, their eyes popping at the agonies that were burned into their minds forever.

Enriqueta ached for the children, the tale so harrowing that the flimsiness of books – paper and ink, not care or love, or the trusted bricks of good family – hardly seemed a worthy salve at all.

Once convictions were made, and the malevolent forces expelled from Sainte Catherine, the first thing Foncé and his charitable group did was to donate funds to clean and purge the building, and employ a proper, qualified and decent matron to oversee the children. They paid for a cook to prepare simple but nourishing food, and a doctor was enlisted. He treated each poor child in turn, dressing their wounds and applying compresses to their impacted teeth and swollen cysts which clotted against their brittle grey torsos. The doctor wept privately at the damage caused to the little girls and boys, many of whom could no longer walk, their pelvises so mutilated and crushed by the wicked actions of their ungodly predators.

Months passed, and conditions at the orphanage were immeasurably improved. Disease no longer ripped through it so viciously. The children were clean and well fed. More pivotally, they didn't live in ceaseless fear and anguish. They had proper beds to sleep in, and no longer had to endure the clatter and scrabble of rats at their feet, the death rattle of another child as they expired next to them, or the brutish tread of the army of villains, the noise of a new party of people come to feast on them.

The matron that Foncé had hired didn't have time to be a tender woman. But she was firm, fair, cheerful, and of sound moral stature. Cook was a sensitive and kindly man, finding time to talk and play with the children once his duties were over. He could be found at the end of his shifts in the backyard, rolling marbles over and over with the little, mad souls, who rocked and chewed at the air, never uttering a sound. They gummed on the biscuit ends he fished from his pocket and mewed in delight when he sung them an old song.

'I'm ashamed that I didn't know any of this. I walk down that road often. I suppose I knew of it in Paris too. I saw children and beggars scuttling about. I knew of poverty – I ignored it there. I ignore it here in Lyon.'

The teapot was cold and empty. It wouldn't be long before Madame Bardin began to talk of lunch.

'How could you know the depths of the depravity and torments that took place, Mademoiselle Tennant? None of us did. Of course, we are none so simple that we thought orphanages were pleasant places. We know the fate of a motherless child is a hard one. But we could not have known how truly terrible it was. It was kept hidden. The place was governed by the criminal and the insane, and the corrupt. The eyes of the law were kept well shielded.'

His pocket watch caught rays through the garden windows, and she felt light and uncaring about the hour. It could have been any hour. Birds still sang, oblivious.

'Enough of the terrible tale, the history. Although we are satisfied that at least Sainte Catherine is now decent and habitable, and the children's physical needs are well met, it is their spiritual and cerebral requirements which require attention. Also, now that happily, fewer children are dying, we are a little overcrowded, though that is something which I alone must address. A new building is necessary at some point but will be costly. Something for Madame Faucher to consider, I imagine', he added, smiling.

Enriqueta thought of Adelaide Faucher, her breasts brimming over her dress like a pudding of pearls, throwing out franc notes to a sea of grimy hands, while the shell of her toenails wriggled over her chaise longue.

'We have converted one of the rooms into a classroom, as I told you the other evening. We need to furnish it with books and writing materials. The children must learn; they must be equipped to work. The usual employment for them would be as house staff or farm hands, and for this at least they must be basically literate and numerate.'

She remembered why she was there.

'Reading is indeed the key to all learning, Armand. Everything else comes after. People don't need to love books, and neither should they. As you say, not everyone loves nature. Or music. Or company. But they need to know how to undo the confusions of language. And it is a confusion.'

'This is why you are so needed, Mademoiselle Tennant! Madame Bardin, in her wisdom and generosity, has offered to any suitable books that she comes across in her business dealings. A wonderful gesture, it will allow us to start a library for the children.'

Enriqueta smarted. Madame had always considered children's books an annoyance. They were of little commercial value to her as she was unable to sell them for much at all. She believed that most children were spoiled, idle creatures who should not be indulged with such fripperies as books and playthings. The children's books that arrived at La Castilla as part of the mixed boxes were snatched and thrown to the burn pile at the back of the house. Enri and Maddy always ensured that they were rescued without Madame Bardin's knowledge before they were torched, and placed in the grateful, chubby little hands of Maddy's many nieces and nephews. Enriqueta kept her counsel and said nothing of this to Armand.

'I suggest that I come to La Castilla weekly and assist you in sorting and cataloguing the books. You have vast experience in this, and I have none. You can recognise truth and worth and quality in them, whereas I do not. I'm afraid all books look the same to me.'

Enri laughed, thrilling at the praise, and basking in the feeling of being useful to him. For so long she had felt untethered. Without direction, days drifted into months. This would be meaningful, measured, eventful. It would give her purpose.

Madame Bardin chirruped at the door, asking if Monsieur Foncé would stay to dine with them.

'If I may, could I reserve that invitation for another time. I must get back to the city. I hadn't realised how late the hour was.'

He kissed Madame Bardin and walked with Enriqueta to the door. A family of doves were busy in the yard, white and pure against the mud of the ground. His horses were bored and impatient, scuffing the birds with their heels.

'We shall be working together; can I call you Enriqueta?'

Her name spun like sugar from his lips. The words of warning from Jules fluttered and died in her. Behind the muscle and height, Jules was only still a boy, with little experience beyond the confines of La Castilla. His fervent affirmations rang hollow, as she stood before Armand in the fading sun, the moon risen like a token in the east. Jules's distant voice was there, somewhere in the recesses of her mind but it all now seemed so unfounded. All she took from her time with Armand today was good. His sense of charity, his passion for his work, his patience.

'Of course, Armand.'

'Then goodbye, dear Enriqueta. Until I see you next.'

His man opened the door to the carriage, the navy doors varnished and glinting. Foncé waved from the window all the way down the long track of the driveway, out onto the road back to Lyon. She waved too, her arm aching until he disappeared.

Sleep came in short, exhausting bursts. Her mind swarmed with images plucked from every moment of the day. Jules featured in her dreams – running from her, jumping over the low walls of the garden and somehow, preternaturally, leaping over the fields and villages that lay between La Castilla and the city. Children, in monochrome, screamed in silence, locked up in palpating walls and trapped under crude beds, reaching their hands to her heart, which she found in her own palms, beating and pulsing thick red blood through her fingers. She woke intermittently, cold with sweat and an unquenchable thirst, before falling back into a dreadful half sleep when her dreams came to feast on her once more. Finally, some respite came and the last dreams that bloomed before she woke were as vivid, but joyous. She was walking through the streets of Lyon with Armand-arm in arm, lips at lips-stopping at shops she had seen but never entered, bright cafes she had passed in real life and longed to visit. There was some vague ending before she woke suddenly, panting and alert, her eyes opened, just as the smudged image of his kiss drifted from her.

La Castilla, Late Summer 1870

ENRIQUETA COULD BARELY CONCENTRATE. Glum and quiet, she picked at the cake that Maddy pressed on her. Too tired by the end of the day to join her and Jules in their usual late supper, she forewent the games of cards and shared bottles of wine, instead retiring early to bed. It was nearly harvest time, and Maddy and Jules were tired too, spending their early mornings and evenings in the fields while it was light enough, earning extra money to see their ageing family over the winter. The house was subdued. Madame Bardin was in Biarritz, and there was little activity. Armand's next visit was three more days away, and Enri fretted that there would be nothing to show him. No books had arrived for some time, and she was growing anxious, listening out for the carts every day. Without the books, there was no progress to be made, or work with him to be done.

Taking the briochette d'hier from the brown paper, Enriqueta placed them into the pan, the butter golden and foaming. She had the bowls ready, and grated the chocolate into them, the thick milk coming to a boil.

The crunch of their boots on the gravel came at the window. Jules and Enriqueta were back from the fields. The bread slid from the pan as they sat down, wordless and famished. The comforting scent of the pastry filled the room, and the chocolate drifted into the air. Breakfast was the least important meal for country folk. Sweet and short, with just enough in it to sustain them until lunchtime.

It had taken some time for Enriqueta to ally herself with the Lyonnaise way of eating. In Paris, with her friends, they only ate breakfast at the weekend. Saturday and Sundays, there were trips to cafes for almond croissants and cakes in gold paper boxes. On normal weekdays, Enriqueta, Jeanne and Marie-Anne had just fruit and coffee and had gone to work, suitably faint and hungry, always thinking of their figures. Lunch really didn't exist, but they ate together well under the careful watch and expertise of their maid Clementine each evening.

In Lyon, breakfast was treated like a medicine. It wasn't lingered over but was perfunctory and purposeful and hasty; a chore to be completed before the work of the day began in houses and fields. Only after seeing Maddy and Jules gobble down their croissants had Enriqueta realised her long garden breakfasts were part of a sort of special treatment as an outsider – une Parisienne.

Conversely, the midday meal was taken with gravity. The vast Lyon lunches amazed her. The household stopped, and the tables laid with speed. Outside when it was fine, and in the stables when it wasn't. The horse hands, gardeners, laundry women, cleaners, cooks, stable boys and Jules, Maddy and Enriqueta all gathered together and the air was filled with chatter and the clatter of plates. While the wages were so low, the tradition that the great houses still fed the workers once a day was welcome, although Madame Bardin had frequently threatened to banish the convention.

There was always soup or salad first, leaves with a poached egg and mustard dressing, or followed by gras-double or cardon à la moelle. Lunch always ended with beignets de fleurs d'acacia or galette bressane. The first time Enri had tried to consume all three courses she could barely stand afterwards.

This was a meal for workers who needed fuel and fats. Standing and sorting books all day, arduous and boring as it was, did not merit a three-course Lyonnaise lunch.

She instinctively ran her hand over her waist, wondering if it had thickened. It was an irony that she had recently become more preoccupied by her figure here, in the Lyon countryside, hidden from anyone, than she ever had been while dwelling and moving in Paris, the vainest city in the world.

She reproached herself for indulging in something so shallow. Prayers pushed aside, her first morning moments and in the final light of each day, she gazed into the mirror, checking for any glints of grey, scrutinising her forehead for lines, her eyes for shadows. The bewitching murmur of romance had turned her against herself, and she despised every one of her garments. By far the worst offender in her meagre wardrobe was the tired grey dress, so offensively plain and rough to the touch. Pulling it on, she dragged it into place in anger, deciding she would wear the tatty old thing just one more time before it was consigned with scorn to Maddy's ragbag. The glorious pen of anticipation sketched an idea – a trip into Lyon with Jules and Maddy, spending a rare, hidden afternoon browsing the shops while Madame was far, far away on one of her business excursions.

Enriqueta toyed with her plan as she worked in the Blue Room, tweaking elements of it this way and that, smiling to herself as she turned the notion over. She embellished it with detail, adding a trip to sit under the red and white awning of the Corner Bar, or a lunch in Place Bellecour, with wine and water served cold under the city's sun. She saw herself walk into one of the dressmakers, where she would consult with Maddy, holding a bolt of silk aloft, yards of lace ruffled in her hands. A beautiful fern green dress, with black felt-covered buttons on the jacket, and a round, bright white collar with matching detail on the cuff. It would be a sublime replacement for her dull grey frock, and it would be smart enough to wear into town. If she could afford it, she would order more: one in a pale coffee brown, one the colour of a ripe peach.

The knock on the door sent one of the heavy bound maps out of her arms to tumble to the floor. A gritty puff of dust gusted over her chest and face. One of the delivery men peered round.

'Sorry, mademoiselle. Jules let me in. He's helping the lads unload. Younger than me, isn't he. Anyway, I'm just letting you know there is a lot for you today. You'll want some of this space clear on the tables.'

The men hauled the boxes in. She hoped that some of them might contain children's books. Joyfully she pulled out one after the other, their bright colours and sweet characters lighting up the room, glowing with cheer and innocence against the sombre backdrop of the shelves lined with grey, brown and black.

Cinq Contes Droles, Peau D'Ane, En Guerre!, Le Poisson d'Avril, L'Oeuf Magique, 30 Proverbes pour les Enfants Sage. There were boxes and boxes of so many different types, and multiple copies of the more popular ones. They were not the most modern, latest children's titles, but they had been immaculately cared for and were in beautiful condition.

Enriqueta was elated. She had begun to despair, doubting that Madame would ever be able to get enough books in time for Armand's next visit. A fear of disappointing him had fixed in her; an agonising belief that her link to Armand would be untethered by Madame Bardin's inaction.

She handled the books gently, as though they were delicate infants themselves. Thinking of the eager souls that would unfurl them, releasing wonder and learning and comfort, she placed them carefully in piles; gentle stacks of hope. There were more to come, as the men went to and from the carts; so many, they could not even fit onto the tables, and they had to leave them stacked in the hallway. She heard Jules shout his final farewells to the removal men as their carts beat their way down the driveway.

Jules was red faced and sheened with sweat.

'Bloody big haul she's managed this time, Enri. She put a note in. It's all from one place. A wealthy family with a large brood and a string of private governesses. The children are all grown now with offspring of their own, so the Madame of the house wanted rid of the whole lot.'

'But wouldn't her grandchildren have wanted them? This is an astounding, wonderful collection to give away when there are children in the family that would enjoy them.'

Jules looked at her archly.

'You know what the rich are like, Enri. They want the newest stuff, the latest things. They will be spending hundreds of francs at the nearest bookshop as we speak, filling their empty shelves.'

Jules was right. Had the need at the orphanage not arisen, these beautiful books would have been wasted, probably left to burn on a far-away bonfire while the owners went shopping, filling their carriages and providing their maids with aching backs and disgust.

'Oh, and the other good news is that she is staying away for a bit. Having a holiday by the sea. Apparently, there will be another delivery in a few days' time.'

The front door clanged again.

'One of that lot always forgets something. It will be a pouch of baccy or a pencil or something. Back in a minute, then we can get to work. I'll ask Maddy to do us some tea.'

There was the tap of fine leather in the marble of the hallway, rather than the thud of a work boot. Jules's voice was gruff.

'Monsieur Foncé for you, Mademoiselle Tennant.'

The dark cast over Jules's face showed his anger.

'Enriqueta, my sincerest apologies for arriving unannounced.'

She caught Jules grimacing at the use of her first name as he left the room, letting the door slam behind him. Irritation passed through her when she glanced down, trying to compose herself. The dreadful grey dress clung to her torso uncomfortably, the skirts scuffed with dust. She had not expected him for two days long days, and she noted, miserably, that one of the buttons on her cuff was hanging by a thread. She didn't need a mirror to show her that her hair was in disarray, her bun sagging limply and damply at her neck. The morning's dab of face powder was long gone.

'Do come in, please. Sit down'

His magnificent name stuck in her throat, unreleased, for fear that Jules might well be glowering, stiff behind the mirrored door.

'It's wonderful to see you again, Enriqueta.'

He sat on one of the few small chairs that there was still space for, looking elegant and expensive, his long frame draped over it with the grace of a reclining statue. His form gave her Sundays in Paris, looking at the *Marcellus as Hermes*, and a thirst for Montmatre wine and ice-creams scented with rose.

'Madame Bardin wrote to let me know that the first dispatch of books would be here today,' he continued. 'Finding myself with an unexpected afternoon free from meetings or other tedious commitments, I thought it might be a nice thing for us to be together when they arrived. I am a little late, but I raced to get here, I assure you.'

The pulse that started in her heart when he had entered the room radiated through her as he came nearer to her. All the pedestrian atmosphere of La Castilla lifted again in his wake.

'But I thought maybe Madame Bardin would have told me about the delivery too. I could have prepared for its arrival.'

The oversight was deliberate; another of Madame's tiresome games. It entertained her to be sly and hurtful, directing all in her absence by the power of her pointed omissions. Madame Bardin threaded minutely cruel episodes throughout her days, imparting a subtle oppression over those she knew she could exert power. She practiced disingenuity with an expert ease, always framing her spite and twists as innocent misunderstandings or blameless forgetfulness. There was much pleasure to be had in the puppeteering of a small world when intellect was lacking.

And though Jules was young, he was male, and a long-standing servant, as much an integral part of La Castilla as the gilded stairway monkeys. And Armand Foncé had been a pillar of Madame Bardin's circle for years, holding up her façade of authority and entertaining her fantasies of worth. A man of towering influence and reputation, he was social nectar to Madame Bardin. Both Jules and Foncé, by virtue of their sex and their usefulness to her, ranked higher in status than Enriqueta ever would. Despite her education, her experience, her good character, Enriqueta Augusta Tennant was only a woman.

'We shall make a start together today, then, Enriqueta? If you want to?'

Want. What did she want? The oddity of the word thumped like a drum in her.

'Enriqueta?'

Unmistakably, she saw his eyes flicker over her body. Could he see how much she shook beneath her hateful dress?

'Of course. Of course, I want to.'

His smile shot right through her again, as Maddy's neat knock rapped at the door. She carried a tray, with a pot of tea, and plates of *orange-blossom bugnes*, and *tarte aux pralines*, glistening rose pink on the white china. They had come from one of the best bakeries. The donuts were shaped into little flowers, expertly dusted with milled golden sugar. Maddy swivelled her eyes toward Armand, and he laughed.

'Yes, they are from me. I didn't think it was polite to arrive both unannounced and empty handed. I called at Patisserie St Vincent on the way. Please, have some.'

Without Madame Bardin in residence, the house always warmed and loosened with each day she was gone. Rules were slackened, windows opened and the days swum easily without her. The gardeners smoked sitting down and cracked their trugs of pastis out earlier than usual. Jules and Maddy started their days later, and ended them later, sometimes staying over in the spare rooms after too many hands of cards and too much wine enjoyed with Enriqueta in front of the parlour fire. When the sheets were pulled tightly and the bathrooms briefly mopped, no one would have ever known they had been there at all, and Madame Bardin was too idle to check.

Enriqueta laughed more frequently and more easily. She seemed to unfurl, blossoming and brightening as the summer season spilled slowly into autumn. The dark green gardens of La Castilla began to bead with moisture in the last of the heat, and the glossy bushes that banked along the garden's edge dropped their parchment flowers and began to push out their fruit.

Since the books had arrived, Armand had been visiting every Monday, Wednesday, and Thursday. A routine emerged, and Maddy instructed Jules to order bakery deliveries. He didn't question it, and the cakes arrived on these days along with the other provisions. Jules said nothing about the cost that they added to their weekly bills, knowing that Madame would display a rare generosity, as it was in her interest. Enriqueta rushed to the morning grocery cart like she had never done before, helping to take out the cans and the flour, the household provisions and the cleaning salts, and then finally looking into the front seat to the apricot-coloured boxes from St Vincent, tied with silver grosgrain ribbon, heralding his visits in all their sugar and almonds.

By the third week, the task of cataloguing the titles was complete, with each copy wiped with soft cloths, damp with mint and lavender. They laid each one out on the trestle tables at the window, and once they were dry, Armand and Enriqueta had numbered and stamped them, detailing each one in a record book.

Car, vois-tu, chaque jour je t'aime davantage, aujourd'hui plus qu'hier et bien moins que demain.

Armand had printed special library plates for the orphanage and together they tacked them in the inside covers, proud with the stamp of St Catherine in gold and blue. The small rhythm of passing things to him filled her ordered mind and her passionate heart – a duality which elevated her with utter joy. Every tiny aspect fired her; the scent of the ink on the stamp, the bubbled blots of the gold paint as it dried, and the way Armand's foot would occasionally collide with hers. Him being near made her brave and she allowed herself to impress him with her knowledge. She told him of her life in Paris.

Oh! Si tu pouvais lire dans mon coeur, tu verrais la place où je t'ai mise!

The Blue Room was warm, and they sat down for the first time in hours. Their backs stiff, their necks rigid. There were few chairs that were unoccupied by packages, but they were at least near the window. Aches sank further into their spines, while crickets clicked outside, and the late air was still.

'Enriqueta, shall we sit for a time in the other room? Where we were together at the party?'

There were no objections to be had in the silence of the house, with Madame Bardin away and Jules and Maddy on an errand in town. Enriqueta could hold every one of those steps in her memory, only five or six, his hand at her elbow, guiding her as he quietly opened the mirrored door into the dining room. Out of use, the curtains were drawn, the room shadowy and silent. She heard the click of the latch on the door, and the waxy smell of spent candles hung in the air as she stood, shaking; waiting for him to come to her.

Armand's face was swallowed by the darkness. As he stepped closer, she shut her eyes to the ballroom smell of him – ash and musk and amber. Her eyes were still closed, the room quiet but for the gasp of his breath as he pulled her up by her waist and found her lips, kissing her and pressing Enriqueta hard against him until there was nothing left for her to think about at all but her the rush of blood through her body, time dropping from her fingers and all of her swelling and alive as they kissed.

La Castilla, Autumn 1870

Enriqueta went to sleep thinking about Armand, and he was still there, waiting in her waking mind when she opened her eyes to each day. She had taken to undressing in bed, under the covers, her body moving under her fingers in the sliding pink sun of the morning.

Her face was clear and bright. She had started using all the ointments and oils that Maddy had pushed on her for so long and she imagined they had begun to take effect. She was sleeping well. Her work was meaningful. And everything in her world had shifted.

Her appetite started to fade, and although she still loved preparing early breakfasts for Jules and Maddy, she felt a burning distraction in her core. She made French toast for them all, but her slice lay curling in the pan, long after they had left for the fields, her eyes at the distant towers of Lyon, like she had no mind at all. The biscuits Maddy made for her were half eaten then tossed to the birds. She came to the house lunches, serving more than she ate, pushing pieces of quiche into her mouth to stop the constant, gnawing feeling of longing in her stomach. She could think of nothing, or no-one but Armand.

Then, one lunchtime, the barn began to swim in her eyes. Maddy leant over her, patting her face.

'Enri, Enri, wake up!'

Moments after she fainted, Enriqueta felt the hands on

her, lifting her up. She could hear Jules's voice, low and full of direction. Someone was carrying her across the silk of the open air, and though her eyes were closed, she knew she was out of the sun, and into the cool quiet of the house. One of the groundsmen was bearing her up the stairs. Tread by tread, he took the journey carefully, steered by Maddy's instructions.

'Careful with her now Jacques, she's not well. She's as white as a sheet!'

Her head swung and bobbed as the man curved up the staircase. Enriqueta's stomach and head turned, dizzy with a febrile sickness that rose, burning in her throat.

She lay on the bathroom floor that night, her head rippling with heat, while her body shook with cold. Enriqueta retched hourly, spent from effort, her raging thirst exacerbated by her sickness. Maddy sat with her. She undressed Enriqueta, noticing how slim she had become beneath her old, stiff clothes. Her shoulders were spiked up in her chemise, and her ribs were clear under the slippery satin. Her arms and legs in her bed clothes were not strong and sturdy anymore, but thin and soft.

Enriqueta fell asleep. Maddy dragged the coverlet and pillows from the bedroom and made a bed for them on the cold tiles, cradling her.

Maddy disappeared early to start her duties downstairs, leaving the healing balm of sleep to mend Enriqueta and fight whatever had struck her down so badly. Hours later she woke, cold and confused, feeling a clumsy hand scuffing against her brow. She could smell the dark, penetrating perfume before she opened her eyes.

'Poor dear girl.'

Madame Bardin purred; her breath acrid.

'Thank goodness I am back. I checked on you often last night. I watched you sleep. Like a mother.'

Enri flinched as Madame slowly drew her fingers along her

body, barely clothed but for her underwear, the blankets thrown off in the night. Her mouth felt dry and stuck, and she could hardly refuse as Madame gripped the nape of her neck, pulling her into the glass of water at her lips. She drank, dropping her eyes from the intensity of Madame's gaze, so close to her own. Her tether on the time had been lost in sleep.

'Oh, oh, I can see what concerns you, dearest. He has been and gone. I could not bring myself to raise you, even for our Armand.'

Panic shot an arrow through her, followed by crashing disappointment. Enriqueta sank back into the floor, cold and hard without the fur of sleep, despite the layer of the coverlet. Her head was dizzy with the exertion and sweat beaded over her lips and under her arms.

'Don't fret, don't fret! I have told him you are indisposed. He will call again tomorrow, if you are well enough.'

Madame's face contorted into what she fancied was a semblance of empathy.

'I believe you and Armand have become close.'

Enriqueta felt sick again. The skylight, which Maddy had propped open to let the fever escape, bought in the bleak, keening plea of an animal in labour. The grim and dangerous passage of life, in stark sounds through a window. Enriqueta thought of blood, and remembered reaching out to her mother, only to find her gone, all of the time. She remembered calling out, eleven years old and bleeding into bathrooms of white china and hallways of wealth, curtains flipping in the breeze where Juana should have been.

'Let's get you into bed, dear. You need your beauty sleep if we are to expect a visit from your monsieur tomorrow. And apart from your dalliances' – she lingered on the word, curling her red lips – 'I need you to keep up appearances. This tiresome orphanage project has put me back in touch with a few important people. Let's not waste our chances.'

She patted Enriqueta briskly, then pushed her up, chivvying her into her bedroom. Enri sunk into the cold of the sheets and shut her eyes, willing Madame to leave. At last, feigning sleep, Enri heard Madame go, with heavy, uneven footsteps pounding down the endless stairs.

Another day passed until Enriqueta woke again.

'It's me, Enri. Try and sit up. I've drawn a bath for you then you must eat.'

Maddy had wisely ran it cool and unscented. Letting her tired throat sink into the water, the water pooled in all the spaces in her body; her stomach concave and her thighs wasted and narrow. The backs of her hands were veined and dry. She was too weak to worry about missing her work with Armand. Missing Armand.

He has come and gone. He has come and gone. He has come and gone.

In the parlour, Maddy and Jules moved quietly around her. Madame Bardin was gone again on another trip, and the house was at peace. Maddy arranged the drinks, pouring water and light port for Enri. Jules ladled onion soup into her dish. It was steaming, rich with goodness. Maddy and Jules had watched their mother make onion soup for as long as their memories could stretch. Madame Beauchene baked beef bones in the oven for hours so that they singed golden, the marrow roasted and supple. She added water, again and again, only draining it off when it was amber, dotted with pools of rich yellow grease and scraps of meat that had floated from the bone.

Madame Beauchene was a wise woman who taught her children at the apron. Jules had learned the correct way to cut an onion by the time he was five years old, and he tumbled them into the pot with a master's ease. Real Lyonnaise onion soup took time. He had begun this one while Enri was still in her stupor.

Jules melted the duck fat and kept a sidelong eye on it, careful that it didn't start to smoke. He added a bundle of thyme, turning it, scenting the pan and the grease, colouring the rings of onion from white to gold to bronze, three inches thick in the pan. As well as the beef stock, there was the chicken stock. Like all good French home cooks, Madame Beauchene had also taught her children to make her own, superlative version. Every household honed their own method.

A small roast capon was a frequent family meal, but the housewife knew how to get every last bit of goodness from the bird. Like his mother, once he had stripped the meat, Jules cooked the bones and the skin at high heat. He added water, which turned amber over the fire, rich with the fat and jellied from the protein in the bones. The stuff from the roast – half lemons, heads of garlic, peppercorns and bay leaves all simmered together.

Pouring the chicken and beef stock onto the onions, he spooned in a generous lump of beef lard, a jug of water, and two slugs of thick yellow brandy. He sliced the old baguette thinly, spreading it with a trace of mustard, pressing it with shards of gruyere, and toasted them until the cheese bubbled.

Afterwards, Maddy read to her. *Madame Bovary*. A copy had arrived in the cart last week. Jules stopped clipping the hedge, Emma's torment and obsessions singing from Madeleine with all the mysticism a new tale brings.

But in her life, nothing was going to happen. Such was the will of God! The future was a dark corridor, and at the far end the door was bolted.

Enriqueta looked at her apple tart and watched a fat fly feast on the perfect roundels of the fruit, clicking its back legs together in satisfaction. The incessant song of the merle, a coven of mothers haranguing their broods and pecking at childish beaks, sounded above them.

The passion, ecstasy and delirium that the heroine ploughed her world for, Enriqueta felt as keenly as if Emma Flaubert herself had flung her cloak of agony over the garden. The treacherous secrecy of disappointment, muffled in the skirts of women everywhere, binding their feet and stitching their lips shut.

When night fell, Maddy slid around Enriqueta, drawing the curtains and pulling the blankets tight. Sleep meddled with her, shutting her off from herself then pulling her back to her most potent ideas, leading her to stories and framing them in a future, Armand presiding over every pathway, standing magnificent in the house of her mind. Emma Bovary's voice, from pages, replaced that of her mother in her mind.

Haven't you ever happened to come across in a book some vague notion that you've had, some obscure idea that returns from afar and that seems to express completely your most subtle feelings.

By midday, each day, the Blue Room was dark, the threat of rain casting slate clouds across Lyon. The chill of the window beneath her palm was comfort. Enriqueta's heart fluttered as the low rumble of thunder moved in towards the house. She heard the front door slam and Armand's distinctive, mellow voice, low against Maddy's light, nervous patter. The laundry needed gathering from the lines before the rain ruined it all.

The mirrored doors bounced his image this way and that, and the scent of weather and amber bloomed in the hallway. He took her in his arms, kissing her head.

'So, you have been unwell, my love.'

His lips found hers, and she felt him smiling into the kiss. In his arms, she was a rose, tugged and shuddering, her fingers splayed and dropping behind her like petals.

'You've missed me, you've missed me.'

Armand spun his long fingers up her spine, down onto her

hip and then to her throat, tracing his hand to her breast. He whispered into her neck, unboxing promises, and it felt to Enriqueta that Eden had opened, the hot sun of his persuasion burning her skin and bruising her lips.

'You surprise me, dear little Enri. Such a serious girl. But in my arms, you come alive.'

Never had La Castilla felt emptier, the absence of all others and the sublime centre of silence a gift. Armand guided her to a sofa and pulled her towards him.

'Do you want what I want, Enriqueta?'

His hands roamed over her, lifting her skirts as he kept on kissing her, holding both her hands with one of his.

'Don't push me away. Let me.'

He was insistent and it didn't take long. While she had not touched one part of him, but for his lips, he had explored every bit of her, his hand working between her thighs, as she shuddered beneath him, his mouth pressed on hers to quieten her. He put her dress back into place.

'I can't stay, my love. I have an appointment in town.'

Dismay twisted in her.

'I could come – Madame Bardin isn't here. If it was our work for the orphanage—'

'Once more, I think, Enri. You are beautiful and ripe – let me.'

Love, she thought, must come suddenly, with great outbursts and lightnings,-a hurricane of the skies, which falls upon life, revolutionises it, roots up the will like a leaf, and sweeps the whole heart into the abyss.

The gleaming wheels of his cart spun the dust of the driveway to meet the rain as it fell, and Enriqueta thought of the mud it would make. Her skirts stuck against her thighs with the ghost of his handprints, all tenderness gone, leaving solitude, as cool and sharp as flint.

La Castilla, November 1870

S HE LET HER HAND DROP to her waist, lying on the bed in the peace of the sun coming from the window. Enriqueta thought of his fingers on her when relief and guilt came, her body thudding. The habit was still new. It was a way to pass the time, and know him, have him be at her while she waited for him, never sure when he might arrive again.

He jumped from his coach to grasp her and kissed her hard.

'Are we going somewhere, Armand?'

She had only seen him in the confines of La Castilla. Between books, he unhooked her, hurriedly sliding his hands over her skin, up her thighs, his ear cocked to hear the warning creak of a door or the unwelcome step of a boot. He listened as he watched her, and she saw through her closing eyes that his smile was triumphant, and it urged her to let herself go limp again and again, to please him, to be his small conquest amid the dust and duty of dictionaries and the bright smiles of the children dancing in rings on the collections of nursery rhymes.

The horses cantered west of La Castilla, into the open countryside and along yards of ancient track. The cart slowed, turning into an apple orchard beside a little house, behind the sketch and tangle of trees, black against the white winter sky. It was only a cabin, but smoke drifted from the chimney. It had been prepared. Armand said a few words to his man and unloaded some baskets, taking them inside.

The air in the orchard was still and cold. An owl, readied for night by the darkness of the day, hooted and a toad launched itself heavily by her feet. The late afternoon sun was spent, pooled weakly in spots, laced with the bones of the trees. Armand and his man exchanged farewells, and Enriqueta fixed her gaze on the toad. The man swung himself up on his horse, and she wondered if he wanted to laugh at her, throwing Armand a salute of congratulation.

The orchard smelled of the old fruit on the ground, collapsed with decay, seeping their sugars into the soil. Her eyes were closed to the dappled sun as she felt him take her hand in his and lead her up the wooden steps and inside the cabin.

It was only one room. He poured wine for them, the soft chug of it decanting, a steady red beat, into glasses. She was fascinated to see him move around, somewhere other than the hallways of the house, or bent over the books of the Blue Room. He was too tall for the low ceilings, but curiously domesticated in surroundings he knew so well. It was enchanting, to see him opening the red curtains that hung in the tiny window, and leaving the others closed.

'This is all my family's land. The lodge has been here for as long as I can remember. It was used by my grandfather, my father. All the uncles. Now it belongs to me. The game hunt around here is rich.'

She took the wine, a long draught slipping down her throat. It didn't quell or silence the drag of doubt, and there were ghosts of women everywhere. The magenta scarf he had whipped from the hook, crushed into the wine rack. A little pot, enamelled with an ivory carnation, on the windowsill. She recognised the expensive brand, full of beeswax and fine carmine. The two glasses he had used were not taken from the cupboard; he had plucked them from the sink, buffing them clean as though they still held yesterday on their brittle rims. The owl cried into the dusk, and Armand drank, staring hard into her eyes over the rim of the glass, stroking her arm.

'You are shaking, Enri. So sensitive, so beautiful.'

He put her glass down onto a table and held her close to him, lifting her and finding her lips with his, pulling her down onto the low divan that was covered in cushions, stitched with silk robins against faded oak leaves. She hardly dared to open her eyes, a jolt of fear gripping her as his kisses became more urgent, and his hands roamed her body over her dress.

She freed her mouth, trying to talk as he kissed her neck, undoing the buttons at her throat.

'I don't know, Armand. I don't know.'

For an infinity of passion can be contained in one minute, like a crowd in a small space.

He stopped her with his kisses but didn't stop himself, and once again, Enriqueta found herself unwilling or unable to resist. She had spent so many unhappy months, restless and bored and lonely. She had no plans for her future, and her past was long gone. All that she could think about was now, as she felt the weight and the heat of his body on top of hers. Where once she had been a reserved, there was now relentless wanting. She thought only of him, and any warnings that rang in her mind she suppressed, listening instead to the raging hunger she had for moments with him. As they lay together under a thin blanket, she let him pull her on top of him again, as the sun sank in the trees around them.

She was the amoureuse of all the novels, the heroine of all the plays, the vague "she" of all the poetry books.

After the orchard, Armand came to La Castilla more frequently, and as often as they could, they took their trips to the cabin. At her request, he had dispensed with his man for the outings, driving them there himself. Seeing him master his horse, his firm body rigid and strong in his shirt sleeves, made her quiet with longing, and by the moment they arrived each time at the little house, it was Enriqueta who reached out first as he dismounted. She dared to ask him as she lay against him,

'Could I come into Lyon with you soon? To see the orphanage. Or, just to be useful to you. I'm sure Madame Bardin would allow it.'

He shook his head sadly and covered her with kisses.

'Not yet, darling Enri. Not yet. I want it to be perfect for you.'

It was a small comfort that she had the company of Maddy and Jules for their evening meals and shared games. Jules continued to eye her warily whenever there was a passing mention of Foncé, but he kept his counsel. He abided with his promise that he would not mention his suspicion of him again, and he didn't. He hovered over Enriqueta with the gentility and silent strength of a guardian angel; watchful and devoted. Maddy, in her innocence and excitability, was unaware of the warning words that had passed from Jules to Enri those weeks ago. She mooned over Armand, girlishly praising his good looks and fine dress to Enriqueta, who smiled but hugged the words of admiration close to her heart.

Her bedroom at La Castilla was no longer just a lonely place to hide. Prone and hot at night, her mind ranged over possibilities. She allowed herself to conjure things with him that were to come. She longed to hear him say he loved her, as she was sure she loved him. If this wasn't love, why did she only think of him constantly, and cherish every second she spent at his side and in his consuming embraces. She thought of him like a possession – when he was not with her; what did he do, where did he sit, what did he talk of- who did he talk to? And what of, what did he talk of. *Who, What, Where.* Where was he when he was not with her.

*　　*　　*

It was a love she could feel in her fingers, drawn from a place of exquisite simplicity, far from the tangle and grind of her mother's love – yet she heard Juana's call in her. Reprimanding her and mocking her. When she turned in bed, at the top of the house, her mother was there, shaking her sad grey dress at her in fury.

The smooth folds of her dress concealed a tumultuous heart, and her modest lips told nothing of her torment. She was in love.

They spent another morning together, as had come to be usual. They had finally got to the last books in the boxes of the second huge delivery. Armand sat back on his chair, rubbing his hands together and stretching his arms that were, like hers, sore with the efforts of the day.

'Well, what an achievement! That's it, dear Enri. I think for the time being, our work is done.'

He turned to her, his smile dazzling.

At first, she was puzzled, then a gnawing fear took hold of her.

'I don't understand, Armand.'

She forced her voice to ring with lightness, while terror clanged, turning all that was good and making it sour.

'Surely there will be more books to come once Madame has returned from her next trip. I would have thought that by the end of the week the men will be here with more?'

He smiled broadly, the sunshine of good breeding seeping from him. He shook his head, pulling her close to him. He was as polite as his forefathers always must have been.

'We have all we need now. The committee is delighted. We have enough books for all the children, and if we keep them carefully, I don't believe we will need to add to them for quite some time. We simply can't store more.'

His pause was as deliberate as a gold coin thrown up in the

air, and he leaned to kiss her, his lips cool and dry.

'I could not have done any of this without you. You are a marvel. A saint.'

While Enriqueta was pale with the burden of confusion, Armand was animated, striding around the room, talking of how excited the children would be when the books were delivered to the new classroom.

'Could I not come with you to take the books to the children? I should so love to see the orphanage; the classrooms where the children will do their learning. I'm sure Madame Bardin would not mind me coming with you one afternoon. I would be helpful.'

Her voice tailed off, as she saw a shadow crossing his eyes. He broke into his smile once more, taking her face in his hands. She said it again. 'I could be helpful.'

'Darling, that is a splendid idea. But not yet, I'm afraid. So much is still in disarray, and while I must ensure that all the books are moved from La Castilla to Sainte Catherine as soon as possible, the classroom is not quite ready yet. The books will be stored in the ante room for the time being. There really would be no point in you visiting us just yet.'

Images of the wealthy and glamorous who had swarmed round him that evening at the party appeared to her. She felt acutely plain and ordinary, and furious that she hadn't yet rid herself of the awful plain grey dress that she still wore and had sworn to cast aside by now. Somehow, there hadn't been time to make her trip into town. Her days had been spent pining for Armand. Waiting for him or being with him or missing him; the dreams of new dresses had been put aside in her haste to relish every second she could with him.

'Don't look so glum, Enriqueta! You are so much more beautiful when you smile.'

It was a command; a brittle timbre to his voice.

Who, What, Where. Who was he with when he was not with her.

'As soon as the classroom is finished, we will have a grand opening, and you will see the books in all their glory. You could be a guest of honour.'

His kiss was brisk. A pallid touch on her cheek.

'I should go now. I have a meeting with the committee. I will see you soon, I promise.'

He plucked at the fabric at her bosom, the edge of the seam tatty with age.

'Time for a new dress, Enri.'

Enriqueta nodded into his shoulder, and she trailed behind him to the door, shame and pain as her company. His shining carriage spun him off to Lyon, which, at that moment, was entirely another country.

La Castilla, December 1870

ARMAND HAD NOT VISITED La Castilla for ten interminable days. Mornings were unbearable and unending. Enriqueta pushed her breakfast brioche round her plate, shaking her head as Maddy tried to offer her other things to tempt her. Maddy had used up all her repertoire: baked eggs, yoghurt, walnuts in sugar, even plain day-old toasted *ficelle* with her mother's freshest strawberry jam. Enriqueta's stomach was twinging and empty; she left the table hungry.

With no word or instruction from Armand, she faced the tedium of returning to tasks that had no end. The bright books, covered with images of dogs in hats, birds on trains, fairies in forests, were all gone and she was back to standing alone amid dun-coloured albums and dusty grey maps. She raked over their last conversations, reminding herself of how busy he was. She tried to reassure her frenzied mind. He had so many meetings. He was an important man with a committee to satisfy and an orphanage to attend to. And all his other projects and businesses. Committee members stood upright, black suited and stern, thrusting through the persistent misery that puddled and brewed in her. The orphans, skeletal and clasping their rags and crag ends of bread tottered, broken boned at the door of her heart.

She could hardly bear to think of them together in the cabin. The things they had done together, the words that had been said.

Her heart remained empty once more, and the procession of days all alike began again. So they were going to follow one another, like this, in line, always identical, innumerable, bringing nothing!

She wondered about writing him a letter. She could ask Jules to deliver it for her. But where to? She had no address for him. The orphanage? Trying to sketch out the sentiments she would write, the favour she would have to ask of Jules. Undoubtedly, the rest of the household at La Castilla must have noticed Armand's absence. She could tell from the pained look on Maddy's face that the girl knew something was amiss. She straightened one pile of books and moved on to the next. She would write to him tomorrow, or the next day. Maybe his glistening navy carriage would swoop down the drive again. Maybe he would appear at the front door soon anyway, and all would be well. Maybe he would take her in his arms and invite her to dinner and society would turn their heads in wonder and warm appraisal as he held her hand over one of Lyon's finest damask tablecloths. She would have her new dress. Maybe he would tell her he loved her and would ask her to marry him. Her best writing paper floated in her hands; whether she should keep it to send her sister- plead with her for advice-or risk committing herself to him in ink.

Brushing dust from her palms onto her apron, another idea jumped into Enriqueta's head, and she felt her heart lift. The new dresses she had planned to buy. She could do the two things at once. If Jules took her into town, she could drop a note at Sainte Catherine's, then spend an hour or two at the seamstress's shop. It was a perfect plan; next time Armand came to see her she could surprise him in the gown she had dreamed of.

She left the Blue Room and walked towards the parlour to seek out Jules. He was usually back from his errands by now and she wanted to ask him the favour before she lost her nerve.

As she passed the mirrors of the hallway, she heard Jules and Maddy in the parlour. His voice was raised, and his outbursts were punctuated by a higher, panicked sound from Maddy. Enriqueta strained to hear what they were saying. It was no good, the door was too thick.

She had never, ever heard the siblings have even the slightest cross word, never mind this sort of fractious volume from Jules.

'Are you both alright? Maddy? Jules, let me in, will you?'

The sudden hush rang louder than anything else.

'Please? I'm worried.'

'Leave it alone, Maddy. Just drop it. Nothing to do with us,' she heard Jules say.

Maddy opened the door and she was pale, hurriedly wiping her cheeks with her sleeves. Jules's head was bowed, his shoulders stiff in his cheap shirt.

'What is it? What's going on?'

The siblings glanced at each other; there was fear and apprehension in Maddy's eyes. Jules rose with a long sigh and pushed his hair back from his forehead.

'Sit down, Enri. Maddy, can you see to the horses? It's cold – can you go and put some hot blankets on them. At least on the foals.'

'No need for her to go, Jules. She clearly knows whatever it is you are going to tell me. We are all friends, aren't we? Let Maddy stay. I can go to the stables with her shortly.'

Jules poured them all a drink.

'It's nearly that time anyway.'

The foals keened across the yard, calling out for warmth. Enriqueta longed to leave the parlour and go to them and wrap up their shaking velvet bones with her grey dress and the steaming blankets that were draped in front of the parlour fire. She rubbed her fingers together, thinking of the satin of their tender new ears twitching for her.

'We were arguing because Maddy didn't think I needed to tell you that I had seen Armand in town this week.'

The slow creep of dread began to flutter in Enriqueta like an autumn moth. Emma Bovary was near again, whispering into her ear, confidante and ally.

But the most wretched thing— is it not?—is to drag out, as I do, a useless existence. If our pains were only of some use to someone, we should find consolation in the thought of the sacrifice.

'I'm sure you did see him, Jules. You are in Lyon most days, and that's where Armand lives and works. I don't see what there is to argue about.'

Jules drained his glass and poured another.

'I've seen him twice this week, Enri, around the Place Bellecour.'

Maddy sniffed, grasping Enriqueta's hands, which had begun to twist together on her lap.

'I said not to bother you with it, Enri. I am sure Monsieur Foncé has many lunches and meetings with all sorts of people. I know how dear he is to you, and you to him. I didn't want any upset between you.'

Maddy's cheeks were pink with strain and the hopeless naivety of youth. But also, could she not be right? Armand was a busy man, with countless contacts and responsibilities. He was not hers alone. And hadn't he assured her, over and over, when they laid together in the cabin, that she was for him, in the way that they shared, the way that was most important?

Jules opened a bottle of brandy, the seal cracking as he twisted it.

'It didn't look like a business meeting, Enri. Either time.'

The cat jumped onto the table again, and Jules struck out at it, pushing it away from the bread with a force that was unlike him.

'I'm sorry. I am sure there is an explanation. Indeed, I expect Monsieur Foncé will visit any day now. I should think the classroom will be finished soon and we can all go and see how it looks.'

She tried hard to keep her voice bright and she almost believed what she was saying.

'I'm going to bed, if you two can manage the stables. Please, both of you – be the dear friends you are. Don't argue any more, certainly not over something that involves me.'

As she left, Maddy glanced at Jules, a burn in her eyes.

'Don't look at me like that, Madeleine. I know what I saw and I know what he is. I have known it for a long time, and I know him. He will bring her misery packaged in a box of promises, and I don't know how to save her.'

LONGFORD 1870

JOHN SHUFFLED THROUGH THE POST, scanning each letter, hoping to recognise the handwriting, to feel the bump of the little bee beneath his fingertips.

'I'm disappointed, Peter. I had hoped Miss Tennant would have replied by now.'

'Don't be downhearted. The post could be delayed. She is such a good match for the position, let's not give up on her yet.'

John sighed. 'Maybe we should look through all the letters again. There have been a couple more that have arrived. I need someone in place soon, especially if I am going to take Martha away. It could be the last chance—I don't know how long she has left.'

There was a loud thud from above them. The desire to run to Caroline was overwhelming. He missed her so profoundly; the loss was an illness. His heart galloped with pain, and he tortured himself with wild imaginings. She was a woman of powerful desires. Maybe she had let his memory slip from her soul, while she opened her little white door. As the milk cart clattered past, did she pull another man towards her, allowing him to bury his nose in her soft, scented breasts. Did he hold her hair, heavy as night, in his fist, as John had? The swell of fear and the poison of envy rose in John as he pictured his darling woman, moaning in ecstasy beneath a younger man.

'I'll go, John. She must have fallen again. I don't think we can leave her upstairs on her own anymore.'

Living without Caroline was like living without colour, or the sun. Seeing her and being with her had meant so much more to him than even he had realised. The promise of her, the expectation of her had been the nourishment and succour that sustained him through the misery of his life with Martha. The exhilaration of choosing the righteous path and leaving Caroline had diminished, leaving nothing but suffering. Even his attempt at finding a companion for Martha had come undone. Nothing was working as it should. He could go back to Caroline – beg forgiveness, buy her brandy in private hotel rooms, strip her and shock her. Spoil it all again, for his life was subsiding into abject sorrow. He was trying, with a might so exhausting that he had forgotten what rest was. He was looking to find Martha help, to seek a salve for the misery of her final years. None of it had yielded anything good. He eyed the keys to the carriage lock. He could go to her now. John willed Peter to come back down from tending to Martha, not caring anymore that he could so easily slip back into his old, shameful behaviours.

'What is it?'

Peter was flushed, his eyes strangely bright.

'She's fine, John. A bit of a tumble. She was trying to find something, and she knocked her little writing desk over.'

'Right. Could you watch her? I need to go out. An errand. A couple of hours.'

John kicked his slippers off, reaching for his boots.

'You might want to see this first, John. Look what fell out of Martha's desk drawer.'

He held the letter up. The one John had written all those weeks ago, stamped for Lyon. Crumpled, but unopened and intact.

'Take it with you now, John, to the post. There is still hope, after all.'

John put his boots down.

'Peter, would you mind posting it for me? I've changed my mind. I will stay in. I should be with Martha. As you say, there is hope, after all.'

La Castilla, 1870

S HE DIDN'T SLEEP AT ALL. Enriqueta saw three o'clock come and go and rose at five o'clock with the birds. The morning was promising to be clear and fine, the robin in the yard hopping like a symbol.

Jules was young and inexperienced. What looked like an odd situation may have been innocent to a more nuanced eye. Context was all, and it was probable that Jules, rushing by in a carriage, his eyes wide with the youthful bias to scandal, had been mistaken. Foncé was a confident man who had many female admirers, but that was just a small part of him. That was the way he was.

Yet worry itched at her. Visions of the way his eyes had swept across the room at the party, his longer glances eliciting lingering, meaningful smiles from other women in the room. She recalled her unease as she had seen him stoop to whisper into ears, brush a tip of a finger on satin elbows and kid gloves, laugh indulgently at witticisms she was not close enough to hear. She had seen his lips curl with satisfaction at something Madame Faucher had murmured.

Enriqueta suppressed the memory, smothering it with activity, writing a list of the things she needed from town: buttons, soap, a box of Callison D'Aix for Madeleine.

'Are you alright, Enri? You're up early. I have coffee ready if you would like some.'

'Can I come into town with you this afternoon, Jules?'

Jules scrubbed the sink harder, his voice hardly audible over the scratch of the wire brush.

'Of course you can. If that is what you want.'

'I need some new dresses. While I'm in town, I will leave a note for Monsieur Foncé at Sainte Catherine's. I am sure the classrooms will be ready now. I'd like to see them.'

As she had hoped and expected, the morning bloomed brightly; the sun blazed, splintering the winter. Jules got the cart ready to leave for Lyon, and Enriqueta clasped the note in her hand. Though the atmosphere between her and Jules was taut, Enriqueta was undeterred, asking him which the best streets and boutiques were to go to for fabrics and dresses. As they trotted into the traffic of Lyon, Jules slowed the horses.

'Which way, Enri?'

'Let's go through Bellecour. If we stay to the left of the square, it will take us out to Sainte Catherine's.'

Jules breathed deeply, as if to say something, but he kept his silence and his eyes to the road, staring so hard ahead like he wanted to ignite the whole scene into oblivion with his stare. He turned the cart into Place Bellecour. The horses cantered through, the beat of their hooves bouncing off the sheer brick of the buildings. But for the noise of the wind, and the animals, there was no sound between the two of them. Then Jules felt her hand on his arm but couldn't hear what she was saying above the wind. She shouted, and grabbed his hand.

'Stop, Jules. Stop!'

Without even looking, he knew. Without her saying a word more, he knew. Jules slowed the horses to a halt and turned to Enriqueta, following her gaze. Her eyes were round with shock, and her face white, her mouth open.

Armand Foncé was sitting beneath the broad parasol of L'Encart. The bouchon was busy, but he stood out distinctly, as he did everywhere. His fair hair gleamed, and he wore a beautiful pale blue jacket Enriqueta had never seen before. A scarlet handkerchief bloomed from his breast pocket. Armand poured wine into his glass, and that of his companion, whose bare shoulder he stroked with his fingertips.

'Enriqueta—' Jules said softly.

It was the same place he had seen Armand with the woman last week, and he had never wished more that he had been mistaken. But there could be no questioning it. The girl in Foncé's arms giggled at something he whispered in her ear. Armand caught her laughing lips with a kiss, his hand pressing against the swell of her young bosom.

'Wait, Jules.'

Her voice cracked under the strain of the pain that was curling through her mind and her heart; licks of the fire of agony. What is the burn of betrayal- pain that sticks and shouts and lingers. Jules saw that she was shaking, and that tears spilled from her eyes. The horses stamped; hot breath billowing in the cold air.

'Oh, Enri!'

There was a peal of laughter from the girl, ringing like a beautiful bell across the crowds. The sky was a bright, seaside blue, and the girl's voice sparkled with the unfettered joy of new love. Enriqueta knew the sound well. Emma Bovary and her mother reached out for her heart, offering the touch of pity in grief.

Where did it come from, this feeling of deprivation, this instantaneous decay of the things in which she put her trust?

The shock came to Enriqueta like a punch, as the girl turned, and the smack of recognition came to Enriqueta. Mademoiselle Faucher, one of the many guests who had clung to Armand's every word, his every gesture, the evening of the party. She was like a doll, childish against the swell of his chest. Her face was exquisite, her features as if drawn by a feather in fine, golden ink. Her lips were painted rose pink, and Enriqueta watched them fall into his kiss with force, seeing the coral tip of a tiny tongue dart from the girl's mouth into his. She saw his handsome face, the one that had hovered above hers so many times, shaping a lustful smile. One she had recognised, until this terrible moment, as belonging solely to her. Armand pulled Celeste closer to him, kissing her passionately with vigour and urgency. And also with joy, the smile remaining on his lips even as his mouth roamed hers.

The torture of humiliation sped through Enriqueta's body into her loins, which burned. A sickness spread as images of her own form, white in the lamplight beneath him, flashed like a cheap bankside sketch, flung into the air. Her foolishness took the shape of a demon, shaking from her all pride and goodness, and the world around her became dark, normal things moving with spite and corruption. Though her legs were shuddering like milk beneath her, she climbed from the carriage and walked towards L'Encart. Jules did not attempt to stop her, but put his head in his hands, overcome with the pain he felt for her.

Down from the height of the vehicle, the sight of them was obscured by the people that passed by her. She went towards them, glimpsing slices of them through the parasols, the strolling families, the buskers, and the light calls of reunited friends. There and there again, snatches of the girl's face in his hands, then again, her lips lifted to his. Pink and blue in quick frames against the crowds, the red handkerchief flashing, like a warning. Closer and closer Enriqueta stepped, until the street had cleared and she found herself at their table.

Enriqueta could not stifle the sob as it broke from her. They pulled apart. The girl was flushed, her pretty cheeks pink, and her lips glistening with his kisses. Turning and seeing Enriqueta in front of them, Armand looked confused for a moment, but quickly set his face to his memorable, impenetrable smile.

'Enriqueta!'

The girl threw out a laugh, so clear and voluminous that all at the table next to them looked round. She spoke to Armand in a mock whisper, and with the scorn of one born into endless wealth and astounding beauty.

'Well, she is not as plain as you suggested, darling!'

Enriqueta shut her eyes tightly, feeling herself sway. Her hands had been gripped at her elbows so hard she could no longer feel them. A gust blew through the street, carrying Armand's scent to her, and the viciously pure, expensive perfume of the girl, elemental in the breeze. Enriqueta felt like nothing – insubstantial and inadequate, her body so empty that the same little wind could pick her up and drop her anywhere. She would fall, and break into a million glass pieces like the glass of the party, her heart and mind fracturing, the debris of agony across the shining tiles of Lyon.

'Are you quite alright, Enriqueta?'

Armand's hand on her arm didn't heat her like it once did, but it felt like violence. Enriqueta opened her eyes and pulled away from him with a force that caused the table to rock. The red wine spilled, bouncing up in an arc over the cream bloom of the girl's breast. The liquid sunk into the tapestry of her bodice and her marble face contorted into a sneer.

'My God! She is as odd as you said, Armand. My new dress!'

For a moment longer, the world twisted again from all Enriqueta thought she knew, as she watched Foncé pluck his handkerchief from his pocket, patting his lover with a familiar tenderness that robbed Enriqueta of all hope. She heard Celeste mewing in complaint and watched Foncé's eyes dart between the two of them. Standing over the couple, Enriqueta felt so profoundly apart from the world, she hardly felt her body at all.

From somewhere in the restaurant, little black-and-white

waiters hurried out with brushes to sweep the shattered glass and steaming cloths to clean the table. In the chatter and the clatter, Foncé stood, tall against the scorch of the sun, and Enriqueta turned and walked away, back to Jules and the carriage. She hadn't said a single word.

Jules wrenched her into her seat and she groaned, her suffering overtaking her, tears dropping from her eyes, her mouth soundlessly mouthing her misery. Jules clasped her with one arm, whipping the horses into action with the other. They left Place Bellecour at speed, Jules holding her close, her body sagging and bouncing like a ragdoll against him. When the roads narrowed, he pulled the horses to a stop, and she was unwell, her face bilious and chalk white. As she was bent over and sick at the roadside, Jules found his handkerchiefs and his hip flask and he sat her down, wiping her face. In her grief, she was docile, able only to breathe.

'I'm so sorry. I'm so sorry, Jules.'

The horses hung their heads, panting. A robin alighted on one of them, and in kindness, the horse didn't shake him away.

'I have been so foolish. You tried to warn me.'

A fresh moan of pain escaped her.

'You were in love, Enriqueta. It makes a fool of all of us. Believe me, you aren't to blame.'

All of the sickening trysts, hidden from her, out of her sight; the performance of love, while she was trapped in the gilded, fearsome cage of La Castilla, gifting Armand Foncé complete security in his secrecy. He knew she didn't have the freedom to come into town, to see him, or interrupt his dalliances. The circles in which he moved, populated by the elegant and wealthy, were too sophisticated for anything as base as feeling. Too refined and too occupied to be bothered by irritations such as attachment or anything as pedestrian as loyalty or love. Enriqueta despised herself, for all her desires and soured plans.

Don't you know there are some souls that are constantly tormented? They need dreams and action, one after the other, the purest passions, the most frenzied pleasures, and it leads them to throw themselves into all sorts of fantasies and follies.

'He underestimated me, Enriqueta. Worse, he underestimated my loyalty to you.'

The sun was covered in thick stone clouds, the sky darkening and scenting the air with the story of snow. It would fall overnight. The horses blinked at her, shaking their manes as she shivered. Jules helped her back into the coach, swaddling her in a blanket.

'What about your new dresses?'

She shook her head, unable to meet his eyes.

'I don't need any new dresses now, Jules.'

They began the journey away from the city, back up the hills to La Castilla. Enriqueta stared over the fields as the snow began to swing from the sky, flakes like ash and cinder. The only movement was in her fingers, which twisted and tore at her shopping list. She let the tiny pieces go and the cold afternoon wind caught them up from her fingers. They floated off into the grey skies, mimicking tattered confetti.

A bared hand passed beneath the small blinds of yellow canvas, and threw out some scraps of paper that scattered in the wind, and farther off lighted like white butterflies on a field of red clover all in bloom.

La Castilla, 1870

THREE LETTERS AND A POT OF COFFEE on the table in front of Enriqueta, more complete and substantial than anything else that her pitiful life had for her. Two nights without sleep had presented her with devastating clarity.

The first letter was addressed to Madame Bardin: her resignation. She had not given any notice, as it appeared that she had lost the capacity to feel anything at all. When love left her, it took with it guilt and loyalty, and the desire for propriety. Grief feasted on the carcass of all other things, and to care for anything anymore was an indulgence she could ill afford.

The second letter was for her sister, Leocadia, asking her to expect Enriqueta in London in two weeks' time. The third was a reply to the post she had opened in the gloaming of the night, when its whiteness on the chair by her bed glowed in the moonlight like fabric. It was an acceptance of an interview at Longford Hall, Stretford, in the city of Manchester, and it was addressed to Mr John Rylands.

MANCHESTER, JANUARY 1871

S ORRY TO MITHER YOU, LOVE. I have your tea here.'
Of the countless things that Enriqueta had worried about before arriving in Manchester, fathoming the Mancunian accent had not been one. She smiled at the lady with the huge brown teapot. The tangle of keys at the woman's waist clacked when she walked.

John Rylands had written to her over Christmas, at Leocadia's home in Kensington. He had arranged for her to stay at the Mitre Hotel, in the centre of the city, close to the cathedral.

The proprietor's wife was mercifully and unstintingly kind, and returned her smile, patting her arm and settling the pot in front of her on the table. The tea was strong and amber. There were also pastry cakes, small and round, full of tiny currants and sprinkled with sugar. Enriqueta could not be sure that her eagerness to eat them was because of their novelty, or because she had eaten so very little since leaving La Castilla. For the first time in weeks, food felt like pleasure again.

Leocadia tried so hard to tempt her with delicacies and their favourite childhood foods. She had cooked her all that she was able to with what she could buy in London: empanadas, ropa vieja, arroz con pollo. Christmas arrived quietly: games were played and candles lit. Over the two weeks she had spent with her sister, a memory of hunger emerged, and the rice smelled good again. Yet it only took a glimpse of Armand Foncé in her mind, towering and remarkable in robin-egg blue, to make her body curl back into dread.

As Christmas sloped into the new year, the sisters spent their evenings wandering round Kensington, arm in arm. They returned to the house at dusk, the neat, boxy English dimensions soothing to Enriqueta after the vast chill of La Castilla. Leocadia's husband tended to the children and made sure they went to bed so that the siblings could talk around the fire, Enriqueta staring into it blankly, finding childish consolation in the ordinariness of the flames. A kind man, Alex was the match for Leocadia that Enriqueta had believed Armand would be for her one day.

Enriqueta took joy in Leocadia and Alex's two children, and found solace and peace in the noisy domesticity of the household. But in the bruises of her heart, she resigned herself to a different sort of life. One without a husband, children or passion. Better to have loved, she told herself, as she watched her sister and brother-in-law exchange kisses.

Everything, even herself, was now unbearable to her. She wished that, taking wing like a bird, she could fly somewhere, far away to regions of purity, and there grow young again.

Over days and nights in Kensington, Enriqueta found the strength in her voice to confide in Leocadia about Lyon. The red curtains of the cabin fluttered behind the pain of her story.

'I gave in to him, Leo. I was so very foolish. I believed he would marry me. The wedding in my head, the years I conjured. I was mad to think he wanted me forever, when all along, every moment, he was eager for opportunity, everywhere. With all of them. I wanted children. I wanted him to love me.'

Leocadia was knitting her another pink cape, in fine, close silks. It was a soft strawberry pink, and Alex wondered if she would ever finish it. She willed herself to thread it together with love, not anger, but seeing her sister, so gaunt and pitiable, made every click of her needles ring with fury.

Enriqueta found determination and a deep need to add detail to detail, layering all the parts of the sad tale on top of each other as she recalled them. She purged herself to Leo, not losing any aspect – however intimate or devastating – and Leocadia listened, as the fire kept burning and the rosy cloak took shape.

'Have you written to your friends yet, Enri? You should. You must. I know how horrible it was, but Madeleine and Jules should know that you are safe and improving. With the way you left, they will be worried. And missing you.'

She had booked her passage to England the day she had written to John, and her bags were packed soon after. Madame Bardin had shown her deep displeasure by ignoring Enriqueta completely, not even acknowledging her if they passed in the hall.

Once, Enriqueta would have been sensitive to a cold reception, but she was hardened in her grief, and kept on with the task in hand – to quit Lyon as soon as she could. She no longer cared at all what Madame Bardin thought of her. It was Madame who had pushed her together with Armand, knowing full well his true character, and was also doubtless a part of his tawdry unions and social pantomimes.

In her darkest hours, Enriqueta had obsessed over a possible and terrible truth – that the affair had been part of a sordid and elaborate plan by Madame Bardin to ingratiate herself more deeply into Lyonnaise high society.

Had she been a transaction between them? Did they ever discuss it, plan it, agree to it? Or did the dreadful story just take a life of its own, as she unwittingly played a supporting act to their two main characters. And when not needed anymore, did they just kill her off, signalling an end to their plot? Did he caress her with gritted teeth, moved by thoughts of Celeste?

Enriqueta winced, her heart churning. It was excruciating to think of how freely she had given herself to him. Shame burned in her like a torch.

Once, over the last grim days in Lyon, Armand came to the house. She heard the familiar, smooth sound of his carriage before she saw him. She went to one of the top-floor windows.

Foncé jumped from his carriage, landing with his usual sanguine grace, so familiar to her that it hurt to look at him. Jules shot out of the front door before Armand could make another step. Enriqueta was too high in the house to hear what was said, but she could see from their movements that the exchange was rich with anger. First from Jules, who leaned so far towards Foncé, stabbing a finger, punctuating the air, that Foncé had to crane backwards. His body was rigid, then after a beat he responded in fury too. Jules pushed him hard and Armand Foncé crumpled to the ground, the blow unexpected. Farmer Luc called from across the field;

'You deserved, that, you deserved it!'

Foncé stood slowly, clearly winded. He brushed himself down, sleeking his golden hair back into place. He said something to Jules, then put his hand out to him, offering it to him to shake. Jules turned his head and spat hard on the floor, just inches from Foncé's polished black boots. Enriqueta never uncovered what had been said. All that hung in the air was the slam of a door and the clatter of horses, whipped so hard that they raced down the drive, the gravel spinning into the air beneath their terrified hooves. Where once she had seen charm, she saw cruelty and a ruthlessness that made her doubt her belief in God Himself.

She could have asked Jules for every detail before she left for England, and she knew he would have recounted them to her, but she chose not to. The parting was difficult enough. Madame had, very purposely, left for another of her trips, as though it were just another day. Thus, she avoided saying goodbye to Enriqueta, and did not even proffer her the dignity or grace of a genuine farewell. Enriqueta no longer cared.

Enri's bags were loaded into the cab and Jules and Maddy took it in turns to hold and kiss her, and then they came together as a three, squeezing each other hard, tears on their faces. She had never dreamed her time at La Castilla would end this way, so dark and tawdry. She promised to write to them, but it was only with Leocadia's urging, and with the balm of her kindness, that Enriqueta had finally sent the letter, pushing it into the post box before she boarded the train to Manchester.

The Mitre's lady cleared away the tea things, trying to press the last Eccles cake onto Enriqueta.

'It's nippy out, miss, but the sun is shining. You might have a walk around the cathedral before Mr Rylands arrives. Your lovely pink cloak looks cosy enough. No rain either, for once.'

Stepping out into the morning, Enriqueta turned her head up to the sun. The Gothic cathedral was handsome and silent in the heart of the city, making her long for the chapels of Paris. A familiar atmosphere, shared by churches the world over, settled over her, as commanding as a prayer. The dark air, laced with incense, and the echoes of the movement of someone holy and unseen. She had felt so limp since she had left Lyon, as though she dared not to feel anything anymore. She associated anything akin to sensuality with her time with *him*. She bathed quickly now, not allowing any sort of sensation to stir within her body. She had lost her joy in nature, weather, music, conversation. She had not picked up a book in weeks, not risking the turmoil that even the mildest romantic storyline could induce. Still, Emma's ghost followed her, across the seas, and lingered by her side in Manchester.

She had no idea by what wind it would reach her, toward what shore it would bear her, or what kind of craft it would be

– tiny boat or towering vessel, laden with heartbreaks or filled to the gunwhales with rapture. But every morning when she awoke she hoped that today would be the day

Enriqueta read the leaflet she found inside the church porch. A collegiate church, the cathedral had spanned the ages and been noted in the Domesday Book. During her time in Lyon, learning had been stifled and suspended, and the flimsy booklet in her hand filled her with an aspiration she had not touched in a long time.

She read about the famous medieval woodwork that had survived, to be surveyed by scholars who travelled from all over the world, drawn to the manor house of the cathedral. The manor that had once housed John Dee, Magus and Astrologer to Elizabeth 1, and still stood as Chethams School, which had a superlative library, the first public one in the world, containing the largest and most fascinating range of books in the land. Enriqueta longed to visit it, and was heartened to feel the stirrings of normality blink into being.

Learn to Live and Play.

An hour had slipped from her. She only had minutes to get back to the Mitre before Mr Rylands arrived.

The lady of the hotel arranged a table for them, dressing it prettily with a white cloth and tea things. At precisely ten o'clock, the lounge door opened and a very tall, slim man swept into the room. He was younger than she had imagined, and he offered a hand, before shaking hers with vigour.

'Delighted to meet you, Miss Tennant. I am Peter O'Hara, Mr Rylands' assistant. Sincere apologies, Mr Rylands is delayed slightly. This always happens when we come into town. There is not a street we can walk down, or a place we can visit without one of his many friends or business acquaintances stopping to greet him. Nature of the beast, I am afraid. He was at pains to send me ahead to assure you that we were here as agreed.'

The lady of the hotel came back to pour their tea, with a plate of little cakes.

Peter took a sip and sighed with pleasure.

'I was ready for that. Please, after you, Miss Tennant,' he said, offering her the plate. She hesitated.

'These are a delicacy of the region, and they certainly look like a fine example. The great Manchester tart. Pastry, with jam, custard, lemon and brandy. Do try one.'

She told him about the Eccles Cakes she had that morning, and how she was pleasantly surprised that the patisserie of the north of England seemed to rival the cakes she had enjoyed so much in Paris.

'Praise indeed. Ah, I believe I see John arriving now.'

At that moment, as the clock in the lounge of the Mitre Hotel clicked to two minutes past ten, on 3 January 1871, rain fell on the cathedral and a bell ringer, late and delayed by a new baby, pulled hard and sounded out the peels, which rang across Manchester and Salford. Molly Owen, the maid at Sinclair's, began shucking oysters for the lunchtime customers. The boys at Manchester Grammar School stood for the Latin master, and Mark Addy dove into the River Irwell, saving his second person of the new year. Manchester thudded with politics and clanked with industry, and Enriqueta set her eyes upon the man who was to change her life; nearly as much as she was to change his.

'Miss Tennant. Forgive me. I hope I never keep you waiting again.' His eyes were a searing and vivid blue. 'So, let me tell you about Longford. Unfortunately, Mrs Rylands-Martha-is unwell. Until recently, Peter's wife, Leone, has been able to care for her, with our assistance.'

The fabric of his black suit was finer than anything she had seen. Even in Paris.

'Of late, her condition has worsened,' he continued, 'It began some years ago with acute melancholia but now my doctors believe she has declined into a state of mental and physical dementia.'

Enriqueta nodded, but she was no nurse, and had no experience of tending to someone whose mind and body were failing. Her Manchester tart was left unfinished. She checked Mr Rylands' shoes, a maxim her mother had instilled in her. His wealth shone from the stitching at his toes.

'Leone has done a fine job of looking after my wife thus far. But she does not have the time to attend to Martha to the degree that is required. Leone is the Head Housekeeper at Longford and I rely on her to ensure the smooth running of the entire house, and to oversee the wider staff and their families in general.'

John spoke of his staff and of Longford Hall with reverence and tenderness and an unexpected murmur of envy ran through her. She had been without praise or thanks for so long, she hadn't realised how much she yearned to be wanted.

'Thus, I find myself in need of someone else. Another person I can trust and rely on as much as I trust and rely on them.'

His shirt was as white as story-book snow, finished with the fine eye of an experienced tailor. The enamel of the bees on his cufflinks shone as he poured them all more tea. Enriqueta's heart ached for Jules and how devotedly he had cooked and catered and cared for her. His bunches of thyme, his favourite knife and the bloom of hot steam on the dawn windows of the pantry.

'Mr Rylands, Mr O'Hara. I have no training as a nurse, and no experience. There surely must be others with better skills than I.'

'Indeed, there may be, Miss Tennant, yet I have more to ask of you. The position is not solely to care for my wife. In fact, that would be an impossible, onerous duty which I could not impose on one person. No – her care will still be shouldered in the most part by myself, Leone and Peter. You would provide us with occasional respite and be another person to act as company for her. The more her health degrades, the smaller her world has become. She needs another face, another spirit around her.'

His eyes on her were fixed and unceasing, it was unnerving and intoxicating all at once. For so many months she had been invisible, and then came the attentions of Armand. A hideous, rotten construct. Mr Rylands's scrutiny felt like the shine of the sun.

'I have many plans to deal with, both in business and at home. One of these projects is to build a public hall in Stretford, near to where Longford Hall is situated. If all goes as it should – and it will – the building will house a public library, with books that the local people can use completely and freely and without charge.'

Warmth stretched through her. Books. Her passion and her most original love, so nearly driven from her by the relentless tedium of her work at La Castilla.

'Is it beginning to make more sense to you, Miss Tennant?' Peter smiled at her. 'We couldn't believe our luck when we read your credentials. It was like you were made for us.'

John ran his ran his hands through his hair, a gesture that made her wonder what sort of man he was when he was when he wasn't empire building, bent over boards with architects, or overseeing sites of men and machinery.

'Peter speaks his mind. One of the many reasons he is so important to me. He's right – the role is unique and requires a person of character and a considerable skill. Your experience of managing the book business in Paris, coupled with your time in Lyon collating and cataloguing such vast, unpredictable collections is precisely the expertise I am in dire need of.'

The cathedral bell clanged again. Need. Enriqueta was unaccustomed to being needed.

'You have much to think about, Miss Tennant,' John continued. 'We can close our meeting here unless you have anything to ask of us. We would like you to visit Longford. You must see the place before you make any decisions. Peter will make all the necessary arrangements, of course, and extend your stay here until you make your choice. I'm sure that once we are gone, you may have many questions. I thought that you could come to Longford in two days' time, where we can talk further.'

The teapot was empty and the bells had stopped ringing. A circus troop crossed Blackfriars bridge and lovers tucked their clothes back in to return to their stalls at the Corn Exchange and argue the toss about the price of parsnips. Mr Rylands picked up his gloves.

'Also, I have left instructions for a carriage so that you can enjoy your time in Manchester. Our magnificent city has many troubles, but it is still a beautiful place.'

A command. John turned to her as he reached the door. She already felt familiar with his profile.

'Miss Tennant, the great Chethams is just across from here. A woman of your interests and learning would very much enjoy all it has to offer. I have arranged a tour for you tomorrow. Of course, you are not obliged to take it. But it is yours if you want it. Ten o'clock.'

John smiled at her once more as Peter opened the door onto the square beyond, where the market stalls had filled. Cauliflowers were piled high, and a man with brown paper bags under his arm pulled a woman close to him, swinging her into his kiss.

As the clock turned eleven, Enriqueta did not know that life would ever be good to her again. She did not know that the years would stretch, full of achievements, events, promise and dangers. She would never be able to piece together exactly what she did that day after Peter and John had left the Mitre Hotel. She supposed she might have walked out again, as she had done that morning. Maybe she had slept. Maybe she had taken out her stationery box and written to Leocadia, to Marianne, or to Jeanne. Had she steadied herself enough to write to Jules and Maddy again, pouring out her news and hopes and fears.

The evening, however, remained clear to her, etched in memory like Indian ink. She came down to dinner in a dress borrowed from Leocadia, with her sister's scent, vanilla and rose, around her like a charm.

There were a few other diners. Single businessmen, and a chattering family nearby, man, wife and three children. Sarah beamed at her from behind the bar.

'Miss! Do sit down. I have things for you from Mr Rylands. What a gent he is. So handsome. Good morals too, all he does. Oh, I do love looking at him. Moves nice. His arms! Lovely eyes too. Never heard a bad word against him in Manchester. Come love, sit down.'

Enriqueta was presented with a neat, olive-green folder, stamped with his name. It bulged and she opened it to find documents and leaflets –things to see and do in the city.

'John has left spends for you with my husband at the desk. And left us instructions for your dinner. My boys, Jim and Tommy, do the kitchen. Tommy was trained in all sorts of French cooking, but Mr Rylands insisted you try some of our Manchester dishes.'

Sarah had been kind to her since the moment Enriqueta had arrived at the Mitre, and Enriqueta was emboldened by the Manchester stout she was sipping. Glad to be in the warm company of a kind woman, she pulled a chair out for her.

'I gather Mr Rylands is a man of means and influence. I'm ashamed to say I still don't know what his business is though.'

Sarah chuckled, leaning back in her chair.

'There's not much business that isn't his business in this town, my love!'

Sarah got her own glass and another little pitcher of ale, chugging a few more inches of the stout into both their cups.

'Such a fine, fine man. A private sort, if you will. He cares about the city, and he means to change things. There is a lot of good here in Manchester, and a lot of bad too. Me and Paddy and the lads – we are lucky, but there's thousands that aren't. Not a penny between them and nowt to show for their hard labours. Angel Meadow, over that way; thousands of people in squalor.'

Sarah drained her glass.

'Manchester needs people like John. Now I must see where your dinner is, miss.'

She winked, and in her squeeze of her arm, Enriqueta felt the most curious feeling of being at home.

Enriqueta was pleased to see the onion soup, the croutons she knew so well replaced with fat suet dumplings, crisp at their edges and salted with mutton lard. Sarah's eldest, Tommy, replaced her empty bowl with another. 'Our famous rag pudding, miss.'

Enriqueta was alarmed to see another vast plate before her, with a slab of swollen golden pastry as big as her forearm, along with a steaming plate of cabbage. The Mitre was quiet that evening, and after some urging Sarah agreed to sit down with Enriqueta. She cut the rag pudding expertly, spooning the rich mince and crust onto her plate.

Sarah took a small slice too, and the two women sat as amiable acquaintances sharing a supper. The Manchester rain clattered on the roof, and the family from the neighbouring table held their baby aloft under the porch of the front door, and she paddled her feet, taking swipes at the drops as they fell from the sky. The men from the market were generous to each other, tankards jostling and spilling at the bar. Sarah cleared their plates.

'Oh miss, I've kept you up. Get to bed. I'll send our Jim up with your bottle.'

There was a tentative knock at the door. Jim outside; one arm aloft with the hot water bottle.

'Here y'are, miss.'

He bent, retrieving a steaming bowl from the shadows of the hallway.

'Mam said she thought you might want your pudding. Night miss.'

Enriqueta was astounded to see yet another offering of suet pastry, thick with syrup and swaddled in a slick wash of cream. She ate it in bed, reading the leaflets, happier than she had been for months.

The dinner, good company and cosy room made for deep and sleep, and it felt like the merest moment between her blowing out her candle and the Jim's tremulous voice again at her door. 'Miss, Mother has drawn a bath for you. Your breakfast is coming so she says to get up now. Miss?'

'I'm awake, Jim, come in.'

The small boy shuffled into her room, unsure. His sweater was robin red, and he picked at where it frayed at the cuffs. He coughed, tickling his fingers at his thighs.

'Come on, miss. Our Tommy will get the best of the bacon if you don't rush.'

Jim was dark like Jules was, and Enriqueta reached out and clasped him to her. She kissed his delicate head. His hair smelled sweet, of coal and soap and cooked milk. She heard his breathing as she pulled him closer.

'Do you not have any boys, miss? Or girls?'

'I do not, Jim.'

'Do you not have a husband, miss?'

'I do not, Jim'

He pulled himself away from her, quizzical and outraged.

'Do you not have any man at all, miss?'

The bells of the cathedral chimed, low and mournful. The rain had stopped overnight, but it had left a flurry of drops on her window, patterning the glass as they dried.

'No, Jim. No man, no husband. No boys or girls.'

'Well, you should have! My Mam said it was a waste. You're pretty and clever. I don't think you are as pretty as Mam though. Do you like her hair? I do the curls in papers for her.'

Enriqueta laughed and kissed him hard on his crown.

'Oh Jim. I would love a boy just like you. Just like you. Could you show me where my bath is, please.'

She wondered how long Leocadia's dresses would fit her. The English breakfast was a thing to behold. She thought about her breakfasts in Paris. The short, potent coffee with the palm-sized croissant as a treat. The Lyonnaise morning offerings seemed extravagant in comparison, with all the bits of sausage, jams, and hot chocolate.

The English breakfast was like nothing she had seen before. Coddled eggs, browned slices of pork, pots of Manchester honey. Bumpy yellow tomatoes, steamed in butter and thyme. Mushrooms in cream, scented with sage. Sliced potatoes, softened and simmered in the brown fat of the meat. Bread, glistening and breaking in pillowy shards.

Sarah poured more tea.

'Eat up, love, there's nothing on you.'

A coachman came to the door, shaking off the morning rain, which had come as the bells had stopped.

'I'm here on behalf of John Rylands, for Miss Tennant.'

Peter was outside the Mitre, waiting for her.

The city dropped away as the main road reduced to single lanes, cobbles turning to mud, and the rattle of carriages giving way to the enthusiasm of birdsong, and a landscape knitted with the poignancy of wintered trees. The city was behind them, and the driver pulled the horses back to a trot. He dismounted, opening the doors to Peter and Enriqueta, into a small, lawned square, with benches and a tea house. A sign over it: 'Gorse Hill Park.'

'Can we speak together for a moment, Miss Tennant?'

The driver lit his pipe, pulling on it with pleasure. He cocked his leg over a wheel and whistled at two girls who were pink with cold, their faces framed with fur hoods.

'I need to warn you.'

Peter's face was grave. One of the girls laughed at the driver and blew him a kiss.

'Mrs Rylands is severely unwell. She is difficult, beyond all you can imagine. My wife, Leone, is an eternally patient woman, but even she is at her wits end. I don't know you, Miss Tennant, and you don't know me of course, and my loyalties to Mr Rylands are without question.'

'I don't understand, Peter.'

The driver tapped out his pipe and dug in his pockets for sweets for the girls. Their fur fluttered in the wind.

'You are young enough to have your own loves and family. Longford will consume you, as it has us. I'm torn – you are everything we need but I know that once you commit to the place, extricating yourself is hardly possible. I must implore you to think of your own future before sinking your roots into Longford. John keeps people. He has a way – everyone wants to please him, and he always gets what he wants in the end.'

Blunt words; stark and at odds with the nannies and prams around them, and the couples walking arm in arm enjoying the chill of the January sun. A primrose-coloured hat flew from a head, and a small girl ran to chase it, her shoes clapping against the freezing ground.

'I understand.'

'I have said enough. It is in your hands.'

'Peter, let's get to Longford. I am hopeful.'

The coach raced down Hedge Lane, turning sharply left into the broad, beautiful driveway of the Longford Park estate. As the trees bent in the breeze, Enriqueta recalled the Latin inscription she had memorised from the cathedral.

Into thy hands, O Lord. I command my Spirit.

The hall came into view. It was an Italianate building of perfect proportions, soft and sympathetic to the parkland. Elegant, and fronted by a grand porch and a sloping staircase.

'John designed Longford himself. Every arch and step and window, placed by his hand.'

Looking up to the top of the building, she thought she saw a figure move behind the curtain, but when she blinked and looked again, nothing, or no one, was there.

'Delighted to meet you, Miss Tennant. I am Mrs O'Hara. Welcome to Longford.'

Leone was a pretty woman, with a generous smile.

'I hope Peter hasn't been putting you off us all, miss. Mr Rylands is expecting you of course, follow me.'

Enriqueta's heart quickened at the same pace that her shoes clicked on the white floors of the hallway. The room was silent but for the steady tick of the grandfather clock. John Rylands put his hand out to her.

'My wife is asleep. I thought that once we have had tea, I could show you the grounds and some of the house. I can answer any questions you may have. I realise that this position is unusual.'

His study was scented with leather and amber. Armand could have been standing in the shadows, surveying the grandfather clock, assessing it's worth. Dabbling his fingers over the books on the shelves, foreign to him, to come to rest his hands on her shoulders, his palms sliding over her hips.

'I do have a question, Mr Rylands. I wondered, does your wife know anything about me? I mean, I suppose she must be very much used to Mrs O'Hara. It might be disturbing for her to be cared for by a stranger.'

John nodded, turning a glass paperweight in his fist.

'Indeed. It's something I have discussed with Leone and Peter. You are correct. Her illness makes her vulnerable, and prone to deep melancholy. She's frustrated. Depressed. It is a small mercy that the episodes come and go, and her moods are mostly governed by a quiet lassitude instead.'

Leone bought tea, and another plate of cakes, striped in white, yellow and pink.

'So, in answer to your important question, yes, we have introduced the idea to Martha. Miss Tennant, this must in no way influence your decision. I am not so presumptuous as to assume you will automatically accept the role, yet we had nothing to lose in raising the idea with her.'

'In fact, she was mercifully calm about it. She did not react as we had feared, but seemed to accept the notion that she may have someone other than Leone for company. If you are ready, Miss Tennant, let's go to the gardens.

Enriqueta heard John's quiet pride in his land, though he insisted that the work and success entirely belonged to his head gardener, Gerard. Enriqueta thought of wealthy men, building and creating and making things with ease and money, time on their hands and in their gift, to gain praise, and admiration of other men. Worlds built around women, where they existed and moved, waiting for doors to be opened for them, and for invitations of marriage presented to them like keys on a ribbon. Time was a different construct for men, giving chances and opportunities, where for women it was a thing to be endured, wasted or spent waiting. She wished she could create and construct, build and library and make a garden, filled with children and trees that were heavy with fruit.

Checking his pocket watch, he said, 'Martha will be awake by now. There is one more thing I want to show you before we return to the house.'

At the centre of the lawn, the ancient red oak was sturdy and magnificent. It stood entirely on its own in the middle of the grass.

'We are unsure of its age. Maybe two hundred years or more. Despite all the changes we made to the land, I could never move or uproot the red oak. It belongs here.'

Enriqueta stretched her neck up to the sky, shielded under the boughs. The red oak rustled its leaves, and she could feel him watching her. John waited, and they shared the feeling of time suspended.

'I will take the job, Mr Rylands, if you want me.'

LONGFORD, 1871

'MISS TENNANT, I KNOW Peter has spoken to you about life here at Longford. I too, want to say my bit. If I may.'

The kettle boiled and Leone settled Enriqueta into the old sofa in the corner. The kitchen was bright and wide. The short arms of the winter day stretched weakly across the tiled floor.

Leone bent, taking her hands. It was strange and simple to feel touch delivered in kindness.

'It won't be easy for you, miss. Mrs Rylands is a difficult patient, and Mr Rylands is a busy man. I barely see my husband for days – even weeks – when they are in the middle of one or the other of their business concerns.'

A kitten balled itself, hugging its tail in front of the stove.

'Pete said you were in France until now. In a grand house, in a good job. I wonder why you would come here to England, and to the north, too. There's not much here for a young, educated lady like you.'

Leone's dark eyes searched hers. The woman smelled of baked bread and fresh laundry, the marks of a mother.

'I'm not being nosey, but what was it that brought you here? You are clearly a clever woman. You could have set yourself up as a proper governess anywhere that took your fancy, or studied your books somewhere properly. Without other burdens.'

Enriqueta didn't even know what the word nosey meant, but she understood that this lady, so new to her, cared for her. The thoughts of Armand that she had so fiercely put in abeyance, came to her, lingering and persistent in her throat and her heart.

Tears came, as they often do under the illumination of love, and she turned from Leone. The kitten sprang onto her lap, nudging at her cheeks as she cried.

'A fella, was it? Oh, love, it happens to the best of us.'

Leone pursed her lips and rolled her eyes.

'Between you and me, I had my time before Peter. I had my heart put through the wringer like you. You don't need to tell me how; I know. I made a show of myself. Risky business, the lot. I know how it goes. I lived it.'

Leone gripped Enriqueta's hands in hers, squeezing comfort from one to the other. The kitchen clocked chimed. A robin, picture postcard with his puffed-out breast, peeked at them through the crack in the window then fled.

'Come now, Miss Tennant. It's time you met Martha.'

Leone went first up the staircase, towards a faint rumble of groans.

'Wait here.'

There were shouts, and over them, Leone's soft, urgent replies. Enriqueta heard the shuffle of movement.

'Mrs Rylands,' Enriqueta greeted her.

Martha was nearly bent double in her chair. Her hair was white, and her skin crumpled. The hands on her lap were juddering and stuttering, restless with the motion of a mind in decline. She raised her head to Enriqueta, with some effort.

'So... you are the new woman.'

She coughed brutally.

'You look his type, sure enough.'

Martha prodded at the air in vain, her fingers weak.

'Seen your sort before. Don't think you are anything special. Not to John. Ha! The husband. The great John Rylands.'

'I'm here to be your help and be your companion, Mrs

Rylands. That alone.'

She dared to run her fingertips over Martha's hand.

'I'm here for you, and Leone. Not for anyone else.'

Suddenly, Martha tilted her head to meet Enriqueta. The two women were brow to brow, and Enriqueta whispered in Martha's ear.

'You don't have to say yes to me. You don't have to accept me, Mrs Rylands. But if you choose to, I will be loyal to you.'

Martha craned her neck towards Enriqueta, a cough wracking her shoulders.

'I never thought my life would be like this. I was beautiful like you. He killed it.'

Leone pushed Martha back to her room.

'John and Peter will be late in town. You should eat with me, miss. If you don't mind the children.'

'Not at all. I would be pleased to be with them.'

'Go and put your feet up in the living room. Rest yourself, Miss Tennant. I'll call you when dinner is ready.'

She was in a deep sleep when Tynan bought her a glass of water.

'Dinner's ready, miss. Mam wants you in.'

Leone spooned the lamb stew onto her plate. Thick with red wine, it sat on top of stewed, salty greens. The meat crumbled under her spoon. Tynan and his sister Bridget, and the little brother Michael, sat at the table too, eyeing her with curiosity.

'Don't stare at poor Miss Tennant, children!'

'It's quite alright, Leone. It's strange when someone new comes into your life all of a sudden, isn't it? It can be a shock, but it can be good, too.'

The Longford driver returned to change the horses, and he lingered in the kitchen with tea, and a bowl of stew. Before he left, the driver pinched Leone's cheek and asked her when she would leave Peter for him. He had told Enriqueta on the way back down the Chester Road to the Mitre Hotel that he had loved Leone for an age, since they had shared dice in the sunlight of the village school room. He said that although years had passed, she was the same to him, as lovely now as she had been five, then fifteen, then thirty then forty. He said he had never found another like her, and never married, and when he sighed and shook his head, Enriqueta understood, seeing and sharing the desperation of the lovesick the world over.

LONGFORD, 1871

TYNAN WAS GLAD TO HAVE A REASON to avoid his morning chores, dashing out with the two letters Miss Tennant had written. One was to Leocadia and the other to Maddy and Jules. She worried briefly about Madame Bardin opening the letter, before it had reached their safe hands, but the feeling passed. Madame Bardin could not hurt or scare her anymore with her looming shadows and heavy tread, her barks and her demands. Manipulation and scheming, and the knots tied tight by cruelty, could not reach across an ocean.

Her room at Longford was bright, and far larger than her room in Paris or La Castilla. Though Enriqueta had been raised in wealth, it had been some time since she had been in a possession of a room so grand. The finest thing was the view at her window, framing the sweeping drive and the green swathe of land beneath. The red oak spread across the lawn, thrusting up from the centre.

What a thing it was, to be here, in Stretford, a place she should never have heard of, let alone walked through, her feet on the grass making it as familiar as family. New places and chances should bring joy, yet they seemed always to be tempered by the melancholy of the passing of time as they happened. If only she could still the seasons just so that she could stop and sit in contentment. But the pace of age was undeniable, and the notion of children of her own felt remote;

lost books full of unintelligible words.

John walked her through the vast spaces of the house; a ballroom, dining rooms, drawing rooms and a billiard room. They were alone in the library, dust motes dancing between them.

'Go on, Miss Tennant. Have a look. After all, this will be your work, not mine.'

It was a silent, smelling the way that only old libraries do – in fragments, dust and leather, aged paper and polish. The scent of study and secrets. John spoke of his mother Elizabeth.

'She believed in the value of education, and I inherited her love of learning. It's in me and I can't ever seem to satisfy it.'

Enriqueta looks at the tracks of books, stiff as soldiers across the shelves and she thought of the army of wealth that allowed knowledge to be indulged capriciously by rich men. They could leap between passions, scouting new languages and allegiances with ease, unrestricted by time or income.

'This library is only one small part of a much bigger strategy. We are short of time today, but I will tell you more when we are together again. Now, I'm leaving for town with Peter. I am sorry that I'm not here for your first day with us, but Leone will be with you.'

'And your wife, sir? How is she today?'

The red oak swayed in the breeze in a dance older than time, greeting the winds it knew so well, and remembered.

'Much the same. But then, what should I expect? I can't turn time. I wish, so much, that I could. I would reverse decisions I have made.'

Enriqueta had been so thoroughly warned by them all, and she was careful to learn from Leone. She watched how she cared for Martha, the way she judged moments, and managed the explosive reactions that sparked so suddenly. Leone was a mother and an organiser, her actions unfettered by hysterics or fear. At the most trying times, under Leone's firm guidance, Enriqueta began to understand how best to convert things from dire to bearable.

The weather was fine and warm for February. Enriqueta explored the endless gardens, discovering daily, new lanes and hidden corners. The old campaigner, the mighty red oak, stood sentry as she wandered, beneath the twist and turn of its unadorned winter branches. As Enriqueta pushed her, Martha fell asleep. Enriqueta revelled in an empty mind, the clang of anxiety no longer filling her head. Sometimes, stimulated by birdsong or the low hum and chatter of the gardeners, Martha was very much awake. Still, Emma Bovary trailed after Enriqueta in spirit, reminding her of her opinions, reminding her how true they were.

Well, quite softly, one day following another, a spring on a winter, and an autumn after a summer, this wore away, piece by piece, crumb by crumb; it passed away, it is gone, I should say it has sunk; for something always remains at the bottom as one would say—a weight here, at one's heart.

The garden seemed to engender a lucidity that she didn't have when she was inside, muffled by the house. She mustered enough energy to explain the parts of the estate to Enriqueta in fond and specific detail.

'The new fellow, Tolan, had some radical ideas when he came to us. He introduced a complicated irrigation system to the meadows. I understood it better than John, you know. John didn't like the interference.'

Martha took satisfaction in the memory of her husband's disgruntled face. She heaved herself in her chair, wiping her mouth energetically.

'Then, Tolan insisted he employed a troop of twenty men, all in full employment as his assistants, and all provided with residence at Longford Cottages. The expense! Not that I am party to the finances these days. Another way to shut me out.'

The kitchen garden was a small balm to Martha. Enriqueta marvelled at her recall of the Latin name of each plant, growing in abundance around them. The soft herbs were drawn back for the winter, but the harder ones – rosemary, bay and thyme – were vigorous.

In these moments, Enriqueta could enjoy her company, and forget the fury and confusion that could, and would, rear up at any moment. The darker moods descended as the day wore on, brother-in-arms to the fatigue that marched through Martha's afternoons. Though the mornings with her were bearable – content sometimes – she was much changed once the later hours arrived.

Enriqueta and Martha played cards or billiards before Martha retired each evening. Their games were sometimes destroyed, as Martha flew into her inexplicable rages, pushing over the table. Enriqueta got to her knees, picking up cards, or pieces, while reminding herself that even this was better than what she had left behind.

Enriqueta didn't always accept Leone's invitation to dine with the family, instead taking her plate to her room. The solitude and the romantic, nostalgic colour of her bedroom made her cry easily. While she battled heroically with the memory of Foncé, he came back to her, a powerful ghost, with the feel of the satin bedspread on her skin, or the scent of her spent bedside candle, as exact in fragrance as the ones that puttered in La Castilla. Tears cooled on her cheek, because she knew that he had never loved her at all.

Enriqueta saw little of John or Peter as the first days stacked themselves into weeks. She watched their carriage bounce down the driveway in the cool first rays of the sun, her forehead pressed onto the wet of her window. A man who never appeared to have a moments stillness, John kept himself relentlessly occupied, pushing idleness away like it was an enemy.

To see John striding across the lawn towards her late one Friday morning was unexpected. Enriqueta was in the herbarium, taking clippings for Leone's recipes. Assuring scents of thyme and rosemary fixed themselves to the air. She looked from the plants and back to John as he came closer. The kitchen kitten had followed her and pulled at the plants, clawing her skirts for affection. She murmured to the herbs, mindless songs of love, and to the kitten, the scissors hot in her hands.

John was dressed in his black suit, but without his jacket. His shirt sleeves were rolled up.

'Leone has asked for cabbages too, so I volunteered,' he laughed. Finding a shovel, John began to dig into the patch nearby, where the cabbages were netted. John dug hard at the earth next to her and she could hear him breathing near to her shoulder. The cabbage came away easily from the earth, soil coating his hands.

'There was something else. I mentioned when we first met that your duties would extend beyond the care of my wife. Your skills would be wasted if that is all you did for me at Longford.'

He cradled the kitten, and it rumbled with contentment against his throat.

'I showed you the book rooms when you first arrived, but there has not been a moment since for us to discuss the libraries. The business has the terrible habit of occupying every waking moment. I can apologise, but it will never change. But there is a lot for me to explain – to discuss – with you.'

He passed the kitten to her, and the little thing bobbed her head between them, loyalties confused.

'Will you have dinner with me this evening?'

The animal mewed, and reached out to John. Her tongue darted to lick his cheek.

'Yes, of course.'

'Very good. I have a meeting this afternoon. I'll be back in time for us to have dinner together at seven o'clock. Peter and Leone are long due an evening off, so they have asked Mrs Tolan, Gerard's wife, to oversee the kitchen tonight.'

Seeing herself in the mirror as she dressed- Enriqueta was stern and determined never to be the person that she had become in the wake of Foncé's destruction. That was behind her; she had left that miserable, tattered, suspicious being in France.

All she had seen so far of John Rylands was that he was a good, intelligent man – brilliant even. He had his business, his home and his wife to care for, and she dared to feel that she might be safe here. She envisioned herself ageing gently at Longford, being useful for as long as she possibly could. No shocks, no scandal, no threats to her spirits. No men, like captains, commanding her with their beauty and their fingers and palms over her. Just a docile, Godly life. She planned to save, to spend as little as she could. After all, there was no need for fancy dresses anymore. She had enough hats and pencils to last her until she died. With her savings, she would eventually find a little cottage to retire to, and that would be all. She would live the remainder of her days there in happiness and health, mending her dresses and keeping her bonnets and notebooks carefully. All darkness, and all passion, lay where it belonged. In her past.

She was faithful to her words, enjoying her conversations with John, unimpeded by any fanciful nerves or wavering confidence. She sunk into their discussions about his libraries with easy pleasure. After so many months of only being able to deal with books as passing commodities, their talk felt like home.

'The aim is to make a proper, lasting catalogue of the contents of the Longford libraries. I have long had a significant share of the ownership of the Portico collection in Manchester.

The fastidious records the librarian keeps there are exactly what I want the Longford system modelled upon.'

Pride, without boastfulness, shone from him. His investment in them was as personal as it was financial.

'I had hoped that by now the billiards room would be converted into a space dedicated to the theological collection. Miss Tennant, I am sure you know how quickly time passes. I mean – it frustrates me. I am not where I want to be with the library.'

He turned the stem of his glass in his fingers, then poured them both more of the Madeira.

'Every year, I tell myself it will be my sole project, my priority. But other things push to the fore. Procrastination and delay don't sit well with me at all.'

John knew Greek, Latin, French and Italian. These were languages she had mastered herself, and they moved on to discussions about their travels, and the countries they had both visited. When the discussion veered dangerously toward her time in Lyon, Enriqueta tensed, fearful that he would question her departure as Leone had. The candles flickered between them.

'Miss Tennant, I hadn't realised the time. Get some rest. I have papers to prepare for Peter. There is something else, but it will have to wait.'

A curious thing, when it comes; disappointment. The absence of what a person wants to happen, or thinks they want. Climbing into her bed, Enriqueta felt her old friend worry come again, then she slept. She never heard the tread of the boards outside as John passed her room hours later, a smile lingering on his lips and a new lightness in his heart.

LONGFORD, JULY 1871

'GOOD MORNING, ENRI! Just in time. Peter and John left for town at seven, so they're gone from under our feet. The children have gone off too. Now what can I get you for breakfast?'

The two women sat with mugs of tea and crumpets, and Leone yawned, rubbing her eyes.

'Did you have a nice evening? Were you late home?'

'It must have been gone midnight. Later maybe. We don't get much time off all together. Not because John won't grant it, but because my Peter won't take it!' Leone spooned jam onto the crumpets. Strawberries from last summer, bruised with time and liquor. 'So when we do, we make the most of it. We went into Chorlton, and while Peter and Ged went for a few ales in the Horse and Jockey, me and the children went over to my sister's.'

Leone was a local born and bred in Hardy, one of the small surrounding villages. Her sister, husband and three children had worked hard to afford a cottage on the green in Chorlton. Frank Beswick had a good position, for life, at Bancrofts Farm.

Only in his thirties, he was managing the vast majority of the men and the operation, and the owner, James Bancroft, was happy to leave nearly all the responsibility and decision making to Frank, while he busied himself with his greater passion for politics. The Beswick children had all attended the Village School on the green, which was just a stone's throw from their home. Having the children out of the house had enabled Clara to develop her own little market garden business, renting a small plot of land from the Lloyd estate nearby. She turned out to be a fine horticulturist, having learned much of the medicinal properties of plants at her mother's knee, learning some excellent techniques and propagation approaches. A competitive and ambitious woman, Clara was proud that she had a reputation for producing the best, freshest, most delicious potatoes in the region.

Clara Beswick sold most of her produce in the hamlets, but she often sent the surplice down the river to Manchester to be sold at Smithfield market. Her trader told her that all he needed to do was shout out 'Clara's Crop! Clara's Crop!', and his stock would be sold out in minutes. She grew other vegetables, but above them all, her pride and joy were her herbal crops.

Clara Beswick was the most talented and respected herbalists in the locality, and her abundant, year-round crops were used by the local apothecary extensively. The nearest medical doctors lived in Urmston, and at the opposite side of the township, in Withington. Even if the locals were to travel the distances, these medical men were more expensive than most could afford. The doctors in Manchester, with their surgeries and offices, were even further beyond anything they could dream off.

Local people relied on natural remedies, tinctures and oils concocted in the premises of Lightly Simpson, on the row. It was to him that Clara took her wares, delivering him new, fresh bundles of her herbs in her barrow every Monday morning.

Her knowledge of botany and herbology was extensive, enlightened and precise. She advised him on the exact proportions to use for each treatment, and the quality of her plants made for potent and effective medicines.

She grew plants for their antiseptic qualities, and they were bound into ointments and oils; bee balm, anemone and burdock. There was a herb for every ailment, many with a multitude of applications. Lavender, Catmint, Chamomile and Mugwort were incorporated into treatments for women; for labour pains, nerves and monthly ills. The farming community and elderly shared a passion for feverfew, which was used to treat aches, pains and arthritis. For the farm hands too, lambs ears acted as a field dressing on stings, bruises and injuries. Mint was a staple for the housewife, which she could employ liberally to children with stomach upsets or toothache, and for herself, combined with lemon balm to wipe over her face to promote a fresh complexion.

Bowel disorders, piles, pimples, influenza, rheumatism and gout. All and more could be soothed and often cured by the formidable powers of Clara Beswick's plants. She kept bees, her honey rich and fruited, full of the goodness of the local plants. Those suffering hayfever, chills, or a cold came from miles to buy the pots of honey that would last them the year, drunk in tea for their chest ailments, or smoothed onto the scratches and grazes on their children's knees, the magical salve knitting together the damaged skin.

It was Clara's honey that Leone spooned into her tea, and it was reviving her jaded spirits, her shadowed dawn eyes regaining some of their sparkle.

'Did you enjoy your dinner? Hope old Anne Tolan didn't talk you to death. She does go on.'

Enriqueta laughed.

'I did, thank you. I don't think I had realised how much I had missed talking about – I don't know – all sorts. Mr Rylands has such a knowledge of things.'

'He does. It's so easy in this world, and this town especially, to use your God-given brains for selfish purposes. Most of the powerful men of these parts do just that. But not John Rylands. He does good quietly; even the people of

Manchester don't realise.'

Leone sighed, spreading her bread with honey.

'There are so many sad things about the way Mrs Rylands is now. It's easy to forget, seeing the way that she has become, that she was a big part of all his efforts for change. There is no way you, or anyone, could know of all the work they did together to make life better for so many of the unfortunate people of Manchester. She supported him in all his great plans. It wasn't that many years ago either. They did so much for the orphans, opening up a house for girls in Webster Street, then a bigger one near Greenheys Chapel. They opened up a servants' home around that time too, looking after respectable folk in the working classes, where they could board and lodge.'

Enriqueta continued to half listen as Leone wistfully listed all the admirable projects, but her mind had lodged and stuck on the mention of the orphanages. The gall and tyranny of feeling- thundering against progress and halting it, tying itself to the coattails of optimism only to drag it backwards. Despite her slowly, but very surely, beginning to find contentment and a meaningful place here in her new life at Longford, Armand Foncé continued to jar into her mind at the most inauspicious moments. The strangest, smallest thing that sent her backwards – in her mind and heart – into his arms in the cabin. A scent, or a sound, or just a word. Orphanages.

She was cast from the warm kitchen back into regret. All that work and time, all her passion and fervent hopes. All she had given to him, offered him so easily, without question. She was the thin red curtains of the cabin, that he could open and close as he wished.

Leone hadn't noticed how far Enriqueta had drifted away from their conversation as she began clearing the dishes and when Martha's shout came from above them, Leone groaned.

'Come on then, Miss Enriqueta Tennant. No rest for the

wicked. Let's have the morning together with her Ladyship, then you can get on with whatever he has got you doing in that library of his.'

After her mornings with Martha, the afternoons in the lofty rooms of the library were a retreat. A small voice whispered to her: *One day, you foolish girl, this task will be finished. You won't be needed by Longford. Not needed one little bit by the good Mr and Mrs Rylands!* Sometimes the voice was so loud that it paralysed her, like the rich call of her mother, and she would force herself to stride to the red oak, running her shaking fingers over its deep bark, making sure the tree was real, or that she was real. Reminding herself that Armand, and her mother's memory, were seas and mountains and sugar fields away.

A picture of John and Martha Rylands formed before her as she worked through the collections. The whole series of *A Lady of England* by Elizabeth Charles, and *Daisy* by Susan B Warner. A collection of travel writing, so large it formed a story of trip after trip around the globe. Closer to home, there were guides to the Lakes, the Isle of Wight and North Wales. Enriqueta imagined the holidays and adventures taken by the couple in happier times. Belgium, Germany, the Netherlands, Egypt.

The Pursuit of Knowledge Under Difficulties sounded so unfathomably serious and worthy it made her smile. A lighter aspect emerged in a range of books on hobbies and pastimes, *Billiards for Beginners, Gardeners Monthly, The Muck Manual for Farmers and Manchester Walks*. Enriqueta wondered if John Rylands could dance.

Chaucer, Shakespeare, Pope, Milton, Locke, Dryden, Wordsworth, Byron; men of words for men of words. Military histories, textile and industrial histories and an array of specifically local books: *Reminiscences of Manchester 50 Years Ago, Manchester in 1844.*

There were copious books on the plight of prisoners and

children. Also, on law reform and progressive, inclusive ways of improving social ills and the lives of those who John knew made up the crowds of the neglected and vulnerable. His books spoke for him and wrote his story; a man driven by big business and surrounded by wealth, yet so keenly aware and despairing of the injustices in the world around him.

She had never met anyone like him. He seemed not to sit in judgement of anyone, but conducted himself with generosity. Enriqueta compared Armand to him, and she felt an urgent shame when she did. How shallow, entitled and glib he had been. The scales had gone from her eyes, as though being in John's presence had shown her what goodness in a man really was. Despite the surface appearance of Foncé's charitable efforts, she knew now that they were little more than an entertaining distraction for him, and a way of imparting a false sense of grace and munificence to those he wished to influence and impress for his wider, commercial gains

Everything was a lie. Every smile hid a yawn of boredom, every joy a curse.

Enriqueta had given so much of herself to him, in every way, and now she could hardly comprehend any of it. She could recollect that, in the moment, he had seemed so sincere, so startlingly genuine. In his arms, she had believed him when he had said he loved her. That expression alone was enough for her and served as a talisman, a testament to what she believed was goodness. It had been a promise of a future. She never would have let him take her to the cabin if she had not believed that she meant everything to him.

Every few weeks, when John was in his office at the hall, he asked for her. Their meetings felt like the seasons; spring and summer for her.

'You are working so hard, Miss Tennant, and I want you to know how much it is appreciated.'

Amber, leather, tea; air full of him.

'Mr Rylands, it doesn't feel like work at all.'

The way he leaned on his desk, his shoulders against his suit; she looked at his shoes and his hands and she touched her face, thinking she could feel something again.

'I think maybe I hadn't realised how lonely my life had become before I was welcomed to Longford.'

She hardly dared look at him.

'You should call me John, now. I want you to.'

Her breath caught in her throat. She longed for the distraction of the kitchen kitten, or his robin, that came like grace.

Want.

'And now for more tedious business, Enriqueta'

The grandfather clock chimed liked a companion to her name on his lips.

'I have to go away. For some time.'

Enriqueta had not expected the news, and it arrived like a blanket.

'Do you leave soon?'

'Yes. In two days. I need to make some plans and put a few affairs in order. Peter will act for me while I am in Italy.'

'Italy?'

'Yes, I have offices all over. There are some untoward practices that I need to address. With urgency. Fortunately, I can trust most of my people implicitly, and it is through the wise actions of some particularly judicious individuals that this has come to light.'

Enriqueta's mind spun webs around a ridiculous notion of envy for a country and people that would have him. Italy, while Stretford and Longford would be without. She would be without him.

'Is there anything I can do? I could help you prepare for the trip?'

'Always so wise, Enriqueta. And kind.'

She had never much liked her name, and especially here in England where it sounded foreign and unwieldy. Yet from him, it was beautiful, crafted from crystal and dance. He made it new, ridding it of sad, mottled history and wringing out of it the voices of her mother and step-father.

'Thank you – it's all in hand. I will leave instruction with you for the next stages of things here.'

He poured brandy for them both, pushing a glass to her.

'Which leads me to what I really want to say.'

Want.

She was thankful for the strong liquor.

'I wonder whether you are working too hard, Enriqueta. You are far ahead of where I thought you ever could be with the library. I consult Peter and Leone, and I find that you have not had one day off in weeks. You care for my wife with the patience and grace of an angel, yet you seem to have no respite yourself.'

'I'm not sure I need much time for myself, John.'

John swept his hand through his hair. She realised that she hadn't thought of Armand for days. When it had all first fallen apart, her hours were interrupted, imploding with the agony of his memory. There seemed to be no respite from their might, reminiscences as agile and as vibrant as the real moment had been.

'You are a young woman, Enriqueta. Leone will gladly take you into Chorlton. There are things I'm sure you would like – dances, gatherings at the church. Teas, women's groups, music evenings.'

The idea of people and evenings made her rigid, and Armand emerged, lighting a flame at her side, luring in the ghouls and wolves of society. The band of fear, swollen with players, struck up in her and Armand conducted it, his fair hair swinging and his beauty unfaded.

'I don't know if I want to socialise much. But thank you.'

She thought for a brief, mad moment that he would reach

for her. She thought she might cry. John sat as still and stately as ever, before murmuring, 'Of course. Leone always says I interfere too much.'

'It's kind of you to think of me. I have been absorbed in the care of your wife and my work, the books. I suppose I might say I was content with my lot.'

'A good thing! Comparison can indeed be the thief of happiness. That I know well.'

She felt so desperately sad for him, his eyes misted with a pain that she knew. She wanted to say something to solve him, or salve him.

'Maybe I shall join Leone on a trip somewhere soon, if she didn't mind.'

She could hardly imagine stepping out and meeting people. The land, the gardens, the books, nests made of grass and cocoons of paper. She doubted she knew how to be in society anymore, the poison of parties and dance drowned in the dark syrup of Lyon.

In her bed, her eyes began to close to the sounds of Peter and John gathering the horses, very early. The thud of the carriage door and the horses objecting to their harnesses, whinnying into the dampness. She listened in hope John's voice, but there was nothing more to hear but the beat of her own heart.

LONGFORD, SEPTEMBER 1871

SEPTEMBER BEGAN IN MELLOW ways, the bold ardour of summer slumping into the first hues of decay. The sun, opal and diluted, lingered on and the days cropped themselves discreetly. The geraniums bloomed on valiantly, and the hedgerows were bright with lime-coloured hops.

With John's departure to Italy, the clemency and good temper of the seasons flew away in a rage. All warmth was blown from the air by booming winds, bending the plants and trees of Longford, making misery of their shapes. The skies over the estate jostled with leaden clouds, bloated with rain that never came. The earth sent up a dank fug, and the scent of bonfires and hearths filled the grounds. Without the comings and goings of John, action subsided, and all was subdued; growing dormant.

Yet despite the damp ground and the dearth of bright flowers, Martha insisted on her daily turn around the gardens. Leone wrapped her in blankets, pushing a hot water bottle through her woollen wraps onto her lap with the promise of tea and cake when they returned. Fortunately as the weather changed, Enriqueta received another package from her sister, Leocadia, full of beautiful winter clothes: coats, muff, boots and hats. Although they were no longer in vogue in London, they were perfectly adequate for suburban Manchester.

After some months at Longford, Enriqueta knew how to

be content with the angry monologues that characterised her walks with Martha. She knew where to stay silent and listen, and she recognised where she should interject to try and soothe. Exertion exhausted Martha, and threw her into sudden, deep sleep, making the outbursts, inflamed with vitriol and ire, at least short lived. Accusations about John, the grave and relentless disappointments of her life, spewed and relished. She said he had stolen her beauty, a piracy that had left her as ruined as her wedding dress, to which she had taken a blade on the tenth anniversary of their marriage, the cuts on her palms oozing red onto the lace.

'You have no idea what I endure. Living under the shadow of that damned, pathetic woman. Dinah. All my life it was Dinah, Dinah. I could see her in his eyes as we laid together, all the time trying to impregnate me as he had done her. Greed. All driven by greed.'

Martha spat on the ground, spittle catching on her chin and foaming at the corners of her mouth. Enriqueta pressed on towards the warmth and the distraction of the begonia glasshouse.

'And I never had a chance against all his other women. Oh no! When I started to refuse him, he got it elsewhere. Everywhere. There is probably not a whore in Manchester, and beyond, that he hasn't mounted. He has the vigour of a horse, that man.'

Enriqueta hardly listened to Martha's outpourings anymore, no longer wondering what parts true, and what parts were not. Distinguishing veracity among the details of a dark remembered fairy tale was impossible. At the beginning, she had considered consulting Leone, but she had stopped herself. It was bad enough to have to hear it all; it left her with no appetite to discuss the tawdry details any further. The Rylands were bound together by legality, habitual loyalties, bent by acrimony and the regret of wasted days. Doubtless it would carry its sadnesses and secrets with it when – and if – it finally expired. Romance, with its long days and fine promises, was dead to the Rylands, as it was to Enriqueta.

With John abroad and Peter occupied with business, Leone was often called out to help with the countless matters that bloomed like fruit on the estate. Be they domestic, arable, educational or medical, Leone seemed always to have time and an answer. And where she did not, she knew someone else who would. Martha's care, in the main, was left to Enriqueta.

A dreadful night had begun benignly. At only seven o'clock in the evening, it was wholly dark outside. Leone had left Enriqueta alone half an hour previously, after putting Martha to bed. She had gone to attend one of the families who lived in the estate cottages. The woman had given birth the night before, and although both mother and baby were well, there were still small tasks and ministrations necessary for them both. Leone had left with a basketful of soft, old, pressed linen and clothes for the baby, as well as pies, bread and butter.

The house was quiet, occupied only by Martha, in bed, and Enriqueta, sitting in the living room she shared with Leone and Peter, writing letters. She wrote at length and regularly, to Jeanne, Jules and Maddy, and Marianne in Truro.

The rain began to patter against the windowpane – lightly at first, then in swollen drops. The gentle tap swiftly turned to a steady thud, a cloudburst over Longford. She thought of Leone and wondered whether she had a coat to shield her. But Leone was an unfussy woman, used to the vagaries of the Manchester weather.

Sealing the envelope, Enriqueta was about to write the address for La Castilla when there was a startling string of blows to the front door. The sound boomed through the house, a manic, demented pounding. Enriqueta's letter fell from her hand, and she stood carefully, her legs made of paper and air, her voice dried away. The hammering at the door went on, and then shouting began, barking above the rain that clattered harder against every window.

The banging didn't cease, and below it the voice came more clearly, though it was muffled by the clamour of the storm.

'Father! Father! Open the door! It is me, John Garthwaite! Father!'

Enriqueta's hand shook, her fingers hovering over the whorls of the great front door. The grandfather clock chimed in John's office, and she longed for him. She thought of John's hand on hers, and his way; always finding answers and solutions, and seeing paths through every severe tribulation. John Garthwaite, his son. His name had been mentioned in terse conversations between Peter and John, but Enriqueta had never met him, or seen him visit the house. The pounding resumed under her palms, and prayers pattered in her.

Oh, Father. Father. Be at my side, Father.

'For God's sake! Please, Father! Let me in! Damn, I am being chased!'

She put ear against the door, the thick wood a barrier between them, yet she heard him groan in desperation. Swinging it open, a blast of rain sprayed Enriqueta, as he bore down on her from the mouthing darkness. Roughly pushing her aside, John Garthwaite slammed the door behind him. The storm, the rain, and all others behind him barricaded out, trapping her inside Longford with him. He leaned against it, gasping, his head in his hands. In the gloom of the hallway, she saw that his face was savaged. Blood was smeared all over him, trickling from a tear in his lip, and from the deep gashes gaping across his forehead. His eyes were milky and crusted, and his clothes were ripped and caked in mud. Water dripped in a slew from his tattered clothes, making pools of grey liquid, tinged with the iron rust of his blood, dark on the marble floors.

His words came in stuttering slurs.

'Who the hell are you? Where is my father? I need to see him, now!'

He lurched at her; his fist bared.

'Now!'

She willed herself not to cower before him.

'Your father is away.'

John was in her mind like a soldier, guarding her with the safety of books, the chimes of clocks, the leather and brandy and teas of his office and with his voice, summoning courage.

'I am Enriqueta Tennant, in his employment here at Longford Hall.'

John Garthwaite let out a long mewling groan.

'That's no good to me, woman. I am being chased. I need money!' He grabbed her shoulders, roaring into her face. She could smell fetid alcohol on his breath, mixed with the metallic, alarming scent of his blood.

John Garthwaite shook her, and the shock of men, and of their violence tolled deep within her.

'Fetch me some money! Get me money, stupid woman! Move! If they find me, they will kill me. And you – they will kill you too.'

Enriqueta was rigid, made blank by terror. There was a screech from above, and both of them turned to look, John Garthwaite dropping her.

At the top of the stairs, Martha stood. Frail, luminous and ghostly in her nightdress, she was holding a heavy vase above her head, her arms shaking and bent with effort.

'Get out of my house, John Garthwaite! Get out!'

The vase spun in the air and came crashing down near them, the shards of the glass splintering like terrible ice across the hallway. Garthwaite bellowed again, pushing Enriqueta back onto the hard, dangerous floor. From above, Enriqueta could hear Martha emitting a keening howl. John Garthwaite rocked on his boots, then moved to come down on her and Enriqueta shut her eyes tight, raising her arms and speeding through a last prayer in her head.

Father. Father. Oh, my Father.

Peter O'Hara burst through the front door and pulled John Garthwaite's head back into a lock. Peter squeezed hard; his face fierce. John Garthwaite's face turned puce, his mouth grimacing in effort as he tried to struggle free. After a few moments, he went limp in Peter's grasp.

Peter's driver ran through the door, eyes wide at the scene before him; a tableau of blood and destruction.

'He's not dead, Will!' Peter shouted, his hands still at John's neck.

'Here, help me get him tied and into the cab. God knows what has happened here tonight but I want this devil gone from Longford.'

Peter glanced up at Martha, who was slumped on the top stair, eyes glassy, mouth slack. He shook his head in angst and sorrow. The colour was gone from Enriqueta and she was dirty with blood and mud.

'Enri, I am so sorry to see you like this. I'm taking him back to where he has come from then I'll be back, immediately. Leone should be back soon, I'm sure. The rain is stopping. I'm so, so sorry. I can't forgive myself for not being here.'

Will and Peter lifted John Garthwaite, and the blood from his face dripped away, mingling with the wet floor, smearing it with violent stains. The broken glass cracked beneath their feet as they tramped to the door, straining at the dead weight of the man.

Minutes after the men had departed, Leone rushed in to see the chaos, and Enriqueta, pale and shaking amongst it. It was only then that Enriqueta looked to her own hands. They were cut, and much of the blood she saw diluted on the tiles was her own, and the lap of her grey day dress was turned black from it.

LONGFORD, 1871

'DRINK THIS, ENRIQUETA.'
Leone pushed a bottle to her lips; one of Clara's herbal tonics.

She surveyed the dreadful scene with the swift and calm efficiency of a woman who was an expert at managing a crisis. After shutting and bolting the front door, Leone helped Enriqueta to the chair in front of the fire. Her hands were still bleeding, and pin-pricked with slivers of glass. Ruddy purple blisters rose around the cuts. Leone rushed to Martha, taking the stairs two at a time, her wet skirts grasped over her knees. Martha appeared catatonic, staring into the distance. There was no angel, or God, or John, to clean up the vestiges of the hell around them.

'Come on, Martha. Drink this, dear. More. And into bed with you. Lean on me.'

Leone flew back downstairs to tend to Enriqueta and her wounds. She cleaned her hands tenderly, picking out the shards, running a tentative thumb over each graze. Dabbing Enriqueta's hands with lint and witch-hazel, Leone murmuring soothing words each time she winced.

As she finished, wrapping Enriqueta's hands in gauze and bandage, Peter returned. Enriqueta heard them talk in the hallway in urgent tones, over the crackle of the fire. The swish of Leone's brush in the hall, clearing the dirt and bloodied glass under John's black overcoat which hung over his office door, exquisite and neat.

'I need this.'

Peter drained his glass of brandy and leaned to refill it. His jacket steamed in the light of the fire. Running his hands over his face, he held his head in his hands.

'We should never have left you alone. I never thought John Garthwaite would appear at Longford again.'

He knuckled his shoulder, trying to ease the pain in his back.

'He's a mess, that lad. John was estranged from him some time ago. I mean, completely.'

'Are you hurt, Peter?'

He shook his head.

'It's you and Martha I am worried about. And John. God, I dread to think of John. What he will say. It was never his choice for it to be like this. It has caused a great deal of pain for him, for years. John Garthwaite has chosen a route through life that is beyond the control or approbation of a very loving, eternally forgiving, father.'

The morning brought Enriqueta familiar sadness, and her old friends, trepidation and fear, which she correlated with her time at La Castilla. A sense that whatever her position, she was still a stranger, not party to the strains and secrets of the house she resided in. Always 'the other', always 'the outsider', truths and histories and people locked like dairies with keys and doors, incarcerated within families.

A form of John, dark-suited across the seas and presiding over some foreign meeting, flicked in front of her eyes. And of her mother Juana, who would have taken her pistol from her underskirts and shot John Garthwaite down dead long before he spoiled the white floor. Her father Stephen, who would have picked up his little girl and ran with her through Manchester and past mills and fields, to safety, wherever that was.

Longford Hall appeared deserted. There were no noises from the kitchen, and as she had passed Martha's bedroom, it was empty; the maids had been and gone already, the bed remade.

A shuffle came from the office, the reassurance of drawers opening, and footsteps across the rug.

'How did you sleep?'

'Well, Peter. Clara's remedy worked.'

'Given the appalling events of last night, we decided you may need some rest. Martha rose early, and unfortunately has a distinct recollection of John Garthwaite's appearance. Leone and Tynan have taken her for a trip into town. Doubtless, it will be short lived as she tires so easily, but a run around some of her favourite places will do her some good, I hope.'

Peter poured her tea, and she drew her robin-red cloak closer.

'I owe you further explanation, Enriqueta. It's a difficult position, with Mr Rylands away. He is a private man. The disintegration of his ties to his son, both business and personal, well, it has been a continual blight on his life. On his heart.'

'I understand.'

'Relations between John Garthwaite and Mrs Rylands were always fraught, throwing John between them in an impossible position. By pleasing one, he riles the other. A terrible, endless carousel of strain and sorrow. Many aspects of John Garthwaite's life troubled John, though he tolerated them. Garthwaite has a penchant for always taking the darkest and most hazardous path.'

He swore at the milk when it slopped from the jug. The curse was hard and foreign from his gentle mouth.

'I know I can trust you, and that Mr Rylands does in the same way. Implicitly.'

His praise gleamed, shining a light in her as though it had come from John himself, across hills and water, a string to tie them when everything else was fraying loose.

'Latterly, John Garthwaite has begun a descent into a most heinous, damaging addiction. The only thing he cares for now is laudanum. He is in its grip, and it has taken everything from him. His money, work. His good health. Friends. His father. He once had everything – all the fortunes and favours of the world.'

Enriqueta recalled the opium addicts who huddled in the moonless streets of Paris, those that she and her friends would avoid. Piles of men and women, and children, slumped in rags in districts that were governed by rats and infection. They lay in piles for warmth, their bodies cadaverous and ravaged, fuelled by nothing but the mad poisons that crawled through their veins. Men became thieves, women prostitutes, and infants were sold as quickly as they slid, or were pulled, from their mothers.

'There's nothing left for him, nothing more that John can do to save him. Believe me, he has tried everything.'

'I can imagine' she replied quietly.

'John has patience. Determination. He has attempted all cures and respites to draw him from his tawdry life.'

Leone shouted a greeting through the window.

'I have written to John this morning to tell him what happened.'

'Oh! Peter, I don't want him to worry. He is so far away from home.'

'I needed to tell him. I'm responsible for everything when he is gone. Responsible for you. Longford. Thanks to your presence of mind, and Leone's quick actions, Martha and you are mostly unharmed, thank God.'

She curled up her hands. Leone's neat bandaging seemed unnecessarily formal in the calmer light of a new day.

'It could have been catastrophic. Again, I am so sorry.'

'Peter, I am well, I promise. But Mrs Rylands, is there anything I can do for her?'

'Nothing more than you do, and have done for her already. She trusts you too, Enriqueta; high praise from someone in such a world of distress and confusion. Let's all have dinner together tonight.'

Martha wanted to play cards. Dark emeralds hung at her ears and Enriqueta wondered if they were a gift, given in the early flushes of love by John himself. Ripples, like yearning, distracted her, and her fingers at her own lobes told her she had nothing to adorn herself. Her mother had tossed gems and ring at her like they were pebbles to play skip with, but Enriqueta had left them all when her stepfather had cast her from Cuba. They were probably still there, tarnishing in a half open drawer.

Gaiety sometimes blooms from the sour soil of disaster, and Martha was cheerful, playing with skill and wit. Enriqueta glimpsed a younger person, instead of the woman Martha had aged prematurely. How she might have been when her health, her mind, her circumstances had been buoyant. Maybe John had kissed her neck as she slipped the emeralds on, laughing with the thrill of the newlywed bed. Once, there must have been mornings and nights together, capturing the same moments she had shared with Armand. Admiration and the shock of another's skin in moonlight, clothes falling, the surprise of the other's beauty after time apart. The wild tug of wanting the smallest word. The intoxication of a new smile that signs the beginning of love.

The beef stew was prepared with vegetables from the estate, Peter was generous with the wine, even allowing Tynan a little. Bridget's favourite pudding, a lemon meringue pie, flavoured with Gerard's prize fruit. When Martha suddenly tired, her shoulders slumping and her eyes drooping, Enriqueta took her to bed. Her hair unpinned, it lay in threads on the pillow.

Tiredness made her cold, and Enriqueta took the red shawl from her shoulders and laid it on her.

'Enriqueta?'

'Yes, Martha.'

'Lots of things ruined us. John Garthwaite was one. But there were lots of others. Things said and done, that can't be unsaid or undone. Our marriage is long dead. He knows it too.'

Martha shut her eyes, her breath laboured. The clock on her dresser was beautiful; enamelled with shepherdesses skipping by lambs. It had lost its tick when Martha had thrown it at John one hot, angry summer. Enriqueta thought Martha had fallen asleep, but her mouth began to move again. She picked up a hand and gestured weakly to a small box near the clock.

'It's a gift. For you, from me. Go downstairs and open it later. I'm tired now.'

First times for all things come with caution, and when Enriqueta bent to kiss Martha on the brow, she felt her heart pound as fast as it had with the distant passions of her past. The thin bones were cool beneath her lips.

'The marriage- we thought it would cure us both and remove the sorrows. A widow and a widower, not leaving any room for love to happen. Errors, and regrets. The time we spent in battle, but I must leave it all in peace. There is nothing to be done about other days. There is only one way to happiness- we must all find our own peace.'

LONGFORD, OCTOBER 1871

B Y OCTOBER, EVERYONE DOUBTED they would be lucky enough for one of Manchester's famed Indian summers. The seasons shifted too far determinedly into autumn to bounce back into clemency. Enriqueta's walks with Martha were shorter, the air clipping at their limbs, and between them, Enriqueta was in the library, working through John's list of instructions at a pace. Leone came to fetch her for dinner, when hours had passed and hunger had begun to claw. Her face, poking round the mahogany doors, called out to rouse her, from a back stiff with sitting, her fingers ridged with writing, and her arms sore with moving the piles of books.

She heaved a chair next to Enriqueta, her eyes shining like polished stones.

'This has just come! Oh, wait on, Enri – pass me that!'

The leaflet was bright with the inks of autumn. A sketch of a marionette bobbed over the page.

Leone opened one of John's French–English dictionaries.

'*Le Fete de la Moisson*! Harvest Festival, we call it! Tombola, puppet show, ale stalls, goose dinner, John of the Harvest! We have to go. The whole village will be there. There are shows, and dancing, and all the market gardens have stalls out with things to buy. We can go with my sister, Clara, while Peter minds everything here.'

Dancing.

What idea did she have anymore of saying her name to strangers, or remembering the steps to a jig, so new that only the youngsters knew how to tap and turn when the fiddles struck. Her youth was left in Paris, where she had held it like a goblet, offering it for the poor swap of promises. Moments that only served her now as a reminder that maybe she wouldn't be held again, or feel the urgency of a man at her neck, or hands in her clothes, and a voice in her ear telling her that she was beautiful. Armand Foncé had ruined her, spoiled her with his skill and left her fixed and suspended in a trough of disappointment. Cloistered at Longford, she didn't need wider society, nor wanted it. Being out in the village, especially after dark, held no appeal.

'I'm not sure. It has been so long. I don't know if I would spoil it all for you.'

By Saturday, Leone prevailed and she was persuaded. Though the walk to Chorlton-cum-Hardy down Hedge Lane was not long, Peter took them in the carriage. Leone didn't want to waste any of the evening or her good shoes on foot.

The streets swelled with families strolling, packs of children playing and couples, linking arms. Leone waved at Clara.

'Oh, doesn't it all look lovely!'

There were crowds of people queuing at the stall in front of Clara's cottage, the line snaking and bunched, contentedly unruly, chuntering with gossip and laughter. Toffee apples on sticks, jars of jams and marmalades, chutneys and pickles, bright in their red-and-white checked cloth caps. Alice, Clara's youngest child, went up and down the row with a tray, so that people could try things, the greedy boys taking more than they should. Sarah, her eldest, took money and passed out the sweet apples, punnets of fudge and slabs of pound cake. The boys eyed Sarah from behind the ledges of their bread.

'Hello, you two!' shouted Clara. She called back to the

house as she whipped off her pinny.

'Your turn, love! I'm going for a wander with our Leone and Enriqueta.'

Flanked by two popular public houses, the Horse and Jockey and the Bowling Green, the green was a meeting place for all local people. The grass was soft, the trees and bushes tender, offering cover under dark for couples of all kinds. In between the two pubs were smaller beer houses – shop fronts which served ale from the keg to swig at home or for the men that grew impatient at the busy bars. All establishments, big and small, tabled or humble, were struggling under the weight of customers. Men pulled at their hipflasks while they stood in line, the young and the bold kissing their girls while dribbling whisky through open lips, holding them tight and hooting to the sounds of the bands.

Entertainers of every kind were vying for attention and coins. Stilt walkers strolled slowly and majestically, teetering over children and frightening the toddlers, their beards twisted with beads. Fire eaters, hemmed in by crowds, spun their torches into the air, before slipping them down their throats. Jugglers and paint spinners, foreign and daubed with red, threw their props high into the yawning night sky. Seamlessly and simultaneously, they winked at the ladies and yelled across heads to each other in tongues that made the local women's eyes spin with desire. A diminutive old man, his face painted chalk white and in a suit of scarlet, directed a dog in a golden ruff to jump through a hoop and walk in circles on his tiny hind legs.

Leone and Clara knew all the local traders, and it was one of them, Mary Wilton, who called the three of them over.

'Here you are, ladies. This will warm you up!'

Mary poured cups of amber cider, and news slid back and forth as quickly as it was sipped. Leone, bright in a citrine weekend dress, laughed in the gold of the lanterns. Away from the hall, the company of women relieved the tedium of usual days, hot stoves and cooling cakes. By the third cup, Mary recalled every local birth, death and marriage that had occurred of late, and more besides.

The Horse and Jockey was often used to host inquests and trials, and Mary was well informed of any nefarious news. Violent skirmishes, bitter divorces, surprising convictions, infanticides, men publicly shamed for dalliances with the wives of their brothers. Mary's eyes rolled as she nudged the women, cocking a brow towards a portly young man as he ambled past.

'See him. One of the Farmer Higginbotham's lads. Him and the other carters went to collect dung in town, ended up drinking at the Bishop Blaize while a bear bait was on, and left the pile by the road in Salford. Well, it's him that in the dung now – he is to be tried next week, alongside the landlord of the Blaize. A right to-do.'

Mary poured more of her cider, pressing them to chink their glasses.

'Your good health, all'

She turned to Enriqueta.

'Look me in the eye. Show me you lovely face, Enri.'

Ribbons of young women and batches of young men circled the green and each other. The girls' faces gleamed against the flames, the firelight licking and lighting their youth, giggling and moving together, arm in arm. The young men stared and strutted, with the confidence and swagger of their ages. Though she was not much older than them, Enriqueta felt remarkably apart from them in every way. Observing the easy confidence that emanated from them all, and the long looks that shot between them, punctuated by shouts and jokes, there was a heavy envy within her. It had been a long time since she had felt truly young and carefree. She yearned for the white streets of Paris, while all around her was verdant, English, green.

One of the groups of young men stopped by them, their leader doffing his cap to Leone and Clara.

'Mrs O'Hara, Mrs Beswick, Mrs Wilton, good evening.'

He stood a pace in front of the other lads, who hovered, kicking dust, their noses in their cups. James Holt made children of them all. He had a dark lick of hair, and his face was far away from his peers, with cheeks cut from a finer mould. His eyes moved from Clara and Leone, sliding over Enriqueta.

'Hello, James, have you seen our Will about?'

Clara clinked her cup with his.

There was a snigger from one of the boys behind him, and James silenced him with a glare.

'Not lately, Mrs Beswick. I'm sure he'll come back for the dancing though. I'll fetch him for you as soon as we see him.'

'You're a good boy, James Holt. I just want him to do a bit on the stalls so that the girls can be free for a dance.'

James gave her a dazzling smile, his teeth white and even.

'And will you be dancing, miss?'

Dancing. The word skipped in Enriqueta, greeting the cider that bloomed in her breast. How she loved to dance. Torches spun around them. Sugar, burned cedar and gunpowder laced the thin fog of fire smoke. The cider rose in her, touching her tongue.

'Yes, I think I will.'

James Holt nodded to her directly and Enriqueta felt the jolt of impulse, like a scorned sister, flood her body. Holt backed away from the women, his group trailing behind him, scruffy children at the coattails of a soldier.

'I know that lot – my Will may be up to no good somewhere with some young lass. I hope they all keep themselves tidy. Last thing I need at my age is a baby back in the crib.'

Leone threw a laugh into the air.

'Oh, give over, Clara. We were the same at their age. It's natural. They aren't bad lads.'

Musicians and acting troupes moved around the green, caps in hand. Fiddlers, in turquoise silk and emerald velvet bounced through packs of tipsy farmers, red faced and jovial. One of them was held aloft, bucking on muscled shoulders: John of the Harvest. All around Enriqueta, laughter sprang, song swaying in places. With a sudden scraping and the thump of shifting furniture, the landlord of the Horse and Jockey began to clear the space in front of the pub for the dancing. His practiced whistle shot through the circle of his fingers like a line across the green, and men came to heave the tables and chairs under the eaves. The brass band and fiddlers assembled, colliding against each other to find spaces for their elbows and their instruments.

'Let's have another drink for courage', said Leone, the thump of the drum and euphonium pounding through the floor to their feet. The vibration that shimmered through Enriqueta was so evocative that she was cast back to the dances at La Castilla. The two settings were wildly apart. Here, the ground beneath her feet was damp and fertile, grass and mud churned by the crowds. At La Castilla, the floors were glassy with polish, clicking at her satin heels. There, the Blue Room ceiling had sparkled with diamanté swags, and silvered netting.

On Chorlton Green, it was the stars that glinted above her, peeping through the rolling autumn night skies, sometimes obscured by the drifts of bonfire smoke and sputtering lanterns. Here, the green was populated by ordinary working men and women, not the bloated, privileged Lyonnaise. Granted, some here were wealthier than others, and had finer dress and manners. There were also the labourers that striked, silencing the machinery of the city of Manchester just as industry took hold, halting looms and rioting, the frenetic energy of the French Revolution still giving them ideas of power. Peterloo cast a long shadow, where twenty people had been slain so easily, next to hundreds more who were irreparably injured. Thomas Walker, who had stood in the grounds of Longford before John, had roared at the injustice of slavery, of the rampant discrimination against Catholics and Jews, and of the 'Christian wickedness' that bloodied hands and money. Walker and Paine, Priestly and Clarkson pushed and bellowed for repeal as Manchester rose, at the forefront of righteousness and reform.

Yet they were all joined by common things. The place, the land, the produce; being together and seeing the same good people on the same good days. At La Castilla, the parties served as a magnet for the rich, cynical, shallow and greedy. Chorlton-cum-Hardy was riven with a seam of goodness, fathered by the city of Manchester. Recognition and a community that gathered for every high day and holiday, funeral and sickness, the surprise of an unexpected birth, and the bleak planning after a death. The joy of children, and small things. A population that was unified in feasting, drinking, dancing and song, tiding a neighbour's grief with care; only waiting for the next celebration, or chance to cook a pig. People that cared for each other's children as if they were their own. The village was knitted with old blood and the new faiths of friendship and marriages across the farms and fields.

The dance floor began to fill, and Enriqueta watched with a bystander's fascination. Her eyes roamed, and then suddenly, from the far side of the Horse and Jockey, James Holt strode slowly into view. The moon greeted his conviction, whitening his skin, turning it alabaster, his black hair jet and long over his forehead. Even his clothes hung on him differently to his peers; a jacket slung over a shoulder, his white shirt unbuttoned against his chest. He walked with the easy assurance of a man so thoroughly and finely built that all the girls swung their eyes toward him as he passed. Enriqueta's eyes betrayed her as she looked at him too, at his fingers, long and pale against the blue scarf at his neck. Heat burst in her like a curse, as she remembered the press of fingers that weren't her own.

The music was loud, and the crowd in front of the pub jumped in jigs and reels, laughter and whoops of filling the night air. Clara and Leone strolled away to the stalls selling sausages cooked over coals, and geese turning bronze on the spit. Enriqueta had no hunger, the damp smell of chips and vinegar sharp around her.

She fought to take her eyes from him as he moved through the crowds. Men parted to greet him, pulling him in with generous shouts and handshakes that spoke of admiration and envy. Elevated, standing among but apart, the blue of his scarf shocking her over the throng of the horde. The younger girls marvelled at him, blinking as though he were made of starlight too fierce to linger upon. The older ones spoke to him, and Enriqueta's ribs tightened unpleasantly as she saw one of them move her face towards his, whispering a joke while she spun a lock of hair over her parted lips.

Enriqueta turned away, and when she looked again, he was emerging from the crowd, pulling Sarah Beswick firmly behind him. Was it loss that she felt, there, so crudely inside her? Sarah and James stood face to face, their eyes casting about each other as they spoke. Enriqueta's heart ached, and she didn't know what to do with the pain that was taking all her thoughts back to Armand. The ecstasies of his despicable cabin, when she had been free to ask for what she wanted, and to do all he wished. As her nails whitened her palms, her sadness was melded to the bold fury of abandonment, her hands springing from their fists to take the cider pitcher and refill her cup.

Enriqueta saw that he had Sarah Beswick in his arms. The young girl span, her amber curls fanning out around her. She had the same look on her face as her sister had, a vision of pleasure, her face flushed and her eyes glimmering. Her body was supple in the circle of his arms.

The band shifted into a polka, and Enriqueta's heart responded. She lowered her eyes, her face hot with the memory and shame of being in Armand's embrace. A shadow fell across her, blocking the cast of the moon.

'Miss Tennant, isn't it? Will you dance with me, then?'

Etched black against the orange of the fires, James held his hand out to her, taking her cup from her and wrapping his long fingers around her wrist.

She had never been held so closely while dancing. The pressure of his chest was stiff against her, the scents of the night moving as they turned: apple and cinnamon, hot wine and warm bodies liberally doused in cologne. The torches and fires threw sparks; giddy bursts of gilded fairies. The melodies of the fiddlers and the saxhorns crooned on the green. Briefly, she was in her Havana childhood again, where nighttime, dance, fire and every kind of sorcery were integral to her world.

When first song segued into the next, James didn't let her go as she had expected, but pulled her closer and put his lips to her ear. She felt his breath, sweet with wine, as he whispered, and an appetite, which had been lost to her for so long, emerged for the very thing that she had run so far from.

LONGFORD, 1871

The wistful, wintery call of a robin and his mate floated over Longford's dawn. Speaking to each other, silvery and yearning from tree to tree. The dancing had left a legacy of aches in Enriqueta's limbs.

She had danced with James from the moment his hand had taken hers to when, some hours later, Leone slid to her, saying Peter was there to take them home. The music of the band echoed in her, and she could conjure the weight of James Holt's arms around her. The drizzle of dawn seemed to insist it had never happened. Disappointment sunk over her when she realised that, for now, all excitement was spent. After hiding from adventure for so long, the taste of it was nectar. There was much work to be done in the library, and her duties with Martha remained the same as they did yesterday, and the same as they would be tomorrow. Not every day could not be made up of dances. Air that was rich in shavings of gold and evenings surging with music were not for the likes of her.

But every morning when she awoke she hoped that today would be the day; she listened for every sound, gave sudden starts, was surprised when nothing happened.

Washing and dressing, she shook her frock and the sad thoughts from her mind, padding at her pockets for her keys. It was a small bunch, but it included the keys for all the glass-houses that she visited with Martha.

Searching her skirts and jacket, scouring her table, her desk, and her pockets; they were nowhere. On the floor, under the bed. She looked in the same places again, panic flashing every time she threw the chaise cushions back.

'Peter, I can't find my keys anywhere. Please can we look in the carriage? They may have fallen out of my pocket there last night. Oh, I can't have lost them!'

The red oak was proud, shrouded in the silent haze of the fog. The two of them stepped out into the wet of the autumn morning, the mist rolling across the vast plain of the estate. Enriqueta shivered in her red shawl as Peter delved around the cab.

'Not there, I'm afraid. Come on let's get inside for some tea. You'll freeze out here.'

Tears bit at her throat. All her dancing and carousing was idiocy, and the punishment was fair.

'Oh my, Enriqueta. Please don't upset yourself. These things happen. We have other keys. There was nothing on them to say they belonged to Longford, was there?'

The teacup shook in her hands.

'I'm sure the whole district is littered with keys buried deep through the ages dropped from pockets and bags and distracted hands, Enri.'

'There was no address or name on them but there was a ring attached with my initials on it – a parting gift from Jules and Maddy in Lyon. Someone could identify the house from my name!'

'I'm sure that wouldn't happen. And in any case, we should find the keys to get your gift back – doubtless it's very precious to you. I have meetings this morning but I won't finish too late, so I can ride down to the green before it is dark and have a look then.'

Enriqueta started to catalogue the Rylands Old Testament

tracts. The voice of the first incarnation of God, fearsome and burning with judgement, boomed at her from the pages of Proverbs.

Can a man take fire to his bosom
And his clothes not be burned?

The windows of the library on one side made a clear length against the sweep of the drive. Enriqueta looked out to it, on and off, all day, without reason. She picked up books and put them down.

'You will wear your shoe leather out with all that pacing. Come and have a minute with me in the parlour. Bridget has made cake. I know you weren't sure about coming last night, but I think it did you good.'

Leone poured yet more tea.

'And the way you dance; I think if Peter hadn't come along to spoil the fun, James Holt would have kept you dancing all night!'

'It seems like it was long ago now, Leone. Time passes too fast.'

'It does when you are having fun. You can see why he is the talk of the town, can't you. Such a handsome, charming lad. He seemed to be sweet on you, that's for certain.'

Tynan craned his neck round the door, and spying the cakes, crammed a whole one into his mouth.

'Did you want something lad, or just come to nick our elevenses? Women's talk in here – not for you, cloth ears.'

'Sorry, Ma. Someone here for Miss Tennant. Shall I bring him through?'

'Hang about, Tynan. We aren't expecting anyone. We're busy – who?'

Tynan wiped the crumbs away.

'James Holt, Ma.'

Hot pins of nerves pricked Enriqueta, the centre of her

falling to liquid.

'Speak of the devil! Yes, bring him in.'

James wore an emerald-green scarf, bright against the sable drop of his hair. Last night was long gone, the magic of darkness when Enriqueta had been careless and unabashed, so far removed from where she stood on the hard tiles of the parlour. She hated her cotton dress and glare of the sun, making a theatre of her every imperfection. Leone spoke for her.

'James! How lovely to see you. What can we do for you?'

The slow smile that had played upon his lips while they were dancing last night spread over his face. He took Enriqueta's little bunch of keys from his pocket, her silver initials safe in his fingers.

'I found them after you had left. On the ground where we had been dancing.'

We.

Their ground – the trampled grass that served them as they held each other, that had captured her keys in the closure of mud, that had bought him here in his scarf, delivering another whisper of promise.

'I wanted to come sooner. I knew you would be worried. It's been so busy in the village, clearing up after the festival. They needed my help. I couldn't get away to give them back to you before now. I cleaned them for you.'

He handed them back, taking her hand to place them in her palm. His hand on hers felt like a wonderful sort of damage.

'Such a very pretty ring. A gift, from someone who admires you very much, I imagine.'

'I'm grateful. Thank you for returning them,' Enriqueta said, before remembering Peter.

'Oh dear, Leone, Peter will be on his way to the green now to look for them!'

'Don't worry yourself, Miss Tennant. I'm sure I'll find him.

It's the Bowling Green he favours, is it not, Leone?' James said.

Leone laughed.

'Can I get you anything before you go, James? Have some cake, here, before young hollow-legs gets to them again.'

'A glass of water, Mrs O'Hara, please.'

Leone bustled off to the kitchen, and the door creaked shut like a secret.

'I enjoyed dancing with you very much, Enriqueta.'

His voice was low, nearly a whisper.

'I have thought of nothing else.'

His eyes looked directly into hers, and Enriqueta felt she was being embraced again. She could feel her herself shaking.

'Leone's lad Tynan knows where I live. And I visit Will Beswick often.'

James trailed his finger down her arm.

'Can I ask you something, Enriqueta?' He held her face, his hand round at her cheek. 'You're not in love with the old man, are you? I can tell you, I could keep you better than he does. I have plenty of money. We are old Chorlton. Old Manchester. Come out with me again. You are wasted here on dust and books and good works. Do you not get bored?'

Leone returned with his water. He drank it in one go.

'I hope to see you again in the village soon, Enriqueta.'

She clasped her keys so forcefully that as he left and she opened her hand, she saw her own initials branded onto the flesh of her palm.

LONGFORD, NOVEMBER 1871

WINTER SETTLED UPON MANCHESTER in all its familiar
damp, misting the buildings grey and leaving the streets
constantly, blackly, wet. October's gusts had seen off the last of
the leaves, and the trees on the estate sketched their branches
onto the freezing fawn of mornings. The gardeners cleared the
grounds for winter—the interminably longest season, some
years reaching well into March. The market gardeners of south
Manchester grumbled, watching their Jerusalem artichokes
drown and their pigs grow too bad tempered to mate.

There was little to see in the grounds, and even the glasshouses lost their appeal to Martha and Enriqueta, their walks
thankless, sunless and dank. Rain and rain, bulging the rivers
of the district, flooding Hedge Lane where the Rough Leech
Gutter flowed down Acres Lane, filling Blomley's fishpond
and making a mess of the milking sheds at Clough Farm. Ged
Tolan despaired when his irrigation systems appeared not to
be as robust as he had hoped. He prowled around the gardens,
muttering darkly, leaning on hoes and barking at children. The
countless brooks and streams that underpinned the district
rose, rustling their waters over all they could reach and spewing
silver fish across Oswald Fields, where they flapped until the
woman whose gardens lined the stretch took a spade to them
to relieve them of their struggles.

'Where is he? Where is John?'

Martha picked at the tangerines Leone bought her, spitting out the pith. The lamps in the parlour were lit, though it was not yet midday.

The whole household felt his absence and was much altered and adrift without him. John was rarely gone for this long, and though Peter made a fine second in command, he could never impart the calm authority so well possessed by John. Decisions had to be made, documents signed, funds cleared; most of this executed in isolation, without the inviolable direction of John. When he wasn't out at meetings, Peter was in constant occupation of the office at the house, working there until the early hours of the morning. As she passed the room to retire to bed, Enriqueta would see him at the desk, eyes red with fatigue, his shoulders stiff with responsibility.

Life in the cottages and out on the land was awry without the familiar figure of John, his sturdy brown work boots pulled over his black suit, striding to greet them all, knowing the children by name, and charming the dogs with treats from his deep pockets.

There was no one to discuss her progress in the library, her ideas and learning. Enriqueta was lonely without him. While he had been away, she had come up with thoughts and plans that she longed to share with someone – yet he was the only person who would understand and encourage her. The only one she wanted to impress. She shone under the light of his praise and without it her world was dull.

It was good news that amidst all the drudgery and plodding darkness of early winter, there was talk of another event in Chorlton.

'We are going, aren't we, Ma?' implored Tynan.

'Will says the bonfire is huge this year and that there will be more fireworks than ever. And we are old enough to join the parade now, too.'

Leone raised her eyebrows.

'You can't go on your own, Ty, but we can all go together. That includes you too, Enri. Your first Guy Fawkes Night!'

Enriqueta could hardly pretend reluctance after her dancing at the Harvest Festival.

'No arguments, Enriqueta. We will look after you, and we will have a grand old time!'

Leone sorted through old costumes and masks for them all to wear, explaining to Enriqueta the bonfire, the procession, the costumes, the fireworks, and Guy Fawkes himself, and the effigies that the villagers made in his infamous memory. Enriqueta had not been in the village since October, and the last she had seen of James Holt was when he had pressed her keys to her hand. She fluttered like a bird, wound tight with anticipation, thinking of the crowds again, and the danger of darkness, and of a man who had made it clear that she was a thing he wanted.

Back from the village, Leone would mention with a wink and a smile that James had asked after her or had questioned when she might next be on the green. Enriqueta grew warm at their teasing; Holt was too young for her, too handsome, too profligate, and after Foncé, she would not put her heart in harm's way again. Yet every time she heard Holt's name, or facts were scattered about him like careless diamonds, she crumpled with expectation.

Leone insisted on tradition; that they all dressed up for the occasion. One of Peter's uncles had been a mariner, and Peter looked magnificent in the ancient merchant seaman's uniform. Tynan dressed as a pirate. For Enriqueta, Bridget and herself, Leone took out some fancy Spanish skirts and shawls that she had made years ago, along with jewelled masks and earrings.

They bundled themselves into the coach, squeezed up against the Guy that Tynan and Bridget had spent days making, stuffing it with straw and old newspapers until it was fat. Ged trotted them at a lively pace down Hedge Lane, the houses lit with coloured Chinese lanterns, and Guys lolling mad eyed on doorsteps and at windowsills.

Turn Moss was already heaving with people, packed together like dolls in a box, waiting on the blast of the trumpet to start the procession. Disguised as masquerade characters, there were clowns, jockeys, courtiers, tarts, Bedouins and Titanias. The women and girls, swagged and ribboned, glinted and flitted in the torchlight. Through the air, thick with smoke and noise, came the loud rumble of drums and then the peeling of trumpets from the firemen at the front. It was flanked all along by the burliest of the village men, Viking stock, and also the squat faced squad of the Anglo Saxons. Flaming tar barrels were passed back down the edges over their heads, and Enriqueta saw they came over her, the acrid smoke billowing, burning her eyes.

The Horse and Jockey, the Bowling Green and the Traveller's Rest sagged with flags, bunting and lanterns. The steady boom of the drums at the front guided them onto The Row, and towards Hardy Meadows, where the bonfire stood waiting, unlit. It towered dangerously, touching the sky.

Torches and stakes driven into the stiff, ancient mud of the meadow, circled it in a band of gold. Village marshals, sashed and serious, wandered around the site, making the lantern fires contained, sure that no naughty children or inebriated youths could sneak through the chains. These were famously hazardous nights, and after many terrible accidents, the local wardens, councillors and constabulary had shouted over each other for hours until hard rules had been made and new bylaws scratched into heavy books.

Children swarmed to the warmth of the baked potato men's tin carts, and rows of tipsy men hung outside Jeremiah

Brundrett's shop at Lane End, where is smiling wife Elisha flipped bacon into bread rolls, making her sandwiches famous as only the generous can.

'Parkin! Treacle toffee! Gingerbread men!' shouted from beneath the stallholders' caps, the loudest coming from Clara, her voice high and clear above the men. Her mulled wine was renowned for its strength and sweetness. Thick and burgundy, it was spiced with cloves, dried orange and nutmeg.

A collective roar heralded the arrival of 'the bonfire boys', who flung the flaming tar barrels, grown too perilously hot to hold, into the base. The fires were the pride of each village, competing with one another year on year as to who could build the highest and grandest of all. The townships of Chorlton, Hardy and Martledge were particularly celebratory as they had won in the locality, as judged by the Mayor of Manchester the day before. The pitches were fiercely protected on the days and weeks leading up to the fifth of November, as years gone by had seen brigands and troublemakers from rival villages (invariably, Didsbury) set fire to the pile. The vicar at St Clements had sworn he had seen them dance naked in front of the flames, and proclaimed that they were surely disciples of the Devil.

The tar barrels exploded when they hit the tinder base of the bonfire, which had been judiciously laced with sinfully flammable liquids. The crowds groaned in pleasure and the trumpets blasted, the flames climbing and licking quickly up the stack. As the heat of the flames reached out, Enriqueta turned her face away.

When she did, the flames ebbed out and in, and she saw James Holt. Disguised though he was, in an ebony cloak and black mask, he was unmistakable to her. The gleam of the scarf around his throat was pearl in the darkness, and Enriqueta swayed with the swing of the fire. She saw his hand go to the shoulder of the girl who stood before him. She should have turned away then, but she didn't, and he raised his head at that moment, looking straight at her through the throng. He withdrew his hand from the girl; said something brief, and without looking back, he strode towards Enriqueta, with eyes as certain and sure and black as the night around her.

'Ah, James! Always a pleasure to see you, son!'

Peter shook his hand and Leone kissed his cheek.

Looking to her feet, Enriqueta felt him come close beside her, his hard arm brushing against her shoulder, a whisper of danger and a warning that again, she was standing near to something perilous. He hardly needed to turn at all, picking her hand up from where it rested at her waist, his fingers brushing her skirt as he did.

'Miss Tennant. I am so pleased to see you again.'

She felt like wax; unmovable wax, and he held her hand just a moment longer than he should have, breaking spells and making spells with gestures so slight she thought she was slipping from lucidity.

'Peter! Your women need more wine. Follow me.'

The night sky cracked with a rainbow of explosions; one after the other they bloomed and receded against the blackness, leaving imprints. The air hung over Hardy Meadows in pagan ghosts, ripe with gunpowder and smoke, perfume and wine. A lad ran past, and Leone laughed, because he looked so much like Tynan, but it wasn't him at all. It was another tall boy, disguised as they all were, running rings round the fire in their hats and their masks, their teeth stained grey with treacle.

Enriqueta strolled alone, edified that since the Harvest Festival, a few of the locals smiled and waved at her, stopping her to say hello. She bought another cup of mulled wine and a cone of something she had never had before. Cinder toffee. Putting it deep into her pocket, she tasted it as she walked around the field edge. Sweetly rough in her mouth.

Out of the black yew hedges, James Holt was by her, walking next to her, striding like velvet to her pace.

'You keep disappearing from me, Miss Tennant.'

His candour – there again, taking her voice away. She wished she could be bolder, lighter, less careful. She longed to be like the girls she saw him laugh with. Her mind ticked with the wind ruffling her scarf, and her hands and soul remembered with ferocity just exactly how she had been. In Lyon, so wildly in love, in a constant state of thirst for a man, and in a madness she could grasp again, happily.

'Do you not want to dance with me again?'

But if she had ever any playfulness in her, surely it was all gone now. She was a mouse, timid and quiet. As if reading her mind, he spoke quietly, lapping at her silence in the darkness.

'I know you are not as shy as you think you are. No one who is truly bashful could dance with me the way you did.'

The warm wine took hold in the cold night. They walked together towards the music and James coaxed her into conversation, making her laugh. While he never took his eyes off her, she knew that all eyes were upon him. Groups of girls strolled past, nudging and whispering, unabashed at looking him up and down, licks like tongues on ice cream.

Sarah Beswick called a greeting to him, her astonishingly plump lips sounding his name out like it was hers to give. Enriqueta felt matronly, foolish in her Spanish dress, in the shadow of Sarah's blue gown, which was scattered with silver stars. A pewter-coloured coronet sat on Sarah's loose, lustrous hair, glossy with the tincture of youth, flicking across the milk white of her face in the breeze. Yet while Enriqueta burned under the mocking gaze of the girls, James seemed not to notice them, or if he did, he was so accustomed to their attention as a usual part of the landscape of his life that he gave them no thought.

The rousing first chords of the polka struck and he drained

his cup. 'Drink up, Miss Tennant. Dance with me.'

Dance with me.

It was though there had been no days, no nights, no moments since last they had danced together. The floor was tight with revellers. Some of them, Enriqueta thought she recognised, but identities were blurred and confused by props, costumes and masks. The jewel-coloured dresses of the women turned as they swirled in the glow of the fire, and the eyes beneath the masks flashed in the gloaming. James's face was perilously close to hers, their masks nearly touching, his hand curled at her waist, a round arc. Once or twice other men stepped forward to request the next dance, but each time James spun her away, pressing her fast against him.

'I need a drink. Walk with me, Enriqueta.'

Vigour had made her thirsty, and she drank deeply, while his arms were taking her away from the crowds.

The coppice at the back of Hardy Meadows was in darkness, too far from the lamps and the fires, and the noise of the celebrations were distant, stifled by the shuffle of the wind in the ash trees, white army around them. James took his mask off, his eyes black and narrow, the moonlight a sheen against his skin. With one hand, he raised her mask from her face, and with the other he pulled her to him.

He was able to hold both her arms to her side and take her face in his other hand, keeping her still as he kissed her over and over. She struggled against him, and as he moved his lips over her neck.

'James, no! No!'

'It's worth the fight to hear my name on your lips. Say it again.'

Rage turned to strength as Enriqueta broke her arms free, pushing against the tree of his chest, a wall of wood under her hands. And as quickly as he had begun, he ceased.

'I'm sorry.'

He kissed her; his lips as light as mist on her skin.

'You taste of sugar.'

She hardly dared to move in case it stirred him again.

'Is there someone else, Enriqueta?'

She shook her head and his hold on her tightened.

'Still old Rylands on your mind? In your heart?'

Holt pushed his hands at her breast.

'But you still resist me.'

'You could have anyone you want, James. I am not the one.'

His fingers, that had been tender, pressed on her cheeks like a claw.

'You are. I have not thought of anything but you since first we met, and then we danced. I watch for you every day, on the chance you may come to the village. When I see the Longford horses come through, I pray it will be you. I ask about you. I look for you.'

She was molten, fire in her and fire around her. Where she had been solid wax, she was melting.

'I am not the one. I am not your one. I am not your one.'

His mouth was against her ear, his voice low and urgent, though there were none to hear him but her, and the whispering ash grove that enveloped them. Leaves, in their brittle drifts, cracked under her feet as she tried to step back from him.

'Don't listen to what they say about me! I am a good man. I could be faithful. You are what I need. All those others – they are feckless and fast. I need someone like you: steady and calm and kind. I need you, Enriqueta.'

She pulled herself away, a high wind whipping her hair that had come free in their struggle.

'No, James. I want more than that. I don't want to be needed.' She looked at him, his hard beauty gleaming in the moonlight, and she felt an overwhelming sorrow. 'I want to be loved.'

*   *   *

Enriqueta ran. The breeze gained strength and caught the words he shouted after her, whirling them into the air, so she couldn't hear them clearly at all, and by then she was further and further from him, her skirts in her hands and her boots slick with Hardy Meadow mud, running back towards the mouth of the fire.

Walking the grounds of Longford pale and defeated, Enriqueta cared little if she got cold or tired. Peace was in a parcel of someone else's possession. Leone recognised the despondency of heartache, and she saw it drawn on her dear friend's every movement. Enriqueta's resolve swung wildly. One moment, she was certain that her instincts about James were real, and valid, and right. The memory of Foncé loomed over her, persistently and insidiously informing her every decision. And how bitterly she regretted. Like James, he had claimed to have needed her, yet he had used her, in so many ways, most heinously.

She turned it all over in her head, and it tortured her. She was twenty-eight years old and had already thrown months of her life away to a man who cared nothing for her. Life was short and James Holt claimed he wanted her. There could be a marriage and children. She could be cared for and cosseted. She looked down at the books on the table. Piles and piles of them. Stories of language, adventure, maps. Trees, dances, dinners, farms. Kitchens. Spaces and parlours peopled by generations and lights blown out, allowing couples to reach for each other and make more.

Would her days be made of other people's stories, someone else's memories bound in leather and stacked beneath her ageing palms? Or should she take the hand of a handsome man and break the shackles of loneliness. How she envied those feckless girls James Holt had spoken of. Free of complication and angst. Free to love and kiss and throw themselves around with a lust for life and loving, unabashed and unfettered by guilt and sadness and confusion.

A soft knock patted at the door of the library. Enriqueta wiped her eyes and sat up straight. She could not bear for anyone to know the depths of her sadness. Leone sat down by her, a large brown box in her hands. She kissed Enriqueta.

'This could cheer you up, love. It's dinner time soon. If you want anything.'

Leone left her alone with the parcel. To see his inimitable fine, sloping hand, and his distinct coal grey ink, and her name and the Longford address. Postmarks and stamps thickly applied; the parcel magically safe on the library table before her, all the way from Italy. To see his handwriting – every slope and slip of his pen conjured a feeling of absurd fondness.

Opening the box, there was a letter and a heavy, square object wrapped in paper.

My dear Enriqueta,

It was with great sadness and concern that I heard of the events concerning my son John Garthwaite and his ill-judged visit to Longford Hall. Peter wrote to me at once. I understand that Peter has gone some way to explain to you the very difficult circumstances between me and my son.

I am truly sorry and that you had to endure such a terrible thing, and I hope that you can find it in your heart to forgive me for not predicting it, or preventing it. You are a cherished and important part of the Longford family, and I pray that the events of that dreadful evening will not make you rethink your position with us.

I had hoped to return to Manchester straight away. Regrettably, I am not yet able, but I can assure you that I am

*doing everything in my power to resolve the situation here.
Then, I will make the journey back to my business and the
estate with haste.*

*Until then, I have sent you a small token of my appreciation
and of my sincere apologies. I know we have spoken together
in the past of how fond you are of Italy, so while you cannot
be here to experience it as I am, I am sending a little of Italy
to you.*

Yours, most sincerely,
John Rylands

She read his letter over and over, nearly forgetting about the
gift. The writing box was made of veneered walnut, inlaid with
maple and ebony, and finished with brass fittings. Two crystal
ink bottles, and a fine, silver fountain pen. It was lined with
pink satin, and contained a sheaf of writing paper, an address
book embossed in gold and pencils of numerous weights. The
scent of the wood healed her, and for the first time in days, she
felt hunger. She stood to go and join her friends for dinner.

LONGFORD, CHRISTMAS 1871

TYNAN AND BRIDGET RAN THROUGH the ballroom. They trailed the paper chains in loops, racing across the floor. Christmas was coming to Longford.

Leone passed the last and largest star to Enriqueta. Two trees were delivered from the forests of Delamere – one for the ballroom and one for the entrance hall. Days before, Peter and Tynan had dragged boxes of decorations down from the attic, and the women had carefully unwrapped each one from its tissue paper. John had purchased them from all around the world: Krebsglas from Germany, Murano from Italy, Baccarat from France. Each one was unique, from blown golden stars to baubles the size of a fist, etched with snowy Alpine images. They glittered, next to the sliced oranges that the children dried by the fire, dotted with gold paint and hung from the tree with silver string. The house was full of the scent of the oranges and plum pudding. Martha had fed it with French brandy since the end of November.

Many of these customs were entirely new to Enriqueta. She sat each evening with Leone, looking through *Cassell's Family Magazine*, while Peter and Ged were sent out onto the Ees to drag back boughs of evergreen and ivy to swag over the mantles and staircases. The children tied them with gold brocade and pushed tissue flowers amongst the foliage. Father Christmas stopped in Chorlton-cum-Hardy, magnificent in his shiny black boots and crown of Holly, looking uncommonly similar to Thomas White, a former landlord of the Horse and Jockey and a good friend of Frank and Clara's. A huge box from L. W. Lyle, the stationers in Manchester arrived, full of Longford Christmas cards. This year, they were decorated with the Lancashire White Rose, curled with evergreen and robins. Enriqueta sat with Martha for hours as she wrote her name and John's at the bottom of each one. Her hand shuddered, their names skidding illegibly on the expensive cards like a waste.

On Christmas Eve, the candles lit the trees. The service at St Clement's had included carols, and Leone kissed Tynan under the mistletoe so vigorously that his hat fell into the fire.

'Let's play Snapdragon! Your father will be home soon, I promise.'

Leone snuffed out the lights and Bridget fetched the bowl of raisins. Martha poured over half a bottle of brandy and lit the bowl with a flourish of unsteady matches. Enriqueta went first, reaching amongst the little blue licks of fire. The room glinted, softly scented with the greenery and burned fruit. A family of geese, who had lived in the backyard of one of the Longford tenant houses, spat fat in the oven, and Leone worried that she should have peeled more potatoes.

'Are you starting Christmas without me?'

Enriqueta's fingers burned in the bowl on hearing John's voice, halting the hour and catapulting the children into his arms. Peter stood behind him, white with exhaustion and smiling. She watched it all, each person embracing John in turn. He was immaculate in his black suit, his thick hair swept back, no indication of miles travelled, or the sleeplessness of other countries. The round hollow of relief and joy at being near him again turned in her. She helped Leone with the plates for the table, picking up and putting down, using the hands that so desperately wanted to reach for him.

'Crackers- I forgot the crackers!'

Leone was pink with pleasure as Peter slid his knife over the first goose.

'Be a dear, Enri, can you get them? John will be back down in a moment and I want it all perfect for him. Oh, what a wonderful thing it is to have him back with us. Longford complete again.'

The crackers were still in the box by the porch. The hallway was silent, and all that sounded was the tick of John's grand-father clock. The candles on the tree nudged an amber glow against the tinsel and stars, that glimmered in the ebb of the shadows. She heard his tread on the stairs, and she shut her eyes to the bliss of his nearness.

'I didn't get a chance to greet you, Enriqueta.'

'And nor me, you, John'

The still of the Christmas tree, the flicker of the candles, the distant happy voices sat in the air between them. The blue of his eyes was dark.

'Thank you for my beautiful gift.'

He raised a hand, and withdrew it tightly to his side.

'Everything I said, I meant. Truly. When I received Peter's letter, I was mad with worry. I convinced myself that you would quit here. Leave us. Leave me.'

Enriqueta felt a surge of tears, shaking her head.

'Enriqueta?'

John's voice, deep and isolated in the empty hall rang starkly with her name.

Enriqueta?

How many times had she heard her name whispered urgently from thankless men. All she wanted was a very simple love – she hadn't asked for or needed or prayed for the pink whispers of romance or the grim compulsion of loveless grappling. She hadn't invoked mystery or deception or mean hands in the dark, or the attacks; rather, she dreamed of love in the cradle of a marriage, a warm bed and the body of a man she could adore. She wanted children to raise, and hold, as precious and small as gold coins. Something like a thin future fluttered always in her imagination – where there was a baby, faint in her mind, and a husband, a ghost of a dream by her side. But the man before her was already a husband, and belonged to someone else.

'Come, Enri. Leone will be wondering where her crackers are.'

John sat at the top of the table, Martha at his side. She whispered into his ear, rousing herself to pull the crackers with the children over the plum pudding, blazing blue in the darkness. Enriqueta wondered where James was. Probably basking in the adoration of a young beauty, letting his fast charm and Holt wealth seduce her and make a misery of her. Enriqueta knew that the hearts he had broken were piled high throughout Manchester, discarded and burned like spent fireworks.

John stood to toast them all, pouring the children a small glass of Madeira.

'Happy Christmas! Peace and joy to all of us.'

John held his wife's hand, and his eyes met Enriqueta's, and she felt a terrible hopelessness hover between them. When the doorbell rang, it was shrill, making Martha jump. Her glass of sherry toppled.

'Who could that be?'

'I'll go, Leone.'

John stood.

The carol singers that had huddled on the hall steps most evenings last week would be with their own families now, round the fires of Urmston, Chorlton and Whalley Range, pleased to have a brandy in their palms in place of the church charity bowl. The delivery men had sent the final boxes and parcels with their boys the previous evening. The vintners and brewers had come to fill the cellars with seasonal bottles at the beginning of December, and were snoozing in front of their lavish hearths, or mauling their cheerful wives with the joy of the season, full of black pudding and Manchester rum. The thrumming at the door was the thud of bad news.

John's harrowing cry fired like a shot from the hallway. Peter pushed his chair back with such force that it fell, and the fat around the goose stuck on the plates. He ran to John, pulling him from the floor and cradling him in his arms. There was nothing so bleak as seeing someone so ordinarily fearless weep like a child. His halls and his charities, his churches and his millions, his land in Germany, and France, and his parquet floors in Italy crumbled like the sandstone of the brickworks, wet and useless in his grief.

John Garthwaite was found dead in an opium house in Hulme, a few short miles away from Longford. Such was the high regard held for John Rylands in the criminal underworld, the shiftless, despicable baron who presided over much of the drug trade in Manchester had delivered the news himself. It was his own pallid, pocked fist that had struck hard on the hall door and pulled at the bell.

John sat in his office and cried on and off until daybreak for his son, only yesterday a babe in his arms. John had been a tender, devoted father to all his little ones, and the pain of their untimely deaths, so many in infancy and now John Garthwaite in wasted adulthood, bore down on him with indescribable agony. It was no surprise to him that Martha had retired almost immediately once given the news, unmoved by his passing. John saw Dinah by his side, and his beautiful, golden baby boy held close to his chest, safe and impervious to all peril.

ANGEL MEADOW, JANUARY 1872

THERE WAS NO COMFORT in morning, as there was no sun. John trudged through the estate, and his workers worried. The dogs ran to him, blinking and nudging him for biscuits. The children pulled at him for stories and hung on his neck, nesting into his shoulders, offering ways out of grief.

John had always taken the days after Christmas as a brief holiday. This year, he was already worn from travel, and the sudden death of his son had brought the deep exhaustion of loss. Pain turned to anger, which fired an impetus for industry. He woke one cold morning with his mind fortuitously clear, and entirely fixated on work.

But charity precluded business, and John knew that the vicious month of January was the worst for the poorest of Manchester. After enduring a pitiful, hungry Christmas, the coldest weeks came, with the most inadequate housing, food or clothing. John spent the early days of each year going from house to house, collecting the toys, clothes, bedding and kitchen things that people no longer needed or wanted. His tenants were not rich, but they were generous, giving their things freely and with good hearts. Beyond the estate, he visited the truly wealthy of the locality, and the Longford outhouses and sheds filled with old saucepans and bedding, faded rugs and the linen of dead grandmothers.

The wagons were loaded. John's head ached; his weak

resolve straining the sinews of his body and the will of his spirits. Wood Street loomed over him like a threat. He missed Caroline with a raging despair. His wretched heart pounded at the thought of her opening a door to him, cheeks flushed by her heat, her hair palmed in his hand, her body rising against his. He thought of Martha, his wife so undone, so changed, more in need of his loyalty than ever. He tortured himself with his guilt, not even daring to open the cupboard of the hot memories he had.

'Would you come with me today, Enriqueta?'

The idea was madness. She would provide some kind of guardianship for him. With her there, there would be no chance of him doing something, in a moment. What purer person could there be to be with him at Angel Meadow. With Enriqueta by his side, he could not run to find Caroline, or question people to seek her out; find out where she had fled to.

And if he found her, he would not be able to drag Caroline urgently back to her Ancoats house, with the fire burning and the brandy taken as they could and would be reunited in her worn, white bed. The coverlet – scented with faded lavender and patterned with violet checks – billowed through his mind. He closed the image with a brisk and painful blink. She had bought it with her very little money. It agonised him to think of all Caroline had given him – a wealthy man. Even in her bed, with her past and her present, she spent what she could ill afford on an eiderdown to cover them both, and to assuage her shame at her status. She had loved him.

'Of course, John. Where are we going?'

'I need to go to Angel Meadow.'

Enriqueta had heard of it – a place entirely defined by all it lacked. Poverty made fast work of its people, who lived short and ugly lives. Something of what she was thinking must have shown on her face, because John's expression changed.

'You should stay behind, after all. Attacks happen. I can't risk anything more. I can't risk you, Enriqueta.

The fabric of his jacket under his hand reminded her of Paris.

'Let me come, John.'

He shook his head.

'Another time maybe. When Ged is free to come with us.'

'Please. You don't need to father me. I can come and help.'

He recognised in Enriqueta his own brand of obstinance. John's eyes were sore with lack of rest. It was labour to clear Caroline from his heart, and he had worked harder, travelled longer, devoted more time to the things he believed to be good: God, learning, his business, his home. The effort he expended into being a better person and quashing his demons left him depleted.

The clouds broke, and the sun dazzled him when he took Enriqueta's hand to help her into the carriage, her fingers firm on his nerves. The sun's rays shifted and lit her face, rosy in the cold. Her lips were full against the pale fur of her borrowed jacket. While the horses stamped against the cold ground, Enriqueta's eyes fluttered. He lingered too long looking at her, unusually flustered before his animals, their reigns dropping from his hands. Steering the carriage out onto Hedge Lane up towards the Chester Road, then Deansgate and into town, the clatter of the horses' hooves was welcome in the silent space where he had so sorely meant conversation to be.

'Angel Meadow was once a wealthy place. It was built for merchants and people of means. The houses were mansions, with gardens and orchards and views over the Irk, which was clear and full of fish and eels which were the best in the land. The Lord of the Manor, Oswald Mosley built mills and bakeries. He had one of the best wine cellars in the city and Style Street and Old Mount Street were famed for their elegance. Unimaginable, now. Heaven inverted to hell.'

John pulled the horses to a trot, sweat steaming from their spines. He allowed himself to steal quick glances of her, silhouetted against the string of red-brick houses that ran in a streak along the Chester Road. The sun was risen, an orange disc, casting a blush of gold onto the heart of her face. Her dark complexion was flushed by the wind, and with the fur framing her, she became an ice princess from a storybook.

'Look at you; I feel like I should hide you from them all.'

In truth, what he really wanted to do was reach into the fur of her hood and kiss her and show her what he was. What he could do to her to bring her happiness. The latent wanting for Caroline had blended with a sudden recognition of the beauty of the woman so near to him. She fascinated him, and he could hardly believe that she existed in his house, breathing the air that he took in, stepping over his tiles.

As his years passed, he was sure that he would outgrow his instincts. He hoped to leave his ungovernable passions in all their destruction and grip, in seasons behind him, but despite his age, they refused to ebb. He recognised the feeling, so sewn into him, of the danger and the exhilaration of seeing beauty, in all its small explosions and turns of phrase, and the shifting – a turn of a page – from the pleasantries of affection to uncontrollable desire. It had come in a moment. The horses panted; they needed water.

'The Irish came in for work, alighting at Victoria, and heading the Angel Meadows to find cheap boarding and a community. It wasn't a place built for so many. They are falling at a rate we can't keep up with. Children are dying, daily. The effluence from the Tanneries, the Dyeworks, the Tripeworks and the Breweries are swilled into the Irk, and the waters the people have to drink are fetid and diseased. It's rife with cholera, typhoid and influenza.' Soon it would be all laid out before her, and the miasma of decay would herald it before she saw it. It was the odour of desperate humanity; of bedsores and dead rats, suppuration and the rank fluids of disease.

John pulled the carriage to the loading doors of Wood Street, the streets clear because of the early hour. A couple of his men were outside, waiting with boxes. The foreman's arms were thick with the muscle under his shirt. Jacketless even in the chill, he thumbed at his braces as he stared at Enriqueta, chewing on his pipe with wet lips. Shards of irritation bit at John.

'Samuel, we are short of time. Load, will you please.'

The foreman pulled his eyes from Enriqueta and flexed his arms. John paced the paving, and rain began to spot it.

The carriage turned towards Victoria and people skittered through the streets and the weather. Rushing to work, or trudging home, their thoughts of sleep at odds with the white haze of the morning. And for a moment, through the trails of people wandering up to the square, John thought he saw her. There – her dark topknot bobbing, her bright shawl like a flower in the grey of the crowds. His eyes searched again, blinded by the low morning light – Caroline Castiglioni was gone. John's heart thrummed to the thump of the horse's hooves, and he quickened their pace with a brutal yank.

The stench of Angel Meadow rose before they had turned their final corner, a gust of rot and fetid, sour materials. Despite the stench, John saw that Enriqueta's face was smooth and placid. She didn't recoil or wince, or press him to turn back to their world of clocks and books and blue china plates. The horses slowed at the entrance to navigate the narrow paths, bustling with people and animals. It was stultifyingly overcrowded. Matchstick figures, gaunt and ravaged, lay slumped in the doorways of the public houses, grasping their drink to them. Enriqueta read the names-unfathomable to her- as they moved through. *The Exile of Erin, Tara's Hall, The Harp and Shamrock*.

'I try and resist complacency, Enriqueta, but you can see that despair runs through it.'

Some of the inhabitants raised their hands and heads to greet John, smiling to show blackened gums and broken teeth. All semblance of cleanliness was impossible without sufficient water, and every person was covered in grime, the children's faces black with ingrained dirt. Even the babes in arms, clutched to the thin bosoms of so many of the women, were silent scraps of nothing, swaddled in filthy rags, with none of the robust energy or disgruntled cries of well-fed, healthy infants.

'Laudanum. They call it 'Mother's Quietness' here. Every druggist has his own blend, and the stronger they make it the faster it sells. It keeps the children silent while their mother's work in the mills, and it distorts the poor creatures, swelling their skulls. They have no appetite, but for more of the drug as they are unable to cry out in hunger, many of them perish through malnutrition.'

Here and there, narrow pigs packed into pens nudged each other disconsolately, with hardly any space to move. As they passed the *Flea and Firkin*, the door thudded open, spewing out a tumble of drunks, tattooed men shoving against each other. The pub door swung shut, trapping a din of singing and swearing.

The pubs and the beer houses were nothing like the ones around Chorlton and Martledge, which were smart with shining paint, clean windows and barrels of flowers at their doors. There were no ruddy-faced landlords or plates of crisp pork ends to share on the bar, or people talking of politics and husbandry, kindly to each other's children and ordering sausages from the countless pork butchers for their next parties. Here, the public houses were as squalid and dishevelled as the one-up one-down lodgings that they flanked.

John navigated cautiously, with the experience and knowledge of a man who knew he was wealth amid poverty.

The Rylands carriage rocked as it passed through the alleys, hit by the inevitable missiles thrown back and forth amongst children, scuttlers and drunks. The vehicle was juddered and thumped, and John saw that Enriqueta's face was taut, and her knuckles held in paled fists on her lap. 'No one, no matter how brave, unshockable or experienced, could fail to be astounded by the wretchedness of Angel Meadow. Especially when you think of the riches in Manchester that flank it. Manchester's shameful, distasteful secret. Hold on to me, Enriqueta.'

Turning down one of the roads behind the Firkin, they drew near to a more open space. Gravestones jutted from the ground, some tipped into chaotic, makeshift pathways.

Children tried to play; bony little bodies attempting to hide and jump and make pathetic fun amongst the fallen stones. There were mounds of earth pitched all over, some of the boys at the top, playing King of the Castle. Beyond the cemetery stood Arkwright's Mill, that gave employment to the meadow, belching steam and the racket of looms, clattering into the air. The River Irk, bubbling like the Styx, crawled along, thick with slime and effluence.

'John! John!'

Daniel Hearne's voice rang clear and mellow, sweetness over hell. His arms were open to John as he came out of the nearby ragged school building. A fierce and magnanimous priest from Waterford, he considered it a good day in the meadows if there had only been six murders. He slept with a mahogany stick in his hand, and half an eye open.

Daniel Hearne oversaw much of the charitable efforts; a thankless, pitiable task, yet his supreme good nature and innate optimism kept him there, hoping and saving and having to endure death upon death. Beaten babies, ravaged children, murdered women, men kicked to death with such force that there was nothing left of their heads on their shoulders. It was daily, and nightly life to Daniel, and he was called on for every reason. Violence streaked through the place like poison, and crime throbbed like blood. There were fights and deaths every day, some between families, gangs, and scuttlers – professional fighters who provided the streets with cheap, tawdry and vicious entertainment, and lorded over their packs like Kings. They filled Manchester Royal Infirmary with their wounds, and they made an epidemic of their violence.

Daniel would be the one to attend the dying, or send for the medic. Often, the doctors and midwives never arrived, too afraid that their bags would be stolen, so it was left to Father Daniel to bless the blue babies, dress the gaping wound of the gang lord, tend to the last miserable breaths of a woman in labour, dying with a baby only half out of her skeletal body. More than once, he had been called to administer over women raped to death by the very men who had killed them, wringing out their laughable tears in their bloodied hands.

The luckiest children were those who were only hungry, infested with lice and crawling with ticks. The rest were damaged by birth or the fact that they were born of their own grandfathers – incest rife, and fuelled by cramped housing, opiates and drink. Daily, the dying lay ready for burial on the path outside the school. They were dumped there by family who could afford nothing but the waning energy they had to drag the corpses over the ruck of the pebbles and broken glass.

There were more than thirty thousand paupers' graves at Angel Meadow. The cemetery outside Daniel's school, which was so bulging with bodies, served as a hellish play place for children by day, but at night, it was stalked by grave robbers and thieves. They plundered it for the rich mulch it yielded and the bones of the dead, which they sold to the glue factories that were dotted all along the Irk.

Daniel spent hours he spent trying to educate the children

of the Meadow (and not least the hours he spent going from door to door, alley to alley, each day to gather them up), he was continually trying to form ambitious plans of how he could lift his people out of the dire poverty that kept them trapped until their miserable deaths. He dreamed of extending the Charter Street ragged school to accommodate more classrooms for adults as well as the children, and imagined a gymnasium, where the young men could compete in empowering their bodies, instead of brutal street battle.

'Good to see you, John. And to meet you, Miss Tennant.'

Daniel leant into John.

'You shouldn't hang around today. Jerome Caminada has been down with his new Constable. Fella called Stanilous Brierley. Poor sod-wet behind the ears- has no idea what he has coming. Anyway, they have word that there is going to be a ruckus later. He overheard it in one of the blood houses- Welsh's Court. Back of Victoria.'

'Do you know who it is?'

'Yes. The Bengal Tigers and the Meadows. The Meadows have Jemmy the Black fronting them now. They call him the Young Phenomenon. Champion of the Lightweights. It is a all over a dossy, of course. Charles Burn's girls, Eliza Leather and Kate McTighe. Jemmy had the both and the word is out.'

The two men took the boxes of books, blankets, clothes, toys and household things into the school while Enriqueta sat in the safety of the cab, horribly aware of the expense of her clothes and the blooming health of her person. A trail of children had noticed the fine Rylands carriage and gathered round it, knocking at the windows, and pulling at the doors. A little boy, his face blistered and distended at one side – a hand-sized bruise covering his cheek – was shoved to the front of the crowd. He was pressed to the carriage door, gasping for breath.

'Please! Children! Move back! You will get hurt!'

Louder, Enriqueta implored them as the boy began to whimper.

'Please! He will be crushed!'

Suddenly, a roar went up into the sky from one of the nearby alleys. Whistles and whoops and stamping feet all sounded at once, and the children clapped their hands in glee.

'Fight! Fight! Fight! Fight!'

They scattered, leaving the little boy slumped in the mud at the carriage door. He was so still, his eyes shut so tightly, for one terrible instant Enriqueta thought he had expired – the breath blown out of him by the rabble. He stirred.

'What is your name, little boy? Let me help you up.'

Aiden Walsh was rarely spoken to with quiet kindness. He had to strain to hear her. He wondered if she was a queen. He longed to touch the soft stuff around her neck. Tenderly, Enriqueta lifted him, feeling the sinews of his armpits like wire underneath his shirt. Even standing, Aiden was bent, one leg turned and crooked. There was something beneath him; a half-empty wooden box of stubby wax crayons, which must have fallen from one of the boxes.

'I'm waiting for Father Hearne and Mr Rylands to finish in the school, Aiden. Shall we see if we can draw on that piece of stone with these?'

Aiden crouched near her, drawing some careful shapes, choosing yellow and red. He circled it with the short black piece of wax, looking tearful as it snapped in his fingers.

'My mother and the others were burned by a fire. In our house.'

He bit hard at his lip, which were raw and speckled with dried blood. Most of the skin on his face and his hands were shiny with the healed blisters of a terrible burn.

'I need to get back. My uncle will come out looking for me.'

'It's a good thing you have your uncle to look after you now, Aiden.'

Aiden Walsh flinched.

'He's not my real uncle, miss.'

A rumble was building behind St Patrick's church. Aiden stood with the creaking difficulty of an elderly man. His bruise, over his burns, looked tender and new.

Enriqueta gathered up the crayon ends with their box.

'Take these home with you.'

Aiden made a noise, small and old in his throat.

'Thank you, miss. I can't. They'd beat me for them. Not worth it.'

Aiden hobbled away, hardly robust enough to carry the weight of his crayons and the tilt of his gait.

'Enriqueta, we need to go.'

'John, hurry yourself, I can hear them over Olive Street.'

A wall of howls and whistles slammed into the air. The Tigers trooped abreast, blocking the end of the road. They stamped in unison, their narrow, brass-tipped clogs clanging on the paves. Over their puncher's caps, they sliced at the air with knives, pokers and cutlasses, firing sling shots of sharpened bottle tops. Only fourteen or fifteen, they had the marks of manhood, with pipes dangling at their lips. Sunlight glinted rainbows on the sequins sewn in tracks down the sides of their flared sailor's trousers. Putty shops were a rich source of the scuttler garb, and the mariner's belts they bought, studded with brass, could be whipped off and used as munition.

'Look, John. The girls are coming in now. Jesus, we're in for a bad one here.'

The scuttler girls flocked in from a side lane like birds. They had a uniform too of black and grey shawls, short skirts, pink stockings and clogs. Their arms were etched with the names of the bad boys they loved, catalogued in rows, a narrative of tussles in the dark lanes behind Strangeways.

'Come on now, John, move yourself. Get yourself and your

lady gone. It's going to kick off. Move out, John, now. Turn left
and take the back way through Crown Street. It will be clear.
Go!'

The streets turned green and the air was sweet as the Rylands
carriage cantered out of the city back towards Stretford.

'I hope you know, Enriqueta; I make sure that none of my
employees, in any of the Rylands mills or any that I work with,
suffer situations such as those at Angel Meadow. I have inspectors that visiting the dwellings of every single one of my people.
If we find that they are inhabiting slum lodgings, we provide for
them and move them and their families.'

Enriqueta thought of money and men, and the luxury or
choosing to be good. There were orphans scattered about the
globe, and women heaving out children only to start again,
short minutes beneath a man yielding more months of work,
goodness leached from their bones.

'There are ruthless men who profit from misery. They claim
they are doing the city a great justice by locking the Irish
and the travellers and the poor born natives into the grind of
low-paid work and despicable conditions, saying that they are
keeping the workhouses clear. It is a shame on Manchester and
a disgrace; something I strive to improve in my lifetime, even in
small ways.'

Aiden, the boy she knew that she would never see again,
stood in her mind's eye, unsteady on his bowed leg, his dear
face sore with burns and bruises inflicted in hatred by a man
who kept him as a toy to beat and abuse. Her heart ached for
him, and for all the little children everywhere who lived and
died in misery. She thought of Sainte Catherine, wanting to tell
John about it and to say how much she wanted to do something
– anything – to help.

The clouds above Chester Road raced, gunmetal grey. John
pushed the horses, the smell of their effort rising with the bitter

tang of threatening rain. The mere hint of the thought that he might have seen Caroline in town made him overwhelmingly saddened. His days of kissing and longing were over, and though there was a beautiful woman in Enriqueta as close to him as he could have wished for, he had made the promise to himself and to God, a Herculean effort, that he would live out the remainder of his days as the decent husband Martha was legally entitled to. The rain came, and John shouted at the horses to hasten. The puddles across Hedge Lane would fill quickly.

Manchester, February 1872

THE DAYS LOST TO UNMEMORABLE cold and bleached winter skies, John was in his office as he was out at meetings with Peter. He was home at the hall more than was usual; his office door kept shut for large parts of the days and evenings. Enriqueta found herself waiting for him to emerge. She stared at his office door, waiting for the clock to turn. She watched for him across the lawn in his boots, just as she listened to his tread on the hallway beside her bedroom at night. She rolled in her sheets in front of the moon, the cotton twisted and damp at her breast.

The winter had been gracious. There were a few days of heavy snowfall, which had kept all but the hardiest gardeners off the land. No one was ever idle; there were indoor jobs to be done, animals to care for, barns to sweep out. John oversaw it all, while balancing his business both home and abroad.

After a week of icy grounds and blank skies, there was a sudden, overnight thaw. The household woke to a blindingly sunny day. The lawn was spotted with pools of ivory snowdrops, and through the hedgerows and ditches poked the beginnings of golden celandine. The warmer wind caught the early perfume of the daphne, which in days would begin to show itself in shy violet, pink and lilac. Peter bought pots of cyclamen for Leone, and the narcissi bloomed under the red oak, in time for her birthday.

'We always go into Chorlton for get together with Clara and the family. A few friends. You will be coming too, Enri!'

They were about to leave, booted and wrapped in their hats and scarves, when John's door opened.

'I think, if you don't mind, I shall come with you all.'

It was nearly unheard of for John Rylands to take any sort of leisure time outside the house. And if he did, it was never so local or so pedestrian as a stroll into the village. He met his business friends at their homes, or in towns or restaurants, and he was often obliged to entertain while abroad, but Peter could not recall the last time John had walked into Chorlton, merely to enjoy himself.

'You'd be more than welcome, John, of course. We all need a bit of frivolity here and there. You and me and the lad could visit the Jockey for an ale or two while the ladies have their chat.'

Peter, pleased with his idea, locked the house.

Clara and Frank embraced John and pulled him into the cottage. John had paid for all three of their children have tutors every Saturday. On countless occasions, he had called for doctors to attend the family; when little Alice was perilously ill as an infant with scarlet fever, and when Sarah fell down the cellar steps.

The Beswick parlour was decorated in pink felt bunting for the birthday, and the small table, squeezed into the bay space of the front window, was full. Fruit jellies, cakes, milk jellies, a baked ham and plates of sandwiches. Though it was early, the days were short, and Frank poured the wine.

'I'll get another bottle. Enriqueta – there is ice outside, Will chipped it yesterday. Can you fetch it, love?'

The yard was cold after the warmth of Clara's front room. Enriqueta bent to shovel the ice into the jug, picking the bigger bits up with her fingers.

'Lovelier than ever. Even when you are doing Clara's chores for her.'

The jug in Enriqueta's hand stuttered the ice over the courtyard. James Holt bent to pick up the shards and lumps, and dropped them one by one into the pail, watching her. His dark hair was stark against the grey skies. The clouds rolled behind him and a nuthatch whistle sounded like tinsel across the green. He grasped her wrist, pulling her to his chest.

'You are shaking. Let me kiss you. Let me.'

Enriqueta's hand was cold, her fingers white and wet as James Holt slid his lips around them.

'Please, James, let me go!'

The clouds tipped and his lips were soft. He pressed her mouth open, his fingers raking through her hair. The nuthatch called again, mournfully, searching for a lost mate. James Holt pushed the back door closed with his foot and Enriqueta leaned against it. She could make it the last kiss of her life, and if it were that, she could allow him. Things seemed to happen to her regardless. She could allow herself. Enriqueta closed her eyes, his mouth on hers, all reason dropped in the sweet shock of the moment.

At the Horse and Jockey, Peter raised his glass to his company, and John, Frank, Will and Tynan all took long draughts of the dark bitter. As was so often the thought of the overworked, overwrought mind, John wondered why he did not indulge himself like this more often. What a tonic it was to be in the company of easy men, in a warm, clean pub – the tug of business and letters and marriage so blessedly out of his reach.

Will turned at the call of his name and the gust of cool air through the door.

'James! Join us.'

His head was bowed beneath the low ceilings. Poised and

perennially unhurried, James shook each of their hands, and waved to the barman for another round, flourishing a thick band of notes. Looking directly at John, his black eyes burned with confidence, his fingers slick with choices.

'Not often we see you in these parts, Mr Rylands?'

John smiled evenly, disguising the unease he felt around Holt. But more than that, history informed all and he had in him anger enough to punch the whole rotten clan. What had gone before between James's father and John was long past, and unknown to anyone but the two men themselves. And Dinah, buried with her babies and moments. John doubted that even the boy James knew much of it. Nevertheless, his memory was long and strong, and Holt's son, standing there before him so bold and youthful, looking just like his father Joseph, goaded dark recollections from his mind.

'I passed by your place, Frank. Said my birthday greetings to Leone. I had a favour to ask of Peter to pass to you, Mr Rylands, but better if I speak to you directly. If you don't mind, sir.'

It was unclear whether the bow of his head, tipped toward John was affected or genuine. Every time he saw a Holt, John saw his Dinah; frightened and imploring, willing to be defiled rather than die.

'Go on.'

James smiled broadly, taking from his pocket a pencil and notebook. John remembered Dinah recounting the moments she had spent at the mercy of Joseph Holt. Holt had tried his hardest to push her into submission. He held her captive as a girl for hours in one of his many dark sheds, pulling at her clothes, ripping them as he bit hard on her shoulder. It was an exercise in sadism. Holt's progeny, standing before him, was as beguiling and physically arresting as his father had been. John had never forgotten Dinah's shame and distress when she had told him of the endless minutes in the sheds, as they turned to hours and the sun sank. She told John how cold she had been; the small thing of being without her jacket becoming important amidst the enormity of horror. Holt had threatened her and frightened her, the monumental courage of his wealth and local standing, and of the cloak of his charm, making him impervious to her tears and pleas.

Soon after they were married, John had sought him out, chosen an evening when he knew Holt would be walking down Dark Lane alone. He made a mess of his arrogant face, leaving his own fists bruised for weeks. Holt didn't come near Dinah again and stood at a taut distance from John when invariably their paths crossed in the township. Yet the deep hatred John Rylands had for the Holts still festered, rubbed into life again by the boy James before him.

Peter gestured for another round of ales.

'One of our boys is down on his luck. Said I would write his name and address down for you. If you and Ged might have anything he can do.' said James.

'His good lady wife has just had twins, which makes six children in all. We've given him as many hours as we can, but he needs more work. There is nothing much on the farms, or the factory, so I thought I'd ask on his behalf. I can vouch for him. Not the sharpest tool in the box, mind, but a hard worker at least.'

'Working a bit too hard in the bed, sounds like' said Will.

Peter cast a warning glance at Will, but the men laughed, nevertheless. Time ticked on in the Horse and Jockey, the men naturally separating into groups, with the younger set – Will, Tynan and James – gathered together, noisy and tall. The talk between Peter, John and Frank drifted towards their business, and what was occupying their days to come. As sure as night follows day, and money follows industry, their moments of levity were never meant to last. Looking at his watch, John took up his coat.

'We should be getting back to the hall.'

It was later than he had planned, and giving the landlord's son some coins, he asked him to go and fetch them a cab. It was dark and John didn't want the good cheer wasted on a cold walk back up Hedge Lane. As they were leaving, and hailing their goodbyes, James called out, his voice buoyant and loud, oiled with the courage of beer.

'Oh Peter, I saw Enriqueta outside at the house. She was called back too soon for me to ask her what I meant to.'

'What's that then, lad?'

'A dance. Tell her James Holt wants to dance with her. Again.'

The bustle of their exit hid from view the set of John's face. A shudder went through him – her name thrown so carelessly from Holt. He swallowed the bitter taste of disgust, and walked, his boots grinding on the salt and slurry of the winter grass. Seeing Enriqueta through the window of Clara's parlour, her head thrown back in laughter, and her cheeks flushed with beauty and happiness, the picture of Enriqueta dancing in James Holt's arms sketched itself hastily and potently before him.

The first spots of colour that had pricked the lawns through the slush gained strength and unfurled. John was at work at dawn, his energies sharpened by a determination to quash any feelings he had that he could not tether. Never again would he confuse himself, complicate his life again. Sully himself. He had navigated his way from that raging aspect that burned inside him when he had ended it all with Caroline Castiglioni. He was proud of that. The hot days, bound in bedsheets, face turned from his marriage and his God; he had cast them away, telling himself all the good things it meant to be free of the burning shackles of lust. But here it was, undeniably. His heart—his mad, uncontrollable heart— treating Enriqueta as if she were his own.

From under his desk, he bought up a long, slim black box. It was the bouquet of scented silk roses he had bought for Martha, and his card; 'Yours, John'. Decorated in blue periwinkles, simple and sadly stark on the thick cream paper, stamped with the mark of Valentine's Day.

Hat in hand he went to leave for town, when he saw the envelope on the carpet at the foot of the door. Coral, with hand-drawn turquoise flowers on the edges. A single name written on the front, Enriqueta, in a hand he recognised instantly, the very same that had scribbled down the name and address in the Horse and Jockey. Forget-me-nots. James Holt.

When Enriqueta returned from her turn around the glass houses with Martha, she bought her into the drawing room to thaw near the fire. Leone beckoned her from the hallway.

'John has asked if you will join him in his parlour when you are ready? I will see to Martha, love.'

There was a glass of wine at her place opposite him at the desk.

'You look frozen, Enriqueta. Drink that and warm yourself.'

John wandered about the room. He picked up his glass and put it down, only to pick it up again. The grandfather clock ticked.

'I have been thinking for some time that Martha would benefit from a trip abroad.' His face turned to the window. The robin that nested with his family in the red oak, sprung onto the sill.

'When I mentioned it to her some months ago, she seemed to be agreeable to the idea.'

His sentences were deliberate, heavy with the weight of things much bigger than his words. Sighing, he pushed his palms together like a prayer, pressing hope hard in his hands.

'I had not expected to be away so long in Italy. It was unfortunate, unforeseeable. I regret it.'

Enriqueta sounded the word in her mind and it spoke loudly. Regret.

'I have noticed that her health is declining, at a pace that seems to have hastened. Maybe when I am here, I notice it less. My time away—I return and it is all a shock again. It's easier for me to keep up a pretence that she is not failing, that her mind will somehow regenerate.'

His words stood against the tap of the hands on the clock.

'I can't delay it any longer. I am going to make plans for a trip to France—where she said she wanted to go. She enjoyed many, many happy times there and as travelling goes, it is one of the more straightforward passages.'

The wine was useful. Enriqueta poured more for him.

'I'm sure that you and Mrs Rylands will have an enjoyable trip. I can promise you too, that you must not worry about everything here. Peter will look after all your concerns, and I can carry on with our work. I can prepare her. Pack her things for her.'

John's hands were clasped so firmly that his knuckles whitened.

'I want you to come, Enriqueta. To France.'

The clock stilled briefly before it chimed, solid and soft, the thud of another hour passed. Time was a thief, slipping out of the windows of days on a breeze.

'I have thought about it over and over. It's not a trip I could do alone. You know that the way Martha is, it would not be wise nor possible for one person alone to try to care for her. I can't take Peter away from the hall or the business, and there is no one better than you. She trusts you, Enriqueta. I would even say she has found, in her own inimitable way, a true fondness for you.'

He gave a hollow laugh.

'It doesn't sound like much of a holiday, the way I say it. That said, I can promise you that the place I have in mind is wonderful. My friend's house—in Normandy—is large and comfortable, in beautiful countryside. There are gardens, and a library. There is history, and there are beaches. I have thought so much about this. If you look after Martha, I, in turn, can look after you.'

She thought of sand, and France, and being by him, in another country. Longford would tick like the clock, consistent and solid, while they shared different skies.

'I don't need your answer straight away. I have ambushed you. You need time to think it over. I am going to book all the tickets in a few days.'

Even the singular word tickets landed like a thrill.

'I ask you, Enriqueta, because you are such a fine and gentle aide to my wife. In all these last difficult years I hardly ever dared dream I could find someone to live here - give themselves so uncomplainingly and completely to the role of her guardian in my absence. Yet you came like an angel, and I could not have wished for someone better.'

'And Enriqueta, let me impress upon you – if you decide not to accept the invitation, I shall understand. I'd still be able to take Martha, by hiring a nursemaid for this side of the travel and one at the other. The trip would still go ahead, so please don't let that concern influence you. Just think about it.'

He slid the window up and threw a handful of seeds that he kept on his desk, out towards the robin, who bobbed his head in thanks.

Tears warmed at the back of her eyes, pricking and blurring her vision. Little did he know, would he ever know, how grateful she was for her life at Longford. And how grateful she was to him. He never needed to know how lost she had been before she had found a home here. He never would. She could not allow it. Gone, past. Gone, buried deep, a closed book of years and chapters strewn to waste. Books burned in Paris, the story so feebly concluded in Lyon.

Their eyes met, and there was so much she wanted to say. She felt herself trembling, and prayed he wouldn't notice, thinking that she only had the nerve to reply as briefly as she was able. She would never be a mother, and she wanted to cry out, ask God for the grace she knew she should have, ask Him to take away the anger she felt for the Universe, that had put men in her way and halted her chances of children. John, against his desk, and the robin at the window waited, their eyes on her.

'Thank you. I must go. It's late. Good night, John.'

FRANCE, MARCH 1872

A S HE WENT TO TOUCH ENRIQUETA, John stopped himself.
The sign by the road read 'Menil- Hermei'. He turned to
her, realising as his hand hovered over her that it should be
Martha he roused first. He worried that on waking, Martha
would be enveloped in confusion. As unpredictable as she was,
he imagined every scenario, from anger to upset. Yet thankfully,
as she woke, her face lit in delight. The journey had been long,
but they had at last reached the place, so dear to them both,
and so full of the sharp, sweet memories of a long-distant and
fragile happiness.

'I remember it here, John.'

Her eyes, wet with tears and illness, blinked rapidly, as she
scoured the road from the window, consuming it with a tenuous
recollection. But the clarity was fleeting, and it receded again,
her expression clouding and closing once more.

'The house – is there a house here?'

A fist of grief tightened around John's heart. Her memory
was failing fast. It was torn, a moth-eaten mind made of scraps
and frail smudges of sense.

'Yes. Just around the corner now, Martha. We are in
Normandy. In France. The place you loved.'

She blinked at him again, content yet oblivious to any
construct of time or place.

Enriqueta stirred, and on seeing the vast wrought iron

gates opening to a sweeping drive, broad and gold in the sun, she thought for a sickening moment that she was back at La Castilla. She breathed, releasing the dismay. She was safe. This was not Lyon.

Chateau des Ducs rose from the Normandy landscape, colossal and outstanding. Built of pale stone, it was structure of curves and towers, its front façade gleaming with windows, neatly shimmering in rows. Enriqueta took Martha's hand in hers.

'It is beautiful, Martha.'

The horses padded down the driveway, grateful for the soft yielding sand on their hooves. A lady in a white bonnet and the apron of a housemaid came down the steps to the carriage with open arms.

'Eloise,' murmured Martha.

'Jean-Luc said you would be here today for us. It is wonderful to see you again, dear Eloise.' John kissed her three times on her cheeks.

He introduced her to Enriqueta and the lady spoke in rapid, animated French.

'Delighted to meet you, mademoiselle. Welcome to Chateau des Ducs. Monsieur, you are always on time. Lunch is ready. Claude will see to your bags. Come, come, leave them in the carriage. Follow me. You must eat!'

A dark, tall boy rushed past them, stopping only to quickly kiss John and Martha. John laughed.

'A young man now, Eloise! He was as high as my knee when last I saw him!'

Lunch was served in the orangery. The glass house was sweet with the mint that burst green from the pots around the edges of the room. An iced aniseed drink was nectar to Enriqueta; she tried not to swallow it all in one draught. The radishes were cold and brittle, sliced with wafers of butter on top, salt scattered liberally over them. Enriqueta hadn't realised how much she had missed French food. Never would she say it, but the food at Longford was something so far removed from this. Dishes bound in suet and dried fruit, all meat and potatoes, pudding and pies. Ale and dumplings, custard and scones, gravy and stews. The sharp, nearly indigestible root fired against her tongue.

There were rillettes to follow – deep pink shredded pork pressed with peppercorns and wrapped with thin Bayonne ham, still scented by the green grass on which the fat pigs fed. The ficelle broke in her hands, the shards of the primrose crust shattering in her fingers. There were salads: Beet leaves, deep purple and mustard, scattered with wincingly tart red onion. Hens' eggs, the size of a fist, quartered and strewn amongst mâché leaves, studded with fat cubes of sizzling lardons. A dish of peas, gilded with butter and roasted lettuce. A quiche, quivering, its cream just set, on watercress. Finally, a piece of ham, sticky with lemon and honey, carved at the table by Claude.

Eloise filled their glasses with a flinty Muscadet. She sat with Martha, cutting her food and listening to her mild grumbling. In and out, Martha was at one minute illuminated and the next confused and listless. Yet Eloise did not heed the difference, sitting patiently with her, stroking her hand, as if the wild swing of her temperament was the most normal thing in the world.

They lingered over their lunch. Cheeses were bought out, then the cakes and sweets. Martha's head began to nod, and Eloise took her up by the arms.

'Come on, dear Martha. Let's get you to your room to rest.'

John and Enriqueta both stood, but she brushed them aside.

'Let me take her. It's been some years, and I'm so glad to have her.'

With Martha and Eloise gone, it was quiet in the orangery, but for lazy buzz of the insects at the door.

'A digestif, I think.'

Before she could answer, John was at the sideboard, bringing with him two tiny, blush pink crystal glasses and a round bottle of Calvados. She shook her head, laughing.

'I can't, I'm sure. I think I should rest too. The wine was enough.'

Her head was swimming. The wine had been stronger than she had grown accustomed to in England. He insisted, pouring her a small glass and raising his.

'I am very glad you are here, Enriqueta.'

His blue eyes we impossible to avoid, and the brandy was sweet. She brushed the mint at her side with her fingertips, and it released a bloom of green into the air.

'Let's meet again at dinner, Enriqueta. It has been a long few days. Try and sleep for a while.'

Enriqueta woke at six o'clock, her mouth dry and her limbs heavy. A melody came from somewhere in the house. Her frock was new, in navy-blue silk, caught at her shoulder with a silver clasp. Waves of contentment emanated from her like a song.

John and Martha happened to come from their room at the same moment. John was holding his wife close to him, and she leaned into his arms, white and tremulous. Without asking, Enriqueta stepped forward to assist them. They descended the stairs together, arm in arm, Martha flanked by the two of them, her skirt blowing in the breeze of an open window.

'Your dress is beautiful, Enriqueta,' said John.

Enriqueta felt a joy she didn't feel she had the right to possess.

The dining room was strawberry pink, and panelled with ancient oak. Crimson hot-house roses sagged in the heat of their brass bowls. Although Martha was tired, and ate little, she was clearly untroubled and at ease, distracted by the good familiarity of the place. She resisted John's pleas to sit with them, wanting to wander the house, tracing her fingers over the windows, tables and ornaments. She drifted from the dining room, buffeted by the placidity of her failing mind, and from their seats John and Enriqueta could hear her opening and closing doors, pacing the house with her slight, shadowy movements.

'What would you like to do while we are here, Enriqueta? There are day trips to lakes and houses, or I could take you to the markets.'

They toured and walked, eating ice cream by the lake at Rabodanges, exploring the severe Norman castle in Falaise. Martha tired easily, and they returned to the chateau by three o'clock each afternoon for her to sleep before dinner.

Enriqueta was reading on the patio, after a morning spent in the markets, choosing gifts for Leone and the children. She heard the low rumble of a carriage in the distance, and she called to John, thinking the visitor might be his.

As the carriage drew closer, Enriqueta strained to see the two figures seated in the back. A dark young man and a golden-haired girl close to him. Her heart caught in her throat. The coach stopped, and with a click of the door, Jules stepped out, his hand outstretched to help his sister, Maddy.

Dropping her book, Enri ran to them. She picked up her skirts, not even pausing to put her shoes on, and ran to them, the tears sliding from her eyes, her breath coming in burning bursts, the sand padding hard and thickly under her bare feet. She pulled them both to her, her tears falling into the soft, childish strands of Maddy's hair. For some time, the three held on to each other.

'I don't understand. What is the miracle that brings you here, into my arms, in front of my eyes? I have missed you so much!'

John spoke from behind the little group.

'I wrote to them, Enri. I invited them.'

Without thinking, Enriqueta threw her arms around his neck.

'You good, kind man. Thank you, thank you.'

John held her for a moment, his hands firm and warm on her waist. Feeling his body for the first time against hers, she pulled away quickly, and he smiled down at her, and let his hands lift from her.

'Come now, come in, Jules. Maddy. You have had a long journey.'

The afternoon was gilded. Enriqueta basked in the company of her friends, hardly believing that they were there, next to her. Jules had grown so tall, his once birdlike frame broad and strong, his arms and torso muscular and solid. Maddy was still slight, but her face and figure had filled and bloomed into beauty. She was as innocent and guileless as she always had been. Alone for a moment, while John showed Jules around the wine cellars, she nudged Enriqueta.

'You never mentioned how very handsome your master was, Enri!'

'Maddy! What a thing to say. John is not my master. I work for both Mr and Mrs Rylands.'

The sense of his touch just hours before caused her heart to drum.

'While they are gone, Enri. I need to speak to you.'

Maddy took Enri's wrist in her hand, pulling her close.

'It's about Armand. Monsieur Foncé.'

His name shot a spear through Enriqueta. An archer's bow pulled back before her.

'I don't know how to tell you. Monsieur Armand has asked me to teach at Sainte-Catherine. Oh, Enri it's always been my dream to be a teacher, even, maybe, a governess one day. And it would mean I got away from La Castilla. Jules said I should tell you as soon as I could. Please, please don't be angry, Enri! I shan't do it if it means I lose you.'

The world seemed to spin – only briefly – before stilling. Enriqueta thought of John, and kindnesses, and chances that slip from us all. The corners of life unturned, and the people that are missed, meant for us but who left their houses an hour before they should have, or who looked the wrong way in a crowd. She thought of how much she wanted everything that was good for everyone. She thought again, and again, of her blood forming children that could lie, swaddled and warm in her arms. Ache – the most interminable ache of not having the one thing she wished for, that came so easily to others. Her children, with the souls and profiles of ages, died and floated from her before they were born.

'Angry? Madeleine, I could never, ever be angry with you and of course you should teach. You must.'

The mention of Armand Foncé had hurt her at first, like a sting, but to know that life for all of them was moving, altering in all its permutations and opportunities felt curiously as it should be. She understood herself, and knew that fearing Foncé and her memories had become a pernicious habit. She took Maddy into her arms, feeling her stiff little shoulders like arrows in her dress.

'Jules was right. He is always right, I know that. He is wise. He is kind. A young man now, and a good, faithful brother to you. We are both so lucky to have him. On your return to Lyon you must accept the job immediately.'

Jules returned with John, and bottles of champagne from the cellars.

'I see you have talked. We should celebrate. All of us together.'

John raised his glass to Enriqueta. 'To friendship and to love. To new beginnings.'

The days were filled. There was tennis to play, and the gardens, and books. Moliere came back to Enriqueta, with all his might, moving Emma Bovary aside.

Vivre sans aimer n'est pas proprement vivre.

The sun shone on them. Martha appeared content to do little, spending most of her waking hours lying on a chaise in the orangery, listening to Eloise or Enriqueta read to her. She was confused on and off, asking who Jules and Maddy were, then forgetting just as quickly. Distress departed, and she even displayed small, limited signs of affection towards John, sometimes taking his hand, or calling him 'dear'.

As the weekend drew near, Eloise told them of a dance that was taking place by the lake at Rabodanges, to celebrate *la Fêtes des Mères*.

'Please, Enri, can we all go?' said Maddy.

'The decision must be Mr Rylands', Maddy. We are his guests.'

Putting his paper down, John said, 'I hear that you are a remarkable dancer.'

'Oh, she is! She was the best dancer at the parties we had at La Castilla.'

'I'm sure that is an exaggeration, Maddy,' said Enriqueta, staring at her book. The words swum at her fingers.

I must learn to be content with being happier than I deserve.

The bank of trees that surrounded the lake at Rabodanges twinkled with lanterns. The music from the band was sweet in the night air, scented with marshmallow and candy floss. Mutton roasted on spits, and there was a circus tent, striped red and white, serving pitchers of wine and amber, clouded ciders. A crowd swirled together in front of the musicians.

The melodies were elegant and French, the instruments different enough to the bands she heard in Chorlton to give it the Gallic sound that she had forgotten she missed. She stood with John, watching Maddy and Jules spin together across the boards. Already, as new faces to the local picture, the pair were attracting the murmurs and nudges of the other youngsters, grouped like flocks of coloured moths around a flame.

John's face was concealed in the shadows of the evening, the lanterns lit in the trees behind him, shimmering gold amongst the leaves.

'Dance with me, Enriqueta?'

A waltz began, and he clasped her to him, leading her to the swoop of the strings. Her face was pressed to his shoulder, and his lips were close to her ear as he whispered,

'Madeleine was right, Enri. You are a marvellous dancer.' He paused. 'And Holt said the same.'

John held her tighter as he said it, and felt her, as he knew she would, pull her breath in surprise. She stiffened in his arms and when the music finished, John released her and she saw that his eyes were glittering, made navy blue by the night. Words unsaid hovered between them and she felt as though she were tipping, perilously out of herself and into something she had never expected.

The rest of the evening went without John and Enriqueta dancing together again. He had seen some acquaintances of the village by chance. Jules and Enriqueta toured the stalls and tents, whiling away the balmy night propped by ciders and roasted nuts from white lace paper cones. She couldn't help but keep glancing his way through the crowds, her gaze searching for him. She thought it seemed his eyes were looking to her too, and they met through the sparkling evening shadows of the lakeside.

It was no surprise that Maddy and Jules secured another meeting with the friends they had met for the following night. Jules worried that John might think him a shoddy guest, running off with the local crowd on one of the last nights they had at the chateau.

John laughed, indulging the pensive, social insecurities of youth he recalled so well.

'I can't think that you have much time or opportunity for leisure in Lyon. Of course you must go. Enjoy yourselves,' he said, pressing a crisp franc note into Maddy's hand. The pair lingered nervously, Maddy shifting her feet and wiping her palms on her skirts.

'Go! Get your shoes on. Martha is tired, and Enriqueta and I will dine together and enjoy the end of the holiday. I am unused to dancing, and I can feel aches I had forgotten I could possess. Now go, get ready. I will drive you down to the village.'

Enriqueta watched the cart trot down the drive from the terrace, where she was sipping a Chambord that John had given her. She drank deeply, trying to order herself. Nothing more had been said of James Holt. She had read to Martha, pleased by the dull distraction of the book, a tedious and unedited local history of the area, blessedly dull and void of any sort of romance.

His words about her dancing; typically John, they were just fact; but the way he said it – the fact that he had said it – indicated something, and she turned the thought over like a stone. She winced at the thought that someone may have seen her grappling with James in the coppice that night, pushing him off and running from him. And worse, maybe whoever it was didn't see that part at all. It was entirely, painfully possible that the passing envoy had heard them on the wind, and turned just in time to see him kiss her, and nothing more. A kiss, which in the shadows of muddled retrospect could have looked like a lover's kiss, one that was wanted; one that was prompted by her. In Clara's yard, when sounds of nuthatches and the burn of the ice at her fingers had made it all happen, when she was lonely and sad enough to risk the kiss, her friends just a door away.

It stuck like a web. Sensing herself begin to be swamped by the old confusion and bleak worries she had cast away in Lyon, Enriqueta resolved that the best and only thing would be to speak to John on his return from the village. She would clear herself in his eyes. Never again would she let her name or soul be sullied by another wretched man, least of all James Holt. Like Foncé, Holt was a man who used the situation and opportunity to take his luck with her, and more than once.

John laughed when he recounted to Enriqueta the way the young people were arranged around the marketplace, artfully displaying all the insouciance of youth and some awkward, tentative attempts at sophistication. He poured them both glasses of Chablis, the bottle cold and dusty from the cellars.

Eloise served them dinner: Normandy pork, prunes, and roasted apples, blanketed in an Armagnac and cider cream sauce. There were greens and baked mushrooms, with little pats of local cheeses afterwards.

Now, away from the dance, she wondered whether all she had fretted over was unreal and ridiculous. James Holt was far away. That moment may have been made of dust after all, whereas the dinner table and talk with John was real and flesh.

The house was quiet. It was not yet late and Maddy and Jules weren't due home until the last cab left the village, some hours yet.

'Shall we walk in the gardens? It's a lovely night, and still warm.'

Through the side door of the orangery was the rose courtyard, which was an unearthly white in the light of an enormous pearl moon. It was noiseless, but for the shuffles of night's nature, and the far-away, low peel of settling cattle. The air was rich with the perfume of early rambling roses, tumbling across and down the walls like the drape of a wedding. Startlingly green ferns lined the pathways, their fronds dipping in the breeze.

At the end of the path was hidden stone grotto. A roofless room, its grey walls quilted with the same roses, holding their scent like a secret. John looked to her, taking her hands in his.

'I wanted you alone.'

Seeing her face in the moonlight, John's voice stilled. He measured his life and his words so carefully, but love, the beautiful demon, had stolen his senses again, and he could ignore it no longer. A storm had gathered in him, and he had to speak, and let her do what she would with his words.

His fingers shook as he brushed a lock of hair from her brow; clear and smooth like marble. The globe of the moon reflected in her eyes.

'I must explain to you. Last night – my foolish words. All day, I've thought of them, and of you, and worried that I had spoken so madly out of turn.'

He sighed hard, pushing back his hair, wrenching his eyes from hers to cast them around, searching for the right phrase in the bricks of the wall, as if words would spring from the blooms, deliver themselves to him, and hold fast in the air on his behalf.

'It was him that I heard from – directly. Holt. That you had danced together.'

He brushed his thumb over her lips, entranced by the plump warmth of her mouth beneath his touch.

'I tried to dismiss his goading reports of you. I am in no position to have any claim over you but for your position at Longford, Enriqueta. But then, I saw the card that arrived for you on St Valentine's day and I knew it was from him.'

The memory landed like a thud. She had opened the card with Leone. After a cursory glance, she had disposed of it, not wanting any further connection to the man. To any man, at that moment. For all she knew, James Holt's card could still be there somewhere amongst the rubbish for burning, with the leaves and the old newspapers, the breakfast eggshells and the discarded kitchen peelings, garish and suggestive and rotting in the heap.

'I don't ask for your understanding, but I wanted you away from him, Enri, and I stole you with me here to France. I was gone too long in Italy, and I fear all of the fault of this lies at my door. He picked you up like a gift I had put to one side.'

He caught her in his arms, pulling her close, his scent swimming over her as it had the night before on the dancefloor.

'You must think that I am a mad, selfish man.'

He felt her head shake against the notion at his chest, and he held her harder.

'You are a young, incredibly beautiful, clever, woman and I am old for you, and bound by marriage. This will not change but as I danced with you last night, as your soft hair was against my cheek and your perfume was making havoc, I couldn't stop those jealous words escaping me.'

She raised her arms and held him and they stood together, for a long time in silence, the roses rustling around them. An animal called out to a family, a sad, longing sound in the pitch black of the trees beyond the grotto walls.

'Please, dearest Enri, please forgive me. Forgive my foolish words. Forgive my feelings. Forgive my pointless candour. Forgive my impotent ardour and the awful envy that I have no right to display. Forgive me for all of these things, I implore you. I adore you. I adore you with every bit of me and I don't know what to do with any of it.'

Enriqueta cried onto John's shoulder, wracked with the sad realisation that all he said chimed with the wild love she felt for him too, a love that she had suppressed but had shaped itself into something that was so huge, it was beyond her control. She had taken her love and made it pliable, turning it and moulding it and forcing it into something flat and made only for friend-ship. Yet it was far from that, and she knew it so keenly now, in his arms, his body hot and hard against hers.

John held her, looking over her face, wiping the rolling tears from her cheeks.

'Does this mean I have to go, John? Leave Longford? Leave you? All of you?'

'God no! My beautiful girl – I couldn't let you go. Ever.'

He stopped himself, hearing his own voice raised, and threatening to let more, dangerous words tumble over them both. He breathed deeply, trying to stop the tears that filled his eyes. The battle was violent and helpless.

'What I have said is a burden to you, and I am so deeply sorry for that. You are a free woman and I dearly want you to continue your life and duties at Longford. Can you do that? Please say that you can. Have I made it impossible for us, Enriqueta?'

Wretchedness was etched on his face, and her heart and soul longed for him to reach for her again.

'Of course I can carry on, John. I can't think of anywhere I would rather be than at Longford. That will never change.'

His smile was weak, redolent of relief and small hope.

'I don't know what we do. I assure you, with all my heart, I will never ever take liberties with you or cause you discomfort.'

The animal, a mother, cried out again.

'It's taken all my strength not to kiss you.'

He looked so desperately sad that Enriqueta very nearly decided their fate for them herself, stealing herself not to raise her lips to his. She bent her head purposefully down and away, denying them both.

'Know this, John Rylands, that I feel as you do. Everything you feel, I feel as equally. Every time you think about me, I am thinking about you. And when you missed me, I missed you too. I miss you even when I know you are near.'

She allowed herself to brush her hand lightly across his face. Misery twisted her heart. John's eyes shut with joy at her touch, and he raised his own hand up to hers, to fasten it to his cheek for a moment longer, wanting it never to end.

In silence, and apart, they returned to the house, just in time to hear the giddy lilt of Jules and Maddy as they crunched up the drive. John gave Enriqueta a last glance, sealing the silence between them, locking their secret, and offering it up to God. He was sacrificing again, in order to sanctify himself.

Maddy and Jules came in, out of the rain, which after such a warm and sultry evening, had finally begun to drop from the sky.

LONGFORD, 1873

Both Enriqueta and John kept their promise to each other and didn't speak of what had passed between them in Menil-Hermei. The turmoil that swirled inside them both in unison was a lived agony, tying their days in the hopelessness of impossibility. Unhappily, both thought that the other had somehow recovered, and that what had occurred had been an aberration, incited by foreign climes and now best forgotten. A madness, maybe, the enchantment of florid and beautiful surroundings. A temporary display of insanity, best relegated to the past. The result of two broken hearts alive to the seduction of chance.

And life back in Longford was full of new, hampered ways. Both worked hard at behaving as things ever were, for fear that one or the other would reach a point where their delicate life together was no longer tenable. Though the situation was brittle, the notion of a life away from each other was utterly unbearable. They continued, with a discreet tenderness and friendship, administered with fervour. They walked by each other with the innocence of children, and the careful propriety that had been born of the acutely difficult and freshly onerous position they found themselves in.

Often, Enriqueta caught John watching her yearningly, a stitch of pain crossing his brow. While she longed to reach and smooth it away, her hands were pinned with duty. Their work, as it always had, required them to be frequently alone together, and in these hours she felt nearly mad with desire for him. Her heart had been captured by his admission in Normandy, and now she saw him wholly, for the man he was. Beyond and above all his good character and his precious, dynamic mind, she consumed his handsome face, his lean, muscled frame, his blue eyes. She had been witness to his most secret, honest passions, and while she battled to control herself, his words had been branded on her forever.

John saw further than the sum of her quiet, thoughtful mind and her clever ideas. He saw her beauty, shining like a beacon from every corner of his world. Her face, golden and exquisite, drew his gaze inexorably. If she moved too close to him, it was all he could do not to seize her, and he imagined his hands over her body, taunting himself dreaming of what she would look like if he stripped her, took her into his bed and turned the lock on the door. He knew that to act on any of this would never be possible, but, equally, he could not be parted from her now. To have to live his life like this, unable to be true to his passion was half a life, but was nothing to the torturous thought of being completely without her. The idea of a life without Enriqueta Augusta Tennant sickened him, and he resolved to be eternally and truly grateful that he could at least live his life alongside her, bleak as it was.

John turned and turned at night, listening for her going to her room. Hearing the touch of her tread on the floors, he fantasised wildly about her in bed with him. He caused himself endless suffering picturing her in the arms of another. A different, younger man than he hovered over her in his mind's eye, and he felt ill at the thought of her shuddering in pleasure beneath the vigour of a menacing, handsome shadow. Obsessively, in mania, he attempted to prepare himself for what he believed was the inevitable event of a man coming for her, snatching her away from him. The imagined seduction sliced open his heart and his mind, yet there was nothing to be done. He had no claim but employer and friend over her. Enriqueta was not his to covet. She was not even his to love.

And to his private fury, James Holt was staggeringly persistent. True to his predatory bloodline, he kept his hunt up for Enriqueta like a lion paddling its prey with a treacherous, perfidious paw.

'Has Holt been here of late, Ged? While I've been away?'

'He has, sir.'

Rage pulsed through John.

'For what reason, Ged?'

Ged rolled his eyes, turning his cap in his hands.

'He's a lad, sir. Came with cakes and excuses.'

The dried mud broke off in Ged's fingers as he picked at his boots.

'They'd make a nice couple. Him so good-looking. And your Miss Tennant such a beauty.'

As John burned with the tinder of outrage, Enriqueta grew pale, and Martha descended further into her private madness. Her face seemed to sink overnight, and she stopped eating very much at all. She mouthed at spoonfuls of warm milk, sometimes taking crusts of bread in the richest gravy Leone could make. Dutifully, Leone mashed the youngest vegetables with the pork fat she kept in the cold room, pressing in the precious oils of the hard herbs, rosemary and thyme, pushing the mixture through her muslin to make the most nutritious liquor she could. Trying to tempt Martha to eat, she took apples from their straw covers and simmered them in honey and cinnamon, feeding her as she had fed her own infants. She folded the soft apple into a puddle of cream and gently tipped tiny dots of it towards Martha's pursed lips, though she knew it would be wasted again. In the backyard, the bluebottles became fat on the pig's bin.

John moved around his wife, not knowing what to do. He mopped her brow and tried to feed her too. When Martha had enough energy to talk, he roamed around her fractured memories with her, piecing together scenes true and untrue, agreeing to even her most unfathomably insane, scattered recollections, making new truths of their life together.

Enriqueta and Leone spent their days differently, in accordance with the tasks that attending to the weak and frail bring. Between the normal routine of housework and cooking, and incidental, shorter hours in the library, they were with Martha. On one of these days, as they pushed Martha out into the chill buttermilk light of the morning, the tall, straight figure of James Holt strode up the drive. Leone nudged her, blithe and knowing nothing of what had passed between John and Enriqueta.

'Oh look out, Enri. Your young man.'

Enriqueta's heart sank, her spirits following. She tensed as James neared, and Leone drifted away, mumbling stories about a cow in calf at the main shed.

At that moment, John Rylands came to his office window. He looked out onto the estate, from the lodge to the steps, seeing Holt – like a poison – on his Longford lawn. John's fists were gripped, wetly hot and rigid in readiness, at once pained and angered by the arrogance of his youth and his beauty. With nothing to be done, he watched Holt swagger towards Enriqueta.

'How are you, Enri?'

John moved out of his office and to the entrance steps, hearing Holt's bold tones float over his land.

Face downcast, Enriqueta stalled Martha's chair.

'I'm well.'

James raised his hand to Enriqueta's cheek, stretching over Martha, who was supine and asleep in her wicker chair. John watched, an agonising bile rising in his core, as Enriqueta turned from James, shrinking from his long fingers. John pounded across the gravel, his heart aching in his throat. James Holt lunged forward to take Enriqueta's shoulders.

'Enriqueta!'

James and Enriqueta turned. Smirking, James released her, holding his hands up in a charade.

'Gallant Rylands! Come to save the maid!'

John glowered at him, holding his fists fast to his body. James grasped Enriqueta by the waist, and she cried out.

'Ah! I see,' said James slowly. His black eyes shot between John and Enriqueta, weighing them both with the dark art of a treacherous man, assessing a tension, taut like wire.

'You don't see anything, Holt. Do you think it acceptable to seize any woman you choose, without their approbation or willing? It may be something you do to the poor girls of the village, but I forbid it on my property and with my people.'

There was not a shadow nor flicker of shame on the young man's face.

'Your people? Or your woman? You make yourself very clear, Mr Rylands.'

James stepped away, casting a glance at Martha, mercifully still sleeping in her chair.

'My best wishes to your wife.' His words were ice. 'I know she suffers.'

Holt left nothing on the Longford lawn but the pervading scent of his cologne, and a dark cloud of despondency. Tears welled in Enriqueta's eyes, and John grimaced, shaking his head. It was more than he could bear to look at her. He sought words, but they evaded him. Taking the handles of her chair, he turned to take Martha back to the house. Something inside Enriqueta broke.

Longford, February 1873

T HE VALENTINE'S ROSES FOR MARTHA were a shy, blush-
coloured pink. John slid the box under his desk, as he
had done each year of their marriage. She had slept for days
now, and her face had wilted, the skin on her fine-boned face
drooping and grey. Her hair, once a righteous boast, was sparse.
Ill health had aged her beyond her sixty-nine years, and John
had begun to forget what her voice sounded like, unable to
recall when she had last used it.

Enriqueta moved silently around Martha's bedroom.
Martha had been not well enough to cause the disarray she
used to, and the room was tidier than it ever had been. No
gowns in silky puddles on the floor, no face powder peach and
smeared on the dressing table. No glasses or cups teetering
on the desk, or shoes with their lining cocked out of the heel,
strewn on the rugs. The order saddened Enriqueta, and there
was a part of her that missed the mess and the chaos. As trying
as Martha's tempers had been, at least where there was fury
there had been life. A tangible, energetic life full of noise and
pain, days and movement. The way she was now – a silent husk
– was without substance and pitiful. Martha's hand was papery
and cool beneath Enriqueta. Her breathing was so noiseless it
could hardly be detected at all.

It was in the silence of Martha's room, her heart aching with
the grief of her situation, that Enriqueta decided she must leave

Longford. She had thought – prayed – that she and John could find the strength to exist together in friendship. Bound by love yet separated by it at the same time. A wave of nausea tumbled over her at the thought of starting anew, away from him, never to be near him again. She didn't try to stop the tears, and as she wept quietly, Martha's hand suddenly tightened over hers. Enriqueta knew it was a movement made in love. As their eyes met, Martha smiled. The clocked chimed seven and Martha's grip softened. A moment after the clock struck, Martha Rylands died.

Enriqueta ran down the stairs to John's office.

'Has she gone, Enriqueta?'

His voice was small.

'I need to go to her.'

John took Enriqueta's hand, the first time he had touched her since Normandy. Enriqueta hovered at the bedroom door, watching John as he bent to kiss Martha's head. When Peter and Leone returned to the changed house, Leone cried. She said she wished that she had done more for Martha. The usual, wasted words of the grieving. John would not hear of it.

'She loved you, Leone. And you, Peter, and the children.'

'And you, Enriqueta. She loved you and you added so much to her life. For which I will forever be grateful.'

The four were quiet then for a time around the bed, until the undertakers arrived. Respectful and dour, the men were head to toe in black, from the high shine of their shoes to their stovepipe hats. Martha was moved slowly, covered in a sheet, leaving the doors of Longford for the very last time.

Martha Rylands was buried with Dinah Rylands in the family grave at Southern Cemetery, at the crossroads of Didsbury and Chorlton-cum-Hardy. The February sky was clear, a cerulean sweep over the gathering, and the sun shone, as so often it does for a funeral, over the few that were there. Martha had no family anymore but John and the household. The working men of the estate, flanked by their wives and families stood like soldiers. Stiff in their grey serge and black polished boots, they hoped for a pint and a pie afterwards. Ged Tolan bore the coffin, with Frank, John and Tynan.

'My wife's good works, on behalf of our charities and foundations speak for her. And all she did for the people of the estate: the babies she helped to deliver, the children she taught to read, the sick and the aged she tended. She was a woman of surety and true charity.'

Enriqueta bowed her head, finding that after all, she missed Martha. She missed being useful to someone.

The ceremony was short, and the party retired to Longford for the wake. There were sausage rolls, thick ham sandwiches, respectful platitudes, and plenty of strong, sweet sherry. As the last guests walked down the driveway, John took to his horse. Work was a salve and he threw his mind and body back into his duties and the business of churning activity. He was not a man to stop. Another son and another wife buried, in mere months of each other. At breakfast, Enriqueta saw that his cup was not where it should be.

'Peter?'

'He is gone, Enri. For some weeks. There is a new contract to be drawn up in London for a property in Kensington, and the office there needs him. There is also the business of the ship canal. I have seen his diary for the next few weeks: meetings after meetings.'

She put her bread back on her plate.

'He should have told you himself. I'm sorry, Enri.'

With Martha gone, and the work in the library nearly at a close, what use was she anymore at Longford? Enriqueta pushed her cup aside. A numbness settled within her, a horrible, supernatural feeling of disconnect in her step. What once had seemed such a genial place, so close to her, now felt like foreign quarters. The beloved scent of the library –wood and rose oil and polish and papery dust – brought her a sickness. Redundant. She had to find a new reason to exist again.

Chaque jour ma raison me le dit; Mais la raison ne règne pas en amour, tu sais.

Enriqueta opened her writing set, the burnished wood gleaming beneath her fingers. She could almost hear his deep, assured tones. She longed for his voice next to her ear, his arms around her just as they had danced so perfectly together in Normandy. The memory ignited in her a fresh wave of agony. Breaching all her senses, it caused her to crumple, and she cried tears of anger, causing the ink on her page to bloom in grief.

Before the day was out, Enriqueta had written at length to Leocadia. A plan of sorts had formed in her fractured mind. She would quit Stretford and go to Kensington, where she knew that she would be welcomed and housed by her sister. There were private schools on every corner of the district. The children of the wealthy would sit by her knee as she read them stories and guided their little hands, fingers in paint, knees scraped and hymns sung. She could almost convince herself it could one day bring her happiness. She could meet someone and marry. It wasn't too late, and he wouldn't have to be the best of men. He might at least be kind, plain, and steady.

The future didn't really matter much in youth, when time stretched ahead with overwhelming generosity. But as moments made months and months formed years, chances were absorbed and choices grew lean. Foncé had been a foolish, painful indulgence and John Rylands, an impossibility. If there were ever to be another man, her expectations would be rightfully low.

Her mind saw a baby on her lap, gurgling. The house was

small and humble, her husband lumbering and placid, leaving at eight o'clock, returning at six. The food was pale and unseasoned, and there was no wine anymore, no cellars or deliveries, no shops or new shoes, no books or debate, no trips or discussions or interesting libraries and glasshouses with plants – only tea and water and banal conversations about the neighbours, or the weather, or the small advertisements in the local paper. She blinked away her tears, banishing them. This was a time for stoicism and valour. She pulled her suitcase from beneath the bed, and with a shuddering sigh, Enriqueta began to pack.

LONGFORD, 1873

L EONE FOUND THE NOTE on the kitchen table, long after she should have. She had decided to make Enriqueta a proper breakfast. Enriqueta had looked so gaunt of late, her dresses loose around her neck, and her wrists like reeds in her sleeves. For the first time since Martha's passing, Leone woke in cheerful spirits. In truth, she didn't have the patience for grief. It was not something she could admit, but she found it hard to maintain an afflicted sadness; it went against all her instinctive buoyancy, and gravity bored her. Martha was gone, and as far as Leone was concerned, a suitable period of mourning had passed, and it was time for levity once more.

In one of her magazines, Leone had found a recipe for an omelette, a light Persian dish that the French had taken as their own. Leone was delighted with herself. Clara had given her a little pot of dried tarragon that she had in her pantry. Though the receipt had stipulated fresh, green stuff, she was sure that the dried would suffice. It smelled of spring; aniseed and pepper.

Beating the eggs, Leone hummed a tune that she had heard the children singing over and over recently, obsessing on the one melody, as children habitually did. The robin perched at the open sill, tipping his smart brown head quizzically.

Flirting, he shuddered his wings at Leone before bouncing off into the white morning sky. Following the instructions, Leone poured the egg into her pan, hot with pork lard. She had already prepared the mushrooms in the fat, and they were aside, slick with juice and specks of parsley. There was a little Cheshire cheese left over from the new year, which had kept well in brown paper, and she grated that in too.

Her hum turned to a full song, and Leone danced around the kitchen, enjoying the company of her own voice, adding all sorts of vibrato to 'List to the Convent Bells'. Delighted with her efforts, she slid Enriqueta's omelette onto her favourite blue plate. She went to call up the stairs and noticed the note. In a thick buff envelope, it was addressed to her. There was no mistaking Enriqueta's elegant hand and her lilac ink.

Dearest Friend, my beloved Leone,

I cannot begin to tell you how you and Peter, and the children, have brought a joy to me I never thought possible. You made me so welcome at Longford, and you have allowed me to feel like part of a family.

It is with sorrow and difficulty that I write you this letter. With the passing of Mrs Rylands, and with my work at an end, I must leave Longford Hall now, and all my treasured friends. The chance for me to come here was always so remarkable, fate working at its finest. I knew my stay would be for a finite period, but my heart will stay with you at Longford.

Leone, you know that my sister Leocadia is well placed in London, and she has kindly offered me a home there for now. I am confident that I can find a position, so that I can pay her and her husband my board at least. I will be glad to be with the children, but I will miss you all profoundly. Please, forgive my sudden departure. It was more than I could bear to speak to you about it all, and it is a decision I have not come to lightly.

A final plea – pass on my greatest, highest regards to John. He can never know how much Longford means to me.

Yours, forever

Enriqueta Tennant

Leone held the note for some time. The paper shuddered in the breeze, which came in and cooled Enriqueta's breakfast. Leone stared out to the garden, her eyes fixed on the blank sky over Longford. The robin returned, hopping boldly through the open window. He bobbed his head up and down, wondering why his mistress, so pretty in her apron, was crying over an omelette that was hardening slowly against the plate.

She ran up the stairs two at a time; Enriqueta's room was empty, as if she had never been there at all. Not a trace of her – no smudge of powder on the dressing table, nor a stray bed sock beneath the eiderdown. Leone flung open the drawers and wardrobes with force, where the coat hangers swung, clattering in her wake. The bathroom was empty and pristine, no hairbrush, no cold cream, no ribbons or soap. Leone sank to the floor. Her best, dearest friend was gone.

Enriqueta alighted the packet boat as it neared the basin at Manchester Piccadilly. It was busy; she was so unused to the noise and bustle of the city. There was no chance for her to indulge her sadness, regret or uncertainty. She was only eight hours away now from Leocadia, and unless she willed herself to stay firm, she would break all over again. John, and all he meant to her, was a closed room in a house in her head, and a door she dared not open.

Someone pushed into her, racing for the train. Her bags were cumbersome, their hard edges clipping and bruising her thighs and ankles. Enriqueta was sore and tired, her skirts cutting into her waist and her boots rubbing against her toes. She had to be brave, she told herself, but all she wanted was John near her, the image of his face ambushing her. She ran with her heavy load bashing against her, and she boarded the train. The conductor squealed his whistle and with a chug and blast, the train left Manchester, bound for London.

KENSINGTON, 1873

LEOCADIA HAD PREPARED the bedroom for her, with a new glass vase and roses, still wet from the garden in a posey jar. It was pretty, untarnished by any feeling or recollections. The quilt was an expensive sprig print and the sheets were worn and soft, good Egyptian cotton, ironed and scented with lavender spray. The first day Leocadia let her sister cry herself to sleep. She felt thin; Leocadia stroked her arms for hours, almost feeling she would wear them out. Enriqueta had always been the more delicate of the two, and Leo listed things to her husband to order, oats and cream and red meat.

Over the next few days, spinach was delivered in bundles, beef ribs arrived in brown paper, hot salmon came in trays from the fishmonger. The children baked tins of almond pies, glass bowls sodden with pears in syrup and finished with suet crumble. Leocadia encouraged Enriqueta to walk, pacing around the district, unspeaking, stopping at ponds and cemeteries, churches and markets, and cafes for glasses of red wine and pots of tea. She pushed her into bed each night, and she opened the mornings with white plates full of eggs, tiny triangles of toast and pots of her own chilli sauce.

Enriqueta pushed them aside, and all her plans of work halted. Leocadia whispered urgently to her husband over the baby vests drying near the stove.

'She is ill! Call for the doctor! Can you not see?'

Her husband answered evenly.

'She's heart-sore, Leo. Nothing to be done. She will get over it in time.'

Alex beckoned to Leocadia to come into the privacy of the kitchen. He pulled a letter from his pocket.

'This came. When you were out walking with her. I didn't know what to do with it. I wanted to ask you.'

Leocadia turned it over in her hands.

'It's not from Leone, or Maddy or Jules. I know their hands. Oh, Alex, I don't think it could be anything good? Maybe we hide it.'

'We can't do that! It is not ours to hide. We should give it her. Just make sure you are there when she opens it. It could make her bad way worse.'

The sisters sat on the bed. Leocadia lit more lamps as Enriqueta's eyes, like all other parts of her, had lost their strength.

My sweet Enriqueta,

I am writing from the Holt House on the Row. You remember it, I'm sure. The big one, and bigger now we have built more orchards and buildings at the back. I used to watch for you from the window, and I still do, despite knowing that you ran away.

I need you to reconsider what you are doing. I feel sure we should be together and I am not a man to give up what I believe should be mine. I will come and find you, and remind you how it felt when I had you in my arms. I am sure you think of me, like I think of you.

Yours, soon,
James Holt

Enriqueta's health worsened after receiving the letter. Alex raged with anger while Leocadia went between the too, whispering hard words of calm to him, and tending to her wretched sister, whose nerves were so badly undone, that she cowered whenever she heard a knock at the door. She spent longer and longer in the safety of her white bed.

'I am in half a mind to get up to Manchester to see this Holt character face to face. That bloody letter is a threat, Leo! Look at her! Just when she was getting better. She is a mess. Damned if we are all going to jump every time the poor postman knocks!'

Leocadia took the wine from his hand.

'I've been thinking. Maybe I should write to John. Tell him about Holt. Him saying he will turn up here. Enriqueta so ill.'

'God, no!'

He took his wine from her and swilled it back.

'She was making efforts to start again here. Longford, John – all of that – it broke her heart and now she has all this on top. She needs to get well. A new start. Maybe some easy work somewhere. Kensington is littered with libraries. Just leave it all well alone, Leocadia. Tomorrow could be a better day, and then there could be another.'

Summer crept into Kensington like a thief. The neat garden woke, the rich green leaves of the clematis were vigorous, scrambling over the walls. The nicotina and the lavender burned beneath the sun, sending billows of their faded scent into the breeze. Enriqueta played with the children in the small, blooming back garden. Harriet kissed her wetly, her fat little hand pressing on her breast.

'I love you, Aunty Enri.'

'And I love you too, dear Harri.'

Enriqueta held the warm child to her and breathed in the scent of the meadowsweet of her hair. Her dreams of children were far from her, little ghosts floating from her body, wisps of hope, not ever even turning to say their goodbyes. Life had betrayed her, making her think she might deserve the happinesses that others seemed to attract with such sickening ease.

There was a sharp rap at the front door. Enriqueta swung Harriet onto her hip, the child struggling and giggling in her arms. Both Alex and Leocadia were out, the first time since the Holt's letter had arrived. The knock at the door came again, causing the cat to leap and knock over the hallway flowers. The water flooded over Enriqueta's bare feet, but she didn't move. Again, the knock came, harder now and Harriet tugged at her aunt's hair, and the cat complained for food. If she had been alone, she would have run to the safety of her white bed, but her charges made her brave.

Opening the door, shock hit her like a hand. Unfathomably, John Rylands stood before her. She let Harriet down by inches, then heard her scramble away to seek out her brother.

Enriqueta stood, her hand meshed to the doorway, all her senses colliding, buffeted by the warmth of the late August air.

'How could you leave me?'

His voice was exactly as she had known it, deep and resonant and urgent. He looked astonishing, lean and handsome, his eyes bright and blue, his jaw set hard.

Pushing through the door, John took her in his arms, his mouth against her hair, his hands gripping different parts of her, as if checking she were real. She held onto him and for some time they stood in the narrow hallway, breathing into each other. She felt faint with a maddening sensation of relief and desire, profound ecstasy to be once more in the same exquisite space as him.

'Now I have you again, I hardly want to let you go for a minute. Do I, Enriqueta? Do I have you again, despite you running from me like I am an enemy? How could you leave? Do I have you again. Say I have you.'

'You do, John. You do.'

'I have sat brooding for weeks, longing for you. I stopped myself, thinking you wouldn't want me. But I had to come, Enriqueta. I had to come for you. Tell me you want me as I want you. I can't bear it. There is no life for me if it is a life without you.'

He bent, taking her face in his hands, like it was his own heart, and kissed her. Summer worked around them, trees and leaves nudged and tickled by swarms of their angels, warm and filled with blossom and joy.

'We need to talk, Enri. We need to talk, and plan, and not ever be without each other again. Let me send a carriage for you to come to me tomorrow evening.'

She nodded, the smile on her face reflecting the song of wonder in her.

'I will not think of anything else until then, as I haven't since first I found you gone. Oh, Enri, when Leone showed me the letter – and you must forgive her that, I was beside myself. You left Longford – and my heart shattered. Life is nothing without you by my side – it is a hard and pitiless place full of missing and longing. Nothing without you.'

'I know. I know, John.'

She kissed him, and the sun was warm on their faces.

Leocadia and Alex returned to the house to find Enriqueta entirely changed, so altered, from gloom to luminosity, from despondency and despair to hope.

The sun rose in such a perfect milk-gold orb, it was as if it had appeared solely to shine on her. The world Enriqueta occupied was a new place. Leocadia began pulling out all her finest dresses and drawing hot tubs of water.

'The bath salts I bought you,' muttered Alex. 'Go easy on them.'

Leocadia chose her sister a gown, bought only weeks before and as yet unworn. Enriqueta protested, laughing with pleasure at her dear sister's unceasing generosity. The skirts were shot silk, patterned faintly with a printed rose in a deep purple over a pale, twinkling lilac. The bodice was in a darker shade, plain and made of a rich, smooth satin. Leocadia arranged her hair with all the care born of historical bonds, a sister's fingers that knew how to shape and pile and pin. The late summer evening was warm enough, but Leo wrapped the robin-pink shawl she had knitted for her around Enriqueta's shoulders, just in time for the Rylands carriage to pull up outside the house.

John had taken one of the private dining rooms at Brown's, with French windows that opened onto the small rose garden at the back. As he waited for her, he thought of the moments they had shared in Normandy. He thought that evening he had never seen her look so enchanting, but he had been wrong. As she walked into the room, she stole those images away and replaced them with a staggering beauty he had never seen in her before. Enriqueta looked at him with the same sight, it was as if she had never seen him before.

Enriqueta was shy around him, nervous of the torrent between them. He was cautious, as though too quick a move or too direct a word would send her fleeing from him again. The candles flickered between them on the table. They ate together and spoke quietly and lightly and carefully of all the small things she had missed in the long weeks of her absence. John answered all her enquiries about Leone, Peter, and Longford. He painted a picture of a bleak scene. Martha's death and her own departure had cleaved two huge changes into the landscape of Longford.

'I don't know what I was thinking – to suppose you were fastened to me so indelibly. It was an assumption I made. I don't think I was arrogant. I think I underestimated how much I loved you.' John sighed, pulling her against him.

There was nowhere for either of them to hide anymore. In the white of the room at the hotel, far away from the occupations of the hall, there was no business, no company, no land. No doorbells or schedules. There were no trees, no offices, no deaths, no work, no library, no hot-houses, no dances on the green, no other country to flee too. Just the room, the table, the candles, the two of them, soldiering on through the frightening and beautiful prospect of a love so definite and so inescapable.

'When I discovered you were gone, I was mindless with grief. I tried to think of a life without you and I couldn't. I couldn't live without you – I had to find you. Even if it was to hear you say you were never coming back.'

She raised a hand, touching his face with her finger.

'I regret causing you pain, John, upon pain already suffered. I didn't know that I would have a place anymore, with Martha gone. It was cowardly of me – I didn't dare face you and hear from you if that were true. I left in a kind of madness.'

'I know about Holt. The letter. I know the nerves and fright you have borne. That family—'

'It doesn't matter anymore. He doesn't matter.'

'If you agree to come back to Longford, that family will always be there. The Holts don't stop. I think he has been silenced for now. The fool – he got drunk enough and had enough ale and bluster in him to tell Tynan what he had sent you. He talked of his train ticket and his grand entrance into Kensington to claim you.'

The endless tussles of men – not for true love but for the game and the win. The story was old, and all she wanted was the good and proper ending.

'Come and stand with me in the garden, Enri.'

The air was cooling, darkening to a hazy dusk, autumn pushing at the heels of summer's end. He pulled her shawl round her, bringing her close to him.

'I want you as my wife. Marry me, Enriqueta.'

Before she could say a word, John kissed her. His lips on hers, his hands stroking her, as though taking his last chance, or maybe his first. Between their kisses and tears, Enriqueta accepted his proposal in the vacant rose garden, while Mayfair sounded, life and triumph around them.

LONGFORD, 1875

JOHN RYLANDS, OF 46 ARGYLL ROAD, Kensington (his London residence), and Enriqueta Tennant, of 54 Gardens Terrace, Kensington (home of Leocadia Fernanda Morison) married at Kensington Congregational Chapel on 6 October 1875. Leocadia and Alex were present as the only witnesses and the only guests.

IT HAD BEEN MANY, MANY YEARS SINCE Enriqueta had put away the childish imaginings of what her wedding day would look like. She had given the notion up completely, thrown it aside like a party dress that no longer fitted. But whatever landscape she had conjured in the past didn't matter anymore, for her wedding day – when it came – was the most joyous thing she could have ever imagined. After the four left the chapel, they went back to Gardens Terrace and celebrated with their wedding cake, a traditional pastel de tres leches and glasses of Cuban rum. John gazed at his bride, hardly believing that all he had longed for had come to pass.

The following day, Mr and Mrs Rylands made the long journey to a short honeymoon in Torquay. The Imperial Hotel rose from the cliff tops of the Devon coastline, and despite the season, they walked the long stretches of Torre Abbey Sands.

Enriqueta slept fitfully each night, her sleep messed by complicated, dreadful dreams. In them, she saw her mother, searching for her in the streets of Lyon. Pieces of her past slotted themselves together haphazardly and threw themselves around her sleeping mind. Over and over she fainted, only to get up to faint again, all in the ties of sleep. She reached across the bed to John who soothed her and let her talk, letting her expose how her nighttime thoughts could betray her daytime happiness so badly.

While it troubled her, it was a comfort that John seemed to have no concern at all about her nightmares. He loved her wholly, and he knew that the place they had found themselves in together had been hard won for them both. On their final afternoon in Torquay, they sat on the terrace of the hotel, looking down at the bay, which twinkled with lights in the clear October night.

They drank brandy, and spoke of love and demons, elements that bookended them both, with love at the door of their futures, and the griefs that dominated their pasts.

John, too, was at the mercy of intrusions. He told Enriqueta that he thought that it was the heavy fruit of lingering guilt. Guilt that ranged and fed upon memory of his precious children, Dinah, Martha, Caroline and the deaths and errors that littered his life like hard rubble. Past mistakes that clouded even the good of his charity and business.

He decided, as he watched his clever, kind and beautiful wife walk across the darkening stones of the terrace, that from this moment he would rise from the the feckless paths of his past, to love her wholly and forever, as he knew she loved him. Theirs would be a shared new dawn, the light of honesty shined to shame the secrets of the past. Enriqueta's nightmares were a product of her shift into peace, and John knew that with his love and care, he would restore her, as she would him. For so long he had been searching for peace and for a love he was free to give and to receive without guilt or restriction. She rid herself of Foncé, telling him all, of the cabin and the corners, of a love so temporary and deep that had fallen into revulsion.

Peter and Leone greeted them at Longford Hall's great door with cries of happiness. John laughed to see the bridal swags covering the entrance, accepting glasses of champagne for them both from the tray that Tynan held. Leone held Enriqueta close to her tightly.

'Oh, how have I missed you, love. I can't tell you how happy we are for you both. Made for each other – that's what I said to Peter.'

The ukelele band that Peter had hired from the village struck up a wedding march as John and Enriqueta entered the ballroom, festooned in Ged's best hot-house blooms tied with yards of ribbons. Clara and Frank came through the crowds to greet them with more champagne, and the delight of those who are continually assured by the good force of true love.

Outside, the Manchester rain began to fall, a familiar, temperate thrum onto the roof of the Hall. The rain didn't stop all night, yet when they finally went to bed, Enriqueta slept completely and deeply. John kissed her as she woke, her expression clear and illuminated by the light of the dawn. They stood at the window looking out onto the estate, Mr and Mrs Rylands, in each other's arms.

'Martha said something to me, John, and she was so very right.' Enriqueta turned to him and kissed him tenderly, touching the emeralds at her ears. Martha's gift. 'She said we must all find our own peace. That is the secret of life. And, finally, I have. I have found my peace with you.'

The sun rose, round on the horizon, and the red oak glowed orange, the broad, ancient branches reaching out to the Longford skies.

Tu es ma paix, mon réconfort, mon salu